The Detective Matt Jones 1........ ~.....

"Stunning emotional force. Ellis keeps everything in focus while building a staggering momentum."
—*Booklist*, Starred Review, *City of Echoes*

"Only really good writers can make you feel so strongly. *City of Echoes* is another bravura effort from the talented Robert Ellis."
—*Mystery Scene* magazine

"*City of Echoes* is an absorbing and entertaining read from first page to last and documents novelist Robert Ellis as a master of the genre."
—*Midwest Book Review*

"*City of Echoes* is a Best Book of the Month."
—Amazon.com

"Ellis eases new readers into the second Matt-centric novel. Having previously suffered betrayal, Matt has good reason to be paranoid, which results in a gleefully tense sequel. His relationships are complex . . . the mystery is straightforward. A persistently gripping thriller with strong characters."
—*Kirkus Reviews*, *The Love Killings*

"With an early focus on the possible murders, Ellis' series entry is more thriller than mystery. The author works this to great effect as the story reveals the burden of unearthing evidence. Ellis generates an impressive amount of suspense. Solid entertainment."
—*Kirkus Reviews*, *The Girl Buried in the Woods*

PRAISE FOR ROBERT ELLIS
City of Fire (Lena Gamble, Book 1)

"Los Angeles under a cloud of acrid smoke . . . Robert Ellis's *City of Fire* is a gripping, spooky crime novel."
—*The New York Times* "Hot List" Pick

"*City of Fire* is my kind of crime novel. Gritty, tight, and assured. Riding with Detective Lena Gamble through the hills of Los Angeles is something I could get used to. She's tough, smart, and most of all, she's real."
—Michael Connelly

"*City of Fire* features a tough but deeply flawed protagonist, a tantalizingly complex plot, fully realized—and realistic—characters, and most of all, a palpable intensity. And if that weren't enough, the bombshell plot twist at the novel's conclusion makes this an absolute must read for thriller aficionados."
—*Chicago Tribune*

"I just discovered Robert Ellis. This book is terrific."
—Janet Evanovich, *People* magazine

"This book is fast, gruesome, and twisted, like a scary Jodie Foster movie. Ellis makes it easy to be terrified."
—*Library Journal*

"A complex portrait of the flawed but righteous Lena by Ellis makes this sure-footed police procedural something special."
—*Kirkus Reviews*

City of Fire (Lena Gamble, Book 1)

"Ellis vividly evokes Hollywood as a place of burning desires, where the boundaries between good and evil are blurred beyond distinction. Ellis's prose is crisp, and his plot moves at a good clip."
—*Booklist*

"Robert Ellis's brisk, complex *City of Fire* is hot stuff. Ellis excels at vivid writing and the expert plotting keeps the reader off-kilter … L.A., which is written about so often, seems fresh in the hands of an original storyteller such as Ellis."
—South Florida *Sun-Sentinel, Best Books of the Year*

"The story is tight, the characters alive."
—*Publishers Weekly*

"Ellis nicely depicts how the unsolved murder of Lena's musician brother casts a specter over her life and work. But *City of Fire* is about its propulsive plot: the ins and outs of police investigation and how the growing horror of a mad multiple murderer loose on the fiery streets of Los Angeles leads to unexpected decisions, layers of betrayal, and a scorcher of an ending."
—*The Baltimore Sun*

"*City of Fire* begins like a roller coaster, building tension, anxiety, and fear. Then it plunges at full speed, spiraling and twisting through scenes that will have hearts pounding and fingers flying through the pages."
—*Mystery Scene* magazine

The Lost Witness (Lena Gamble, Book 2)

"Scorching. Deliciously twisted. Nothing is what it appears to be. Ellis succeeds masterfully in both playing fair and pulling surprise after surprise in a story that feels like a runaway car plunging down a mountain road full of switchbacks."
—*Publishers Weekly*, Starred Review

"Ellis serves up a killer crime tale with riveting characters and relentless twists."
—*Booklist*, Starred Review

"Ellis's elaborate puzzle is a nail-biter to the final page. Great LA settings enhance this high-speed thriller. Recommended for all popular collections."
—*Library Journal*

"Ellis piles on the Hollywood atmosphere and procedural detail, and the end revelation is expertly timed and genuinely shocking."
—*The Guardian* (UK)

Murder Season (Lena Gamble, Book 3)

"*Murder Season*: a terrific sick-soul-of-LA thriller. Before you can say *Chinatown* we are immersed in a tale of mind-boggling corruption where virtually every character in the book—with the exception of Lena—has a hidden agenda. Ellis is a master plotter. Along the way we meet wonderful characters."
—*Connecticut Post*, Hearst Media News Group

"Within the space of a few books, Ellis has demonstrated that rare ability to skillfully navigate his readers through a complex plot filled with interesting, dangerous and surprising characters."
—Bookreporter.com

THE GIRL BURIED IN THE WOODS

A DETECTIVE MATT JONES THRILLER

BOOK 3

ALSO BY
ROBERT ELLIS

City of Stones

The Love Killings

City of Echoes

Murder Season

The Lost Witness

City of Fire

The Dead Room

Access to Power

THE GIRL BURIED IN THE WOODS

ROBERT ELLIS

A DETECTIVE MATT JONES THRILLER

BOOK 3

This is a work of fiction. Names, characters, organizations, places, events, and incidents are either products of the author's imagination or are used fictitiously.

THE GIRL BURIED IN THE WOODS

Copyright © 2019 by Robert Ellis
New York City

ISBN: 9781081999254
All rights reserved.

No part of this book may be reproduced without express written permission from the author or his legal representatives, excepting brief quotes used in reviews.

For more information, visit:
https://www.robertellis.net

Cover design by Elderlemon Design

First Edition: October 2019

Printed in the United States of America

For Nelson C. Rising, the man who changed the face of downtown Los Angeles, and my good friend.

We shall find peace. We shall hear angels, we shall see the sky sparkling with diamonds.

—Anton Chekhov

ONE

NEWS BRIEF (*Los Angeles Times* Staff Writer) Detective Matthew Trevor Jones, the LAPD homicide detective out of the Hollywood Division who appeared to have nine lives, is deceased. The young detective was gunned down by an unknown assailant atop Mount Hollywood. On loan to the FBI from Los Angeles, Jones's body was fished out of the frigid waters in Long Island Sound off Greenwich, Connecticut during a Nor'easter this past December . . .

Matt could almost see the words in the newspaper as he rolled over in bed and tried to shake what had become yet another nightmare. Another lost night in a long line of lost nights. Flashbacks. Night sweats. Ghouls and ghosts visiting his bed. The Grim Reaper checking on him every so often to see if he was *ready*, or was the word *done*. And what about the pain in his chest and shoulder from the four gunshot wounds that were real. The pain that his doctor had said would someday disappear. Someday fade and be nothing more than a memory.

Matt rolled his head across the pillow. Someday he'd forget the four muzzle flashes that had been pointed directly his way. Someday that spike of fear, that jolt of jolts, would take flight like a flock of blackbirds heading for cooler air in the north sky. And with that flock of birds, the sounds of the shots, one after another, the unreal feeling that he'd been hit, and hit hard, maybe even hit forever—maybe those blackbirds could take all of that with them as well.

Someday all those memories might vanish in a hard wind.

Someday his world would become bright and steady, and he could live life the same way normal people live their lives. The people sunning themselves on Venice Beach. Walking along the waterline barefoot. Laughing and talking and rollerblading up and down the bike path. Eating at the cafés with old friends or feeling that certain promise and joy in meeting someone new.

Happiness wasn't an illusion, was it? Happiness was attainable, even for him, right?

He heard something in his dream. It wasn't an answer, or even the Grim Reaper standing over his bed. It was an irritating tapping sound in the darkness. It seemed so out of place. So annoying.

He let it go and rolled over again, seeking drier sheets and hoping for one last cool spot in his bed. As he settled in, the words came back, and he realized that he was reading his own obituary. Dreaming about it as he tried to swim through those ice-cold December waters in Connecticut and make it back to shore. It didn't look like he was going to pull it off. His arms and legs had gone numb almost instantly. The water was as black as the sky, the stormy chop playing with him. He could feel the undertow reaching out for his ankles and feet and trying to pull him to the bottom. He thought he could see a ship burning in the distance; thought he could hear the deafening sound of an explosion as he coughed and choked on the salt water, gasping for air and reaching for—

He wondered why this wasn't enough to wake him up.

Bad dreams were supposed to work like alarm clocks. At least they had in the past—as a boy and even more so since his return from Afghanistan as a soldier. Once he got a feel for the trouble he was in, once he hit the *big moment*, ten times out of ten he would be jolted back to the real world. Why not this time?

He heard that tapping noise again. Was it tapping, or was it a banging sound that just kept going on and on without end?

His body shuddered and he opened his eyes. He found himself staring at the clock radio on the bedside table. It was almost 4:00 a.m., and it sounded like some idiot was throwing punches at his front door. He noticed his cell phone docked to the clock radio for an all-night charge. The phone was vibrating, the name of the caller blinking on and off the screen to the beat of the fool working over his front door.

It was his supervisor, Lt. Howard McKensie.

Matt grabbed the phone. McKensie didn't wait for him to say hello.

"What the hell are you doing in there, Jones? Open the goddamn door."

"Right," he managed, his throat bone dry.

Matt switched off the phone and checked the time again. The sun wouldn't be up for three or four hours. Maybe he was still dreaming. Still in the nightmare.

He got out of bed, adjusted his boxer shorts, crossed through the kitchen and into the living room. He could see McKensie through the window in the street light. The big man with the shock of white hair was shaking his head and looked all amped up, but at least the racket had stopped.

He threw the locks and swung the door open. McKensie brushed past him and marched into the living room.

"Turn on the lights, Jones. I've been out there for ten minutes."

Matt switched on a table lamp and found McKensie sizing him up with those sharp green eyes of his. His supervisor was standing by the slider—the deck behind him still lit up because Matt, for whatever reason, had stopped turning off the outdoor lights before bed.

"You're sweating, Jones. Why are you sweating?"

Matt shrugged. "It's four in the morning, Lieutenant. Why are you here?"

McKensie didn't blink. He was a tough man and, despite his age, still strong and built like a street fighter.

"You saw the department shrink yesterday. You were in Julie May's office in Chinatown. How'd you make out, Jones?"

McKensie's 4:00 a.m. visit wasn't about Matt's first session with Dr. May in Chinatown. The first of what he'd been told when he returned from Philadelphia would be weekly appointments until when? No one would answer the question. No one would even give him an estimate. When Matt pressed Dr. May a second time, her eyes flicked down to her notes and she became quiet. After several moments, she changed the subject and said she wanted to hear him talk about what happened when he'd entered his father's house in Greenwich just two weeks ago. What it had been like to find the father who had abandoned him as a child, dying with his second wife and their two sons before his eyes.

All of them shot. All of them dead or dying. All of them murdered.

McKensie cleared his throat, his voice booming. "You with me, Jones? Or are you sleepwalking tonight? Hey, you're not juiced, are you?"

The memory of his father's death vanished, and Matt looked back at his supervisor. "I'm good."

"Good enough to work another murder case?"

It hung there. Matt had been placed on medical leave. He guessed that rather than make a simple phone call, McKensie had driven out here because he wanted to see for himself—some sort of eyeball confirmation that what he was about to do would be okay. And he had a strange look in those eyes of his. A hard, worried look—more human than Matt had ever seen before.

Matt tried to ignore the man's stare as he thought things over. Someone new was dead in Los Angeles. Someone new was always dead in Los Angeles. Murder had become an epidemic this year, the coroner's office a factory for the City of Angels.

"I'm good," Matt said. "I'm ready."

McKensie laughed and cocked his head. "You're ready? That's not what your shrink said."

"When did you talk to Dr. May?"

McKensie smiled like the devil, his bright green eyes drilling him again. "About an hour ago. I woke her up. She didn't seem too happy about it."

"What did she say?"

The big man laughed again. "She said that you're not good, and you're not right. You're not ready for prime time, Jones. She said you've still got those monsters swimming in your head."

"She doesn't know what she's talking about."

"Sure she does. Don't you think I can see it, too? You think I haven't been there? You think I'm blind?"

"She's a witch doctor."

McKensie cracked open the slider, his eyes brightening. "I heard she's hot, possibly wicked hot, but smart and true."

Matt shrugged, spotted his T-shirt on the couch, and slipped it on. "Okay, if I'm not ready for prime time, then why did you drive all the way out here and wake me up in the middle of the night? I had a good sleep going."

"I'll bet you did."

McKensie paused a moment, then crossed the room to Matt's reading chair by the window and sat down on the arm. When he spoke, his raspy voice was quieter, like he was thinking the words through.

"A body was just discovered partially buried near Dodger Stadium and the Elysian Reservoir in the Buena Vista Meadow picnic area."

"That's not our turf."

"It is tonight. Central needs a favor. Besides, it's just over the line."

"But you and the witch doctor said I'm not ready."

A moment passed. More looking. More thinking.

McKensie got up finally, started to pace, then stopped. "You're not ready for prime time, Jones, but you might be ready for this one. The witch doctor thinks so, too. It's murder lite. The body's buried in the dirt. You get to play archaeologist and dig him out, low and slow, like a rack of baby backs done just right."

Matt thought it over. Other than his inability to shake his nightmares and get a decent night's sleep, he felt reasonably close to normal. Not rock-steady stable, but not in the deep weeds either. That feeling in his stomach wasn't as bad as it used to be, and his headaches seemed less brutal. It had been two weeks since the love killings, right? And he was back from Philly.

He was home. His surroundings were familiar. Working a new case might get his mind off things, maybe even speed up his recovery.

"Any idea who's dead?" he asked.

McKensie shook his head. "Not even a guess. First responders just called it in to confirm the corpse. I'm sorry, Jones. I know you could have used some time off. It's just that we're stretched thin right now. I drove out here to see for myself. All you need to do is take it easy—one step at a time. For all we know the body's been in the ground for thirty years. Once you guys dig it out, let the lab make the ID and close the case. Then you can go back on leave and get some rest."

Matt met the big man's eyes. "Murder lite," he said.

McKensie shrugged, his voice peppered with worry and concern again as he stepped toward the front door and opened it to leave.

"Murder lite," he said. "Just be careful, Matt. Do you know where the picnic area is?"

Matt nodded. "Yeah."

"You need anything at all, call me."

"Sounds good."

Matt took a deep breath and exhaled, watching McKensie close the door and vanish in the night.

TWO

M*urder lite . . .*
   Pretend you're an archaeologist and dig him out low and slow, like a rack of baby backs done just right . . .

Matt shook it off and took fifteen minutes to shower, dress, and make a fresh pot of coffee. Then he filled his travel mug with the hot brew, added sugar, checked his laptop case for meds, slipped his .45 into his belt holster, and headed for the front door. As he crossed the lawn to the carport, he couldn't help but notice the vista. The winds had pushed the marine layer out over the ocean, his view of what was left of Potrero Canyon crystal clear in the moonlight.

The rich vegetation that used to line the basin and steep slopes had been completely burned out by the wildfire. None of the homes on the south rim had survived, and he counted fifteen black spots—fifteen families who had lost everything. He knew that there were five more, but he couldn't see them from this side of the house. He also knew that the wind had carried the flames over to the north side and that his luck had held out. Only two houses burned down, and they were a block and a half up the street.

He felt a chill crawl up his spine—the strong, rank scent of the charred rubble wafting in the way-too-warm-for January air. It was a smell he couldn't get used to. A foul odor in the breeze that wouldn't go away.

Matt let it go and climbed into the car. Pulling onto the narrow street, he eased his way around the curves and down the hill, making a left turn at the light onto the Pacific Coast Highway. Traffic was thin to none, and he could blow through red lights without slowing down. Once he reached the Santa Monica Freeway, he brought the car up to a cool eighty miles an hour, switched on the radio to KNX News for traffic updates, and cracked open the lid on his travel mug. He felt the steam rising into his face and took a quick first sip. The jolt of hot caffeine seemed to clear his mind some, and he settled into the driver's seat. The announcer on the radio was reading a weather forecast that called for a break in the oppressive heat, but Matt wasn't really listening. He was thinking about the park and the body that was buried there. He was trying to keep his imagination in check. Trying to push away all the unknowns that might color his first impression of the crime scene.

He glanced at the navigation system, then took another sip of coffee. There would be no need to enter an address. Matt had worked narcotics before his promotion to homicide last fall. Despite its proximity to the LA Police Academy, the Buena Vista Meadow picnic area, also known as Elysian Park, had been the location of choice for more than a few drug deals on the east side of the city. It was a big space, more than six hundred acres, with tree-lined roads and walking paths carved into the side of the ridge. The picnic area sat on top offering close-up views of downtown Los Angeles to the south and the burgeoning city of Glendale just a few miles north.

Matt checked the time as he picked up the 110 Freeway, exiting quickly onto Solano Avenue and gunning it through a neighborhood of what looked like small homes and apartment buildings. He made a left on North Broadway, and then another on Elysian Park Drive.

As he followed the road that snaked up the steep hill to the picnic area, he was reminded of how remote the park felt. How eerie it all seemed at this time of night. No doubt about it, the oldest park in the city was big enough to get lost in and, he guessed, home to more than a few ghosts.

Matt shrugged it off, accelerating up the hill. After a few moments, he began to notice flashing lights through the tree branches. Rounding the last bend, he spotted a police cruiser parked at the very top before a grassy field littered with picnic tables.

He pulled in beside the cruiser but didn't see anyone around. His partner, Denny Cabrera, wasn't here yet. No one from the Forensic Science Division or the coroner's office had shown up either. Just this one empty black-and-white, idling in the night with its headlights on and its LED light bars flashing.

Something about it didn't feel right.

Matt flipped open the glove box, grabbed his flashlight, and climbed out of the car. Glancing at the picnic tables, he turned back to the police cruiser and gave it a long look. The windows were down, the air conditioner jacked up on high. He could hear the sound of a dispatcher on the car's radio popping on and off at random intervals.

Images surfaced. Memories of what he'd discovered at his father's house just two weeks ago in Greenwich, Connecticut. The two police cruisers he'd seen idling by the entrance covered in snow on a stormy night. The four cops he'd found sitting inside their cars—all four ambushed—all four cops shot dead. It wasn't possible, was it? Something so grim repeating itself so quickly. Maybe he was just feeling jumpy. Just feeling the rush of anticipation as he arrived at a new crime scene and began working a new case.

Pretend you're an archaeologist . . . let the lab do all the work . . . just lay back and everything will be all right . . .

Matt walked around to the front of the cruiser and stepped onto the lawn. The headlights from the vehicle seemed to illuminate most of the meadow, dying out before they reached the trees. And that's when he spotted them. That's when he felt the edge take a step back. Two cops with flashlights were standing in the darkness just this side of a grove of pine trees. An old man who appeared upset was with them, dressed in street clothes and seated at a picnic table. All three were staring Matt's way. As he started toward them, he raised his badge in the air.

"Matt Jones," he said in a loud voice. "Homicide."

Despite the distance, he caught the recognition on both cops' faces, even the old man's, and laughed a little when he realized that his days working undercover were over. Too many articles in the newspapers had been published over the past few months, too many stories on TV. Matt tried to ignore it as best he could and figured that people on the street probably knew more about his life than he did.

The cops stepped away from the picnic table, the taller of the two introducing himself as Alvin Marcs, with his partner, Bill Guy.

Matt glanced at the old man behind them. "Who's he?"

"Levi Harris," Marcs said in a quieter voice. "He found the body."

Matt nodded. "Tell me what happened."

"It's probably easier if I show you."

"Okay," he said. "Show me."

Marcs lowered his flashlight to the grass and led the way to an opening in the grove of pine trees. Then he stopped and turned back to Matt.

"Harris works nights, sleeps during the day," he said in a voice that wouldn't carry. "He's from the neighborhood. He was walking his dog and thought maybe he might find some pine cones in here. Sounds like his dog went crazy."

"Where's the dog now?" Matt said.

"He took him home when he called nine-one-one."

Matt nodded again. "Let's have a look."

Marcs gazed into the opening and seemed shaky. "There's not a lot of room in there. You can lead the way. Once you get inside, it's gonna be about four steps to your right."

Matt switched on his flashlight. Pointing it at the ground, he ducked through the opening in the branches, took a step to his right, and froze. He could see it. Not a body, but human hair, black hair, strewn through the soil. He took a moment to absorb the shock and pull himself together. Then he stepped closer and knelt down. He could see the deep claw marks etched into the dirt by the dog. They appeared frantic, and he could almost hear the dog sniffing and snorting and barking as it ripped away the soil and tried to dig out the body.

"You see it?" Marcs asked in a low voice from behind him.

"Yeah," he said. "I see it."

Matt stood up to take in the entire space. The death chamber. Although he couldn't make out the form of the body buried underneath, he could see a mound of dirt that looked fresh and packed down. From the sparse spread of pine needles, he guessed that the killer had been in too much of a hurry to think about details.

His eyes flicked back to the hair strewn through the soil. The dog's claw marks. It was a horrific image, one that he knew he'd never forget.

Murder lite . . .

His body shuddered, his gut on fire. Maybe he wasn't ready to come back so soon. Maybe Dr. May had been right—too many monsters were still swimming in his head. And he'd stopped smoking two weeks ago, which Dr. May had said might make things worse. He'd given up cigarettes for good, he hoped, but at a time when he needed to be cool, calm, and what was the right word? Oh, yeah, collected. A time when he needed to come off like everything was cool, when nothing about anything was cool. Not even the January air.

He noticed his hand quivering and lowered it to his side. Then the headlights from a car swept through the tree branches and filled the grove of pine trees, the death chamber, with an ephemeral light. Turning away from the grave, he stepped through the opening and switched off his flashlight. He saw his partner, Denny Cabrera, walking across the lawn between a row of tables. Although he couldn't be certain, he thought he heard him say, "Hell of a time for a picnic."

THREE

"You're sure it's not just a toupee?"

Matt felt his partner give him a nudge with his elbow but didn't say anything. The remark had come from David Speeks, whom everyone in the department knew to be one of the best criminalists in the Forensic Science Division. He was a short, stocky man with graying hair and twenty-five years of experience. Now he was kneeling before the grave, eyeballing the hair and claw marks in the soil with what came off like ghoulish fascination.

Cabrera cleared his throat. "That's no hairpiece."

Speeks nodded, still staring at the horrific sight. "Nah, I don't think so either," he said in a voice so quiet he might have been speaking to himself. "I was just hoping we might've lucked out tonight."

Matt leaned closer. "It's too tight in here, Speeks. I want to set up a tent on the lawn. After you guys make the excavation, we'll see what we've got inside the tent."

"I hear you," the criminalist said. "But it's gonna take time, Jones. We'll have to process what's left of this crime scene before we start digging."

"Just do it right," Matt said.

Speeks nodded again. "Are the body guys here yet?"

Cabrera checked his cell phone. "The crew from the coroner's office are five minutes out."

"Tell them they've got time for a cup of coffee," Speeks said. "While they're at it they might as well order breakfast."

Speeks sniffed the soil, winced unpleasantly, then began to stand up. Matt could feel Cabrera's eyes on him as they stepped through the opening in the trees onto the grass and switched off their flashlights. The sky had begun to brighten, sunrise an hour or so off.

"Did you smell it, Matt? Did you see Speeks's face?"

Matt nodded as he met Cabrera's eyes. The smell of death was beginning to work its way through the soil. It might have been faint, but it was there. In the murder chamber. The dead room.

Over the next two hours, Matt and Cabrera worked on ramping up the crime scene. As they took Levi Harris's statement and sent him home to rest, the park was shut down and the entrances sealed off by patrol units. In order to block the view from the news choppers, a tent big enough for a banquet was pitched over two of the picnic tables on the lawn. Fifteen cops in uniforms were recruited to help scour the immediate area and sift through trash cans. Once lights were set up and a handful of criminalists from forensics had a chance to comb through the immediate crime scene for physical evidence, Speeks began excavating the body.

The entire process was recorded by the crime scene photographer in both video and still photographs. A variety of miniature-size trowels, rakes, and brushes were used, sweeping the soil away from the victim's hair and moving it with a small bucket to a box and screen inside the tent for further examination. By 9:00 a.m., a face was beginning to emerge. Two hours later, the horror was truly realized, and it took Matt's breath away.

Speeks looked up at him aghast. "Oh my God," he whispered. "Oh my God, Jones."

The photographer raised his camera and burst through a series of rapid-fire shots, the strobe light burning white hot. Matt felt the hair on the back of his neck stand on end as he knelt down and watched Speeks brush the soil away in gentle but quick strokes.

It was a girl.

A young girl. Sixteen or seventeen years old. And she hadn't been buried for very long. She was so well preserved that she might have been killed just a few hours ago. Still, from the wretched smell in the air, an odor that appeared to be in full bloom, Matt guessed that she'd been in the ground for a couple of days.

But that didn't account for the terror he'd heard in Speeks's voice or seen in the criminalist's experienced eyes. That's not why the moment the girl's face had been uncovered, there was a hush that rattled through the entire crime scene, or why everything seemed to go dark in the light of day.

Matt could feel the anger rising out of his belly as he leaned in for a closer look.

The girl had been beaten, and beaten badly.

Death hadn't been easy and hadn't come quick. She had two black eyes and a ring of bruises around her neck. She seemed so gentle, so slight, so innocent.

So wronged.

Matt felt his partner give him another nudge with his elbow.

"You're shaking," Cabrera said. "You okay, Matt?"

He didn't hesitate, and he didn't need a moment to collect himself. He kept his eyes on the girl's battered face and spoke like Dr. May and Lieutenant McKensie had made the wrong call.

"Yeah, Denny," he said, gritting his teeth. "Everything's cool."

FOUR

M**att tried to ignore the sound of the news choppers** hovering overhead as he stood with Cabrera on a grassy bank by the grove of pine trees and gazed down the steep hill. It looked like there was a private road that picked up where Baker Street ended and ran along the train tracks until it reached a small factory surrounded by a gated ten-foot wall. On the other side of the factory, he could see the railroad tracks leading into a substation, and the Los Angeles River, flowing south toward the city on a bed of broken concrete.

Cabrera stepped closer, checked his back, and spoke in a low voice. "You sure everything's cool, Matt. I thought you got tagged for medical leave. After what you went through, it wouldn't mean anything if you weren't ready. It'd just be a matter of, well, you know what I'm saying, you're not ready."

Matt noted the security cameras mounted on the factory walls before he turned back and saw the worry on Cabrera's face. They had become partners just three months ago, and Cabrera was almost as green as Matt had been. Off to a rough start, the size and weight of the murder case they'd carried on their shoulders brought them together the same way the war in Afghanistan had brought Matt's unit together. Now he trusted Cabrera with his life.

"It turns out I didn't need to go on leave after all," Matt said. "McKensie came out to my place, and we talked it over. I'm fine. I mean it, Denny. We're in this together. Everything's good."

He could see Cabrera trying to get a read on him. And while Matt hadn't stuck to the script word for word, what he'd told his partner seemed like the truth now. Something about seeing the girl's battered face in the dirt made it true. Her death, and the hunt for whoever did this, gave his life a new purpose, a weighty mission more important than himself or anything that had happened to him over the last month on the East Coast.

Speeks stepped out of the pine trees and waved at them. "It's a go," he said.

Cabrera led the way off the grassy bank over to the trees, and Matt peered through the opening in the branches. The crew from the coroner's office had arrived more than three hours ago. The investigator, Ed Gainer, was someone Matt knew and trusted. Matt stepped aside to let the crime scene photographer pass, then stepped back. He could see Gainer and an assistant lifting the girl out of her shallow grave and setting her down in a body bag. After they got her zipped up, she was hoisted onto a gurney and pushed as quickly as possible across the lawn in full view of the news choppers. And then, just as quickly, into the privacy of the tent.

Speeks unfolded a sheet of plastic, laid it over a picnic table, and taped it down as a man and woman from forensics closed the flaps on the tent and rolled in the work lights. Once the tent was illuminated, Matt gave the nod and watched as the girl's body was removed from the bag and lowered onto the picnic table.

A moment passed, and then another, with everyone staring at her—everyone taking it in. She seemed so young. So vulnerable. She was wearing a pair of jeans and a white blouse that remained dusted from the soil she'd been buried in. Her shoes were a popular sports brand, the same style and color Matt wore when he walked down to the bike path on the beach and went jogging. He took a deep breath and exhaled. Ignoring the pungent smell of death in the air, his eyes began eating up the images before him in big bites.

She'd been violated. That much seemed clear.

Her jeans were undone and unzipped, her blouse ripped open with her bra pushed up over her small breasts. But what bothered Matt most were the bruises on her arms. He counted seven. Based on the range of colors against her light-brown skin, he estimated that they varied in age from just before her death to a week or ten days ago.

Matt turned to Speeks. "Let's break out the UV lights."

Speeks lifted a pair of military-grade plastic hard cases onto the second picnic table and flipped open the latches. Inside were four UV LED forensic flashlights with safety glasses for the eight people in the tent. Speeks kept one flashlight for himself and passed the remaining three to Matt, Cabrera, and Gainer.

Matt slipped on his safety glasses. "Kill the work lights," he said.

The tent went dark, and Matt switched on his UV light. When the other lights came up, the girl's dead body began to glow in a mass of eerie purple light.

Matt noticed that everyone seemed to take a step back. He thought that it might be the amount of semen reflecting back at them from the UV light. There was a lot of it, more like the discharge from an animal than a human being. Bright drip marks could be seen all over her zipper and panties, her jeans, and the bottom half of her blouse.

He watched Gainer trying to avoid the dried stains with his gloved hands while emptying the girl's pockets. Two one-dollar bills, a quarter, and a pocket rock for luck. No one said anything as Gainer dropped the items into an evidence bag, everyone's eyes locked on that pocket rock. When the investigator finished, Matt followed Cabrera's light as it panned up the girl's body and stopped on the ring of bruises around her neck and those two black eyes.

"There's something wrong with her head," Cabrera said in a quiet voice. "The angle's off. It's not set right."

Gainer, who was the only one there authorized to touch the body, gave the girl's head a gentle lift. Matt leaned forward to get a better look at the back of her skull. It was battered and crushed in, and he felt himself grimace in the shadows cast by the purple flashlights.

Gainer set the girl's head down. "She's got no ID," he said. "Her neck's broken. She's been strangled, beaten, and she's ice cold. Rigor mortis has come and gone. We need to get her downtown, guys."

Gainer turned to Matt and gave him a long look. Matt understood what the investigator had left unsaid. Matt guessed that everyone in the tent did. They had a major-league problem on their hands now. A girl had been dug out of the ground, and it had been a monster who put her there. A maniac. What seasoned homicide units call a full-blown *motherfucker*. But even worse, as they stood there with the corpse, the killer was free and clear and probably stalking his next victim. He was invisible. And if he could do this to an innocent teenage girl, then he could do it to any living thing, and do it again and again and again.

The words *murder lite* flicked through Matt's head and vanished. When he noticed the girl's watch, he turned back to Gainer.

"May I?" he asked.

Gainer nodded.

Matt checked his gloves, then carefully took hold of her cold, lifeless arm and turned it over for a look at her watch. The lens was shattered, the watch possibly broken in the struggle. While he couldn't be certain before the autopsy, while it was only a decent guess—time, even life itself, appeared to have come to a final stop for this young girl at 4:30 p.m. on January 8. In Los Angeles in early January, that meant it would have been almost dark.

Matt lowered her arm to the table, examining her rough hands and fingers. Her nails were cut short and appeared clean, but her fingertips were scratched like she tried to put up a fight.

He turned back to the coroner's investigator. "Would you mind pulling her jeans down, Ed. I want a look at her legs."

Matt could feel everyone in the room staring at him.

Gainer gave him a troubled look. "Can it wait until the autopsy?"

"No," Matt said. "I don't think it can."

Gainer may have been slightly irritated, but it didn't last long, and with great care, he slipped the girl's jeans off her hips and slid them down her thighs to her ankles. Matt made room for the photographer, then gave Cabrera a quick look.

The girl's legs were bruised—her thighs, her calves, and shinbone. It had only been a hunch, but Matt needed to know. Like the bruises on her arms, some of the contusions could have occurred during the struggle, but most looked as if they'd come before that—within the last ten days.

The photographer moved in with his strobe light pulsating again. Matt took a step closer, adding it all up. Most of the girl's wounds were a part of her life, her history—a monster she may have known.

But just as disturbing was the amount of semen on her upper thighs. It crossed Matt's mind that maybe the killer had spent more time with the girl than he had first imagined. Maybe that's why the killer didn't have time to cover the shallow grave with pine needles. Maybe that's why the grave site appeared rushed. The killer had seen the grove of pine trees, dragged the girl inside the canopy for privacy, and had his way with her. Not once or twice, but until he was done with her . . .

FIVE

Matt switched off his flashlight and returned it to Speeks, then dug his cell phone out of his pocket and backed away from the table. Sweeping through his contact list, he found Howard Benson's number. Benson headed the Missing Persons Unit. Anyone involved in narcotics spent a lot of time working with Missing Persons, and he and Benson knew each other well enough to have exchanged cell numbers a few years ago. Benson picked up on the first ring.

"I've got something," Matt said quietly. "You busy?"

"Let me get to my desk," he said. "You got a body?"

Matt sized up the victim. "A girl," he said. "A teenager. Sixteen or seventeen."

"Maybe younger," Cabrera whispered.

Matt noticed his partner standing beside him. He tilted the phone so that both he and Cabrera could listen without turning on the speakerphone.

Matt's eyes flicked back to the girl. "You get that, Benson? Maybe younger. She's Hispanic. About five nine, and on the thin side."

Benson cleared his throat. "This is LA, Matt. I've got hundreds of missing girls around that age. Where are you? Give me a location. Maybe that would help."

"Elysian Park."

"The picnic area up top?"

"What about it?"

"You're on Channel Five right now. The news choppers, Matt. They're circling the tent."

"Yeah, they are."

"Give me a second," Benson said. "No, I might have it. Sophia Ramirez. She's from the neighborhood. Fifteen years old. She went missing on her birthday three days ago."

Matt met Cabrera's eyes as it settled in. The murder victim was a kid. Her watch stopped three days ago on January 8.

"You got a picture you could message us?" Matt said.

"It's on its way."

Matt felt his phone vibrate, pulled it away from his ear, and clicked open the message. As the picture rendered on the screen, he held the phone out so both he and Cabrera could compare the image with the dead girl laid out on the picnic table. It wasn't easy. On the one hand they had a corpse that seemed remarkably preserved. On the other, a young teen who had been severely beaten and bruised.

"It's a match," Matt said finally, then, glancing at his partner. "A match, right, Denny?"

Cabrera nodded. "Yeah," he whispered. "It's a match."

Matt lifted the phone back to his ear. "We got her," he said to Benson. "Sophia Ramirez."

"If that's her, she lived right down the hill on Casanova Street."

Matt pulled a notebook and pen out of his jacket. As Benson gave him the house number, he wrote it down beside the girl's name and date of birth. When the UV lights shut down and the work lights came back up, he took a quick shot of Sophia Ramirez's battered face. Then he raised the phone back to his ear, trying to listen through the sound of the rotors churning in the sky above. He could hear Benson at his desk—papers rustling in the background, a keyboard that stopped clicking.

"What is it, Benson?" Matt said.

"Just want to give you and your partner a heads-up. Something's going on with this kid."

"Like what?"

Matt waved Cabrera back and tilted the phone toward him again.

"Something's wrong with her disappearance," Benson said. "It didn't happen the way it should've happened."

"We're listening," Matt said. "Tell us what you've got."

"She wasn't reported missing by her parents. That's more than unusual. As a matter of fact, in a missing persons case that's been reported, as long as I've been here, that's not the way it happens. Not when a child's been involved. Usually it's the parents who make the call."

"Who are they?' Cabrera asked.

"Angel and Lucia Ramirez. They never reported her missing."

Matt wrote down their names, thinking about Sophia's black eyes and all those bruises on her arms and legs. "If her parents didn't make the call," he said in a harder voice, "who reported her missing?"

"The principal at her high school."

"When?" Matt asked.

"Two days after she went missing. Yesterday."

It hung there for a moment. A fifteen-year-old girl was murdered on her birthday and no one had said anything. No one had even been looking for her.

Matt glanced over at his partner and could see it in his eyes.

The idea of it was stunning. A human disgrace. The young girl had been abandoned even in death. Matt knew all about being abandoned by a parent because it was part of his past, too. Part of the darkness that still haunted him.

The monsters were waking up in his head.

He tried to shake them off and pull himself together. He thanked Benson for his help, thinking that he sounded like a machine, then walked over for another long look at Sophia's corpse. He watched as Gainer gently pulled her jeans up over her hips, then lowered her into a body bag like a father taking his dead girl home.

Gainer gave him a look.

Matt could feel the storm beginning to rotate through his gut. The bands of thunder and lightning coursing through his body. The monsters in his head were awake now, rising from a deep and disturbing sleep.

Trouble ahead.

He grabbed Cabrera by the arm and walked him out of the tent where they could speak without being heard.

"I'm doing the next-of-kin notification," he said. "And you're staying here to oversee the crime scene."

Cabrera eyed him carefully. "I think that sounds like a bad idea."

Matt shook his head. "We can't do both," he said. "Not now. Not fast."

"But those bruises, Matt. We don't have a clue who these people are. You could be walking into something."

"You're right, Denny. Her killer could be homegrown. There's a chance he could be someone she knew. That's why I think we can't wait on this. We need to do it now."

Matt measured his partner's face. Despite the protests, he knew Cabrera agreed. He turned and saw Gainer loading the corpse into the truck, the two first responders, Alvin Marcs and Bill Guy, standing by ready to help.

"I'll take them with me," Matt said.

"Who?"

"Those guys. Maybe we'll get lucky, Denny. Maybe it ends right now."

SIX

It had become a gray January day. Dreary, and even more strange for Los Angeles, uncomfortably humid with thunderclouds moving in over the city. Matt glanced at his watch and realized that it was almost four. Dusk had already set in, and he hadn't eaten anything since the middle of last night. His coffee mug ran dry nine hours ago.

He was riding in the back seat of Marcs and Guy's cruiser. As he gazed out the window, his first thought was that the people living on Casanova Street were a stone's throw from one of the most affluent cities in the world, yet they were impoverished.

He tried not to think about it. Tried not to feel it. Had his uncle, Dr. George Baylor, been sitting beside him right now, the demented man would have used this rundown neighborhood as some sort of bent justification for the people he'd murdered. And for a variety of reasons, some easy and others not, Matt had a vague understanding of his uncle's logic, his torment, but didn't want to let it prey on him right now.

The Ramirez's home was halfway up the block on the left, a side entrance to the park directly across the street. Marcs pulled in front of the house, switched off the headlights, and turned around in his seat. He seemed a little tense.

"How do you want to handle this?" he asked.

Matt gazed out the window, still thinking it over as he eyed the small stucco house and weighed the risks. The rooms were lit up, the light over the front door switched on as if Sophia's parents were expecting someone. Matt looked up in the dark sky, noting a small satellite dish mounted on the terra-cotta tiled roof. To the left of the house, a short driveway led down the hill to a pickup truck and a modest two-car garage that looked as if it needed a fresh coat of paint.

The front door swung open.

"Oh shit," Marcs whispered from behind the wheel. "Company."

Matt turned and saw a man with a mustache and dark brown eyes standing on the other side of a storm door staring at them. He guessed that the man was Sophia's father, Angel, and from the porch light raking his heavily lined face, that he was more than upset. The man seemed fixated on the cruiser and didn't make a move to step outside and ask why they were here. Instead, he just stood there—still as a statue—brooding and trying to pierce the darkened glass of the cruiser with those eyes of his.

Matt turned back to Marcs and Guy, then pulled out his pistol.

"Here's the way I want to do it," he said as he inspected his .45, checked the mag, then returned the pistol to its holster on his belt. "This may not be what it could be. You guys understand? Don't let your imaginations get in the way of what you're seeing right now. I'm going in alone to talk to these people and let them know that we found their daughter's body. If I need help, I'll shoot you a sign."

Guy gave him a wild look from the passenger seat. "What kind of sign?"

Matt filled his lungs with air as he opened the door and climbed out of the cruiser. "I've got no clue," he said under his breath. "You'll know it when you see it."

He closed the door and started toward the house knowing that the advice he'd just given Marcs and Guy was more for himself than anyone else. As he stepped onto the narrow front porch, the feeling was so strange, so odd—the man just standing there glaring at him. From a distance he appeared short and stocky and strong as a bull. He was wearing a pair of overalls and combed his coarse black hair straight back. When Matt finally reached the door, he got a closer look. The lines on the man's face seemed like they might be more about exhaustion than age because he was obviously still in his thirties. But even more important, he didn't appear to be armed. Matt's eyes ran up and down the man's body, and he didn't see any sign that he might be carrying a piece.

"Are you Angel Ramirez?" Matt said in a firm voice.

Moments passed before the man nodded.

"May I come in?"

Ramirez had an attitude going but eventually acknowledged Matt's presence and stepped aside. Pulling the storm door open for himself, Matt glanced back at Marcs and Guy in the cruiser, then entered the house. He was feeling uneasy, trying to push the images of the bruises on the young girl's face and body out of his mind. He was concerned that even this early in the case, the evidence could be spinning them in a direction they might not be able to overcome.

He kept reminding himself that a monster killed the girl. A monster beat her up and put her in the ground.

He looked up. Angel Ramirez was standing close, maybe too close, and still staring at him with those hollow dark eyes.

"We've been waiting for you," Ramirez said in a gruff voice. "We've been waiting since we heard the helicopters this morning and turned on the TV."

Matt took a step back, noting the shotgun over the fireplace and guessing that it was far too new and lethal to be a family heirloom. He knew the make and model well, a Remington 870 Wingmaster, and had to assume that it was loaded. When he turned, he realized that the room was lit entirely by candlelight and the TV, which appeared to have been muted. Framed pictures of Sophia were everywhere.

And then he noticed Sophia's mother, Lucia. Her eyes were on him as she sat on the couch quietly weeping into a handkerchief. Like her husband, she was well groomed. She wore an apron over what appeared to be a fitted red blouse, and black slacks. But what struck Matt most about her person was her warm face and gentle demeanor—her dark eyes that seemed to work like a pair of open windows, revealing how damaged she was inside.

"You've come to arrest us," Ramirez said.

Matt turned and gave him a hard look. "Why don't you have a seat on the couch with your wife."

The man grit his teeth in anger. "Why don't you just get this over with and take us away?"

"Sit down on the couch, Mr. Ramirez."

Matt watched the man cross the room and take a seat beside his wife. Ramirez's admission of guilt was more than unusual. It came way too quick to be right and true. These people were obviously in shock and grieving. His eyes dropped to Ramirez's hands. He didn't see a single bruise, cut, or even a scratch. He could have been wearing gloves and it wouldn't have made a difference. There was no way that he could have beaten his daughter to death and walked away with unblemished hands. Something was going on here. Something he couldn't see yet.

Matt sat down in a chair across from the couch, making sure he had a view of the front door.

"How many children do you have?" he said.

Lucia Ramirez raised her head and gazed Matt's way. "Only Sophia," she said. "Just our Sophia."

She lowered her eyes again. Matt reached inside his pocket for his cell phone and found the photograph he'd taken of the victim's battered face.

"I need to show you something," he said as gently as he could. "It's not gonna be easy to look at. It's gonna be tough. Maybe the toughest thing you'll ever be asked to do in your life. That doesn't change the fact that I have to ask you to do it."

They were staring at him, their eyes big and glassy. Ramirez moved closer to his wife and wrapped his arm around her shoulder as if he could somehow protect her from the moment. His meaty hands were trembling.

"Are you ready?" Matt asked.

They nodded tentatively, unable to speak. They knew what was about to happen. They already knew what they were going to see.

Matt turned his cell phone around and pushed it across the coffee table. Both Ramirez and Lucia leaned closer, their eyes drifting toward the phone, then locking in on the picture of their dead little girl.

"Is this your daughter?" Matt asked. "Is this Sophia?"

They didn't need to answer. They didn't need to say or do anything. Moments passed. Tears and agony—he could see the dread in their eyes. A certain kind of dark confirmation that their lives had just been ruined. Forever ruined. And in an instant, Matt knew with absolute certainty that they had never abused their child and had nothing to do with her death. They were in mourning but had admitted to committing a crime. From the fear they were still showing on their faces, Matt thought he knew what it was now.

He switched off the phone and slipped it into his pocket. Then he picked up a framed photograph of their daughter from a side table and placed it before them on the coffee table. His hope was that it might help shorten the memory of what they'd just seen. Both Ramirez and Lucia gazed at the new picture, wiping their eyes and cheeks and trying to pull themselves together.

"Your daughter went missing three days ago," Matt said in a quieter voice. "Why didn't you call it in? Why didn't you report it?"

They kept their eyes on the photograph without speaking, the fear on their faces all the more telling.

Matt gave Ramirez a look. "When did you come to this country?" he said. "That's the crime you were talking about, right? That's why you didn't call Missing Persons. You were afraid someone might show up and take you and your wife away."

They looked up from the photograph of their daughter, the fear in their eyes reaching a fever pitch. Matt guessed that their journey began a long time ago, maybe when they themselves had been children, because both spoke English without the hint of another first language.

Matt leaned over the table, measuring them. "Okay," he said. "Okay. We'll never talk about it again. But you've got to understand something. I'm gonna need your help to solve this case. Your daughter's case. I can't do it without you."

They nodded like they wanted to help but remained silent.

"Okay," Matt said. "I understand why you're afraid, but we've got a deal, right?"

He met their eyes and waited for them to say something, but they never did. He glanced at the door, then back.

"Tell me why your daughter had so many bruises on her body—her arms and legs. Who was abusing her?"

Ramirez shot him a look like he didn't understand. "Abusing her?"

"Was it a neighbor? A relative? Someone bullying her at school?"

Lucia met Matt's gaze and appeared just as confused as her husband. "Sophia was very popular," she said. "She was a straight-A student. Everybody loved her."

"What about a boyfriend?"

Ramirez shook his head. "He lives down the street, but he would never hurt her. He wouldn't do this to Sophia."

Matt pulled out his notebook and pen. "What's his name and address?"

"Trey Washington, but he's a good boy. Those bruises on her arms and legs are Sophia's fault. She does that to herself."

Matt stopped writing and gave Ramirez a long look. "She does it to herself?" he said.

Ramirez nodded. After a moment he stood up.

"I want you to see her bedroom," he said.

Matt got up from the chair, glanced through the storm door at Marcs and Guy in the cruiser, then followed Ramirez through the kitchen, down a short hallway, and into Sophia's bedroom. When Ramirez switched on the lights, Matt took one look and understood.

Sophia Ramirez was a skateboarder.

And from the poster-size photographs of her tacked to the walls, the numerous trophies on her bookcase, and the blue ribbons pinned to her bulletin board, a prolific skateboarder with talent.

Ramirez crossed the room, sat down at his daughter's desk, and switched on her computer. Once the machine booted, Ramirez clicked open a window and a video began playing.

"She takes too many chances," Ramirez said. "But it's who she is—a risk taker like her mother. It's how she wins. It's how she thrives. She and Trey shoot these videos together. They want to go to UCLA and become filmmakers."

Matt tried to take it all in and settle. In a single instant, his view of the case had been gutted. Nothing about solving this case would be easy. Nothing about the murder was homegrown. He found a spot on the bed and sat down to watch the video. The shots looked as if they had been made and edited by a professional. After a few minutes, he saw Sophia's boyfriend on a second skateboard and realized that they were taking turns shooting each other. It looked like they were across the street in the park. He could see the picnic tables at the top of the hill, the grassy bank, and the grove of pine trees in the background. As they started down the street on their boards, they made a long jump over a bench and landed on a slab of concrete that had the look and feel of a drainage canal built to carry rainwater down the hill to the river. It was a steep, fast, and harrowing ride.

When the clip ended, Matt turned and found Ramirez gazing at him again. But this time the anger and fear were gone, and his face looked young and clean and filled with love and pride.

A moment passed, the air in the room heavier now as Matt began to sense the totality of their innocence and loss. When he spoke, there was a certain shake to his voice, like he'd tried to reel in his emotions but only made it halfway.

"What was she doing in the park three nights ago?" he said. "Do you have any idea?"

"It was the eighth," Ramirez said. "It was her birthday. We gave her a new skateboard and upgraded her camera. It's a sports cam that attaches to her helmet." He turned and stared at the image of his daughter frozen on the computer screen. A spirit filled with life, and at fifteen, just beginning to bloom.

"She wanted to take a test ride before it got dark," he whispered. "She wanted to make sure everything worked just right. That's Sophia– so happy, so loving, so smart. My wife had made a birthday cake. We were waiting for her in the living room, looking at the gifts that were still wrapped and staring at the door. We waited a long time. Then I went out looking for her. I searched all night but couldn't find her. When I came home, I had this hope, this dream that my child would be sleeping on the couch waiting for me. This hope that all my fears, the nightmares in my head, that everything would be over, and we would go back to being a family again. But it didn't happen. Not like I hoped and dreamed it would. I never saw her again. Never got to hear her call me 'Daddy' again."

Matt could see Ramirez playing the images of his daughter in his mind, then watched as the man lowered his head and started weeping.

SEVEN

W**ork lights were set up,** the crime scene still being processed on what had become a foggy night. Matt got out of the cruiser, thanked Marcs and Guy for the ride, and looked past the tent and picnic tables for his partner.

On the drive back, Matt had called Cabrera to let him know that Sophia had a helmet and skateboard with her on the night she was killed. But even more curious, when Matt had watched the video of Sophia skateboarding, both she and her friend had been wearing knee and elbow pads. Before leaving, Matt had asked Ramirez about it and was told that his daughter never skated without the added protection. In fact, he said that Sophia often wore compression sleeves to support her knees but wasn't sure about that night because the sleeves fit underneath her jeans.

None of these things had been found on the girl's body or underneath the trees. And while it didn't confirm the idea that the killer may have spent a considerable amount of time with her or even corroborate the theory that he removed her clothing and dressed her up again, Matt found the whole thing particularly disturbing.

He jotted down a few notes in his pad, thinking that they might be useful during the girl's autopsy. Returning the pad to his pocket, he saw Cabrera stepping out of the grove of pine trees and caught his eye. As he headed for the grassy bank, he glanced at the tall buildings that framed out the new downtown section of LA, their bright lights blurred by the heavy mist.

"Any luck?" Matt said.

Cabrera shook his head as he climbed the ridge. "These guys went through every trash can in the park this morning when they made their first sweep. No one found a skateboard or a helmet or anything like that. All they found was trash."

Matt grimaced as he chewed it over, wondering why it felt like all this mattered. "What about Speeks?"

Cabrera gave him a slow look. "He left about ten minutes ago. He said it doesn't look good. We've got a few dirt samples, the dried semen, and whatever else they can pull off the body, but that's about it. The hairs they picked up look like they came from the dog."

Matt reached into his pocket for a smoke, then remembered that he'd quit.

"Let's take a walk," he said.

"Where?" Cabrera asked.

Matt pointed to the warehouse set before the railroad tracks at the bottom of the hill. "Down there," he said. "It looks like they're still open."

They walked through the gloom by the picnic tables and started down the street on foot. As they passed the bench Sophia and her friend, Trey Washington, had jumped over in their video, Matt peered through the haze at the concrete canal and estimated it to be a good fifteen feet beyond the bench. He didn't know why he liked the fact that the jump had been dangerous, but he did. A risk taker, her father had called her. A risk taker like her mother.

Matt noticed a path through the trees and saw the private road that followed the train tracks at the bottom of a steep wall of stones and rocks. As they climbed down to the pavement, he thought the road seemed too narrow to accommodate tractor trailers carrying heavy loads. He turned and looked back at the city to get his bearings. He could see the Buena Vista Viaduct just a hundred yards behind them. Once the private road passed beneath the bridge, it became Baker Street, and finally North Spring Street, rolling through the outskirts of Chinatown into the city.

Cabrera turned back and pulled a bottle of water out of his jacket. "What about the girl's family?" he asked.

Matt shrugged but didn't say anything.

"What do they do?" Cabrera went on.

"He's a cabinet maker. He showed me his shop in the garage. She's a housekeeper for a TV director."

"Who's the director?"

"Somebody I never heard of. But I don't watch network TV."

Cabrera stopped in the middle of the street. Matt saw him brooding and could guess what was on his partner's mind. Cabrera was first-generation American. Eventually the storm seemed to pass, and his dark eyes cleared. After rubbing his hand over his forehead and through his wiry hair, he started walking again.

"How do we keep Immigration out of this?" he said after a while. "They could fuck everything up, Matt. They could fuck it up before we even get started."

Matt gave him a look. "This is a murder case, Denny. They're not gonna mess with us."

"That's the point. There's a killer on the street. Immigration likes messing with people. They'd fuck us up just for kicks. They don't give a shit about anything anymore."

"Maybe not," Matt said. "But this is our case, and they're not gonna mess with us. Believe me. It's not an issue here. Forget about it."

They walked around the bend in the dark of night. As the road straightened out on the other side, Matt saw the factory nesting in the fog at the bottom of the hill. Although he could appreciate the torment his partner was wrestling with and knew the sacrifices his parents had made to raise him here in California, Matt tried to put it aside. He was thinking about the security cameras mounted on the factory's walls that he'd noticed earlier in the day. It seemed like a long shot. But they needed a break, and he hoped they might get one tonight.

It took no more than a couple of minutes to reach the facility. Fixed to the ten-foot wall, a small brass sign read DMG WASTE MANAGEMENT. Matt stepped over to the open gate and gazed into the building. Five people dressed in hazmat suits were transferring fifty-five-gallon drums from a cargo container to a platform beside a smaller truck. There was a smell wafting from the place. A foul acidic odor that smacked of sulfur and rotten eggs. To the left of the facility's huge bay doors, he spotted an entrance to the office. But just as they passed through the gate, a security guard stepped outside, noticed them, and switched on his flashlight.

EIGHT

"You guys have an appointment?" the guard asked.

Both Matt and Cabrera raised their badges. Matt stepped in beside his partner, his voice steady and clear.

"We'd like to talk to the owner or manager if he or she is still here."

The guard nodded and seemed friendly as he approached them, panning his flashlight across their IDs. After a brief look, he lowered the light and stepped back, then cracked an odd smile.

"Is this about that girl on TV?" he said. "The one they found in the woods up there?"

Matt nodded, noting that the guard wore a nameplate that read "Tommy" and that there was something not quite right about the man. Matt traded a quick look with Cabrera. When he checked the guard's belt, he was glad to see that he didn't carry a weapon.

"We thought you guys might be able to help," Matt said.

The guard smiled at them again. "They're in a meeting," he said. "But let's go inside and see. Annie will figure it out."

Matt traded another quick look with Cabrera as the guard led the way up the steps and through the office door. Once inside, they entered a lobby with a young female receptionist seated behind a chest-high counter. Her eyes made a quick sweep from Matt and Cabrera to the guard.

"What's going on, Tommy?" she said in a casual voice.

"These are the detectives trying find out who killed that girl on TV. They'd like to speak with—"

He stopped like his batteries had run out and suddenly appeared uncertain.

The receptionist smiled and spoke gently, almost as if she were a parent. "They'd like to speak with who, Tommy?"

The guard thought it over with his eyes down. "Sonny, I guess."

The receptionist looked over at Matt and flashed another pleasant smile. "They're in a partners meeting," she said. "But I think it'll be okay. I just need to let them know you're here."

Matt thanked her and watched her get out of the chair and start down the hall behind the counter. She was young and dressed in a pair of skintight stretch jeans and a black turtleneck with her light-brown hair pulled back in a ponytail. He watched her reach the first door on the left, give it three taps, and enter. When she closed the door behind her, Matt's gaze returned to the counter, where he noticed three trays filled with business cards. It didn't take much to realize that the company, DMG Waste Management, had been named after its three partners—Sonny Daniels, Ryan Moore, and Lane Grubb.

Matt pocketed one of each card and looked up as the door opened and a man with a shaved head stepped out and started walking toward them. He was dressed in a pair of well-tailored slacks and a casual dress shirt, appeared to be in his late thirties, and carried himself with confidence. When he reached the reception area, he looked directly at Matt, extended his hand, and spoke through a smile.

"My name's Sonny Daniels," he said. "How can we help you?"

They shook hands.

"I'm Detective Matt Jones from Hollywood Homicide, and this my partner, Denny Cabrera."

Daniels nodded. "Annie told me this is about the girl. We've had the TV on all day. Come on back."

He swung the gate open. While the guard stayed behind, Daniels led Matt and Cabrera down the hall and into what turned out to be a conference room. Two other men were there, both of them standing by their seats while the receptionist made a fresh pot of coffee. Matt glanced at the conference table. Papers were strewn across the glass surface: schedules, lists, and other documents. A set of blueprints was weighted down by three empty coffee mugs. A TV mounted to the wall was switched to Channel Five News, but muted.

Daniels stepped around the table to a chair between the two men. "These are my partners, Detectives. Ryan Moore and Lane Grubb. Meet Denny Cabrera and Matt Jones."

Daniels patted both partners on their shoulders.

"You three guys are co-owners," Matt said. "Daniels, Moore, and Grubb. DMG Waste Management."

Daniels smiled again. "That's true. Now please, have a seat. Would you like a cup of coffee? Something stronger?"

"Thanks, we're fine," Cabrera said.

Daniels nodded at the receptionist. As she left the room and everyone sat down, Matt took a moment to measure the three men on the other side of the table. Ryan Moore and Lane Grubb were dressed in expensive slacks and casual shirts exactly like Sonny Daniels. And it didn't take much to guess that all three were in their late thirties and probably the same age. But what struck Matt most about them was their presence, their demeanor. They were identical. Like they were brothers. Like they had known each other and been friends their whole lives. They were comfortable around each other. There wasn't an ounce of tension in the room.

Daniels leaned forward. "Please, Detective," he said. "Tell us how we can help."

Matt glanced at Cabrera and took the lead. "We realize that you're here on a quiet street without much traffic, Mr. Daniels. Basically, you're here on a dead end. Still, there's a chance you or your partners or someone who works for you might have seen something. It could be as simple as seeing someone drive by who seemed out of place. Someone on foot who appeared lost or in a hurry."

"When did the murder occur?" Daniels asked.

"Three days ago," Cabrera said.

Matt nodded. "We're guessing around four thirty in the afternoon. It would have been dark."

Daniels settled back in his chair as he thought it over. "You're right, Detectives. The only cars we see passing by are from railroad people driving to and from the substation. But most of the time our gate's closed. The wall is ten feet high, so we don't see much. Like I said, we've had the TV on all day. I've had a chance to ask around. I think my partners will back me up on this because I know that they've been talking to everybody as well. No one who works here mentioned seeing or hearing anything that they would describe as out of the ordinary. The truth is, we're down the hill and can't even see the park from here."

Daniels leaned forward and raised his hand like he had an idea.

"Here's what we could do for you," he said finally. "Most of our crew left at five. Tomorrow, if you'd like, we could set aside time to let you and your partner talk to them yourselves. The TV said this is about a young girl. Believe me, anything we can do to help, we'll do."

Matt paused a moment, trying to hide his disappointment. Daniels was bright, the natural leader of the three, and doing everything he could do to assist them. Matt couldn't help feeling like he and Cabrera were wasting time and headed in the wrong direction.

"How many employees do you have?" he asked.

"We're a small group," Daniels said. "Other than the three of us, and Annie, who's still in school and works part-time, we've only got fifteen employees."

"What about your security cameras? Did anyone check them?"

Daniels turned to his partner, Lane Grubb, who cleared his throat and leaned his elbows on the table.

"I haven't had a chance to go through the logs, but you're welcome to join me," Grubb said. "If it's three days back, then everything we've got is still saved."

Daniels nodded. "It wouldn't take more than ten minutes to set up. We could do it right now."

"That would be terrific," Cabrera said.

Matt watched everyone get up from the table. Daniels opened the door, glanced at the reception area, then led the way farther down the hall. The plaster walls soon gave way to cinder block, the sounds coming from the factory growing louder as they moved deeper into the building. After turning the corner, they climbed a set of steps and entered a room that overlooked the entire facility. Matt noticed the security monitors mounted on the wall below a small video and audio switcher. While Grubb sat down at the computer and began searching his video database, Matt crossed the room to the wall of giant plate-glass windows and gazed into the plant.

He had a bird's-eye view of the entire operation from here. He could see the five people in hazmat suits unloading the fifty-five-gallon drums from the shipping container. But now he realized that the drums were being moved with a forklift to a small room on the other side of the supply shelves and workbenches. Flashes of bright red light were bouncing out of the room onto the floor and walls of the factory. Once the drums were hauled out of the room, they were rolled onto a scale by hand and weighed by three men wearing gloves and safety glasses. A man with dark hair and a beard was standing by the scale making notes on a clipboard and adding a sticker to the top of each drum. Behind him, Matt could see an enclosed garage area where two additional small trucks were parked for the night.

"Not very exciting, is it?"

Matt turned. The comment had come from Sonny Daniels, who had walked over to the windows as well.

"What do you guys do here?" Matt said.

Daniels smiled. "Like the sign says, we're all about waste management. The kind no one wants in their backyard. It comes in by rail. Our people inspect the integrity of the drums, the quality of the welding, and assign each drum an identification number. Then they're loaded onto a smaller truck like that one and driven to a storage facility outside of Palmdale."

"Why the smaller truck?" Cabrera said. "Why not a big rig?"

Ryan Moore, who had remained silent until now, stepped in beside Cabrera. "The storage facility is an abandoned gold mine that's been capped, sealed, and inspected by the EPA. You can drive cars through those tunnels.

But that truck's as big as we can go. It's not that bad really. Each truck has a thirty-drum capacity. Fifteen trips back and forth and we're good."

"The way it smells," Cabrera went on, "I wouldn't want it in my backyard either."

Moore nodded. "Even if one of the drums failed, the mine has been completely modernized and the cap is five feet thick. There's no way that it would ever have an impact on the environment."

"We're up," Grubb said. "This is video from three days ago."

Everybody stepped away from the windows. Matt moved in beside Grubb for a closer look. DMG Waste Management had ten camera positions. Of the ten, five cameras covered the interior of the facility, and the remaining five were housed outside. All ten shots were up, and all ten were synchronized with their time code running at the bottom of the screen.

"This is two in the afternoon," Grubb said. "I'll speed it up by ten. If you see anything that stands out, we can go back over it in real time."

Matt traded looks with Cabrera and sighed under his breath. Like Daniels and Moore, Lane Grubb was trying to be helpful. But as Matt studied each camera, its position and angle, he knew that it was hopeless. The reach of the five cameras mounted on the perimeter wall covered the street on both sides of the factory but focused on the gate and property. Though the base of the steep hill filled the background in two shots, it looked like it was ten miles away and completely out of focus. And when day turned to night, the view across the street went completely black.

Grubb must have noticed Matt's disappointment.

"What?" he said. "No good?"

NINE

And then there was nothing...

Matt was beginning to get nervous, like just maybe they'd have to wait for another murder, another death of an innocent young woman, with the hope that the killer might make a mistake and leave something behind.

Before that happened, before someone else died, he wanted to interview Sophia's boyfriend. It may have been a long shot—the killing so brutal. Still, he wanted to meet the kid and hear what he had to say, just to make sure.

Matt felt the rain on his face as he walked over to Cabrera's SUV and watched him climb in.

"You got the address?" Matt said.

Cabrera nodded, rolling down his window. "What's his name again?"

"Trey Washington."

"I'll see you there."

Matt stepped over to his car and got behind the wheel. Lighting up the engine, he rummaged through his glove box until he found a sheet of nicotine gum. There were eight pieces, wrapped in foil and plastic and glistening in the lights from the dash. A moment passed, and then another, before he sucked it up and tossed the pack of gum back into the glove box.

Not this time. Not now. Or was it really just not yet?

He switched on the wipers, pulled around the trees, and glided down the hill behind Cabrera. Within a few minutes, they made the turn onto Casanova Street and were cruising up the block. As they passed the Ramirez's home, Matt noticed that the lights were out and tried not to think about what was going on inside. The anguish and despair of an unimaginable loss. How did the girl's father put it?

She was so happy. So loving. So smart.

The rain had started to pick up. Matt could see the billowing white clouds in the black sky, the sound of thunder moving closer. When Cabrera parked across the street from the kid's home, he pulled in behind him and eyed the house carefully. He noted the lighted front window but didn't see a car on the street or in the short driveway. Matt pulled his cell phone out of his pocket, speed-dialed his partner's number, and heard Cabrera's phone click.

"What do you think?" Matt said.

"Doesn't look like anybody's home."

"Let's give it a try just in case."

A bolt of lightning snapped across the sky, the entire neighborhood bright like a battlefield under heavy fire. Matt counted a single beat before he heard the thunder cracking and knew from experience that the storm had reached them and was now directly overhead. He could feel his car shuddering from the sound, followed by a strong blast of wind. Shutting down the engine, he climbed out and jogged across the street with Cabrera behind him. He could see a set of steps ahead and took them two at a time until he was standing beneath a modest porch. Moving over to the front door, he gave it a hard knock and gazed through the window above the dead bolt.

A moment passed, and then another with no response.

Cabrera crossed the porch and peered around the corner. "The driveway's empty," he said. "And I don't see anything behind the house. Nobody's here, Matt. No one's home."

Matt knocked on the door again, still looking through the window. The footprint of the house seemed remarkably similar to the Ramirez's home. The front door opened into a small living room. The kitchen would be to the left with the bedrooms in back. Matt eyed the modest furnishings. The TV was switched off. With the exception of a single lamp on the table by the door, the house was dark.

He thought it over, trying to keep an open mind.

Was Trey Washington hard to reach? Or was he trying to avoid them? Matt wasn't sure anymore but acknowledged his growing frustration and dropped the idea.

"Let's get back to the station," he said. "I'll pick up some takeout on the way in. Chinese okay with you?"

Cabrera broke a smile. "The Red Dragon?"

Matt nodded. The Red Dragon was in Chinatown on Bamboo Lane and only a five-minute drive from where they were standing. Both Matt and Cabrera liked the food and were friends with Zhang Wei, who managed the restaurant for a pair of owners who lived in Beverly Hills and had bought the place for twice what it was worth from Wei's grandfather.

"I'll call it in," Cabrera said.

"And I'll get Benson back on the phone and see what he can send us."

Matt pulled out a business card, wrote the words *Call me—It's important* below his name, and jammed it into the door. Then he ran across the street with his partner, flinching when another bolt of lightning exploded over their heads. Matt climbed into his car, made a U-turn, and sped off. Within fifteen minutes he'd spoken to Benson at Missing Persons and was walking out of the Red Dragon with their order and two extra-large cups of freshly brewed piping-hot coffee. That first sip of hot java was more than comforting and, after a day like this one, better than a shot of bourbon. Matt settled into the driver's seat. That nervous feeling was back, and he tried to ignore it as best he could. On any other night the fourteen-mile drive from downtown LA to Hollywood would have used up the better part of an hour. But tonight the storm must have scared people off because he managed the ride in less than half an hour. Two minutes after exiting the freeway he pulled into the lot behind the station and killed the engine.

The rain had become torrential, the sound of water beating against the roof of the car almost deafening. Matt slung his laptop case over his shoulder, grabbed the bags of food, and ran across the lot. Flinging the rear door open, he hurried past the holding cells, stepped onto the empty bureau floor, and found Cabrera in the conference room with his computer already powered up.

"Benson sent over the files," Cabrera said. "It might be worse than we thought."

Matt set the food down on the table, then grabbed a seat and rolled it next to his partner. Cabrera pointed to the screen as he reached inside a bag for the second cup of coffee. Popping the lid, he sipped through the steam and gave Matt a long look.

"Take a deep breath," he said. "The list of missing teenage girls over the past six months is well over a hundred, Matt. But look what happens when Benson narrows the search by type, age, and location. He's using the Police Academy and Dodger Stadium as his center point, then extending the reach by five miles in every direction."

Matt studied the screen carefully. There were five girls between the ages of fifteen and eighteen who had gone missing over the last six months. Aside from Sophia Ramirez, there were two Latino girls, a black, a white, and an Asian. Although race didn't appear to be in play, each girl was identical in every other way. They all looked young and innocent for their age. When Matt skimmed through Benson's notes, he learned that in every case they came from a loving family. In each case the missing child was popular in school, didn't use alcohol or drugs, and had no obvious reason to run away.

Cabrera added another packet of sugar to his coffee. "There's a rumor Mexican drug gangs are kidnapping teens out of LA and smuggling them across the border."

"Maybe so," Matt said. "But our girl wasn't kidnapped. She was raped and killed two blocks from her home."

Matt opened the boxes of Chinese food, made a small plate, and ate quickly. Over the next five hours he and Cabrera put together a murder book, wrote and completed their preliminary reports, and got started on an electronic version of the Chronological Record that they could access and amend from their laptops. Hard copies were printed and added to the murder book, along with color photographs of the five girls who remained missing. Matt printed a second copy of the photos, taping them side by side to the glass window between the conference room and the bureau floor. Below each photo he added a three-by-five card with their names, ages, and the dates each girl went missing.

It was nearly midnight when he and Cabrera finally sat down at the conference table and gazed at the five photos. They were in trouble, that much was clear. Big trouble. And that nervous feeling in Matt's gut had come back with a vengeance.

He turned to his partner, who still appeared mesmerized by the photographs. "You see the problem, right?"

Cabrera took a moment to think it over. "If you're saying there's a pattern, I don't see it. It's not as if these kids went missing a month apart. Our guy isn't howling at a full moon."

"That's not what I'm talking about," Matt said.

"Okay. What are you talking about?"

"Every one of them went missing, right? Never to be heard from again."

Cabrera nodded, his voice breaking. "Somehow we have to find them, Matt."

"And that's the problem. The guy we're looking for takes them, uses them, but doesn't throw them out when he's done."

"What are you saying?"

Matt got out of the chair, grabbed the bags filled with what was left of the Chinese food, and tossed them in the trash.

"He doesn't throw them out when he's finished, Denny. He doesn't leave them by the side of a road or dump their bodies in an alley. They're never seen or heard from again, right?"

Cabrera nodded, glancing at the photos, then turning back. "This isn't like most cases," he said. "Other than the semen and what forensics might find on the body, there's no trail of evidence for us to follow. No sightings, like you said, not much of anything. Is that what you mean?"

Matt sat on the table beside his partner. "There's nothing to see because the victims have been put in a place where no one can find them. You see what I mean? He buries them, Denny. He puts them in the ground."

49

TEN

The idea that a killer could have been working the city completely undetected for months or even years because he buried his victims was more than grim.

Matt unlocked his front door and switched on the lights.

As he lowered his laptop onto the kitchen table and cracked open a beer, he felt his cell phone let out a single pulse. After swiping the glass face with his thumb, he read a text message that had been sent to both he and Cabrera from Ed Gainer, the investigator from the coroner's office. Sophia Ramirez had been moved to the top of the list. Her autopsy was confirmed for 7:00 a.m. tomorrow morning. Art Madina, the best medical examiner in the county, had been assigned the case.

Matt knew that moving Sophia to the top of the list hadn't been easy. He also knew that Gainer and Madina pulled strings when they thought a case stood out. He thought about the way Gainer had placed the girl in the body bag. The care he'd taken. The expression on his face.

Matt took another swig of beer and walked back into the living room. Switching off the lights, he opened the slider and sat down on the couch in the darkness. The view from his living room matched the view from the deck, and he could see everything across the basin from Venice Beach to the tall buildings downtown. The storm had lessened some. He found the sound of the steady rain soothing and watched with fascination as stray bolts of lightning opened up the sky over the city every few minutes or so.

Calculating that he'd been up for almost twenty-four hours, Matt slipped out of his shoes and put his feet up on the coffee table. That odd feeling in his gut was back. He had always been able to trust his instincts. And he wondered why this nervous feeling seemed to be cutting in and out on him all day. He also wondered why he hadn't felt any pain from the four gunshot wounds still healing in his chest and left shoulder. It all seemed to begin when he'd laid eyes on Sophia's hair strewn through the soil under those pine trees.

Was it the shock of seeing someone buried in a shallow grave? Was it the depravity of the crime?

Or was it the *big* thing?

That thing in his life—that thought, that fear—still following him everywhere he went. Still haunting him. Still chasing him through the day and catching up with him every night.

A single question.

Was his uncle, Dr. George Baylor, involved in the murder of Sophia Ramirez or not?

At first glance, it didn't seem to fit. But only at first glance.

His uncle was clearly insane and had murdered scores of innocent people—innocent young women just like Sophia Ramirez. Celebrated for his skills as a plastic surgeon, the doctor-turned-serial-killer was more than capable of changing his motive, or the way he wanted things to look, in order to cover his tracks and satisfy his demented thirst for blood.

Matt finished off the bottle and settled into the couch. He watched the Library Tower, the tallest building in LA that had since been renamed by a bank, take a direct hit from a bolt of lightning. The electrical charge struck the very top of the building and seemed to last for ten or fifteen seconds before it fizzed through the air and died out.

A moment passed as the living room went dark again.

Matt realized that he could see it in Cabrera's eyes today. In every criminalist from the lab who worked the crime scene. From Gainer to Speeks to even the two first responders, Marcs and Guy. He could see it showing on their faces as they examined Sophia's battered corpse in the tent. He could hear it in Howard Benson's voice when he'd called Missing Persons.

Could it be Dr. Baylor? Was it possible that the plastic surgeon had returned to LA and was killing again?

Matt knew that as long as he was a homicide detective, as long as he was alive, this would be his fate, his curse. That until the doctor was found and either killed or locked up in an asylum, he would always be the first suspect. The madman who defied capture and always got away.

His cell phone started vibrating. Though he didn't recognize the caller ID, he switched on the phone and raised it to his ear.

"You awake, Jones?"

Matt tried to place the husky voice, then realized in an instant that the caller was Wes Rogers, special agent in charge of the FBI's field office in Philadelphia.

"I'm awake," Matt said. "What's happened?"

"The story's gonna break in the morning."

Matt got to his feet and started pacing in the darkness. He already had a feel for the answer—it could only go one of two ways—but he asked Rogers the question just the same.

"What story is that?" he said. "What's gonna break in the morning?"

ELEVEN

How a double murder twenty-five hundred miles away could flood Matt's body and mind with relief might be a question he should ask Dr. May someday. Still, that rush of good feeling couldn't be denied.

It was official. Dr. George Baylor was no longer a person of interest in the Sophia Ramirez murder case.

According to Rogers and the FBI, Baylor murdered two people on the same day Sophia had been killed. The bodies were found in a cheap motel in Washington, Pennsylvania, about thirty miles south of Pittsburgh. And for Dr. Baylor, his latest two victims mirrored everything he stood for. He had killed a woman caked in greed, the CEO of a pharmaceutical company who had been in the news lately, along with her paid stooge, a man who claimed to be a clinical professor of family medicine in Baltimore and published bogus articles touting the company in a number of medical journals.

Matt couldn't believe the woman had been so stupid or even psychotic that she didn't see Baylor in her rearview mirror.

According to what Rogers said last night, and what CNN was broadcasting this morning, the pharmaceutical company specialized in a generic medication for children. The cost to manufacture the drug topped off at somewhere between $1 and $16 per dose, but she decided to raise the price to $600. So pleased with herself for pulling off what amounted to a nationwide swindle on children and their parents, she thought she deserved a gift and gave herself one. She increased her salary from $2.5 million a year to $20 million, and no one said or did anything to stop her.

Until now . . .

The doctor must have been drooling as he researched his prey.

According to Rogers, the methodology of the double murder showed that the doctor had been influenced by Andrew Penchant, the serial killer Matt brought down in Philadelphia just two weeks ago. Matt had to agree. With this double murder, Baylor no longer seemed to be going after the children of the greedy to inflict pain on their narcissistic parents. Instead, what first responders found when they'd entered the motel room demonstrated a far more direct approach.

By all appearances, the man and woman had been stripped of their clothing and forced to have sex. Once the doctor was satisfied that they had been adequately humiliated, he injected them with a sedative, slashed their faces into full-blown Chelsea Grins, then woke them up to show them what he'd done.

Matt buttoned his shirt and slipped on a pair of shoes as he played through the murder in his head. He had seen it himself so many times before.

The Chelsea Grin. The Glasgow Smile.

The idea of showing his victims how he'd mutilated their faces was the doctor's particularly cruel way of getting them to scream. Seeing themselves as hideous and disfigured creatures beyond repair wouldn't have taken much more than a quick look in the mirror. And that was his goal. To get them to scream, to see the dread in their eyes as their wounds burst open and they bled to death. The result was a gruesome clown-like smile that extended across the entire face from ear to lips and lips to ear. Something out of a horror movie, but far more vivid and far more grotesque.

Matt took a moment to steady himself. He could see it in his mind. He could see every grisly detail.

Apparently, the doctor selected a motel that had the reputation for being a hangout for local prostitutes. When the cleaning staff saw the DO NOT DISTURB sign on the door, they passed the room by for two days. On the third day, the smell of rotten flesh had become so toxic, the manager peeked inside and called 911.

Dr. Baylor had three entire days to put distance between himself and the crime scene. Even so, his fingerprints were found in so many places in the room, it was clear to Rogers that the plastic surgeon no longer cared about hiding his identity. In fact, Matt imagined that he was more than pleased with what he'd done and wanted to be recognized for it. The choice of the motel was almost inspiring as a finishing touch, and Matt thought he could still hear the doctor laughing in the night.

When Matt had asked Rogers if anything else stood out from the doctor's past, the special agent only mentioned one thing. The male victim's penis. At some point during the murder and while the man was still alive, the doctor had removed it with what state police investigators were calling a very sharp blade or scalpel. Though the crime scene had been processed and all evidence packed up and sent to the crime lab, investigators still hadn't been able to locate the man's penis.

What stood out for Matt was that Baylor seemed to be evolving. Innocent people appeared to have become off limits, at least for now. The doctor had identified two horrible people, two narcissists who thought the world revolved around them and only them, two people who were hurting thousands of children and doing it willingly for the money. Once the doctor located them, they were removed from the face of the earth.

Matt knew that if he were with the doctor, his uncle, his flesh and blood, he'd say the same thing he always said. And Matt also knew that he couldn't argue the point.

The world was a better place with these two people dead and gone. Never again would they be able to hurt children or jeopardize their lives because of the money the families of those children may or may not have had.

Matt checked the time. It was 5:00 a.m.

He had already traded text messages with Cabrera, and they agreed to meet at the station in half an hour, then drive over to the Denny's at Sunset and Gower for breakfast. Although Matt had little experience attending autopsies, he guessed that he and his partner would be better off eating before the three-hour procedure took place. Last time, the experience of watching a medical examiner dissect a human body had been so traumatic, his appetite didn't return for several days. And if his expectations held true, today would be far more harsh than that because the victim was so vulnerable—a fifteen-year-old child.

He tried to put it out of his mind as he locked up the house, tossed his laptop case on the passenger seat, and climbed into the car.

Traffic was light, and within thirty minutes he was pulling into the lot behind the Hollywood Station. He saw Cabrera waiting for him in their unmarked Crown Victoria. Grabbing his laptop, he slid into the passenger seat and they were off.

Despite the coffeehouse on the corner, it was still early enough that they found a parking space at the Gower Gulch Plaza on their first pass through the lot. Matt checked his watch as they entered the diner and were seated by a window with a view of the corner and Sunset Gower Studios across the street. Pushing his menu aside, he glanced at Cabrera, then looked around at the other people chattering away in booths and at the counter. After a few minutes he decided that at five thirty in the morning, there were only three types of people who might walk into a diner in Hollywood. The first group had no doubt just come from the bars and needed food to deal with their high. The second group probably got some sleep, were headed in for work, and needed a big breakfast to start the new day. The third, like Matt, might not be able to explain whether they got to sleep or not. If they did, it wasn't for much more than two or three hours, and they needed coffee and a light breakfast just to keep going.

Matt smiled as he watched the waitress walk over with a fresh pot of coffee. She was wearing her red wig again and, as she filled their mugs, seemed to recognize them as regulars. Cabrera ordered his usual, the bacon and eggs French toast special. Matt handed over the menu and kept things simple: bacon and eggs, over medium, with home fries and two pieces of whole-wheat toast.

When she left, Matt noticed three or four people beginning to check them out from the counter. Wondering what might have happened, he gazed up at the TVs hanging from the ceiling and noticed that every one of them was switched to the story on CNN. Cabrera was facing the window and couldn't see the screens.

"What's with you?" Cabrera said. "What's with the face? We're about to have a real bad day."

Matt watched his partner take a first sip of coffee. "Nothing," he said. "I'm fine. Just a little relieved maybe."

"Why? What's going on?"

"You see the news?"

Cabrera shook his head. "Didn't have time."

"What about the radio?"

"I got up late. I was in a rush."

Matt glanced at the people openly gazing at them from the counter now. He could see the recognition showing on their faces. Two or three people had begun to whisper. One even waved. Matt looked back at Cabrera, then pointed to the TV behind his partner's back.

"Take a look for yourself," he said.

Cabrera turned. The TV journalist was reporting from Washington, Pennsylvania, with the cheap motel in the background. Photographs of Dr. Baylor and his latest two victims were laid over the upper left side of the screen above the words DOUBLE MURDER AT THE SUNSHINE MOTEL. After several moments, they cut away to shots from other cities. Apparently, with news of the greedy woman's murder out in the open, spontaneous celebrations were breaking out in New York, Philadelphia, and Boston. But even more, the story was sweeping west with the sunrise. Chicago was up and running. People were making early-morning plans in Los Angeles, San Francisco, and Seattle. On Wall Street they were already marching, raising their fists in the air and carrying banners that read: "The Wicked Witch Is Dead! The Wicked Witch Is Finally Dead! Thank You, Doctor B!"

The screen cut back to the studio, and it looked like they were doing background on the doctor and the murders that had occurred in LA last fall. Beside the anchorman were photos of Baylor, then Matt and Cabrera.

Matt watched Cabrera turn back, noting the hint of a smile.

"He struck again," Cabrera said in a low voice.

Matt nodded. "The same day Sophia Ramirez was murdered."

"Where?"

"Outside Pittsburgh."

Cabrera glanced at the TV, shifted his gaze to the people staring at them, then turned back and shook his head like he didn't get it. Like he didn't want to get it.

"They love him," he said finally.

Matt narrowed his eyes. "They haven't met him."

When the waitress with the bad wig walked up with their orders, Cabrera didn't seem to notice. Matt lifted his coffee mug out of the way, and she set their plates on the table. Then she looked Matt over and pointed her pen behind her at a man by the cash register cleaning menus with a wet rag.

"It's your lucky day, boys. Manager's special. Breakfast is on the house."

TWELVE

Matt got into his disposable hazmat suit, wrapped the sleeves of the hood around his neck, and grabbed a respirator off the table. As he watched Cabrera getting into his suit, he noted his partner's fingers trembling, his glassy eyes, and guessed that this wouldn't be easy for him either.

The door opened.

Art Madina entered the changing room already suited up and sat down on the opposite bench. "I'm gonna guess that observing an autopsy isn't part of your everyday, so let's go over the rules."

Matt and Cabrera shot each other a look.

Madina flashed a short, dry smile. "I wish I could give you something to mask the foul odor. If there was anything that worked the way it does in the movies, I'd use it myself. But here's what I want you guys to keep in mind. Between what you're about to see and smell from the corpse, we'll be using formaldehyde, so there's a good chance you'll become light-headed. Most people, even first-year med students, feel faint. Believe me when I say that you don't want to collapse in the operating room. What spills on the floor from the corpse is something you never want to touch or have any contact with. You guys understand what I'm saying? I don't want you to tough it out. If you start to feel faint, if you think you're gonna puke, get yourself out of there. You're not gonna miss anything. A staff photographer will be taking pictures and shooting video. Everything that happens will be recorded and in my report."

Madina let it settle in. "You guys ready?"

Cabrera shrugged like he wasn't sure.

Madina laughed out loud as he slipped the respirator over his head and got to his feet. "I didn't think so," he said. "Now let's get to work."

Matt followed Madina and Cabrera through the door into the operating room, surprised that six other autopsies were underway. He tried not to look at anything as they passed table after table, tried not to hear the second ME on the line working his skull saw or the sound of body fluids splashing onto the floor. But then his eyes skipped ahead to Sophia, laid out so helplessly on the stainless-steel gurney at the very end. He looked at her battered face as he stepped closer, her flat breasts and all the bruises ringing her neck. As he eyed her body and the wounds from falling off her skateboard that peppered her thin arms and legs, everything seemed to stop when he reached the massive wound at the base of her skull.

Sophia had been decimated, the attack on her life overwhelming.

He touched her fingers with his gloved hand, so unnaturally cold and lifeless. The smells venting from her body and hovering below the tiled ceiling were staggering, but Matt knew that he could handle it because he wanted to. Because he needed to. As he watched Madina select a scalpel to make the Y cut across her torso, he stepped back, pulled out his notebook and pen, and just let things happen. The truth was that he found the smell of formaldehyde helpful. That in some fundamental way the harsh reality of what he was experiencing had become surreal and almost went by like a drug-induced nightmare. Over the next three hours he checked on Cabrera once or twice and found him staring at the ceiling tiles rather than Madina's dissection of the girl.

But that was okay, too.

When Madina readjusted the body's rib cage and sewed the chest back together with heavy black twine, they'd made it and the autopsy was finally over.

Prior to their arrival and the autopsy, Madina had given Sophia a complete visual exam that included photographs and X-rays of her entire body. Now the medical examiner was walking over to the flat-panel monitor mounted on the wall and gazing at the images the staff photographer had made. Matt paged through the notes he'd taken during the procedure and looked up.

But then Madina turned and gave both Matt and Cabrera an odd look. "Why don't we go into the changing room," he said. "I can pull these images up on the monitor in there, and we'll have a chance to talk."

Matt began to wonder if something might be wrong. He nodded slowly and followed the medical examiner down the line of autopsies still underway. When they reached the door to the changing room, Matt entered behind Cabrera and pulled off his respirator and hood.

"What is it?" he said. "What's happened?"

Madina shook his head and removed his mask. When Matt checked on his partner, Cabrera appeared drained and maybe still a bit groggy from the formaldehyde. He turned back and watched Madina switch on the monitor and pull up Sophia's file. Using a pen, the medical examiner pointed to a close-up photograph of her battered face and cleared his throat.

"We spoke about this during the procedure," he said. "We have hemorrhaging around her eyes and beneath the eyelids, which would seem to indicate that she died from strangulation. When we opened her up, we found that her hyoid bone had been snapped, which backs up our initial findings."

Matt stepped closer, Madina's use of the word *initial* leaving a bad taste in his mouth. "What are you trying to say?"

Madina turned to him. "Cause of death, Jones. Take a seat. Let's talk about it."

Matt could still sense that Madina was holding something back and imagined that whatever it was couldn't be good. He glanced over at Cabrera sitting on the bench by the lockers, then turned to Madina and took a wild guess.

"It's the soil you found in her nostrils," he said. "It shouldn't have been there."

Madina nodded and took a seat on the opposite bench. "And in her throat and lungs, Jones. This was a brutal death. When she went in the ground, she wasn't conscious—she couldn't have been—but she was still breathing. She was still alive."

It hung there . . .

The thought that the girl had been buried alive. He wasn't sure why it felt so personal. Why it felt as though he had been wronged by the madman himself.

Cabrera removed his gloves, wiped his hands over his face, and still appeared weary. "So it's not the strangulation," he said.

Madina turned back to the monitor. "I don't think so. Her leg is fractured just above her left knee. She may have been skinny, but she was strong and in terrific shape. I'm guessing the fracture came early in the struggle and that she was incapacitated."

"You mean that she couldn't get up," Matt said quietly. "She couldn't get away."

Madina lowered his voice. "I think that's probably the way it turned out, Detectives. This was a rage killing. A rage killing by someone who either lost control of himself in the moment or never had it to begin with. What I'm trying to say is that the man who murdered this girl couldn't stop. That's the problem with madness. Once they get started, very few of them can stop."

The air in the room seemed to double in weight. Matt took it in for a moment—the sheer scope of their mission, their case.

"What about rape?" he said finally. "We saw the semen on her clothing. There was a lot of it. It came up in the UV light."

"That's why this case is so singular, Jones. So strange. I can't speak about what was found on her clothing, but her body's clean. There's no evidence that would indicate she was raped or sexually abused in any way. Her genitals are completely intact and completely normal. You saw for yourself. No vaginal rips or tears. No bruising or even reddening. No evidence of vaginal or anal penetration. No cuts or bite marks found on her body. No semen or saliva on her skin, her face, or lips. There's nothing here that points to a sex killing."

Matt was dumbfounded. "Then you're saying it was the trauma to the back of her head?"

"Yes and no," Madina said. "This guy grabbed her by the neck and beat the back of her head against the ground with as much force as he could. At some point during the struggle, or after that, he broke her neck. But like I said before, she was still breathing when he put her in the ground."

Matt shot his partner a hard look but didn't say anything. Neither did Cabrera. The man they were looking for was an animal.

THIRTEEN

Cabrera still appeared numb and didn't say anything as Matt took the wheel and drove the Crown Vic back to the station. Matt couldn't tell if his partner was reacting to the autopsy itself or Madina's results but guessed that it was a combination of the two. He didn't mind really, preferring the din of the freeway while he chewed over what was happening to their investigation. Although it may have only been a couple of days old, every move forward seemed more like they were being pushed five miles back. Matt had to admit to himself that this was only his third murder case. That he didn't have the experience of knowing what it felt like when a case never lit up but just seemed to stop breathing and die.

He didn't know what to make of it. All he knew was that he felt guilty. Like he was letting a fifteen-year-old girl down when she needed him most.

He turned into the lot behind the station and found an open space along the far wall. Cabrera remained silent as he got out of the car and started walking toward the building. Matt shrugged it off and grabbed his laptop but kept his eyes on his partner as they entered through the rear door. When Cabrera ducked into the conference room, Matt followed him in and closed the door thinking he wanted to talk. But Cabrera still didn't say anything. Instead, he took a seat at the table, eyeballing those photographs Matt had taped to the glass last night. The five girls who had gone missing over the past six months. The girls no one had heard from and, Matt guessed, never would.

He pulled a chair out from the end of the table, sat down, and gave Cabrera another look. "You okay?" he said.

Cabrera sniffed his jacket but remained quiet. Matt leaned back in the chair, well aware that the smell of death had permeated their clothing and followed them like a shadow from the morgue.

"You're right, Denny. We smell pretty bad, but other than that, are you okay?"

Cabrera kept his eyes down. "Yeah," he said finally. "I guess so."

"You guess so?"

Matt's cell phone started to vibrate. Digging the phone out of his pocket, he saw Speeks's name blinking on the face and, as he took the call, imagined it would be another grim setback.

"Let me guess, Speeks. You just got off the phone with Madina. You've got something that breaks the case wide open, and you called to give us the good news."

Speeks didn't say anything. Matt turned to Cabrera and saw him staring back at him. Switching on the speaker, he set the phone on the table between them.

"I'm sorry, Jones," Speeks said after a moment.

"Why are you sorry? Just tell us what happened."

"We're at a standstill. We've got no physical evidence. No footprints in the soil, no fingerprints, no hairs or fibers that match anyone other than the victim and the old man's dog. It's almost as if the killer's a ghost. Like he was never there."

Matt thought it over. "What about the semen on her clothing? Madina told us there's no indication that she was raped. But at least you've got something. You've got his DNA, right? You pulled it off the girl's blouse and jeans."

"That's the problem," Speeks said in a shaky voice. "That's why I'm calling."

Matt glanced over at Cabrera and saw his eyes go dark. No doubt about it—their plane had lost power and was going down. Matt took a deep breath and exhaled.

"Tell us why you called," he said.

Speeks cleared his throat, still sounding nervous. "It's not semen, Jones."

Cabrera got up in a huff and started pacing. Matt slammed his fist on the conference table.

"What are you talking about, Speeks? We saw it. Everybody in the tent saw it. And there was a lot of it, like it came from a goddamn horse."

"I know what we saw, but we didn't know what we were looking at. Not until we got back to the lab. It was just a bad call."

"A bad call, Speeks? This is a bad call. I can't take another bad call like this."

A moment passed. When Speeks eventually spoke, he sounded embarrassed.

"I'm sorry, Jones. I really am. I was just waiting to hear Madina confirm that he didn't find any evidence that the girl was violated. The stains we saw in the UV light turned out to be from a goddamn can of Coke. She must have spilled it on herself. It turns out that under UV light Coca-Cola reflects back just like semen. When it dries, they're almost the same color. That's what we were looking at. That's what we saw."

Matt heard Cabrera gasp. As the shock wafted through the air, Matt lowered his head to the table and closed his eyes.

"She's dead, Speeks. She was just a kid. Tell me there's something. Anything."

Another long moment passed, and then another—heavy and acid-like.

"If the killer wasn't wearing gloves," Speeks said finally, "if he strangled her with his bare hands, Jones, then there's still a chance he left enough skin behind for us to work with. It could be in our soil samples. Madina told me that he swabbed her neck. You never know."

"So you're saying there's a chance you've got enough for a profile."

Speeks went quiet again. Another batch of uncertainty and gloom filled the room.

"No," Speeks said in a voice that had gone dead. "I'm saying there's a slim chance. A very slim chance. The kind you can't count on. She was in the ground for three days. That's a long time. Some cases never get going, Jones. They just burn like a wildfire, taking everybody out who's in the way."

Matt's body shuddered, and he switched off the phone. When he looked up, Cabrera was removing the photographs of the five girls who'd gone missing from the window and dumping them in the trash.

"I'm gonna go home, Matt. I'm gonna take a long shower and get into some clean clothes that don't smell like some kid who's been dead for three days. I'll be back in a couple of hours. Then we'll finish the paperwork, turn the murder book over to McKensie, and call it a day. This one's DOA. No sense wasting any more time chasing shadows in the dark."

Matt didn't say anything.

He just sat there, watching Cabrera walk out of the room and vanish around the corner. He heard the back door open and slam shut. Then the din of the bureau floor began to fade, and in his mind, everything went quiet. Numb. He was alone finally. After a while, he got up and dug the photographs out of the trash. He spent several minutes examining them. Once he'd committed each girl's face to memory, he placed the pictures in an unmarked file folder and slipped it into his laptop case. The Chinese food he'd tossed out last night was still there and smelled so nasty it could have been road kill. As he walked out of the room, he thought it might be a while before he ordered Chinese again.

FOURTEEN

Some cases *never get going, Jones. They just burn like a wildfire, taking everybody out who's in the way.*

It wasn't the tang of death anymore. It was the tang of failure.

Matt ripped open the trunk, unzipped his gym bag, and dug through his clothing to find a clean black T-shirt and a pair of jeans. Pushing aside the boxer shorts and a fresh pair of socks, he spotted his shaving kit and felt a wave of relief that he'd remembered to return it to his bag when he got back from Philadelphia.

Driving across town in the middle of the day to take a shower and change into fresh clothes wasn't an option. A thirty-mile round trip between Hollywood and the Westside could eat through more than three hours. And he was too amped up to waste that much time.

He grabbed his gym bag, tossed his leather jacket on the front seat, and slammed the trunk. Legging it back to the station, he burst into the locker room, glanced at the showers that hadn't been working since last fall, and washed himself down at one of the sinks before the mirror. As he got into his jeans and slipped on the T-shirt, he thought he'd done a good job of washing away the smell of the girl's dead body. But when he coughed and cleared his throat, he could taste it in his mouth.

Not death, he told himself again. Failure.

He met his own eyes in the mirror. Then he pushed the moment out of his mind and looked down at his shirt and trousers on the floor. Even a dry cleaner couldn't make them right again. Rolling the shirt in his trousers, he tossed them in the trash, grabbed his gym bag, and walked out.

The activity on the bureau floor made him feel uneasy. He could hear the banter of detectives talking on their phones and to each other behind the six-foot-high partitions. It sounded like they were working cases, earning their paychecks, and getting things done. As he reached the window by his workstation, he could see McKensie in his office talking to someone in the doorway.

Matt ducked away from the glass to avoid being seen.

After giving the rear door an angry heave, he crossed the lot quickly and with full knowledge that he was headed back to the crime scene for another look—maybe another talk with Sophia's parents or, even better, the girl's boyfriend who never made contact with them and didn't seem to be around. As he wove through traffic on Sunset, he tried not to think about the nicotine gum he'd found in his glove box or even the café half a block south of the Skylight bookstore in Los Feliz. An extra-large cup of piping-hot java was only a few blocks out of the way, that is, if he stayed off the freeways and spent the extra time using surface streets.

He could almost taste it—

He turned on the radio to clear his mind, but the news of the day was the same news as yesterday and so abhorrent he switched it off. Within twenty minutes he was speeding up Casanova Street and pulling to a stop in front of Trey Washington's house. He took a moment to center himself as he gazed across the street.

One look and he could tell that no one was home.

Matt tried to shake it off and got out of the car just to make sure.

He climbed the steps and crossed the porch to the front door. He could see the lamp still switched on by the window and stepped closer to peer through the glass above the dead bolt. Everything looked exactly the way it had last night, except for the business card he'd wedged into the doorjamb. Someone had taken his card and, he assumed, read the message but never called.

He tried the doorbell. When no one responded, he knocked on the glass and waited. After a few minutes, he tried to open the door but found it locked. He stepped off the porch and walked around the house, eyeing the windows carefully. The back door had a window above the knob exactly like the front door. He climbed the steps, turned the handle, and found it locked, then gazed through the glass into the Washington's kitchen. He noted the breakfast dishes stacked in the sink and the sponge that still looked wet. There could be no doubt that the Washington's had returned home last night and began their day here before taking off again.

Why hadn't anyone called? He'd left that message on his business card, and he'd used the word *important*. But even more, they had to know that Sophia Ramirez was dead by now. That she had been murdered. So why hadn't they called?

Matt grit his teeth, circled the house, and got into his car. Last night's rain had brought cooler air, and he zipped up his leather jacket and switched on the heat. As he turned into the drive and backed out, he glanced at the house and tried to keep an open mind but had to admit that it was becoming more difficult.

He gunned the engine, then backed off and glided down the street to the Ramirezes' home. As he pulled in front of the house, he saw Sophia's father working in his wood shop in the garage.

The driveway leading down the hill was unpaved. When Matt stepped onto the lawn to avoid the mud, Sophia's father turned and gave him a look. Matt guessed that the moment of fear he saw in the man's eyes was instinctual at this point, part of living a life off the grid while trying to provide for his family. The fear vanished as Ramirez shut down his table saw and turned.

"You have news?" the man said.

Matt nodded and met his eyes. "Your daughter wasn't violated," he said quietly.

Ramirez seemed to wilt and almost stagger, then reached for the stool. Matt could see his mind going as he steadied himself and sat down.

"You okay, Mr. Ramiroz?"

The man paused to catch his breath before lifting his eyes off the floor. "Not really," he said in a shaky voice. "Not now or anytime soon."

Matt let everything settle for a while and looked around the garage. Ramirez had shown him the shop yesterday, but Matt had been distracted and not much registered. Kitchen cabinets were set on the floor in various stages of completion. They appeared to be made of cherrywood, constructed from scratch with enough detail that Matt could tell Ramirez was a master cabinetmaker. When he ran his finger across the surface of a door, it felt smooth as glass.

"Where are these going?" he asked.

Ramirez looked up like he was still deep inside himself. "A new house in Beverly Hills," he managed in a low voice. "They don't renovate anymore. They rip the old place down and start all over again. Everybody wants everything new."

The man's eyes went lazy again. Matt leaned against the workbench.

"I'm having trouble locating Sophia's friend, Trey Washington. Have you heard from him or his family? Do they know what's happened?"

Ramirez nodded. "They were away for almost a week. They got home last night. Trey's inside."

"Inside where?"

"Sophia's bedroom."

FIFTEEN

*T**rey Washington had been away for almost a week . . .*

As cases go, Matt figured that Sophia's boyfriend would have been the last stone in a short line of stones to kick over and see what might be found underneath. But now everything had been accounted for. Everything could be tossed aside. The girl wasn't the victim of a sex killer. According to her father, the boyfriend wasn't even in town. Whoever did the murder left nothing of himself behind.

And Matt was out of stones.

He opened the back door and stepped into the kitchen. He could hear the sound of an audio track coming from Sophia's bedroom, the sound of the girl's voice, the sound of her laughing. When he turned the corner and looked into the room, he could see the kid seated at her desk watching one of their skateboarding videos on the computer. Matt knocked on the door. The kid flinched, and when he set eyes on Matt, gasped.

"Are you Trey Washington?" Matt said.

The boy stopped the video. His eyes got big and he looked frightened.

Matt stepped into the room. "There's no reason to be nervous," he said. "I'm a homicide detective. My name's Matt Jones, and I'm trying to find out what happened to your friend. Her dad told me that you were away. I left my card in your door. Why didn't you or your parents call me when you got home last night?"

The kid stammered. "My father said I wasn't supposed to talk to you. He said he'd handle it."

"Okay," Matt said. "So why didn't he handle it?"

The kid lowered his eyes and began wiping tears off his cheeks. "I don't know."

Matt moved over to the bed and sat down. He noticed the boy's hands trembling.

"Let me see them," Matt said in a calm voice.

"See what?"

"Your hands. I'm gonna prove to you why you shouldn't be afraid of me."

The kid wrapped his fingers together in an effort to conceal them, then lowered his hands to his lap.

"Come on, Trey. Let me see your hands."

Reluctantly, the kid lifted his hands up and held them out for inspection. Matt examined them closely, then looked the kid in the eye.

"Other side," he said.

The kid turned his hands over. The boy's brown skin was soft and smooth and showed no signs of a scratch, cut, or bruise. No sign of being involved in a murder that reeked of ultraviolence.

"You see, kid, I told you so. Your hands prove you shouldn't be nervous."

"How?" the boy blurted out. "Why?"

Matt spotted a box of tissues on the bedside table and passed it over. "Because I'm a fortune-teller," he said. "You were away the day it happened, right? Just for the record, where were you?"

The kid wiped his eyes with the tissue. "San Francisco."

"What's in San Francisco?"

"Nana and Papa."

"Did you have a good time?"

The kid nodded. "Until Mr. Ramirez called . . ."

A moment passed, and then another. Trey Washington was built just like Sophia—long boned and skinny, with a gentle demeanor that matched his angular face. But it was the inside that seemed so unique and striking. Despite losing his friend, his innocent nature seemed to have remained intact.

"How old are you?" Matt asked.

"Fifteen."

"Why aren't you in school?"

The boy's dark eyes rose up from his hands and locked on Matt's face. "Because of Sophia," he said in a soft voice. "Because of what happened to her. My father gave me the day off. I'm making a video for her funeral."

It hung there. It hung there for a long time . . . and as the girl's death and the loss of a friendship settled into the room, Matt watched the boy wipe another batch of tears away from his eyes, then stood up and patted his shoulder.

"You're a good kid, Trey. A good friend. Sophia was lucky to have you."

Matt noticed the bookshelf on the wall by the window and walked over for a quick look. As he skimmed through the titles, he realized that most of the books on the top shelf were graphic novels. On the shelves below were books about film production and stacks of skateboarding magazines. He was about to turn away when he noticed two paperbacks wedged in beside an old *Webster's* dictionary and a copy of the Holy Bible. The first was a book of selected poems by Pablo Neruda, edited by Robert Bly. Matt had a copy of the same edition in his library at home. But when he spotted the book jammed in beside it, when he read the title—it threw him. It was a heavy book for a fifteen-year-old girl to read, a big book to grasp. *One Hundred Years of Solitude* by Gabriel García Márquez, arguably one of the greatest writers of the last century working on one of the greatest novels of our time. Matt owned a copy of this one, too—a dog-eared paperback that he'd taken to Afghanistan with him and read three times.

The memory was a good one. But as he straightened up, he felt a sudden wave of pain rock through his body.

"Are you okay, mister?"

Matt grabbed the bookcase and looked over at the boy, trying to breathe evenly and not show anything on his face. All four gunshot wounds had erupted at the same time. The pain was so sharp and so deep that it felt like he'd been shot all over again. He wondered what triggered the eruption. Was it the physical act of bending over? Or was it the compassion he felt for Trey Washington's despair?

Matt tried to shake it off. "I'm fine," he said. "It's nothing."

"You don't look fine. What happened? What is it?"

Matt returned to the bed and eased himself down, knowing that his meds were in his laptop case in the car. "I was shot," he said.

The kid's eyes got big again, and Matt saw his jaw drop.

"I'll be fine," he repeated. "Show me the video you're making for Sophia."

The kid turned in the chair. "It's not ready yet. I just got started pulling clips—where were you shot?"

Matt leaned against the backboard. The pain didn't have any give to it. His car, the meds, seemed so far away right now.

"All over," he said.

"How many times?"

"Four," he said. "Four times last October."

"You were shot four times?"

Matt nodded and pointed at the monitor. "Go ahead," he said. "Show me the clips. I want to see them."

"But they're not even trimmed."

"Show me anyway."

The kid noticed the gun holstered to Matt's belt and gave it a long look. After a few moments, he scooped up the mouse and highlighted a handful of shots that had been reduced to thumbnail images. Then he pulled the keyboard closer and hit "Play."

Matt's eyes drifted over to the screen, but his mind felt like it was buffeting off the spikes of pain in his chest and shoulder like a meteor bouncing off the clouds on its way to the ground.

His pockets were empty, and he was out of stones.

Could it be possible that the murder of Sophia Ramirez was nothing more than a random act of violence? Was it conceivable that her murder came down to nothing more than bad luck and timing? That she entered the park at precisely the wrong moment? The same exact time a madman turned up out of nowhere? Someone who came and went and left nothing of himself behind?

In the end, was the girl's murder nothing more than fate?

The idea made Matt angry. He turned back to the monitor and tried to focus on the shots of Sophia skateboarding down a series of concrete steps—the joy on her face, her character and spirit in full bloom. He had to admit that he found the clips difficult to watch. But when he checked the boy's face, he realized that it was just him. Trey Washington was lost in the pleasure of the past, drinking in the images of his friend as if he needed them now more than ever. After several takes of a wild downhill ride on the drainage canal, the camera switched on as Sophia carried her skateboard up the road to the picnic area on top of the hill. Matt could see the tables on the lawn in the background, the grove of pine trees on the other side of the meadow.

But then something happened. The camera took a bounce and jerked up and down. Matt sat up and leaned closer as the images became steady.

He could hear someone shouting on the audio track. He could see a man laid out on his belly on the grassy bank screaming at Sophia, then spotting the camera in Trey's hands and jumping to his feet. The man started chasing them across the lawn and back down the hill. Sophia led the way, and Trey kept the camera rolling as they veered off the street into the bushes and through the trees. After several moments, the sound of the man shouting at them faded away, and Sophia and Trey slowed down and turned back. They were trying to catch their breath. Matt could see Sophia smiling through it and heard both of them trying not to laugh.

Matt's body shuddered and he got to his feet. "Who was the man chasing you?" he said.

The boy turned to him. "Some guy. Some weirdo."

"Have you ever seen him before?"

"A couple of times. He yelled at us, and we ran away."

"When did you see him?"

"Ten days ago," the boy said quickly. "Is everything okay? Did we do something wrong?"

Matt shook his head. "What about before that? Had you ever seen him before?"

"No. Never. Just a couple of times ten days ago."

Matt took a step closer. "Play it again," he said. "But this time I want you to hit pause as soon as the camera stops shaking, okay? As soon as you see the guy, freeze the video."

The boy knew something was wrong and became nervous. Still, he managed to find the exact moment the camera stopped shaking—the first clean frame—and killed it.

Matt leaned over the desk, eyeballing the image and trying to keep cool. A man with dark hair was lying on the grassy bank holding a camera with a long lens. A pair of binoculars sat on the lawn beside him. The man looked to be about forty. Matt couldn't tell for sure, but it seemed like he had been peering down the hill and that Sophia and Trey had startled him from behind.

"Do you have any way of zooming in on his face?"

The boy nodded. "Sure."

Matt looked back at the screen as the image began to expand.

"That's about it," the boy said. "Any closer and we'll lose too much detail."

"That's close enough," Matt said. "That's good, kid. Real good."

Matt dug his cell phone out of his pocket and switched on the camera. After taking several shots of the image frozen on the monitor, he lowered his phone and stared at the man's face.

He knew him.

Everybody who worked narcotics knew him. Anyone who read the *Los Angeles Times* knew him.

Robert Gambini was the nephew of Joseph Gambini, the CEO of the Gambini Organization and a notorious crime boss whom Matt thought had retired or might even be locked up in prison somewhere.

But Robert was the face of the next generation. The new breed. Someone who followed his uncle's lead, stayed in the background, worked with the Mexican drug cartels, and had the organizational skills to be running one of the biggest drug operations on the West Coast. A man who had graduated from the Wharton School, a prestigious business school at the University of Pennsylvania, and had the clout to somehow buy a license and open a chain of pot shops in Southern California. It was unclear how he managed to pull that off when everyone on the street knew Gambini's real mission in life was weaning addicts off oxycodone with high-grade heroin that remained infinitely less expensive. Ten bucks' worth of "junk" could still turn an addict into King for a Day.

Matt tossed it over, his stomach churning. Something about this case had been out of order from the very beginning. It had been gnawing at him ever since Madina reviewed his autopsy results and none of it seemed to fit with the crime scene. Something was wrong. Something he couldn't see yet but had the strong sense was there now. It had to be there.

What was Robert Gambini doing on top of that hill?

SIXTEEN

Matt parked under the trees and quickly fished through his laptop case for his meds. Dumping them out onto the passenger seat, he stared at the pill bottles and weighed the odds the way he always had since he'd been shot just two and half months ago. He could risk addiction with the oxycodone or, as his doctor warned him, blow out his kidneys with a hopped-up version of ibuprofen—eight hundred milligrams cut with a buffering agent that required a prescription.

Matt decided on the ibuprofen, tossing the large pill in his mouth and chasing it down with half a bottle of water. He knew that it would take an hour until he felt any relief, maybe longer because too much time had passed before he'd done anything about it.

The idea of waiting for relief that might not even happen put him in a foul mood.

He ripped open his car door and started across the lawn to the grassy bank beside the grove of pine trees. On the other side of the meadow, he could see Levi Harris, the old man with his dog, tossing a tennis ball.

What had Robert Gambini been doing here? And why did he need a pair of binoculars and a camera with a long lens to do it? Who was he spying on?

Matt climbed the grassy bank and gazed over the edge and down the steep hill.

There could be only two possibilities, but he knew that the moment he saw Gambini on the video. Either something was going on near or at the substation, maybe something to do with a drug shipment and a freight train. Or, what? Something wasn't quite right at DMG Waste Management?

Matt chewed it over.

Nothing about the waste management company had the look or feel of anyone trying to hide a drug operation. When he and Cabrera showed up the other night, the gate had been standing wide open, along with the bay doors to the entire warehouse. The place smelled of sulfur and other toxic chemicals that reminded him of rotten eggs. But even more, the owners had welcomed them into their inner offices and been only too willing to help. Matt could remember watching security videos that hadn't been screened or edited first. And the building's overall security was slim to none—the only guard, a dim-witted man who didn't even carry a firearm.

Where was the logic?

Matt rubbed his shoulder as he looked back at the freight trains being fed onto a sidetrack behind the substation. He could see a parking lot carved into the hill, big and wide enough to accommodate trucks. If Gambini had been receiving or moving product on a freight car, Matt doubted anyone would have ever noticed. Everything about the transaction would have seemed routine. And Gambini could have overseen the entire operation with a bird's-eye view from right here, armed with nothing more than his cell phone, a pair of binoculars, and a—

Matt heard something.

He turned and saw Harris's dog race into the grove of pine trees, canter back out, then charge in again like he was playing a game. The dog was some sort of terrier, snorting and barking and making a whining sound. Matt looked for the old man and spotted him hiking across the lawn with the dog's leash tossed over his shoulder.

Although Matt was certain that the lab no longer had any interest in the location, he could still see crime scene tape stretched around the trees. He wasn't sure why the tape hadn't been removed or why Speeks had never mentioned it. Maybe Speeks was embarrassed and just wanted to forget about it. After all, the lab's effort had yielded no substantive evidence and turned out to be a complete failure.

Matt grimaced. Something about watching a dog trample over their former crime scene appeared fitting. Even so, he stepped off the grassy bank and walked over to the pine trees.

"You should probably get your dog out of there, Mr. Harris," he said.

"I thought you guys were all done."

Matt shrugged. "You should probably do it anyway. At least until someone takes the tape down."

"I'm sorry."

"No problem, Mr. Harris. You've been a big help. We wouldn't be here without you."

The old man readied his lead and stepped through the opening in the branches. Matt could see the shallow grave in the soil, the dog digging again and wagging his tail. Once Harris snapped on the leash and gave it a light tug, the dog turned, shot him a look, and whimpered. With a treat in his hand, Harris led the dog out onto the lawn and smoothed the fur back beside his ears.

Matt thought the dog might be a Westie and let it sniff his hand before petting him. "What's his name?"

"Louie."

"That's a great name, Mr. Harris. Hello, Louie."

The old man smiled. "Sorry," he said. "I wasn't thinking. Louie must have caught the scent of that poor girl in the dirt. He's still a pup. He thinks everything's a game."

Matt nodded and watched them walk off. When they reached the street and started down the hill, he stepped through the branches and gazed at the fresh claw marks in the soil above the grave. He was about to turn away when the words the old man had used hit him between the eyes.

The dog must have caught the scent of that poor girl in the dirt.

Those were the words he'd used. The dog caught the scent of the girl still in the soil . . .

What scent?

Matt turned sharply. The earth that surrounded Sophia's body had been removed by Speeks and a variety of forensic criminalists. They might not have had much luck, but Matt knew with certainty that the soil had been examined, sifted, and meticulously combed through for physical evidence. Any soil that required further examination had been taken to the lab. What remained had been left in a pile on the lawn beside the closest picnic table.

Yet Harris's dog hadn't gone near it. Instead, he had raced under the trees onto what was left of the girl's shallow grave. And he'd been excited about it. Barking and snorting and all amped up as he wagged his tail.

Matt turned back to the grave, letting his mind travel freely through the world of maybes and what-ifs. As he let out more line, his imagination suddenly locked in on something so horrific that his heart skipped a beat. Something so dark that when the idea clicked, he could feel an ice-cold chill working its way up his spine.

He searched the ground for a stick. When he didn't see one, he rushed outside, over the grassy bank, and into the woods. He spotted a flat rock and grabbed it, then hurried back under the pine trees. Dropping to his knees on the dead girl's grave, he drove the rock into the ground and started digging the soil away. Quick, hard strokes—over and over again.

He could feel the pain radiating through his left shoulder and across his chest but no longer cared about it. He could hear the frantic sounds he was making and thought of that terrier, digging away with his paws. Growling and barking and all jacked up—not like a dog anymore, but like a man on all fours who had locked in on the scent of an idea. A homicide cop beating back failure. He took another swing, driving the rock deeper and deeper still.

Another swing until he hit something eerily soft.

He groaned and flung the rock out of his hand. He could feel the heady rush of adrenaline as he clawed through the dirt with his fingers.

And then he saw it. Then he clenched his jaw and felt his entire body shudder.

It was a hand. A human hand. In the grave below the earth where the girl had been found.

Matt grabbed hold of the wrist, gave it a yank, and screamed.

An arm broke out of the soil. A human face and the wretched smell of another dead body.

SEVENTEEN

The tents had been pitched over the picnic tables for the second time in two days. The park had been sealed off, and while the news choppers would have liked to move in for their money shots, the air above had been deemed restricted until further notice.

Matt couldn't help thinking about how quiet the crime scene had become. It was clear to everybody here that leaving a body behind amounted to the World Series of fuck-ups, that it had been a team effort, and that the story would wind up above the fold on page one of the *Times* tomorrow morning.

It was quiet, but it was also very grim.

Matt knelt down and watched Gainer and an assistant from the coroner's office lift the corpse out of the earth and lower it into a body bag. The victim was a white male with dark hair, about forty, wearing a long-sleeved flannel shirt and a pair of jeans. As Gainer went through his pockets, Matt noted that the back of the victim's head was soaked in blood, along with his neck and shirt collar. His eyes were covered in dirt but still open and hard to look at. His mouth was open and filled with even more dirt, his teeth jutting out of the soil in a hideous death scream.

Gainer completed his search and looked over at Matt. "His pockets are empty," he said. "No ID. No cash, keys, or credit cards."

Matt looked the body over without saying anything. He didn't see a watch on either wrist or any rings on his fingers.

"Okay to zip him up?" Gainer asked.

"Okay," Matt said. "But once we get him in the tent, I wanna pull him back out, Ed. We can't leave here without having a better idea of what happened."

Matt stood up and followed his partner out from under the trees. Cabrera pulled him over toward the grassy bank and spoke through his teeth in a low, anxious voice.

"What's Speeks gonna do to make sure nobody else is buried in there, Matt?"

"I already talked to him. His guys are gonna probe every inch of that ground. If there's a dead mouse, they'll find it."

"The way things are going, let's just hope that if they find a dead mouse, his goddamn name isn't Mickey."

Matt noted the angst in his partner's voice, then turned to watch Gainer and his assistant wheel the body across the lawn into the tent. By the time he and Cabrera entered, work lights had been switched on and Speeks was digging into his hard-shell cases for the UV flashlights.

The tension was almost unbearable. The air inside the tent so heavy, Matt found it difficult to breathe.

But he let it slide because he had to. No one could go back in time and fix what they'd done or hadn't done. He let it go, then moved in beside Gainer as the murder victim was removed from the body bag and lowered onto the table. Speeks passed out the UV flashlights and safety glasses, and once a tech killed the work lights, the corpse began to glow in that strange purple light.

The first thing Matt noticed were the bright white specks all over the man's clothing—much like the way lint glows under a black light.

"Any idea what this stuff is?" Matt said.

Speeks eyed the body with fascination. "A fabric of some kind. It could be lint from another piece of clothing in the dryer. He could have been wrapped in something. A blanket or a flannel sheet."

Matt traded looks with Cabrera. At least Speeks would have something to work with. When he turned back, Gainer had begun his examination of the corpse. Matt realized that they were on the same page when the investigator started with the victim's hands. His fingernails were dirty, his fingers and palms scratched and stained a dark brown from the soil.

Matt panned his flashlight down the man's legs to his knees and noted the dirt stains on his jeans. "You think he dug his own grave?"

Gainer nodded. "Sure looks like it."

"Let's check out that head wound, Ed."

Gainer adjusted his gloves, then with the help of his assistant rolled the body over. Once he spread the man's hair apart, Matt leaned in with his UV light. He could see what he thought was an entry wound in the lower half of the skull. But it was a small wound—so small it easily could have been missed in the field and never picked up until the autopsy.

Gainer looked at Matt, then back at the wound. "Gotta be a twenty-two," he said. "Something small enough that it bounced around and never came back out."

Cabrera leaned closer. "Something small enough that it turned his brain into scrambled eggs."

A moment passed in that eerie purple light. Everyone watched as Gainer and his assistant rolled the body over on its back and the corpse settled into the table.

"Okay," Matt said finally. "Okay. So what we're looking at is a hit. An execution that Sophia Ramirez more than likely witnessed. Odds are that that's why she's dead right now. The girl saw it. She saw everything, and that's why she's dead."

Matt didn't think that what he'd just said was a surprise to anyone. But there was an image that went with the words once they'd been spoken aloud. An image so palpable that Matt imagined everyone in the tent could grasp it. See it. Feel it.

A man was forced to dig his own grave on his hands and knees, then shot in the back of the head with a single bullet. A fifteen-year-old girl witnessed the murder and tried to run away but fell short.

Matt tossed it over. It could account for the rage they associated with the girl's murder. The idea that the killer had been surprised by a witness. A teenage girl hiding in the darkness. An innocent child overcome by the sight of watching one man kill another man. Someone who saw enough of the heinous act that she could more than likely identify the killer.

It could account for a lot of things.

Matt's mind flicked back to the video Trey Washington had shown him just a few hours ago. He could remember the way Robert Gambini had acted when the two teens startled him. The rage he'd demonstrated as he chased them across the lawn and through the woods.

Robert Gambini.

What would he have done if he'd caught up to them?

Robert Gambini. The new breed.

Someone tapped Matt on the shoulder from behind. When he turned, he saw one of Speeks's techs, a young woman who had been assisting with the excavation all afternoon, standing before him with a flashlight.

"Two officers are outside," she whispered. "They want to see you and your partner. They said it's important."

Matt traded a quick look with Cabrera, then turned back to the tech. "Thanks," he said. "We'll follow you out."

Matt switched off his UV light, removed his safety glasses, and handed them back to Speeks. He watched Cabrera do the same, then stepped outside with the tech. He'd lost track of time and was surprised when he found the sun had set, the sky filled with clouds and a handful of stars. He looked back at the tech, who pointed to two cops standing beside a work light. Leading the way across the lawn, Matt realized that it was Alvin Marcs and Bill Guy. Both wore bleak expressions on their faces. Both seemed caught up in the moment.

"What's up, fellas?"

Marcs glanced over at his partner, then back. "We might have something."

"Something real?" Cabrera said.

Marcs nodded slowly. "A car with a week's worth of parking tickets."

"Where?" Matt asked.

"Down the hill on Elysian Park Drive. The first ticket is dated the same day the girl was murdered."

Matt gave him a look. "You run the plates?"

Marcs's partner opened his notepad and tilted it into the work light. "The car's registered to a Moe Rey, Detective. Thirty-nine years old from Venice Beach. A white guy. Five nine, medium build, with brown eyes and brown hair."

Matt tossed it over. The body had been in the ground too long to tell what color his eyes were.

"What about a picture off his driver's license?"

Marcs nodded again. "I had them send a text message to your cell about five minutes ago."

Matt remembered the single pulse his cell phone had let out while they were examining the victim's head wound. At the time he'd ignored it. Now he dug his phone out—the message waiting for him with a photograph attached. As he highlighted the image, Cabrera looked over his shoulder.

"That's him," Cabrera said. "That's got to be him."

Matt eyeballed the photo and grimaced. "It's him, all right. Moe Rey. On a better day, maybe, but that's our guy."

EIGHTEEN

Moe Rey's house was just a block from the Venice canals. Local police had pushed the media to the walkway on the other side of Twenty-Eighth Street. While the first responders seemed to have everything well organized, the roads in the neighborhood were exceedingly narrow and only allowed for one car to pass at a time.

Matt pulled in behind a police cruiser parked in the middle of the street and killed the engine. Ignoring the lights and cameras, he fished through his laptop case, pushed the oxycodone aside, and opened the bottle of high-dose ibuprofen his doctor had prescribed. Slamming the pill back, he downed half a bottle of water and got out of the car—stoked that the case was beginning to show daylight.

He turned and gave Moe Rey's house a long look.

It was a small white bungalow on the corner surrounded by a low wall and fence. When he gazed down the sidewalk, he could see that the property extended over to the next street and included a two-car garage that wasn't attached to the house. A new wall at least ten feet high enclosed the backyard, along with an electronic driveway gate made of solid metal sheets that couldn't be seen through.

Matt had worked narcotics before homicide. People who ended up dead by execution usually hung with their own kind and had to earn their way to oblivion. Everything he was looking at felt like another sign that Moe Rey might be connected to Robert Gambini in some fundamental way.

He heard a car screech to a stop and saw his partner jump out of his SUV.

"We need to call McKensie," Cabrera said in a shaky voice. "I was thinking about it on the drive over. Two days and every step of the way's another nightmare. We need help."

Matt turned back to the bungalow. "Knock it off, Denny. All we're doing is searching a house. A dead guy's house. Now let's go."

Matt started toward the house, leaving Cabrera in the street. But even before he reached the porch, he could feel his partner catch up from behind. He didn't understand where Cabrera was coming from and, all things being equal, didn't really care right now. He was too anxious to find out who Moe Rey had been in real life. Too jacked up to see how all these odd pieces were going to fit.

He gave Cabrera a quick look as he crossed the porch. The front door was standing open, and inside the foyer he could see the two first responders waiting for them. While Matt clipped his ID to his jacket, he glanced at their name tags—Roy White and Linda Ragetti—surprised that when he'd worked in Venice, they'd never met.

"Tell me what we need to know," Matt said.

Ragetti stepped forward. "Moe Rey's neighbor says he kept to himself. He used to be a teacher, but she doesn't know where."

Matt gave her a look. "Moe Rey didn't strike me as the teacher type. He didn't die like one either."

Ragetti nodded and took a deep breath. "The neighbor said he got a new job doing something else. She told us that he seemed all worked up about it. Excited, like he was holding in a secret."

Matt thought about Robert Gambini again and what it must be like to work a job that has to be kept secret. He turned to Ragetti's partner.

"Did you guys ask the neighbor what the new job was?"

White glanced at his partner, then turned back. "He never told her, but I think you should take a look at the garage before we get started tossing this place."

"What's in the garage?"

"A picture's worth a thousand words," White said, flashing an ironic smile. "I'll lead the way."

They stepped into a living room that had the feel of being furnished from weekend tag sales at the beach, passed through a nondescript kitchen, and went out the back door. Matt noticed that the small backyard was used as a parking area, the grass replaced with gravel. A path of flagstones led to a side door in the garage, which was standing open.

Ragetti walked ahead and switched on the overhead lights. Once Matt stepped down onto the concrete floor, he took a moment to process what he was seeing.

Moe Rey's two-car garage had been turned into a warehouse for what Matt guessed were stolen goods. He counted three aisles of merchandise—the shelving six feet high. Cell phones, cameras and camcorders, home theater systems, computer gaming consoles and video games—all in their original packaging. Matt eyed the inventory, checking labels and wondering what the value might have been when Rey brought everything home.

"What's wrong?" Cabrera said from the first aisle.

"Check out the labels, Denny. See for yourself. Everything we're looking at is three, maybe four years old. It's worthless."

"And that tells you what, Detective?"

Matt froze, realizing that the question had come from Lieutenant McKensie. He turned and saw the big man with the shock of white hair staring at him from the doorway. Behind the lieutenant he could see Speeks and a handful of techs walking toward them from the bungalow.

Matt looked back at his supervisor. "It tells me that Moe Rey was small time, Lieutenant. He was sitting on product no one wants anymore."

McKensie's eyes were still pinned on him. "Anything else?"

"It tells me that this isn't what we're looking for tonight. Moe Rey's execution has to be about something else."

"I agree," McKensie said. "Something else. So let's get started looking for it."

Matt nodded. He knew from experience that the two most likely places to find anything hidden in anyone's home were the master bedroom and the kitchen. He glanced at Cabrera and took charge, asking his partner to concentrate on the bedroom while he combed through the kitchen. By necessity, the forensic team would overlap everyone else and work the entire house. McKensie seemed to be here to stay and, for reasons never explained, stuck close to Matt.

In the past Matt had found that the freezer always seemed like a good place to start. But after half an hour of inspecting everything wrapped in aluminum foil, he and McKensie came up empty. Like the freezer, the refrigerator and cabinets yielded nothing of interest.

Matt opened a set of louvered doors and found a small pantry. There was a cutting board there, along with a counter and sink for food prep. Built-in shelves lined the wall on the left from floor to ceiling. Matt guessed that Rey had shopped at one of the warehouse stores, probably the Costco over on Washington Boulevard in Marina del Rey. The shelves were overflowing with oversize pasta and cereal boxes, canned goods and olive oil, paper towels and enough cleaning supplies to cover a crew working an office building. Matt started with the boxes of rigatoni, picking them up and shaking them. A few minutes later, he could feel McKensie move in behind him.

"How you doing, Detective?"

Matt lowered a box of pasta to the counter, turned around, and gave his supervisor a look. The big man was standing on top of him, and Matt took a step back.

"What is it, Lieutenant? What's wrong?"

"I just wanted to know how you're making out, Jones. How all those monsters are doing inside your head. I'm guessing they're awake now. Awake and probably hungry."

Matt didn't say anything right away. He just stood there and looked the man over. When he spoke finally, his voice was cool, calm, and steady.

"Things didn't turn out the way you hoped, Lieutenant. It's not exactly murder lite, sir."

McKensie's face flushed with color and he laughed. "That's the great part about working for the LAPD, Jones. Every day's a goddamn adventure."

Matt picked up another box of pasta, gave it a shake, and lowered it to the counter beside the last box.

"We're on the right track now," he said carefully.

McKensie shook his head. "Chief Logan doesn't think so."

A long moment passed. It wasn't what McKensie had been saying that lit up the warning sirens in Matt's head. It was his supervisor's tone of voice. McKensie had come up the hard way. Despite his age, he was still tough, with a voice that matched his demeanor. But now the big man was whispering.

"I just came from the chief's office," he said. "He's not happy."

"But we're beginning to see daylight."

"Daylight, Jones? Is that what you call leaving a dead body in the ground for two days?"

Matt tried to get a read on McKensie, but nothing was showing on the man's face. He had a bad feeling about it. Like maybe he was about to be thrown off the case.

McKensie didn't say anything for a while. Instead, he gazed out the door into the kitchen as if to confirm that they were still alone, then turned back.

"The chief agrees with your shrink, Jones. He talked to her. You look tired. You're not ready. He doesn't think you can handle this one. He thinks I made a mistake."

The big man's words settled into the room hard and heavy. Matt didn't think there was anything more he could say that wouldn't seem defensive or weak. He heard someone in the house call out his name. It sounded like Speeks. He looked back at McKensie, who nodded and waved him off. But as Matt started to leave, he turned back and pushed the last two boxes of pasta he'd checked across the counter.

"There's something wrong with these," he said. "They look good, but they don't match the rest. They're too heavy."

McKensie didn't say anything. Instead, he eyeballed the boxes with suspicion, then picked one up with great care, measured the weight in his hands, and gave the box a light shake.

Matt walked out, resigned to the fact that he couldn't control his fate. That whatever may have been said between Chief Logan and Dr. May, whatever the chief and McKensie decided, was a decision he had no power to change. All he knew was that the trail felt hot now, and all of them were wrong.

He was back. And even though the heavy dose of ibuprofen hadn't kicked in and he could still feel the gunshot wounds in his chest, his mind was clear.

He found Speeks in the laundry room. The dryer was stacked on top of the washer, the door open. Speeks was holding what looked like a bright yellow rain jacket.

"Jones," he said excitedly. "I think I found it."

"Found what, Speeks?"

"Watch."

Speeks slid his arm into the sleeve of the jacket, gave it a hard twist, and yanked it out. Tossing the jacket back into the dryer, he switched on his UV light and pointed the beam at his shirt. Matt saw it immediately. The white lint-like specks that they had found all over Moe Rey's body. To the eye, they looked identical in shape and size.

Speeks switched off his UV light, pulled the jacket out of the dryer, and opened an evidence bag.

"Let me see it," Matt said.

The criminalist held up the yellow jacket. "He's got a pair of pants that go with it," he said.

Matt pulled the pants out of the dryer, examined the lining carefully, and read the label. It was a hazmat suit. The top and bottom halves of a hazmat suit. Exactly like the hazmat suits he'd seen the people wearing at the waste management company.

He felt someone grab his arm.

"In here," Cabrera said. "Hurry."

Matt followed his partner through the kitchen and into the master bedroom. A cigar box was open on the bed, and he could see what looked like three or four grams of cocaine and roughly an ounce of weed, with papers and a roach clip.

"Not that," Cabrera said. "Here."

Standing over the bedside table, Cabrera opened Moe Rey's checkbook and slipped a pay stub out of the register. As he passed it over, Matt could feel his gut churning.

Moe Rey had a new job, a new employer, and a nosy neighbor who thought he might be trying to keep it secret.

DMG Waste Management.

Matt examined both sides of the pay stub and read the company's logo a second time.

"How long's he worked there? Can you tell?"

Cabrera opened the checkbook and skimmed through the register. "He's been paid twice. The checks were deposited two weeks apart."

Matt stared back at his partner, who seemed just as staggered by the news as he was. After a moment, he reached for the checkbook.

"We need to show this to McKensie," Matt said.

"I was hoping you'd say that."

They stormed out of the bedroom and through the kitchen, then came to an abrupt stop when they hit the pantry. A photographer stood close by waiting to get a shot. McKensie appeared stiff as a statue and more than edgy. From the look on the big man's face, nothing needed to be said or written down.

The lieutenant had opened the first box of pasta and laid out its contents on the counter by the sink. It was cash—a lot of it—wrapped in a Cryovac bag that had been vacuum-sealed. Matt grabbed the second box, ripped open the packaging, and dumped another Cryovac bag on the counter. His eyes cut through the plastic and locked in on all those bundles of hundred-dollar bills wrapped in bands the color of mustard. All that money.

Enough to kill for. Enough to die for.

Daylight.

NINETEEN

Enough of everything for Matt and everybody else to survive for at least a few more days, but with strings attached.

They had counted the money. Each Cryovac bag contained ten bundles of hundred-dollar bills, and when added together, amounted to a cool two-hundred grand. Crisp, new bills—the ink so fresh it filled the air with a scent only that much paper money can buy.

But now it was 3:00 a.m., the cash entered into evidence, taken away, and locked up.

Matt crossed over the Grand Canal on Washington Boulevard, then made a right onto Pacific Avenue. The marine layer had rolled in off the ocean. Traffic was light to dead, but Matt kept his speed down, stopped at red lights, and wasn't in a rush. Home was only ten, maybe fifteen minutes away, and he found the cool air breezing through the open windows more than refreshing.

He glanced to his left and right, passing a hodgepodge of buildings cloaked in street murals and graffiti that didn't seem to belong just two blocks from the beach. Dated apartment buildings and small bungalows whizzed by, warehouses that may or may not have been abandoned, stores here and there that either looked closed for the night or shut down forever.

Matt let his mind wander. He was thinking about the strings McKensie and Chief Logan attached and wondering why they had called them strings. He was told to lay off Robert Gambini until Mitch Burton, the deputy DA in charge of the Organized Crime Unit, could be brought in for advice. A meeting had been set up for later that morning at 10:00 a.m. in Burton's office. To Matt, that felt more like the right move—not strings.

The two murders in Elysian Park had suddenly become radioactive, yet the case hadn't been traded up to the elite Robbery-Homicide Division. That would have been the right move, too.

So why hadn't the chief and McKensie made it?

As Matt considered the question, he couldn't ignore the fact that he'd had a bit of luck in scoring this small victory.

The murders of Sophia Ramirez and Moe Rey were still on his plate. But so was the mysterious relationship between Gambini and the owners of DMG Waste Management. He thought about Sonny Daniels and his two partners, Ryan Moore and Lane Grubb, and the possibility that their innocence, their willingness to help the other night, might have been completely bogus. The idea that maybe their company was nothing more than a front for a scam.

Matt cruised down the block and stopped at the red light. When the glare of headlights struck his rearview mirror, he saw a Mercedes idling behind him but couldn't make out the driver.

Why was Chief Logan willing to face the music with the media and cover for him, Cabrera, and the entire team from the crime lab rather than clear the deck and restart the case with a fresh crew?

Matt knew the homicide rate was up and that the department's resources were stretched thin. But how thin?

The light turned green. Matt eased his foot down on the accelerator. Checking his rearview mirror, the Mercedes seemed to linger back at the corner, then lurched forward quickly.

Matt looked back through the windshield. The fog was thicker here. Because of the height of the buildings, the road seemed extraordinarily dark and narrow. He checked the mirror again. The Mercedes had made up the distance and was following three car lengths back. They were the only two cars on the road.

Tossing it over, something about it didn't feel right.

He looked ahead, saw the dog park, and made a right on Westminster Avenue. His eyes flicked back to the mirror. The Mercedes was making the turn with him. As the car drove beneath the lights from the park, Matt could see that it was a black coupe. High end, but that didn't mean anything anymore, especially in LA.

He punched the accelerator, hit the end of the block, and made a hard left onto Main Street. Checking the mirror again, he watched the Mercedes vanish into a fog bank, then reappear in the darkness behind him.

Nothing about it was right.

He thought about the road ahead. In another seven or eight blocks the buildings would become commercial. Storefronts, bars, restaurants, and cafés that might still be open. Even if they were closed, the street would be brighter, and there was a decent chance he could get a look at who was tailing him in the black coupe.

He slowed the car down to an easy thirty-five miles an hour and settled into the seat. He made no moves, no turns, no fluctuations in speed. When he hit red lights, he eyed the intersections but never stopped. Checking the rearview mirror each time, he watched the Mercedes roll through the red lights without even slowing down.

He grimaced, then spotted a coffeehouse to the right on the next corner. Even better, there was a bus stop there, the sidewalk well lit. Wrenching the steering wheel, he skidded to a stop at the curb and turned to the open window just as the black Mercedes started to pass by.

There was a man sitting behind the wheel, and he turned with his chin up and an arrogant smile on his face. Their eyes met.

It was Robert Gambini.

The car made a sharp left at the corner, its tires screeching as it vanished up the street and into the fog.

Robert Gambini. The new breed.

A moment passed. Matt looked at his right hand and realized that he was holding his .45. He set the pistol down in the cup holder and spent a few moments committing Gambini's face to memory. Matt didn't think that the video image he'd photographed with Trey Washington that afternoon matched Gambini's presence in the flesh. His dark hair was combed straight back, his face more lean and angular in real life. From the glint in his eyes, the relaxed way he seemed to carry himself, even in the split second he sped by, Matt could tell that he wasn't a lowlife. That the degree he received from Wharton wasn't the result of a bribe made by a rich daddy. Robert Gambini had the look and feel of a successful man in his late thirties. A brutal heroin dealer who was making a fortune and wore well-tailored suits.

He wondered why Gambini did it.

Why would Gambini follow a cop down Main Street in Venice Beach at three in the morning? Why would he show himself to the detective who was most likely hunting him? Why take the risk?

It occurred to Matt that Gambini must have been watching them toss Moe Rey's place. He must have been waiting. He must have known who Matt was.

Matt let it go.

There was no one around. Not a single person on the sidewalk or a car in the street. The cafés and bars were closed, the fog in the cold night air billowing. He glanced at the clock on the dash, then pulled away from the curb. Blowing through another red light, he felt the cold breeze beating against his face and shut the windows. Once the heater kicked in, he sat back and tried to relax. But as he crossed the next intersection, the glare of headlights struck his rearview mirror again and he felt his blood pressure spike.

Gambini had circled the block. The black coupe had just burst through the clouds and was three car lengths back.

Matt knew from the Love Killings case in Philly that crazy was far more dangerous than steady. Crazy was unpredictable. Crazy was like a rabid dog that just keeps coming your way, regardless of the risks or consequences.

Matt reached for his pistol, chambered a round, and held it below the window line. He knew who Robert Gambini was now.

For the next five minutes he kept an eye on the Mercedes. Gambini followed him all the way down Main Street to Pico Boulevard. When Matt made the turn from Pico to Ocean Avenue, Gambini was still only three car lengths back. But then it all changed when they reached the entrance to the Pacific Coast Highway. For whatever reason, Gambini seemed to have had enough. Matt eased off the gas and watched the coupe continue down Ocean. As if to punctuate the end of the night, Robert Gambini, a person of interest in two murders, blinked his lights and tapped the horn before disappearing into the fog.

Matt shook his head. It was almost as if Gambini had escorted him out of the neighborhood and off his turf. Almost as if Gambini thought that LA was his city and he owned it.

Matt turned back to the road and accelerated onto the ramp. As he entered the highway, he looked at the .45 in his hand and decided that he'd better keep it close.

TWENTY

Matt looked at the receptionist sitting at her computer behind the chest-high counter in the lobby at DMG Waste Management. It was 8:30 a.m., and she was speaking to her boss, Sonny Daniels, on the phone. After a few moments, she palmed the mouthpiece.

"They're in a meeting," she said. "Mr. Daniels was wondering if you guys could come back later."

Matt noticed the copy of the *Times* beside her computer, then gave her a look and rocked his head back and forth. "That's not gonna work for us," he said. "We won't have time later. Tell him it's important."

The receptionist got back on the phone. While they waited, he could see Cabrera keying in on the newspaper. The story had broken wide open sometime overnight and, just as Matt expected, had made the front page of this morning's paper above the fold. The headline, LAPD'S FINEST BUNGLE ANOTHER ONE, LEAVE DEAD BODY BEHIND, pretty much said it all. Matt and his partner had been singled out for their inexperience and blamed for the debacle. And while Moe Rey's name as the second victim hadn't been confirmed, both Matt and Cabrera had been seen at Rey's house last night, so it didn't take much for anyone to connect the dots.

The tone of the piece was just as bad as the reality and at times seemed over the top. But what bothered Matt most were the photographs. The article had been cowritten by a crime beat reporter, a woman Matt respected and had spoken with in the past. Somehow, she had managed to break through the police line and enter the crime scene undetected. There were pictures of the tents pitched over the picnic tables at night with their work lights burning. Worse still, the reporter had waited until everyone left, then found her way under the pine trees and snapped a picture of the grave that was more than eerie.

Matt could remember reading the piece online when he woke up after an hour and a half's sleep. Everything about the case seemed bigger, more urgent now.

"They'll see you in a few minutes," the receptionist said, her eyes lifting off the newspaper and meeting Matt's head-on.

Matt turned and gave Cabrera a look. Then the door to the conference room opened and Sonny Daniels walked out. Matt stepped down to the gate in the counter.

"Thanks for seeing us, Mr. Daniels. We just have a few follow-up questions. It shouldn't take long."

"You're more than welcome, Detective. We can talk in the conference room. Everybody's here."

Matt checked his watch. Their meeting with Deputy DA Burton wasn't for another hour and a half, so they had plenty of time. Before he and Cabrera arrived, they had come up with a plan. Matt would ask the questions while Cabrera remained an observer, studying the three partners' reactions and writing everything down. If Cabrera thought Matt missed something important, he was free to jump in at any time. Still, both detectives agreed that this kind of inquiry was all about rhythm. All about pressure—all about the build—then cataloging responses and hoping something unexpected might shake out.

Matt followed Cabrera into the conference room. Ryan Moore and Lane Grubb were standing on the other side of the table just as they had the other night. And all evidence pointed to the receptionist having told them the truth about a meeting. Papers were strewn across the conference table. Matt could see schedules and lists and another set of blueprints weighted down with a ruler and paperweights. Although the room was slightly darker, the TV muted and switched to a cable business channel rather than Channel Five, almost everything was just as it had been before.

Matt chewed it over as he watched Sonny Daniels walk to the other side of the table and take a seat between his partners. Once again, no attempt had been made to cover up or hide any of the papers on the table. Once again, all three partners seemed completely at ease and willing to help—almost as if they didn't have a care in the world.

It seemed so odd.

Matt let it go and sat down beside Cabrera, who was already opening his notepad.

"Our offer still stands," Daniels said. "If you'd like to interview our employees, Detectives, I can make it happen. We can arrange a time."

Matt nodded. "Thanks," he said. "We just have a few follow-up questions for now."

"Go ahead."

Matt opened his laptop case and pulled out a file. Leafing through the papers, he found two photographs of Robert Gambini that he'd downloaded off his phone and printed an hour ago. Two images of the crime figure that included the man laid out on the grassy bank with his binoculars and camera and then running across the lawn as he chased Sophia Ramirez and Trey Washington into the woods.

Matt turned and gave the three partners a good look. When he spoke finally, everything about his demeanor was cool and straightforward.

"What interest would a man like Robert Gambini have in any of you or your company, DMG Waste Management?"

Matt slid the photographs across the table and watched all three men study the images. Sonny Daniels shook his head as if confused by the question.

"Who is Robert Gambini?" he said.

"You don't know him?"

"I've never even heard of him."

"He's the nephew of Joseph Gambini, the CEO of the Gambini Organization, which is just a front for the Gambini crime family. Robert's business is drugs. Heroin mostly. Getting addicts off oxycodone so they can buy his dope."

Daniels leaned back in his seat and looked Matt in eye. "I've never heard of any one by the name of Robert Gambini," he repeated in a subdued voice.

"Well, he's heard of you. He's watching this place, Mr. Daniels. Take another look at these photographs. The binoculars. A camera with a long lens. Robert Gambini's a dangerous man from a dangerous family. They kill people, go to prison, and when they get out, they kill all over again. It's a vicious cycle. These photographs would seem to prove that he knows who you are, Mr. Daniels. And that you have something he wants. We're hoping you can tell us what it is."

Matt let the news settle into the room. He noticed the coffee maker, got up and poured himself a mug while keeping an eye on all three of the partners. Sonny Daniels, Ryan Moore, and Lane Grubb no longer seemed so willing to be helpful. Instead, all three appeared deeply concerned, especially Grubb, who was staring at his hands beneath the glass table. Matt noted the black circles under Grubb's eyes and glanced back at his hands as he returned to his seat at the table. He thought they might be trembling.

"You guys know anything about heroin?"

The air thickened. No one on the other side of the table wanted to be there anymore.

After several moments, Sonny Daniels cleared his throat. "I guess I'm wondering what this is all about, Detective. I just told you that I don't know Robert Gambini. That I've never met him. That I've never even heard of him and have no idea why he might, as you say, have an interest in our company or any of us. And to your question, the answer is no. None of us know anything about heroin."

Matt glanced at Cabrera taking notes, then skimmed through his file and pulled out two more photographs. The first was Moe Rey as they found him buried in the ground in a death scream. The second was another blowup, this time from his driver's license.

"What about Moe Rey?" Matt said.

Daniels shook his head again and laughed sarcastically. "Who the hell is Moe Rey?"

Matt slid the photographs across the table and watched their eyes devour the images. How the man looked when he was alive versus the horror of his brutal death. Ryan Moore finally shot Matt a look and seemed flabbergasted.

"Who is he?"

"Who is he?" Matt repeated.

"That's what Ryan just asked you," Daniels said. "Who the hell is he?"

Matt nodded calmly. "He worked for you. He worked here, Mr. Daniels, in this facility as your employee. He was a low-level associate of the Gambini Organization. He worked for them, too. His body was found with the girl's up on the hill."

Anger was beginning to show on Sonny Daniels's face. "That guy never worked here," he said. "Nobody named Moe Rey ever worked for this company. Why are you doing this, Detective? Why are you making things up?"

Matt slid a photocopy of Moe Rey's pay stub across the table. Sonny Daniels grabbed it, eyeing the stub but also checking the official LAPD file numbers indicating the stub had been entered into evidence.

"Moe Rey worked here," Matt said calmly. "An associate of the Gambini Organization, a friend of the Gambini crime family, worked in this building. And Robert Gambini has his eyes on you, so tell me and my partner what's going on. It only cuts two ways now, Mr. Daniels. Two people have been murdered. And feigning ignorance is no third way out. Believe me, it won't work. Either you're in business with the Gambinis, okay? Or you and your partners are in a great deal of danger because you have something these people want."

Daniels sighed, then grabbed the phone and punched in three numbers. His face had turned a deep red. As Matt sat back and assessed the moment, it looked like Ryan Moore had turned them off and was mulling things over deep inside himself. Lane Grubb still appeared zoned out and preoccupied with his hands hidden below the glass table.

"Who's managing the floor right now?" Daniels said into the phone. He listened for a moment, then nodded. "Good. Send him in now. And tell him to hurry."

Daniels slammed the phone down hard enough to break it. Within two minutes, the conference room door opened and a shy-looking man wearing a hazmat suit without the hood and headgear stepped into the room. Matt guessed that he was in his fifties, medium height and build with gray hair and dark brown eyes.

Daniels didn't waste any time greeting the man.

"Who is Moe Rey?" he said.

The floor manager shrugged. "I've got no idea, sir. Who is he?"

Daniels smiled and turned to Matt. "This is our floor manager, John Malone. John hires everybody who works here. If he says he doesn't know who Moe Rey is, then your Moe Rey never worked here. And you can take that to the bank, Detective."

Undaunted, Matt beckoned the floor manager over to the table with a raised right hand and an exceedingly calm voice. "Come over here for a moment, Mr. Malone. This is serious business. Two people are dead. They were murdered just up the hill here. One was a teenage girl. Do you understand?"

The floor manager turned to Sonny Daniels as if he needed permission. When Daniels nodded finally, the shy man stepped over to the table. Matt reached for the two photographs of Moe Rey, dead and alive, slid them in front of the man, and waited for his reaction. The floor manager's gaze hit the gruesome image of Rey in the dirt with his eyes open, then rocked back over to the shot taken from the victim's driver's license.

"He worked here," the man blurted out suddenly. "He worked here, but his name wasn't Moe Rey."

Daniels slapped the table, astounded. "What the hell was it?"

"Maurice Reynolds," the floor manager said. "He worked here for two weeks, and then I fired him."

"Fired him for what?" Daniels said, aghast.

The man thought it over, his lips quivering. "He was lazy, sir. And I could never find him. He was never where he was supposed to be on the floor."

"Show me," Matt said.

The manager's eyes flicked back to Daniels. Again, after considering the idea, Daniels nodded, then turned to his partners.

"We're all going out there."

Matt picked up the photographs and returned the file to his laptop case. He glanced at Cabrera but didn't hold the look for fear of giving something away. They had been hoping to work themselves into a tour of the factory floor without a warrant—it had been part of their original plan. A goal to work toward, no matter how unlikely it might seem. Matt wanted to look around and get a feel for the place firsthand. But even better, he had one more card in his hand, and that's where he wanted to play it.

Sonny Daniels and the floor manager led the way out of the conference room. Matt and Cabrera fell in line, with Ryan Moore and Lane Grubb bringing up the rear. As they walked down the hall, it was clear to Matt that Grubb was strung out and had issues. His hands were still trembling, and he looked like a man trying to hide whatever might be going on in his mind.

Matt let it go as they stepped through a double set of steel doors into the facility. A bin filled with clean hazmat suits had been placed against the wall. Matt grabbed one, checking the label and confirming that it matched the one they found in Moe Rey's dryer. But before he could examine the jacket's lining, the manager pulled him aside, shouting over the loud, echoey din of the factory floor.

"I'm gonna give you the nickel tour, so we don't need to suit up, okay?"

"Okay," Matt said.

The manager took the hazmat suit and tossed it back into the bin. Then he pointed to a yellow line that had been painted onto the floor and made it clear that crossing it would be a problem. They passed a locker room and several more storage bins and tried to stay out of the way of three forklifts that were loading fifty-five-gallon drums onto an exceedingly large pallet. Matt eyed the heavy cables attached to the pallet and followed them to a crane operated from the ceiling. The smell of sulfur was so rich, so overwhelming that it reminded Matt of a depiction of hell he had seen in a movie as a young boy. Somehow this seemed worse, though, and he couldn't help wondering how much DMG Waste Management might be adding to climate change.

They passed a room where drums were being inspected, their welds X-rayed. A few moments later, a drum fell off a forklift and three men standing close by scattered in panic. A loud alarm sounded from the ceiling. The floor manager pointed to an open side door and waved everyone outside. But before Matt turned away, he saw the liquid dripping out of the container. A chemical so toxic it looked like it was burning a hole in the concrete floor. He watched the men who had scattered run back, picking the drum up and hosing down the floor. He could hear others shouting over the alarm and watched the crane lowering its cargo to the floor.

Matt felt himself being pulled outside into the fresh air and was grateful when the alarm shut down.

He looked around. There were two picnic tables here, both set on a lawn beneath a large oak tree. On the other side of a chain-link fence, he saw the employee parking lot.

"Satisfied?"

Matt looked up and found Sonny Daniels staring at him. Pulling the file out of his laptop case, he set two new photographs down on the picnic table.

"Not yet," he said calmly. "Not just yet, Mr. Daniels. We found these hidden in Moe Rey's house. Each bag is filled with a hundred grand in cash. Crisp new bills. Hundred-dollar bills. What do you make of that?"

Daniels stared at the photographs with a face that almost looked as if it had been flash frozen. Matt quickly turned to check on Moore and Grubb. They were leaning over Daniels's shoulder, eyeing the photographs carefully.

All three looked more than interested.

All three appeared to be mesmerized by the cash, and Matt knew that he'd just struck a nerve. He let the moment ride. Then stepped closer, keeping his voice smooth and steady.

"You guys have any idea how a lowlife like Moe Rey could get his hands on this much money? This much cash?"

No one said anything. After a long moment, Daniels looked up from the photographs. When he spoke, Matt could see the effort it was taking to keep his emotions reined in. Sonny Daniels was seething.

"You said yourself that this man worked for a crime family, Detective. Why don't you ask them?"

Matt met the man's dead eyes and flashed an ironic smile. "We intend to, Mr. Daniels. We do. But let me ask you one more question before we leave. Why would a guy like Moe Rey want to work at a place like this? A place that smells like this? Why would a goon with this much money show up every day and punch in his timecard? If you guys come up with any ideas, you know how to reach us, right?"

No one said a word. Matt nodded, then returned the photographs to his laptop case and shouldered the bag.

"Thanks for your time," he said. "We'll show ourselves out."

Matt looked over at Cabrera and motioned him toward the gate in the chain-link fence. He didn't want to walk through the building back to the lobby and out the main entrance. He'd seen something in the employee parking lot beside the picnic tables. He wanted to walk through the lot and around the building to their Crown Vic parked on the street out front.

He led the way. He counted fifteen cars in the lot, but there were only three that really mattered. The three at the head of the line marked with the names of the three partners. As they passed by, he heard Cabrera say something under his breath. He knew that his partner was seeing what he was seeing but wondered if he had an idea what any of this was worth.

The three cars parked in the marked spaces might be called "high-end" by some, but that would hardly cover it. These cars were exotics. A black Audi R8, which Matt knew from his life in narcotics had a V10 under the hood and sold for just over $175,000. A BMW i8, which sold for about $165,000 without extras. But it was the third car that topped the list. The one Sonny Daniels drove. An Aston Martin DB11, which started at about $210,000, stripped.

He thought it over as they made their way around the building in the warm sun. Despite the rotten smell, business in waste management seemed pretty sweet.

TWENTY-ONE

Matt raised the binoculars to his eyes and adjusted the focus. He was standing beside Cabrera on the grassy bank, eyeing DMG Waste Management and the Aston Martin DB11 that had just pulled out of the employee lot and was speeding up the private road. He smiled a little as he tilted the field glasses up and found Sonny Daniels behind the wheel. He could see the tension on the man's face, the worry, and it felt like confirmation.

"So what did we learn?" he said to Cabrera.

"Sonny Daniels is the boss, Matt. No doubt about it. The other two will do whatever he tells them to do."

Matt nodded, still following the car as it raced up the hill. "Anything else?"

"Lane Grubb's the weak one. The one we need to work on."

"I agree with that," he said. "And he's using."

"How do you know?"

"He's strung out on something, Den. Who knows what? Wanna look?"

"Yeah."

Matt passed the field glasses over. Cabrera pointed them toward the Aston Martin until the car reached the top of the hill and vanished over the other side onto Baker Street. After a moment, he turned back toward the factory and adjusted the focus.

"At least we hit something," Cabrera said.

"We did, but I'm still not sure what. When we got there, they were glad to see us. It doesn't make any sense."

Cabrera laughed. "Maybe they never saw it coming. They were thinking that this was about the girl, and then it changed into something else."

And that was the problem, Matt thought. If the waste management company was cover for a drug operation, if they were competing with Robert Gambini or doing business with the man and involved in the murders of two people, then what Matt and Cabrera needed was still lost deep inside that building.

"I think we should split up," he said. "We need to get SIS involved. You should stay and bring them up to speed when they get here. I'll talk to the deputy DA and see what he wants to do about Gambini. We can meet back at the station."

Cabrera nodded, still looking through the field glasses. "Make the call."

Matt dug his cell phone out of his pocket and found the number in his contacts list. The Special Investigation Section was the LAPD's primary surveillance unit. It seemed obvious that the investigation needed more eyes and a bigger reach. It wasn't enough to say that something was wrong with the three partners at DMG. There was too much gray area. Too many questions.

Was Sonny Daniels telling the truth when he claimed he didn't know and had never heard of Robert Gambini? Was Daniels really that naive? Was he that far out of the loop? Had he never heard of or read the *Los Angeles Times*?

If all that were true, and Matt knew that it could be, then why didn't Daniels want help and ask for protection? And why did he have that meltdown reaction when he saw the pictures Matt had taken of the money? Why were all three of the partners driving exotic cars and wearing their wealth on their sleeves the same way lowlifes do? Why did they want to stand out when they'd be so much safer living off the grid?

"I just noticed something," Cabrera said.

Matt looked over at this partner and saw the concern showing on his face.

"What is it?"

"Here," Cabrera said. "Take the binoculars."

Matt handed over his phone. "I'm on hold," he said.

Cabrera nodded, bringing the phone to his ear. "Down in the lot behind the substation. Check out the black car. It looks like the one you were talking about. The one that followed you through Venice last night."

Matt brought the binoculars up to his eyes and dialed the substation into focus. After a moment, he saw the sun spiking off a windshield and panned across the lot.

It was the black coupe. The Mercedes.

He tried to steady his hands as the sun pinged off something inside the car. Then he tilted the lenses up slightly and fine-tuned the focus.

He caught the smirk. The angular face and vicious smile.

It was Robert Gambini, sitting behind the wheel with a pair of his own field glasses trained on the DMG factory. Matt looked over at the building, then back at Gambini. The man had positioned his car so that he could look through the front gate and open bay doors directly onto the factory floor.

Gambini had picked the perfect spot for the perfect view. A parking lot at the end of the road.

TWENTY-TWO

Matt was still wrestling with the details. Still lost in a sea of possibilities.

Stepping off the elevator with his ID in hand, he told the receptionist that he was there to meet Deputy District Attorney Mitch Burton. When asked to take a seat, he glanced at his watch and realized that he was almost half an hour late. He glanced back at the receptionist, who seemed more like a security guard than anything else. A young cop in uniform with a pistol holstered to his belt and the oversize chest and biceps of a bodybuilder. There was no one else in the reception area. Matt watched the cop pick up the phone and speak so quietly, he couldn't make out what the man was saying. After a moment, the cop hung up the phone and turned.

"Someone will be out shortly," he said.

Matt nodded. A few minutes later he saw a woman walk around the corner and start down the hall with her eyes on him. She looked older than him by ten or twelve years, forty to forty-five maybe, and was wearing a white blouse with a turquoise skirt cut three or four inches above her knees. Her hair was shoulder-length and a mix of light brown and blonde that looked natural enough, though he doubted she spent much time in the sun. She had a pleasant, straightforward, even stylish way about her. As she stepped into the reception area with an outstretched hand, she smiled at him.

"I'm Val Burton," she said. "Mitch's wife. I already know who you are."

She laughed.

"This way, please," she went on. "Mitch is looking forward to meeting you. I am, too."

Matt walked with her down the hall. When she glanced his way, her blue-gray eyes seemed to dance all over his face. Though she appeared immediately likable, Matt couldn't help wondering why she was here. He didn't think she worked in the DA's office.

They turned the corner, passed a conference room and a small library on the right, then stepped into an office suite. Matt understood why Val Burton was here the minute he walked through the door. He stared at the cardboard boxes scattered across the floor. Burton was packing up his office. The deputy DA was moving out.

Matt tried to hide his disappointment as he turned and saw Burton rising from his desk chair.

"Detective Jones," the man said in a cheerful voice. "Welcome. I wish my office wasn't in this sorry state of affairs, but change is good, don't you think?"

Burton leaned over his desk and met his eyes while they shook hands. As Matt stepped back, he noted the stacks of files on the couch, the credenza, and across the windowsill. The prosecutor's desk was littered with papers and files as well, along with row after row of notes jotted down by hand and set beside the telephone. On the walls were photographs documenting Burton's rise to the top of the Organized Crime Unit. Big busts with recognizable figures from the mob, big business, and the entertainment industry that made the papers and wound up on the evening news.

One photograph in particular caught Matt's eye. It was none other than Joseph Gambini himself, being escorted by Burton and four detectives out of a downtown building to a police cruiser waiting for them at the curb. The press had encircled the entrance. Gambini was dressed in a well-tailored suit and somehow appeared dignified. Despite all the cameras, despite the handcuffs, Joseph Gambini looked like a man who didn't have a care in the world. Like his arrest was nothing more than a distraction some underling would take care of before lunch.

"You're moving out of the unit," Matt said.

Burton had been watching him take in the photographs. He shook his head and smiled, his blue eyes twinkling in the window light.

"Not with the cases I've got on my plate, Detective. Organized crime is a burgeoning industry. Especially here in LA, or should I say anywhere else that's a magnet for money."

"Then why are you packing up your office?"

"Some of my personal files are going back to the house, but the whole unit's moving to the other side of the building. We're doubling our staff and need more space."

Matt felt an immediate sense of relief and took a moment to measure the man as he tossed it over. Burton may have been ten or fifteen years older than his wife, but he didn't look it. He still had the spark. The juice. The drive. He stood just over six feet tall, the same height as Matt, with broad shoulders and the trim, limber body of someone who had jogged for decades. But even more, Burton's reputation was stellar. Matt could remember a prosecutor he'd worked a drug case with last year calling Burton the brightest attorney in the building. The murders of Sophia Ramirez and Moe Rey had become more than a challenge, and he'd been counting on Burton's experience ever since McKensie mentioned his name last night.

"I'm sorry I was late," Matt said. "I'm guessing you spoke with Chief Logan and maybe my supervisor, Lieutenant McKensie."

Burton nodded as he slipped on a pair of eyeglasses and began leafing through a file. "I'm up to speed," he said, shooting Matt a look over his glass frames and laughing. "Sort of."

It hung there for a moment. Matt glanced at the boxes on the floor—all the notes and files—and turned back to find Burton watching him again.

"No worries, Detective. I've got plenty of time for a case like this. Where's your partner?"

"We're bringing in a surveillance unit to keep an eye on the waste management company. It turns out all three partners have expensive tastes."

"Good," Burton said. "And I set up a meeting with Joseph Gambini. I think that's where we should start. I spoke with him on the phone this morning. I'll explain everything in the car."

"Where is he?"

"Terminal Island, at least for the next two years. But I need a minute before we go. I'll be right back."

Burton found the papers he had been searching for and hurried out of the office. Matt glanced at his wife, Val, who was clearing a space for him on the couch.

"Please," she said. "Have a seat while you wait."

"I'm okay, thanks."

She moved the stack of files over to a table, then crossed the room to the window. She was staring at him, her eyes dancing all over his face again. She seemed so gentle.

"Do you have nine lives, Detective?"

"You can call me Matt, you know."

She smiled. "And you can call me Val, Matthew. But I've been reading about you in the newspapers."

"I hope you're not talking about what you may have read today."

"I wasn't, but I did."

That smile of hers came back. Matt took a moment, then sat down and tried to relax. Val Burton had a sense of humor and appeared to be as genuine as her husband. When she spoke, her voice was on the low side, like she didn't want it to carry out the door.

"Your father," she said. "All the things that happened to you in Philadelphia. And what about Greenwich? The snowstorm on the water? Most people who fall into the water in December drown. How come you didn't?"

He gave her a long look. "I'm not sure," he said finally.

"Are you okay?"

"I think so."

"But how could you even be close to okay? The paper said you were on medical leave."

Matt shrugged it off and glanced around the office. The idea that Burton was on board gave the investigation a blood transfusion—an entirely new status. Before he had a chance to really think about it, Burton rushed back into the room.

"Sorry about that, Detective. I've got all afternoon open now. Let's get out of here."

The prosecutor walked over to his desk, returning the papers to his file. Matt watched Val move to the coatrack, then help her husband get into his jacket.

"Will you be home late?" she said.

Burton glanced at Matt and turned back. "I don't think so."

She nodded like she'd heard him say the same thing a thousand times. Burton met her eyes.

"I'll do the best I can," he said quietly. "I promise."

Matt gathered his things and started for the door. Burton grabbed his briefcase and led the way out.

TWENTY-THREE

Burton drove a dark-gray Audi SUV that looked as if it hadn't been washed since the rainstorms. As they pulled out of the garage onto the street, Matt slid his laptop case aside and stretched his legs.

"My wife's a fan of yours," Burton said. "She's taking a few days off to help me move. She designs children's clothing. The reason I mention it is that she's got an artist's imagination. She wants to hear about everything she's seen and read in the news."

Matt smiled. "That's okay. I'm getting used to it."

"Good," Burton said. "I can call you, Matt, right?"

"Sure."

"And I'm Mitch."

Burton made a right onto West Temple Street, then another onto North Grand. Within a few minutes they were cruising down the 110 Freeway heading south to San Pedro. Matt had made the trip to Terminal Island many times in the past. Depending on traffic and the number of slowdowns, the twenty-five-mile drive could take anywhere from forty-five minutes to three or four hours.

Matt pulled a file out of his laptop case. "Why is Joseph Gambini our first move?" he said.

Burton thought it over. "Because anything Robert Gambini has done or might be doing wouldn't be with his uncle's blessing."

"Why not?"

Burton glanced his way, then back at the road. "Because they hate each other."

"How is that possible?"

"It's a blood thing. A family issue, and it's irrevocable."

"Are you serious?"

"Robert has nothing to do with the Gambini Organization and never has."

Matt shook his head in disbelief. "He isn't a friend or a player? He has no involvement, no business, no participation with the Gambini crime family at all?"

Burton flashed an ironic smile. "None," he said flatly. "But that doesn't mean that Uncle Joe doesn't know exactly what his nephew is up to. You know what I mean?"

"Why would a man like Joseph Gambini agree to talk to us? Why would he want to?"

"He seemed agreeable on the phone," Burton said. "But that doesn't mean he'll give us anything we can use. All he knows is that I didn't put him away this time. The Department of Justice got him. A federal prosecutor trying to score points, Marvin Sanders. He went after Gambini's bank accounts. He didn't need to do that, but he did. He put Joe away for ten years on charges of racketeering and extortion that didn't add up. But the headlines did, and so did the media coverage. Marvin Sanders is from South Carolina and thinks he's gonna be a senator someday."

"How much time has Gambini done? What about parole?"

Burton checked the mirror, moved into the left lane, and picked up speed. "He served eight of ten and was released. About a week later, he was seen outside one of the casinos on the Westside. He was sipping an espresso and smoking a cigar with two members of a major crime family from New York. They turned out to be best friends from childhood, the meeting by chance. But like I said, Marvin Sanders wants to be a senator someday. For him it's all about the kill. He sent Gambini back to prison for the remaining two years of his sentence and got more of those headlines he likes so much. As you've probably guessed, Sanders is a small-time guy. Our office thought the move was petty and we said so in public, and Gambini knows that, too."

Matt grimaced. There were too many people like Marvin Sanders in the world. Too many people who deserved a hard pushback. No wonder Burton thought the crime boss might talk to them.

He let the thought go, glanced at the speedometer, and saw that they had settled in at a brisk ninety miles an hour. Traffic had thinned out, and they were making good time. Burton had already reached the Seaside Freeway.

Matt sat back in the seat as they turned onto Terminal Way and approached the prison's main gate on the right. Straight ahead was a guard tower and to the left, the parking lot and prison entrance. Matt fished his ID out of his pocket. Terminal Island was a low-security federal prison for male inmates set on the water in beautiful Southern California. Still, it never ceased to amaze Matt how much barbed wire could be wrapped around the walls of a three-story building like this one. He knew that the barbed wire was there for show. That the Federal Bureau of Prisons hoped to dispel Terminal Island's reputation as "Club Fed" after a series of embarrassing scandals. Matt couldn't recall many of the details except to say that six prison officials had been indicted for selling drugs to inmates. Based on the overwhelming amount of barbed wire encasing the buildings—based on the size of the show—that wire had to add up to a lot of drugs for a lot of inmates and, at least for a few, a lot of cash underneath the table.

TWENTY-FOUR

Joseph Gambini was waiting for them in a meeting room. He was seated at a table, wearing a jumpsuit the color of orange juice spilled over light wood and holding an unlit cigarette in his right hand.

"Does my nephew know that you're onto him?"

Matt glanced at Burton, then back at the CEO of the Gambini Organization.

"Maybe, maybe not," Matt said as he approached the table. "He followed me through Venice last night, but that could mean a lot of things."

Gambini shrugged, then turned to Burton. "This is the guy you were talking about?"

Burton nodded. "Detective Jones. Hollywood Homicide."

"The one in the funny papers?"

Burton gave the crime boss a grim smile. "They're not so funny these days, Joe."

"No," he said quietly. "I guess they're not."

A moment passed as Gambini turned to the window. Matt followed his gaze through the bars and thick mesh of barbed wire to a cargo ship that had been stacked with containers and was being led out to open water by a pair of tugs. When Burton pulled a chair out from the table, Matt turned back to Gambini and sat down.

He couldn't help thinking about the photograph hanging in Burton's office and guessed that it was taken twenty years ago when Gambini would have been about forty years old. Despite the time, setting, and circumstance, Gambini didn't seem to have changed much. He still had the look and feel of someone comfortable in their own skin. Someone who lived above the fray and without worries. Someone who knew that in the end, he would survive, and everything would turn out okay. His dark hair was gray now, his thin build meatier, and his brown eyes framed by age lines. But he looked healthy and seemed smarter than most—the kind of guy Matt had always thought he needed to keep an eye on.

Gambini turned from the window and gave Matt a long look. "If my nephew thinks you're onto him, that's not good, Detective. Not good for you."

Matt noticed that Gambini was wearing a gold watch and a wedding band. Both looked high-end and out of place for an inmate in a federal prison. He leaned his elbows on the table.

"What's going on between you and your nephew, Mr. Gambini? What happened?"

The man crossed his legs, then casually rubbed his chin with two fingers. When he spoke, he didn't seem rushed or fazed, his voice low.

"I kept Robert's mother and father out of the family business. His father was a loser. They didn't live that well. I made sure they had enough to get by, but that's about it. Robert always resented it."

There were three paper cups on the table, along with a pitcher made of plastic and filled with ice water. Gambini filled a cup for himself, looked at Matt and then Burton, and filled two more. After a first sip, the crime boss cleared his throat.

"I kept them out of the business," he repeated. "They didn't have the knack." He laughed a little as he thought it over. "In a way, it turned out to be a good thing for Robert. He went to college. He got an MBA from Wharton. But in the end, with all that higher learning, he still wasn't smart enough to see things straight. After he graduated, he came to me and wanted to work for the Gambini Organization. I refused, just like I always had. I refused for the same reasons I refused his father."

Matt noticed that Gambini was wearing a polo shirt underneath his worn-out orange jumpsuit. When he lowered his laptop case to the floor, he shot a quick look at the man's pant legs and spotted a pair of jeans beneath his prison garb. The jumpsuit was like the barbed wire. The whole thing, a ruse.

Club Fed.

He could remember a cartoon that appeared in the editorial section of the newspaper around the time indictments were handed out here at the prison. The single-frame sketch depicted an inmate resting on a chaise lounge by the water while a prison guard served him a gram of cocaine and a glass of wine on a silver tray. The caption read, "Will there be anything else, sir?"

Matt let it go, took a sip of water, and sat back in his chair. "Why refuse to take Robert in?" he said. "Even if we put his illegal activity aside, do the math. Your nephew owns a chain of pot shops. He obviously knows how to make money. Why wouldn't he have been an asset to you?"

Something changed in Gambini's eyes, almost as if storm clouds had swept across the sky of his face and were blocking the sun in his eyes.

"Because he's got the gene," the crime boss said emphatically. "The 'mean Gambini gene.' He got it from his father—my father. And our father got it from our grandfather. He's mean. He's vicious and cruel. He keeps an enemy list. A shit list. He's always got somebody he hates. You ever meet anybody like that, kid? They hate everybody they know they can't beat, right? And they love stabbing them in the goddamn back. That's how they get that feeling of power. That's how their little game works. If they're surrounded by losers, they're the king on top. And that's what makes them dangerous. That's why I didn't want them anywhere near my business. They're crazy motherfuckers. They just don't know it yet."

Matt met the man's eyes. "How come you didn't get it? The gene your brother got from your father. Why not you?"

Gambini must have been thrown off by the question. The storm clouds vanished, and his face cleared. He looked around the meeting room and laughed.

"Because I got this," he said joyously. "I'm living the good life now; can't you see it, Detective? The feds took all my cash. They took my buildings, my casinos, my homes, and my cars. They got my toys—that little prick that nailed me thinks he got everything. But I still got this." Gambini tapped the top of his head with a finger. "I still got what's in here, Detective. And I've had a lot of time to think things over. A lot of time to sit in the sun and work on not getting burned. In two years, I'm out of this place. In one year, seven months, three days, and six hours, I'm free as a fucking bird. Watch me fly, kid. Watch me fly away and never bother nobody again."

Another long moment passed. Gambini drained the paper cup, crushed it in his free hand, and tossed it in a trash basket beside the table. Matt turned to Burton.

"How much of what's happened did you tell him?"

Burton leaned closer with his eyes wide open. "Enough that he can probably guess what your next question will be."

Gambini flashed a scary smile as he measured Matt up. "You ought to be an attorney, kid. You wanna be my lawyer?"

Matt ignored the question and fired one back. "Why do you think Robert is watching the waste management company? Is he keeping an eye on things because he's already in with them and doesn't trust them? Or do the three partners have something he wants?"

The crime boss shook his head. "All things being equal?" he said.

Matt nodded carefully. "All things being equal."

"What the hell could they have that he wants?" Gambini said. "What the hell could they have that he doesn't already have ten times over? I think it's a better bet that Robert's watching something on those train tracks. Something in a freight car that's either there right now or on its way."

Matt gave Burton a look, then turned back. "That doesn't make any sense, Mr. Gambini. If it's about a drug shipment on a freight car, then why was Moe Rey working for DMG?"

Gambini seemed to be genuinely surprised and turned to Burton. "What's one of my couriers got to do with any of this?"

Burton met the man's hard gaze. "Moe Rey was murdered the other night, Joe."

"Murdered?"

Burton nodded. "According to Matt, his supervisor, and Chief Logan, he was executed. They think a young girl witnessed the killing. They were found buried in the same grave up the hill in Elysian Park."

Gambini still appeared stunned. "Moe Rey was a nobody. My nobody. He was harmless. Why would anyone want to kill him?"

Matt pushed the paper cup aside. "We're not sure. But we think it has something to do with the two hundred grand we found hidden in his kitchen pantry."

Gambini gave him a long look. After several moments, he turned back to Burton.

"Two hundred grand?" he said. "Cash?"

Burton nodded again. "Hundred-dollar bills, Joe—banded in packs of ten thousand and sealed in two Cryovac bags."

Matt stared at Gambini and still couldn't get a read. Nothing was showing on the man's face except for the effort Gambini appeared to be making to put it together.

Matt decided to take a guess. "Moe Rey was associated with your family," he said. "You described him yourself as one of your couriers. Are you worried that before his death he'd crossed over and was working for these guys at DMG, or even your nephew?"

Gambini gave Matt a passing glance that seemed to suggest they were so far off the same page, any further conversation would be meaningless. Yet Matt could see the man was still chewing things over. Then, without warning, Gambini stood up like he'd had enough, walked over to the door, and gave it a light tap. As he waited for the guard, he turned back to them. Matt noted the storm clouds. They were drifting across Gambini's face again, his brown eyes dark as night. When he spoke finally, it was more of a low rumble than anything else.

"I think you've turned everything upside down, Detective. My nephew is insane. I think he snapped and hurt the girl, and that's what this is all about. When he realized Moe Rey saw him do it, he lost his cool and decided to kill both of them. Maybe, in his warped mind, he greased Moe Rey just to get back at me. Either way, he dumped them into a hole, hoping that whatever the fuck happened would go away. Only it didn't go away, and now it's working on him. My guess is that he's hunting down witnesses and looking to clean things up. Like I said before, Robert doesn't know how to let things go. He keeps that enemy list, and it sounds like it's growing. If he followed you through Venice last night, I'd bet the house you're invited to the party."

The guard arrived. Gambini gave Burton a hard look, then turned back to Matt with those dark eyes of his. Everything became quiet and dead still.

"Nice meeting you, kid."

TWENTY-FIVE

Burton spent a good deal of the drive back to the city on the phone. According to his assistant, the prosecutor's personal files on Robert Gambini had already been packed up and moved to his house on Mulholland Drive.

Matt didn't mind. He wanted time to process the interview with Joseph Gambini before Burton offered an opinion. He didn't trust Gambini and thought that most of what he'd witnessed had been a deliberate attempt to muddy the waters. He was also wrestling with the fact that his mind and body had become weary, and he needed a decent night's sleep. The muscles in his arms and legs ached. Thoughts were bending into each other. Twice over the past half hour he caught himself in a free fall, only to be jolted awake by one of the many potholes on the freeway or the shrill sound of the ringer on Burton's phone.

He pulled himself together as he felt the elevation changing and saw Burton start the climb up Coldwater Canyon Drive. They were just north of Beverly Hills, the homes almost storybook. But once they made the turn onto Mulholland, Matt had no doubt that they were passing through one of the most exclusive neighborhoods in all of Los Angeles. Just the view of the basin outside the passenger-side window was enough to shake the cobwebs out of his mind.

"We're close," Burton said. "Hopefully Val found the files."

Matt nodded. "Do you think that the prosecutor from South Carolina got all of Gambini's money?"

Burton smiled. "He works in Washington, you know. He's a fed."

Matt shook his head. "Either way, you said he's vicious. Do you think he cleaned Gambini out?"

A gate opened just ahead on the left, and Burton pulled into a driveway before a three-door garage. Matt got out and looked up at the house built into the hills above. He knew that there were people who lived in houses the size of buildings on this road. People who lived in cold, sterile dwellings as far away from reality as their money could take them. But Burton's place wasn't one of them. In one sense it was a modern house—not big or small but just the right size—and well landscaped to keep the neighboring houses screened out. In another sense, though, Burton's home reminded Matt of a country villa in the hills of Italy, a place lost in time and swathed in good feeling.

Matt slung his laptop over his shoulder and followed Burton up a set of stone steps built into the hill. "Do you think the feds cleaned him out?" he repeated.

Burton pursed his lips as he mulled it over. "No," he said. "Joe's too smart for that. If there's one thing I've learned over the years, it's that street smart beats book smart almost always. My guess is that Joe's still got his money—maybe not all of it, but enough to get by."

Matt nodded. "But what if it isn't enough to get by? What if he needs more?"

Burton stopped and gave him an odd look. "What are you saying?"

"Something happened during our interview. I think he gave something away."

"Let's go inside."

Burton pulled his keys out of his pocket, crossed the stone entrance to the set of double doors, and unlocked them. Once they stepped across the threshold, he called out his wife's name. While he got out of his jacket, Matt glanced about the foyer. Through the floor-to-ceiling windows he could see a terrace that included a pool and spa and what might have been a small guesthouse.

"You made good time."

Matt heard Val's voice and turned. She was walking toward them down a wide hallway.

Burton hung up his jacket and closed the closet door. "Did you have any luck with the files?"

"In your study," she said. "They're on your desk."

Burton led the way around the corner to a set of open double doors. As Matt entered, Val met his eyes and mouthed the word *welcome* through a smile. He nodded and turned to watch Burton hurrying over to his enormous desk.

"I don't have much," Burton was saying as he grabbed the first file. "Don't get your hopes up."

Matt stepped into the middle of the room and couldn't help taking a look around. Burton's study was a large space with vaulted ceilings and heavy beams that were finished and meant to be exposed. The overstuffed bookshelves were built-ins and extended along an entire wall. There was a full-size couch here, a large coffee table, and a pair of wingback chairs set before a fireplace. Matt noted the art on the walls, along with a flat-panel TV. But it was the wall of glass that made Burton's study a standout. Matt crossed the room and gazed outside in wonder. It was a view of the entire LA Basin, from the tall buildings downtown all the way west to the Pacific Ocean.

Matt knew that he shared a view of the basin from his own home. But this was different. This felt like the wide-screen version. It was bigger, closer, almost as if he were standing over a game board in the heavens and God had the next move.

Matt turned to Burton. "How do you get any work done in this place?"

The prosecutor smiled, then adjusted his glasses as he stepped behind his desk and skimmed through the file.

"There's less here than I thought, Matt. You worked narcotics. How much do you know about Robert Gambini?"

Matt glanced at Val, then back at Burton. "He never came up in an investigation," he said. "We never got close enough. The trail always seemed to die out before we got there, like he was a ghost."

"He hides behind his organization," Burton said. "He learned that from his uncle. All roads lead to someone else."

"I know what I've read in the papers. Stories mostly about his knack for weaning addicts off oxycodone with high-grade heroin."

Burton glanced at the file in his hands. "And it says here that he graduated third in his class at Wharton. He could have gotten a job anywhere on Wall Street. He could have worked for anyone."

Val stepped over to one of the seats beside the desk. "I hope I'm not interrupting."

Burton shook his head. "You're never interrupting, Val," he said. "What is it?"

"It's just that I read the papers, too. How does a man like that get a license to open a chain of pot shops? You'd think that with all the rumors about his background, he'd have been booted off the list and never given the opportunity to even apply."

That was one of many good questions with no answers, Matt thought. How was Robert Gambini able to manipulate the system and pave the way to running a drug business that was legal?

Burton sat down in his desk chair and gave Matt a look. "What did you mean when you said Joe Gambini gave something away today?"

Matt turned from the window. "I noticed that you didn't tell him about Moe Rey's murder before we got there."

"I didn't want to do it over the phone. I wanted to see his face when he learned the truth. He was surprised. The news shocked him. It made him angry."

Matt glanced at Val again, then back at Burton. "I thought the same thing. But that's where the truth ended, at least for me. I didn't believe a word he said after that. This is about drugs, pure and simple. It's about the execution of a courier, a courier who belonged to Joseph Gambini, and the young girl, Sophia Ramirez, who had the bad luck of witnessing the murder. It's about the two hundred thousand dollars we found in Moe Rey's pantry.

The possibility that the feds cleaned Gambini out and he's gonna need more money when they open the gates at Terminal Island."

Burton tossed the file onto his desk. "And how do the three partners at DMG fit in? What are their names again?"

"Sonny Daniels, Ryan Moore, and Lane Grubb."

Matt thought it over as the sound of his voice faded into the room with open beams and vaulted ceilings that reached two-stories high. Nothing about the three partners made sense or had become any clearer. He remembered the accident in their plant this morning. A fifty-five-gallon drum had been knocked off a pallet and the seal broken. As a toxic chemical spilled onto the floor, the first reaction of the men working nearby had been to run for their lives. Despite everything Matt had learned since, the idea that the three partners were moving drugs still didn't feel right.

"How do you think they fit in?" Burton repeated. "Wouldn't you say that they're the missing piece? What if you're right, Matt? Joe gets out of prison in a couple of years. He's older now, and let's say he does have money issues. Right or wrong, he's got a federal prosecutor who's all over him. Our unit in the DA's office isn't going anywhere soon. What if Joe's in business with these guys at DMG? Some sort of silent partner."

Matt sat down in the chair beside Val. "You're saying that it comes down to a turf war. Robert figured out what they were doing. He's been keeping an eye on the place, we know that. So one day he sees Moe Rey walking out the door to his car in the parking lot. He asks around, maybe he even talks to Rey himself, and learns that he works there. All of a sudden he realizes that his uncle Joseph is involved."

Maybe it was the challenge or even the delight of a free-form discussion, but it was obvious to Matt that Burton loved this. He watched the esteemed prosecutor get out of his chair and start pacing along the wall of glass. He could see the man's wheels turning. He was in his element. Stoked, and in the moment.

Burton cleared his throat, thinking it through as he spoke. "Robert, as the rumors go, runs the heroin trade on the entire West Coast. San Diego, San Francisco, Portland, and Seattle—even Las Vegas. But LA would be his cash cow. It makes sense that he wouldn't want any competition. He despises his uncle, he always has. The last thing he'd want is his uncle muscling in on his business. He becomes angry. He starts to brood over the details until it gets underneath his skin and he's worked himself into a venomous rage. That's when he decides to send Joe a message. One that says he means business. He kills Moe Rey and the girl who witnessed the murder. Today, you and I delivered Robert's message to his uncle. We told Joe that his courier wasn't just dead. He'd been executed."

Matt lowered his voice. "And the minute we told him, the minute we delivered the news, he shut down."

"He did, didn't he," Burton said, coming to a stop behind his desk chair. "Joe got up from the table and called for a guard. He ended the meeting."

"Because we delivered Robert's message."

Burton's eyes brightened. "And he knew."

The phone on the desk started ringing. Burton checked the caller ID and gave Matt a hard look.

"Who is it?" Matt asked.

"Marvin Sanders," he said. "And I'm guessing he just found out that we spent the afternoon with his favorite conviction."

Burton picked up the phone with a pleasant expression on his face, his voice irritatingly calm. Matt hoped that he could see him work a jury someday.

"Hello, Marvin."

Burton listened for a few moments. Matt could hear the garbled sound of the federal prosecutor screaming through the earpiece.

"I'm going to have to put you on hold, Marvin."

Without waiting for a response, Burton pulled the phone away from his ear and punched the "Hold" button down. He turned to Matt, and then his wife.

"This may take a while," he said. "Matt needs to get to his car downtown. Would you mind giving him a lift?"

TWENTY-SIX

Val's car needed gas, so she decided to take her husband's SUV. Matt didn't care one way or the other and was just grateful for the ride. As they pulled away from the house, she offered to stop for coffee, but Matt declined. The Blackbird Café wasn't far from where he'd parked. It was the best cup of hot java in the city and worth waiting for.

He settled in, watching the houses breeze by as Val made her way down the other side of the hill on Coldwater heading for the Hollywood Freeway. She didn't say much, but as Matt looked at her face, he could tell that she had something on her mind.

His cell phone started ringing, and he dug it out of his pocket.

"I'm sorry," he said.

Val shook her head and laughed. "No problem, Matthew. It's your job."

Matt read the name blinking on his phone and switched it on. It was Cabrera.

"What's up?" he said.

"There's a problem, Matt."

"What happened?"

"I'm not sure. Lieutenant McKensie wants to see us as soon as possible. He looks pissed off."

"Where are we meeting?"

"His office."

"I'm on my way. Anything else?"

"Yeah," Cabrera said. "Remember that dim-witted security guard at DMG? That guy who didn't carry a piece?"

"Okay."

"Well, SIS just checked in. They said he's been replaced."

"With who?" Matt asked.

"Three meatheads with Glocks."

Matt let out a short smile as he pictured the partners at DMG seated at their conference table making the decision to add firepower to their security team.

"We got to them," he said.

"Looks like it."

Matt glanced at the clock on the dash. "I'll be there as soon as I can. I'm across town. I'm at least an hour out."

"I'll tell McKensie," he said. "See you then."

Matt switched off his phone and slipped it back into his pocket. Val finally reached the freeway entrance and accelerated up the ramp. Once she found her lane and brought the SUV up to speed, she gave him a look.

"Anything you can talk about?" she said.

"It sounds like we're beginning to make a difference. DMG just added three new hires."

"What kind of hires?"

"Three goons with guns."

Val turned back to the road. Matt could tell that whatever had been on her mind was still there. He settled into the seat and looked her over. She had a natural way about her, and the silence in the car didn't feel uncomfortable at all. It could have been his imagination, but it seemed like they'd known each other for a while. He knew that she was ten, maybe twelve years older than him. He was also well aware that she was Burton's wife. Still, Matt found it difficult not to look at her legs. They were long and bare and spread open slightly, with her short turquoise skirt hiked all the way up her thighs. His eyes rose over the curve of her hips, her flat stomach, and lingered on her round breasts. The top two buttons on her blouse were undone, and he could see her cleavage and a piece of her black bra.

"Why don't you become an attorney?" she said.

Matt looked up and saw her leaning toward him.

"Where'd that come from?" he said finally.

"My husband. He said it to me before we left. Mitch said that he thought you'd make a good one, Matthew. Even the man you saw in prison today said it. Mitch told me that he did."

Matt laughed.

"What's so funny about that?" she asked.

"I'm just trying to figure out what's on your mind."

She gave him a long look. "You'd be a lot safer, Matthew. The people who care about you wouldn't have to worry about you so much."

He turned back to the windshield, keeping his eyes off Val and pinned to the road ahead. She didn't say anything after that, and within ten minutes they were exiting the freeway and winding their way through downtown to the parking garage beside the Hall of Justice. Matt told her that his car was parked on the second floor. To his surprise, Val pulled up to the gate, took a ticket, and drove into the building.

"You don't have to do this," he said.

She shrugged her shoulders without a reply. When they reached the second floor, he pointed to the Crown Vic. Then Val pulled into an open space across the aisle, turned off the engine, and released her seat belt.

The car quieted—the din of the city subdued. Val still had something on her mind and turned, leaning against the door.

"I know it's none of my business," she said. "We just met today, but somehow it seems like I've known you longer than that. Maybe because of the stories about you in the news."

"What is it, Val?"

She glanced out the window, then turned back. "The things you were just talking about with your partner. Why chase three goons with guns in the real world, Matthew? Wouldn't you be safer in a courtroom?"

Matt didn't say anything. He sat back in the seat and gave her a look.

"You were shot," she said finally.

"Yes, I was."

"Well, isn't that reason enough to think things over?"

"Probably."

She glanced at the clock on the dash. "You're gonna be late for your meeting. You better get going. I need to get back to the house."

A long moment passed. He met her gaze.

"Is everything okay, Val?"

She seemed surprised by the question and flashed a crooked smile. "Why do you ask?"

"I don't know," he said. "It just seemed like the right thing to say."

She laughed, glancing at his car parked across the aisle. "You're gonna be late for your meeting, Detective Jones."

TWENTY-SEVEN

Why were Val and Mitch Burton so concerned about his welfare?

Why did he suddenly feel so uneasy about things?

Matt double-parked and ran into the Blackbird Café. Victor was behind the counter, and he ordered an extra-large cup of the house blend with two sugars to go. While he waited, he wondered if Lena Gamble might be here and checked the main room and terrace. He didn't see her and within five minutes was back in the Crown Vic barreling onto the Hollywood Freeway.

He popped the lid on his coffee, sniffed through the steam, and took a first sip. The brew was strong and piping hot, but his mind still felt like scrambled eggs.

What had just happened?

Why was he suddenly overcome with the feeling of impending doom? And was any of this even real?

All the Burtons had really done was show concern for him and pay him a compliment.

Maybe you should think about becoming an attorney. You'd be a good one, Matthew, and you'd be safe. Why not think it over?

He tried to clear his mind and took another sip of coffee. Passing the freeway exit for Echo Park, he checked the side mirror, eased into the left lane, and brought the unmarked car up to a hard ninety miles an hour.

He wondered if he should call the psychiatrist he'd been seeing in Chinatown, Dr. May. Maybe she could help him understand his recent bouts with paranoia. Maybe his sessions with her could continue while he worked the case.

He took another quick sip of coffee, then set it down in the cup holder as he exited the freeway and cruised down Sunset Boulevard. Within a couple of minutes, he was pulling into the lot behind the station. A black Chevy Suburban with darkened glass was idling at the curb. He couldn't see who was behind the wheel, but when he caught a glimpse of the license plate, any personal issues he might have been wrestling with suddenly became irrelevant and vanished.

That impending doom had already arrived. Time to chill out and be cool.

Chief Logan was here.

TWENTY-EIGHT

Matt found a parking space beside his own car, grabbed his laptop case, and hustled across the lot to the rear entrance. He wondered why Cabrera hadn't given him any warning. All his partner had said over the phone was that he thought there might be a problem. Their supervisor, Lieutenant McKensie, seemed angry. But McKensie was usually angry, so that didn't add up to much of a warning.

Matt swung the door open, hurried past the holding cells, and rushed onto the bureau floor. When he looked through the glass into McKensie's office, he saw the chief sitting behind the lieutenant's desk and knew that something grim had either happened or was about to.

He set his things on the chair before his workstation, then took a deep breath and started down the hall trying to shift to an unhurried pace. But as he stepped up to his supervisor's door, the chief's dark eyes were all over him.

"You're late," the chief said. "Now get in here, Detective, and close the door."

An empty seat was waiting for him right in front of the desk. The chief was pointing at it like just maybe Matt had earned his way to the electric chair. When he shot a quick look at Cabrera in the seat to his left, his partner couldn't meet his gaze and appeared worried and shut down. When he glanced over at McKensie seated on his right, the big man's face was as blank as a sheet of paper.

Proceed with caution.

The chief was getting up, walking around the desk, and sitting on the edge directly in front of him. He was staring at him and measuring him and appeared to be mulling something over. When he spoke finally, his voice was so tight and controlled that Matt felt a chill creeping up his spine and almost shivered.

"Why are you bothering the people who own DMG Waste Management, Detective?"

A long moment passed. Matt was stunned by the question.

The chief leaned closer and was seething. "Why are you bothering them?"

Matt gave him a look. "Bothering, sir?"

"That's what I said, Detective. Why are you doing it?"

This was a homicide investigation. The question seemed outlandish. Matt turned to McKensie for help, but his supervisor's face remained blank.

"Why are you looking at me, Jones? Answer the chief's question."

Matt turned back to the chief and met his hard gaze. "They're people of interest in two homicides, Chief. We believe that they could be distributing narcotics."

The chief was in his fifties and had been the prime mover in restoring the LAPD's reputation as one of the best police departments in the country. He was a lean man, steady and tight, with tanned skin and most of his dark hair gone now. But it was his eyes that made him stand out from the crowd. They were almost the color of Matt's .45—black, with a dark-blue glint here and there that had a way of penetrating whoever the chief trained them on like bullets.

"Who are the people you're talking about, Detective? Who are the people of interest in two homicides? Who are the people that you believe are distributing narcotics?"

Matt didn't understand why this was happening. He felt like everything in the world had suddenly turned upside down.

"The three partners," he said finally. "The three men who own DMG."

"Have you seen the drugs you're talking about? Do you have any evidence to back your claims?"

Matt shook his head. "What is this? What's going on?"

The chief leaned closer. "Be careful, Detective. Very careful. Do you have any evidence at all that these people are involved in anything?"

"We think that they may be connected to Robert Gambini in some way, or even his uncle. It's still early."

"Early? Is that how you see it, Detective? You and your partner over here think it's early?"

The chief shook his head in disbelief. Matt watched him get up, roll the desk chair over, and take a seat. He was sitting so close now that Matt guessed he was trying to intimidate him. But why would a cop with his record do this? The chief of police, who'd rebuilt the department from a pile of ashes.

The chief met his eyes and kept them there. He leaned even closer.

"Do you know who Dee Colon is?" he said.

Matt's heart sank as he suddenly connected the dots.

He knew exactly who Dee Colon was, and now he had some idea—nightmare or not—why the chief was trying to undermine their case. Dee Colon was a city councilwoman—the most powerful politician in Los Angeles. But even worse, the woman was dirty—the very definition of a corrupt politician who had been able to beat the odds because of her talent and media persona. It didn't make any difference that she came off like a crime boss. It didn't matter that she'd turned the mayor into her personal go-go boy. Or even that she stood accused of taking piles of cash under the table from more than a dozen labor unions and tech companies, even three movie studios. When the lights came up and the TV cameras started rolling, Dee Colon had a crowd of supporters behind her because she was, as she said herself many times, *the woman of the people*.

Matt stared back at the chief. He guessed that Sonny Daniels had cut a check to the city councilwoman and was making the delivery when he and Cabrera saw him driving his Aston Martin up the hill from their facility this morning.

"Are you with me, Detective?" the chief said. "Do you know who Dee Colon is or not?"

Matt nodded but remained silent—the anger beginning to stir in his gut.

"Dee Colon is trouble," the chief said. "The kind of trouble I don't want, and the department doesn't need right now. She came to my office with the mayor this afternoon. Both of them vouched for the three partners at DMG. It turns out they've known each other for quite a while. She said they were friends."

A long moment passed, the chief's words hitting the office floor like a pipe bomb. Sonny Daniels paid off Dee Colon, and what? The investigation goes away? In what world was that okay?

Matt could feel the adrenaline coursing through his bloodstream now. The rage spinning like storm clouds gathering strength over a warm sea—the kind of wind that blew buildings down. He tried to become still, imagining himself sitting in a meadow in Afghanistan with his rifle aimed at a window half a mile away. The patience it required to wait for the subject to make a mistake and step before the glass for a look outside.

They always made the mistake, he thought. They always stepped before that glass and looked outside.

Matt tried to keep his thoughts to himself because he knew that if he said anything at all he'd be fired. Off the force without a way back.

The chief rolled the desk chair even closer. "I'm not asking you to shut down your homicide investigation, Detective. I'm just asking you to think more clearly, and do it before you act. This is only your third case. I'm asking you to think better than you have in the past. Do you understand?"

Matt nodded again but kept his mouth shut.

The chief glanced at Cabrera, then back at Matt. "Your partner here told us that the owners over at DMG have been only too willing to pitch in and help you. In fact, your partner said that they invited you into their offices on two separate occasions. That they gave you a tour of the place and showed you their security tapes freely, transparently, without a warrant or even a call for legal advice."

The anger was storming through his entire body now. Out of control and in a free-fall rage. Not buildings anymore, but whole cities could be blown down.

"Is that what he told you?" Matt whispered in a hoarse voice through his teeth.

The chief gave him an odd look. "He said that when you showed them a photograph of Robert Gambini, they didn't recognize him. They had never even heard of the man and didn't know who he was. Is that true, Detective? Is that what happened?"

A long moment passed. Another test. Another chance to demonstrate that he was truly on the mend and had somehow managed to regain his self-control.

"Is that the way it happened, Detective? They didn't know him?"

Matt looked down at the floor, then nodded slightly. "Yes, sir."

The chief smiled like he'd heard what he needed to hear. He got up to leave, walked over to the door, then stopped and turned back. Matt couldn't look at him and let his eyes drift back to the floor.

"I'm glad that we had this talk, Detective. I'm glad you understand that right now the department needs your best effort. Sonny Daniels, Ryan Moore, and Lane Grubb are no longer to be considered persons of interest in this investigation. In all probability they didn't see anything and don't know anyone involved but, like good neighbors, just wanted to help. A girl was murdered on her fifteenth birthday and buried in a shallow grave. Now pull back your surveillance team and get to work solving this murder case."

Matt was speechless. He turned and watched the chief walk out of the room. Through the glass he could see him crossing the bureau floor. When he looked out McKensie's window, he saw the man walk down the sidewalk, get into the back seat of the Chevy Suburban, and drive off.

The sun had gone down, and it was dark outside. No one in McKensie's office said anything. No one moved.

TWENTY-NINE

"I'm sorry, Matt. McKensie called me into his office, and the chief was already here. I couldn't get out. I couldn't warn you."

"You don't owe me an apology, Den. What just happened isn't your fault."

"But the chief's been bought. It's outrageous. He's the chief of police."

Matt shrugged. "We don't know that. Not yet, anyway."

"What else could it be?"

"I don't know," Matt said in a low voice. "This one's complicated."

A moment passed.

They were in the conference room with the door closed. Cabrera returned to his seat where his laptop was set up beside a legal pad and a cup of coffee from a fast-food restaurant. Matt was standing by the window with his back turned, looking across the bureau floor into McKensie's office. The lieutenant had tossed everything off his desk onto the floor and kicked it into the corner. When the phone rang two minutes ago, McKensie had ripped the wire out of the wall and tossed the phone into the trash. Now the lights were out, and Matt thought he could see a bead of light glowing from the end of a cigarette.

Cabrera flipped a page over on his legal file. "Did you know that this bitch councilwoman makes fifteen grand a year more than the governor of the state?"

Matt turned away from the window and smiled. "Are you serious?"

Cabrera nodded. "Dee Colon's annual salary is over two hundred grand."

"That's a lot of money for doing almost nothing."

"It gets better. It turns out that two hundred K isn't enough to keep her happy. The *Times* did a story about her last summer. They said that it would take a million bucks a year to cover her lifestyle. Remember that old TV show? That's the title the writer played with. That's the headline. LIFESTYLES OF THE RICH AND NOT SO FAMOUS."

"Maybe she's got family money?"

Cabrera shook his head. "Not a chance. Her parents brought her over the border. She was dirt poor, just like me."

Matt glanced at his partner's laptop, pulled a chair out, and sat down. "What happened with SIS today?"

Cabrera turned to his computer and opened a window to reveal three photographs of the exotic cars they'd seen parked in the lot at DMG this morning.

"They took these shots of their plates."

"And you ran them."

Cabrera glanced at his legal pad. "All three cars are owned by a company called Yellow Brick Leasing."

"Here in LA?"

"Yeah, over on Wilshire. I spoke with the manager. Two-year leases, no problems, and she said all three pay on time. Yellow Brick only leases to VIP types. And only high-end cars. The manager was nice but couldn't say anything more because she's locked in by privacy agreements."

"But you ran these guys, right? Where do they live?"

"All over town. Ryan Moore lives in the Palisades. Lane Grubb's got a place in Hollywood Hills."

"Where?"

"Ledgewood Drive near the reservoir," Cabrera said. "Within a stone's throw of the Hollywood Sign."

"What about Sonny Daniels?"

"West Hollywood, above Sunset."

"What about women?"

"It looks like Sonny might have had a problem in college. He's been divorced twice and probably getting killed with alimony."

"What kind of trouble in college?"

"I'm still working on it."

Matt nodded. "What about the other two?"

"Grubb lost his wife a couple years back. She died at Sloan Kettering in New York, so it must have been cancer."

Matt thought it over. "That could account for why he might be using. He's wounded. It might be the reason he's the weakest of the three. What's up with Ryan Moore?"

"He's still married to his first wife. He's got three kids."

"Anything else?"

Cabrera shrugged. "All three of these guys are the same age. They're forty-five years old. Just from the way they were acting, Matt—even the way they were dressed—I'm guessing they go way back together."

Matt had thought that they might be childhood friends ever since he set eyes on them.

His cell phone started vibrating.

He pulled the phone out of his pocket, crossing the room to the window for another look. McKensie's office remained dark, and that bead of light from a cigarette was still there. He glanced down at his phone and read the name blinking on the face. It was the deputy DA, Mitch Burton.

"You there, Matt?"

"I'm here. What's going on?"

Burton's voice became louder, like he'd just switched over from speaker to the handset. "What did you do to Dee Colon?"

Matt shook his head back and forth. "I'm not sure, why?"

"You must have done something."

"I've never met her, but let me guess. The city councilwoman showed up at the district attorney's office this afternoon. She had the mayor with her. Together they vouched for the partners at DMG and said that they had known each other for a while and were friends. They probably weren't too specific on how long they'd known each other or how good their friendship's been. When they left, the DA stopped by your office and said hands off. The three partners aren't involved in the case and were just trying to be good neighbors to help us out."

Burton started laughing. "Good neighbors. You're a mind reader now. I had no idea."

"The chief just left. He tried to feed us the same story. Hands off."

Burton's voice changed. He wasn't laughing anymore.

"All the same, you must have done something to her, Matt. Dee Colon does not like you. And she's not the kind of person you'd really want as an enemy. She thinks you're a cowboy. According to the DA, she tried to quote a Bogart movie but blew it. What's that movie?"

"*Casablanca*?"

"No. *The Treasure of the Sierra Madre*. She told the DA that she 'don't need no stinking cowboys in the LAPD. And the cops don't need no stinking cowboy to investigate the murder of a girl who was buried in the woods.' I bet she said the same thing to Chief Logan."

Matt didn't know how to respond except to repeat that he'd never met the city councilwoman. Not once. Not ever.

"How do you want to handle this?" Burton asked.

"Carefully," he said in a low voice. "Until we know more."

"I was hoping you'd say that. I was worried you might want to quit."

"Never."

The door opened, and McKensie walked into the conference room.

"I've gotta go," Matt said to Burton. "We'll talk later."

"Sounds good."

Matt clicked off his phone and slipped it back into his pocket. McKensie had a brutal expression on his face and looked like he'd just walked out of a bar fight and lost. Glancing at Matt, the big man with the white hair and wild green eyes turned to Cabrera and grimaced.

"You told me these guys at DMG, the three partners, brought in heat this afternoon."

Cabrera became very still. "Three heavyweights with guns, sir."

"To protect industrial waste?"

"That's what they're saying."

McKensie sat down on the edge of the table, rubbing his chin with an open hand. "How many SIS guys do we have keeping an eye on that place?"

Cabrera checked his legal pad. "Eight," he said. "Two groups of four working twelve-hour shifts."

McKensie looked like he was mulling something over. After a while, he turned to Matt.

"I have a friend over at SIS, Jones. The kind of friend who owes me forever and knows how to keep things quiet. So this is what we're gonna do. From here on out, we're invisible. You're gonna cut the number of SIS guys down to four. One pair working twelve-hour shifts, and tell them to move back. No one can know that they're there. What we're doing is off the books and off the record. You two guys are gonna do the same thing. Your new mantra is *watch, listen, collect* until something shakes out and we've got a better idea of what's going on. Is that clear, Jones?"

Matt nodded. "Clear as a sky with no clouds, sir."

"Watch, listen, and collect," McKensie repeated. "Like you're a couple of nature boys taking a walk through the woods on a sunny afternoon."

He stepped over to the door, opened it to leave, then turned back. "Now keep your mouths shut and get the hell out of here. It's been a long goddamn day, and I'm tired of looking at you two."

THIRTY

McKensie had a way of saying things . . .

As Matt pulled out of the lot, he thought about the number of men and women who he had taken orders from as a soldier in Afghanistan. Here in LA he had worked for more than a handful of supervising officers as a cop, an undercover detective in narcotics, and now for the last three months a rookie homicide detective. Of all the people who directed him and issued orders, McKensie was the one he most admired.

It wasn't just the way he spoke. It was the way he handled himself. The way he saw things and what he stood for.

Matt noticed that the radio was tuned to the news station and switched it off. Pulling up to the red light on Sunset, he wondered how long he'd been working without sleep. After tossing it over, he decided that he felt okay enough to take the long way home.

He made a right turn instead of a left and within a few blocks was gunning it down the entrance ramp and onto the Hollywood Freeway. It would be a late-night visit to the Buena Vista Meadow picnic area. He wanted a last look of the day to think things over. He wanted a fresh view of the crime scene to sleep on.

The heavy traffic seemed like it was headed north into the Valley. Matt breezed toward downtown, exited onto the Harbor Freeway, and then proceeded onto surface streets. Within another five minutes, he was making the steep climb up Elysian Park Drive. When he reached the top of the ridge, he saw the picnic tables and the grove of pine trees on the other side of the meadow and killed the engine.

He popped open the glove box. Grabbing his flashlight, he started to get out of the car but stopped when he heard something.

He could hear voices. Male voices.

He wondered if there were any women on the SIS team. He wasn't sure of the gender makeup and had never thought to ask. All he knew was that if these voices were coming from the surveillance unit, they were a real long way from being invisible. It sounded like they were in the middle of a heated argument. Matt looked around but didn't see any cars in the lot or anyone on the lawn, yet the voices were still there and seemed close.

He got to his feet and shut the car door as quietly as he could manage. Once he thought he had a bead on the direction of the sound, he started across the lawn heading for the grove of pine trees. The voices were getting louder, more heated, but he still couldn't make out what anyone was saying.

He stepped underneath the tree branches and, for a moment, switched on the flashlight for a look at the grave. He knelt down and ran his fingers through the soil, thinking of Sophia Ramirez mostly, but Moe Rey, too. He could still see the condition they were in when their bodies were dug out of the earth.

This is what he had wanted to see tonight. This is what he needed to remember.

He switched off the light and stood up. Sweeping the branches away, he stepped out onto the lawn and started up the grassy bank. When he reached the top, he gazed over the edge and down the steep hill.

He could see them.

Six men standing outside the DMG facility. Despite the darkness, despite the distance, it wasn't difficult to tell who they were. The three partners were standing beside their cars doing the arguing. The other three had to be their hired guns. They were bigger, meatier, and rougher looking. But even more telling, they were standing off to the side keeping their mouths shut.

Matt checked behind his back, then gazed across the meadow. He could see the private road from here and followed it with his eyes from the bridge on North Broadway all the way down the railroad tracks to the DMG entrance and substation beyond. He wondered if anyone from SIS was here tonight. It didn't seem like it. It didn't feel like it either.

He turned back to the factory, letting his body and mind quiet down. As he tried to make out what was being said, he realized that their voices were being amplified by the darkness. But it was a false read. The sound was echoing up the ridge through the trees and mixing with the din of distant freeways and the line of jets just south of downtown making their approach into LAX.

He took a moment to sort through it all. As he strained to filter out the background noise, he thought he could hear Lane Grubb saying how disappointed he was that it had come to this. Something about how Sonny had assured them that there would never be a problem. That there were no real risks involved. Promises had been made that weren't kept. Then Sonny began shouting that the only problems they had were in Grubb's head. That everything was going just as they had planned. When Grubb started to push back, Ryan Moore stepped between the two men and told them to go home and chill.

A freight train started to roll by the substation, wiping out the sounds of the three partners' voices. While Matt watched, he tried to interpret what he had just heard. What was Grubb's disappointment? What were the promises Sonny might have made that weren't kept? But even more, what was the plan, and how could there be no risks?

As the long train stretched through the cityscape, the argument seemed to end, and all three partners got into their cars. Matt watched them begin to drive off when it occurred to him that he was witnessing something important.

The three men with guns standing off to the side.

Matt did a double take. While the three partners were driving off into the night, the three armed goons were ambling back into the building. As

Matt added it up, he realized that these men weren't serving as bodyguards. Whatever they might have been hired to protect was something else and had to be *inside* the building.

Matt found the idea astonishing. How could whatever the three partners were doing defy the possibility of blowback? How could these guys not feel like they were in eminent danger?

It seemed so naive. Or was it some bizarre form of arrogance?

An image of Joseph Gambini sitting in his prison cell pulling strings flicked through Matt's brain, then vanished. He ran across the meadow, jumped into his car, and jacked up the engine. Speeding down the hill and around the curves, he hit the park entrance, pulled to a screeching stop, and looked through the trees toward the bridge and the private road below.

And then he waited.

THIRTY-ONE

It only took a few minutes before the bursts of light began to cut through the tree branches and wash across the interior of the car. Looking down the private road, he saw the three pairs of headlights crest the hill and begin approaching the bridge.

Matt eased his car a few feet forward to open up the view. He watched Sonny Daniels come over the rise first, shoot beneath the bridge, and vanish down Baker Street. It looked like Ryan Moore was following Sonny out in his BMW. But Matt was waiting for car number three—the one lagging behind. Lane Grubb in the black Audi.

He watched Grubb reach the bridge and pass underneath. Even though the moment was brief, Matt could see that he was on the phone screaming at somebody. Like everybody else who uses their cell phone behind the wheel, he'd be an easy follow—an easy target—because of the distraction.

Matt pulled out onto North Broadway and gunned it. Bringing the car up to seventy, then eighty, and even ninety miles an hour, he looked outside his window and could see Grubb cruising down the road on the other side of the train tracks. That long freight train had caught up to them, moving in and out of Matt's line of vision. But even more frustrating, once he cut deeper into Chinatown, he had to slow down, with his view of Grubb becoming totally obscured by buildings.

Matt shrugged it off because he knew that in the end it wouldn't matter. If Grubb was heading for a freeway entrance, he'd eventually have to make the turn back onto Broadway. Matt pushed his speed up, ignoring the sneers and shouts of people trying to cross from the sidewalks. When he reached Alpine Street, he spotted a fire hydrant, pulled over, and killed his headlights.

Within a matter of seconds, he saw Sonny Daniels make the cut onto Broadway. Ryan Moore was right behind him. And then, after a few more minutes, Lane Grubb made an exceedingly wide turn, heading for the freeways as he continued to scream at someone on his cell phone.

Matt waited a beat, then pushed through the intersection. Even five car lengths back on a dark night, the sleek black Audi R8 was easy enough to keep sight of in a world of dented compact cars, vans, and SUVs. Along the sidewalks here, tents had been pitched by the homeless, and Matt slowed down through two intersections. It didn't really matter. Once he hit the freeway entrance, he saw Grubb easing over into the left lane heading back to Hollywood.

The only surprise over the next thirty minutes was when Grubb exited onto Sunset rather than Beachwood Drive. Matt watched him winding his way on surface streets and realized that he wasn't on his way home. He closed the distance between cars to half a block, then fell back again as Grubb pulled into a lot behind a supermarket and parked in the two spaces at the end of the aisle. Matt waited a few moments, watching Grubb get out of his car with the phone still glued to his ear. When Grubb turned away from the market and started hustling down the street on foot, Matt found a place to park and jogged down the sidewalk.

He caught a glimpse of Grubb vanishing around the corner. Once he reached the end of the block, he caught another glimpse of Grubb entering a sidewalk café and bar in an alley behind Hollywood and Vine.

Matt looked around, thinking it over. Without following Grubb inside, it looked like the best view was from across the alley at another café with sidewalk seating and a terrace. Matt rushed across the street and inside the café, choosing a table on the terrace. When a young waitress stopped by, he ordered a double espresso with sugar and pushed the menu aside.

He watched the waitress walk off, then turned and searched through the crowd of people at the sidewalk tables until he found Grubb taking a seat across the street. The man had chosen a table in the shadows off to the side. A table where Matt doubted anyone would notice him.

Moments passed. Then a waiter stepped over to Grubb's table with what looked like a frozen bottle of Tito's vodka and a glass of ice. Matt watched Grubb take a huge pull on the glass, and then another. He appeared upset, worried, and distraught—his hair pushed back and soaked with sweat on what was decidedly a cool night. And he was looking around. At first Matt thought he was eyeing the women seated nearby. But then it occurred to him that Grubb was checking the tables to see who might be watching him. Once he appeared satisfied that no one was spying, he slipped something out of his pocket. A small fold of paper.

Matt's double espresso arrived. After a quick sip he looked back across the street. Grubb had rolled up a dollar bill and was snorting lines of white powder at the table. Long lines. Matt watched the man's body shudder as he wiped the powder away from his nose with his fingers.

It could have been cocaine. It could have been heroin. It could have been a lot of things. What mattered was that it looked like Lane Grubb had jumped off the edge. The man was beside himself.

And now he was loaded.

Grubb refilled his glass from the bottle, taking a sloppy gulp and wiping the vodka dripping down his chin with a napkin.

Out of his mind loaded.

Matt couldn't help being fascinated by what he was witnessing, even if he was the only one watching. This public display occurring in the shadows of a sidewalk café in downtown Hollywood. One of the reasons Matt loved being a detective, one of his most prized reasons, was the opportunity the job offered to study human behavior. To observe the circumstances people may have been dealt or even chosen for themselves, the decisions they made, and then finally the explanations they offered once they were confronted with the truth.

Grubb snorted another long line of white powder. Unfortunately, his waiter was approaching the table this time and caught him. An animated discussion followed, with Grubb snorting another line despite the man standing over his table. A few moments later, Grubb nodded and waved his hands at the waiter as if apologizing, then seemed to put his stash away and clean things up.

Matt wanted to get closer. He wanted to be across the street. He pushed his espresso away and looked around for his waitress. As his eyes searched through the crowd of people seated on this side of the street, his heart fluttered in his chest.

In a world of wolves, distractions could be a real gamble.

Someone else was watching Grubb tonight. Someone seated at a distance and wanting to remain hidden. Someone waiting in the shadows who looked angry and ready to strike.

Robert Gambini was in Hollywood.

THIRTY-TWO

He knew that he hadn't been seen. That Gambini had been too wrapped up in the spectacle of Grubb's public persona to check behind his back. Still, Matt made his way off the terrace and into the café with great care. Once he got his bearings, he pushed open the kitchen door and prepared to identify himself as a police officer. But as he breezed through the room, everyone seemed too busy plating orders of food to notice. Matt spotted the back door, hit the stairs, and sped outside.

He walked around the block, avoiding the two sidewalk cafés and working his way back to the car. Pulling out of the lot, he found an open space by a fire hydrant with a decent view of Grubb's Audi. When he checked the cars parked on the side street, he saw Gambini's black Mercedes in the shadows.

He checked the clock on the dash and settled back in the seat. And then he waited.

Grubb didn't show up for at least an hour, and by then he looked even more wasted. He was trudging up the sidewalk with his head down and appeared to be lost in his own world. Matt reached for the bottle of water in his cup holder, took a short swig, then slid lower in the seat.

Robert Gambini had just turned the corner and was following Grubb up the sidewalk. He was keeping to the shadows, but he was there. Matt looked at the concentration showing on Gambini's angular face, the intensity of his dark eyes. Seeing him on the street like this, he appeared stronger than Matt first imagined. Sturdier and more athletic, but also tougher.

Gambini glanced his way for an instant, and Matt ducked. Peeking over the dashboard, he watched the heroin dealer look away, then turned back to Grubb as he reached his car safely and got the engine started. When the Audi began moving through the lot, Matt turned and saw Gambini getting into his Mercedes.

It didn't take much to realize that something was going to happen tonight. That Gambini had every intension of following Grubb home and making some sort of statement. Matt knew that if it came down to a confrontation, Grubb would lose.

Matt lowered his head as the Audi idled down the street, its monster V10 engine groaning in the night. Once the Mercedes pulled out, Matt waited until both cars reached the corner before easing into the street.

Grubb was cruising up and down backstreets, probably trying to avoid cops and the possibility of a drunk-driving charge. As he finally reached Franklin and then made the turn up Beachwood Drive, Matt knew that he was heading home and dropped back even farther.

Cabrera had updated the Chronological Record this afternoon, including the contact information for each partner at DMG after running their plates. Matt had committed their home addresses to memory and knew that Grubb lived on Ledgewood Drive. The roads were narrow, the curves sharp. But within ten minutes, Matt had made his way up the steep hill just below the Hollywood Sign. He spotted Gambini's Mercedes parked at the curb but didn't pull over until he reached the top of the ridge two houses up.

Matt got out of the car, took a quick look around, then started back down the hill on foot.

Grubb's place turned out to be a big two-story stucco job with a massive terra-cotta roof. A six-foot wall was meant to keep people out, with redwood gates securing the front walk and a two-car parking area. But tonight, Matt found the front gate cracked open and the outdoor lights shut down.

He waited a moment, listening. The neighborhood was quiet. Just a dog barking in the distance. A quiet breeze rattling the palm trees above.

Matt stepped through the gate and eyeballed the property in the gloom. Most of the houses on this street were either built into the air off the ridge and secured with hundred-foot stilt-like pilings or, like Grubb's place, planted right on the edge. While the views might be remarkable, Matt had always found the houses difficult to look at and often wondered how anyone could feel comfortable living inside. During an earthquake a few years back, he'd seen a house a lot like the one next door break off its pilings and tumble all the way down to the canyon floor. At the time, a record producer had been inside with his girlfriend. It had taken the coyotes a single night to find their bodies. It had taken rescue workers nearly a week to find what remained.

The picture in his mind was still there. Still crystal clear and very grim.

He heard something.

A sound coming from inside the house. Something like glass shattering, but bigger. Maybe a lamp.

Matt checked the front door. When he found it locked, he worked his way around the side of the house. Once he reached the back and saw all the windows, he stepped around the corner and faded into the shadows.

Gambini was inside the living room, and it didn't seem like the meeting was going very well.

He had Grubb by the shirt collar and was slapping him around with an open right hand. Grubb looked too high to fight back—too weak—and appeared terrorized. He kept trying to force his eyes shut, almost as if he thought Gambini might not really be there if he couldn't see him. Still, with each hard slap, Grubb's eyes opened again until it looked like Gambini had become bored. Finally, the heroin dealer took a swing with a closed fist and knocked Grubb down onto the couch.

Gambini stood over the man, glaring at him. Apparently, Grubb had made a drink before his visitor arrived. Gambini picked up the glass and poured it all over Grubb's bruised face. After sweeping everything off the coffee table with a single violent stroke, Gambini sat down in front of his victim and took a few moments to size him up.

Matt scanned the windows quickly, wondering why he could hear them so clearly. The windows were shut. When he checked the deck, he gazed through the screens and saw the double doors standing wide open.

"Why are you doing business with my uncle?" Gambini said in a voice so low and rough it sent a chill up Matt's spine.

Grubb looked back and seemed confused. Gambini gave him another slap.

"Why are you in business with my uncle Joseph?" he repeated.

Grubb shook his head back and forth, stammering. "I don't know your uncle," he said. "I don't know what you're talking about."

Gambini slapped him again, harder this time. "Did he approach you, or did you and your idiot friends approach him?"

Grubb was drooling the way users do, his entire body trembling now. "Nobody approached anybody," he said quickly. "It never happened. Don't you understand? It's not real."

Gambini hit him again. "Are you trying to placate me? Are you trying to play me, little man? Do you really think you're gonna get away with this?"

Grubb tried to speak, but the words weren't coming out fast enough. Gambini smashed him on the side of the head.

"Do you really think you can walk into my town and steal my business? Steal my money? Look at you. You're using your own product. You're a loser boy."

Gambini stood up in disgust, then punched Grubb in the stomach. When he doubled over, Gambini smacked him in the head again. A moment passed, with Grubb groaning and gasping for air. Gambini sat back down on the coffee table.

"You're interfering with my business, little man. This is my city. I own it. You need to tell your friends that they're fools. That there's no place at the table for them. Not here in LA. It's time to close up your shop and get out of town."

Grubb's eyes had become glassy. He sat against the back of the couch staring at Gambini but not saying anything. Matt checked the way the window light was falling onto the ground and inched toward the open doors. When Grubb finally spoke, he seemed different and his voice had changed.

"Do you know who you're dealing with?" he said finally. "Do you know who we are?"

Gambini's dark eyes got darker. If he'd had a tail, it would have been rattling now.

"What did you just say?"

Grubb wiped the drool away from his mouth. "Do you know who we are?"

A moment passed with Gambini thinking it over, then—

"Okay, prick, I'll play along. Who the hell are you? Take me to school. Educate me, little man."

Grubb didn't say anything, still measuring his visitor with those glassy eyes. Matt knew that he was misjudging the situation and had no clue who he was dealing with.

Grubb cleared his throat. "What if I could get you fifty thousand dollars?" he said. "Would you go away if I could get you that kind of money?"

Gambini seemed stunned by Grubb's audacity and started laughing.

"What's so funny? I'm making you an offer."

"Fifty?" Gambini said, mocking the man. "Why not seventy-five?"

"Okay. Seventy-five. That's a lot of money. Would you go away and leave us alone for that much cash?"

Gambini was playing with him now. "A hundred would be even better, friend. Something I could sink my teeth into."

"One hundred sounds like a good number to me," Grubb said. "I'll get you a hundred thousand. Cash. Unmarked bills. Any denomination you want. It's yours if you'll go away and leave us alone."

Grubb stuck out a trembling hand as if he'd just made a deal and wanted to shake on it before contracts were signed. Gambini stared at him for a long time. Long enough that Matt realized how dangerous this tough guy really was. Matt could remember Robert's uncle Joseph talking about the "mean Gambini gene." He could remember the warning he and Burton received that Robert was insane. What happened next occurred so quickly, almost in a single instant, that Matt could have never prevented it. Gambini reached behind his back, then lunged forward with something in his hand. Matt caught the sheen, the flash of black metal, then froze as Gambini drove a .38 revolver into Grubb's mouth and pulled the trigger.

Matt's heart nearly stopped. It looked like Grubb's did, too.

A long moment passed. The air in the room, thin to gone.

Gambini got to his feet, all jacked up, his eyes wild like a madman's. Matt looked back at Grubb, who appeared to be in shock and remained completely terrorized—his body laid out on the couch quivering.

Gambini's piece never fired. It didn't need to, nor was it meant to. He stepped closer to the couch and leaned over Grubb. From the sound of his voice, he remained livid. Seething.

"You ever insult me again, you little prick, and a bullet's gonna be in that chamber. You understand what I'm saying? Do you get what's on the line here? This is my turf. You hang around, and you're gonna be a dead body floating in the reservoir. That goes for your two prick pals and times ten for my uncle the day they cut him loose. Don't ever mess with my business; you can tell him that for me. Don't ever mess with me again."

Gambini grit his teeth, then slammed Grubb over the head with the side of his pistol. It was a savage blow, and Grubb went down like a tree. Gambini slipped the piece behind his belt and gave Grubb a long last look.

And then something changed.

Gambini seemed to reach some twisted version of nirvana. An inner peace that was distinctly visible. He straightened his shirt and slacks and checked his hair in the mirror. After shrugging his shoulders, he walked out of the room cool as a man taking a stroll on the first day of spring.

Matt didn't move. He'd read about people like Robert Gambini, people who can switch from light to dark and back again almost instantly. Almost a real-life version of Dr. Jekyll and Mr. Hyde. He'd read about them but never seen one in the flesh.

He waited until he heard the front door open and close. Then the gate out to the street. When he heard a car start its engine and drive off, he made his way over to the deck and entered the house. He wasn't exactly sure if

Grubb was dead or alive. A heart attack seemed more than possible. Walking over to the body, he checked for a pulse and was surprised when he found one.

He remembered the spectacle of Grubb snorting white powder at the café and reached into the man's shirt pocket for that folded slip of paper. Opening it on the table, he dabbed the white powder with his finger and touched the tip of his tongue.

No doubt about it. The faint taste of vinegar, even the scent—Grubb was using heroin.

He took a closer look at Grubb's nose and noted the inflammation. Rolling up the man's shirtsleeves, he saw the tattoo on his right arm and switched on a lamp. The tracks were hidden in the ink, but they were there. When Matt checked his teeth, they were brown and had that distinctively foul odor that comes when they're beginning to rot.

He felt Grubb's pulse again and gave him a long look. It seemed stronger, and the man's breathing sounded steadier now.

Matt looked around the living room and finally stood up. Something about the place didn't feel right, but he couldn't pin it down. He noticed the wet bar and walked over. There was a wide chest against the wall. When he opened the top drawer, he found it empty. When he slid open the second drawer, it was empty as well.

He turned around and took an inventory of the furnishings.

After a few minutes, Matt realized why Grubb's house felt so strange. There was nothing personal here. No photographs, no bric-a-brac, nothing found or collected.

It suddenly occurred to him that Grubb was renting the place. Renting it furnished.

Matt thought he'd noticed a stack of mail on the bar when he first walked over. He glanced at Grubb still laid out on the couch. The man was groaning and beginning to stir. Matt turned back to the mail and leafed through the letters. When he noticed a return address from a real estate company on Wilshire, he ripped open the envelope and unfolded the cover sheet.

There were only two paragraphs, and Matt skimmed through them quickly. The house was being leased from the same company who leased the three partners at DMG their cars.

Yellow Brick Leasing.

It felt like another sign on a road without exits. Another loose end in a case of loose ends. He wasn't sure what it meant.

THIRTY-THREE

Matt raced down Beachwood Drive feeling like he'd finally reached his limit. The windows were open, the cool air blowing against his face, Pink Floyd doing "Wish You Were Here," loud. He needed to eat something, and he needed it badly. Something to fill the black hole in his gut while he thought about what he'd just witnessed and wrote down as much as he could remember for the case file.

He passed the market and café halfway down the hill, then gunned it past Glen Alder Street until he hit Franklin. After making a right, he pushed through heavy traffic for about a mile before turning left onto Highland.

Petit Trois made the best omelet he had ever tasted anywhere here or in his travels overseas. The small French bistro was sandwiched in between a dry cleaner and a pizza shop in a rundown strip mall half a block north of Melrose. Matt had discovered the place while working the night shift as a patrol officer. The anchor for the strip mall was a cop magnet—a Yum Yum donut shop that stayed open twenty-four hours, seven days a week.

Matt pulled into the lot, found a spot beside the trash dumpster, and walked inside. Despite the neighborhood, despite the fact that the bistro only offered counter seating, the place was elegant. Lots of marble and polished wood with mirrored glass and stainless steel to make the narrow room feel bigger.

Matt had met the owners years ago and had become friendly with a female sous-chef who was working tonight and saw him enter. Waving him over, she pointed to a stool on the end and gave him a hard up and down.

"You don't look so good," she said under her breath. "Everything okay?"

Matt nodded and glanced at the name tag she'd pinned to her chef coat. The tag read "Savanna" even though her real name was Emily. He wasn't sure why seeing the tag cheered him up, but it did.

"I'm good," he said. "I am now."

She smiled. "The usual?"

"Thanks . . . Savanna."

She laughed and turned and got started cracking eggs into a bowl. Whenever Matt came here, he always ordered the same thing. The five-egg omelet with Boursin pepper cheese, garnished with chives and sea salt and served beside a butter lettuce salad with a Dijon vinaigrette, shallots, and grape seed oil. When a waiter passed by the counter, Matt added a double espresso and turned to watch Emily make his omelet.

If he had to guess, Emily was probably his age. She was on the small and thin side, with brown eyes and light brown hair, a round face, and a smile that had a bit of magic to it. Although they had never met outside the bistro, he knew how hard she'd worked to become the chef she was, and he'd always liked and admired her for it.

His double espresso arrived. And then the omelet and salad. The food smelled good and tasted even better. After a few bites, Matt decided that he'd return to the station before jotting any notes down on paper about what Robert Gambini had done to Lane Grubb tonight.

He didn't want to ruin the first meal he could remember eating in a week. Besides, the conclusions he'd made in his mind were tagged with forever stamps and would remain unforgettable—

Joseph Gambini had found a way to do business while he served out his time at Terminal Island. Somehow, he'd formed a relationship with the three partners at DMG. His nephew, Robert, didn't want the competition and was willing to do whatever had to be done to drive them off his turf. He had beaten up Grubb tonight and threatened to take the man's life. Robert was also the most logical suspect in the murders of Sophia Ramirez and Moe Rey, which Matt believed, along with Deputy DA Burton, had been a message meant for his uncle Joseph to back off and leave.

Matt tried to clear his head as he took a last bite of food and finished off the double espresso. He looked over at Emily, who suddenly appeared very busy. The bistro had filled up while he'd been eating, and he hadn't noticed. After checking his watch, he realized that the place closed in fifteen minutes and the rush was something of a last call for the night. Leaning over the marble counter, he gave Emily a light tap on the shoulder. When she turned, he thanked her and left enough cash to cover the meal with a generous tip.

He walked out into the cool night air. He felt rejuvenated and refreshed and thought that he had picked the perfect place for a late-night meal. And then he noticed the black limousine idling in the gloom beside his car.

THIRTY-FOUR

Matt gave the black limousine a long look as he stepped off the curb. Then the back door snapped open, and he saw a middle-aged woman glaring at him. Matt's first thought was that she looked mean, angry, maybe even crude. And while she seemed familiar in an odd sort of way, it took several moments to even make a decent guess. The short and round old-world body, the meaty arms and fingers, the attitude tattooed all over her face.

It had to be the city councilwoman. It had to be Dee Colon.

"Get in," she said.

Matt grimaced. "Why would I do that?"

"I'm not asking, Detective. I'm giving you an order."

Matt's eyes flicked through the car. The mayor of Los Angeles, Billy Garwood, was sitting in the front seat beside the driver. Though the councilwoman may have turned him into her personal go-go boy, tonight the mayor looked like he'd run out of "go" and seemed uncomfortable and out of place. Matt's eyes went back to Colon. He could see some sort of knuckle-dragging goon with a pistol holstered to his belt sitting beside her.

Colon leaned out the door. "Do you want me to call the chief, Detective? Do you want me to tell him what you've been up to tonight? That you beat up Lane Grubb and planted drugs in his home? Is that what you want me to say, Cowboy?"

"But I didn't do any of those things, and you know it."

She flashed a dark smile and nodded. "Sounds like a great defense, Detective. The trouble is that no one will ever believe it."

It hung there for a moment in the cool night air beside the trash dumpster. Dee Colon was a psycho bitch.

Matt walked over to the limo, then, reluctantly, slid into the back seat beside her.

"Close the door," she said impatiently.

Matt closed the door as ordered. When the limo pulled out of the lot heading north on Highland, Colon pushed a button closing the privacy window so that the driver and even the mayor couldn't hear what was about to be said.

Matt turned to Colon's bodyguard and guessed that he was in his early fifties. The man had the look ex-cons get after a couple of years living in a cage. His nose had been broken at least twice, and he had a long scar on his left cheek. From head to toe he appeared rough, cheap, and boorish. Matt turned back to Colon.

"What about him?" he said.

Colon glanced at her bodyguard and shook her head. "He doesn't speak English," she said.

Matt took a deep breath and sat back in the seat wondering what Colon had on her mind that required privacy. He could feel her muddy brown eyes on him. He could feel the woman measuring him.

"You were ordered to back off," she said finally. "You were told to leave the three partners at DMG alone. Was there something the chief said that you didn't understand? Were your orders not clear enough? Or do you have issues, Detective? You like to run around the city with your badge and your big gun thinking that you're what? Bigger and smarter than everybody else? Are you Superman tonight?"

Matt didn't say anything. The limo had just made a left turn onto Sunset. When he glanced up front at the mayor, he caught him trying to reel in a smile. It seemed more than obvious that closing the privacy window was just for show. The back seat had been wired, and Colon's go-go boy was listening to everything being said.

Somehow Matt wasn't surprised.

Colon cleared her throat. "You're in a free fall," she said. "And for what? Just think about what life could be like if you started seeing things right. I could help you, Detective. I could make your career, if you'd let me. You want a promotion? You want one? You've got my word; just say it, and Dee Colon will make it happen. That's who I am. That's who I've always been. Dee Colon gets things done, and she takes care of her friends. Good care of her friends. Ask anybody in the city. Ask them and they'll tell you Dee Colon takes care of everybody who takes care of her."

The air in the limo had turned foul. Matt didn't care. He could feel his blood pressure rocketing across the universe. It took a moment to find the right words. Once he had them, he turned to the vile woman and met her gaze eye to eye.

"How much are they paying you?" he said.

Colon froze like she wasn't used to being challenged. Matt could see the venom in her eyes. She was trying to fight off all the anger. Trying to hold back the firestorm.

Matt held the stare. "How much is Sonny Daniels paying you?" he said. "You've got a decent job. You're on the city council. You're way overpaid, but no one's bitching about it so you're in the clear. Why would you want to mess that up by doing business with people like Sonny Daniels? How much more do you need? What's the headline gonna be when everybody figures out that you're part of an illegal drug operation? That you're trying to cover up two murders?"

Colon laughed. "You're in all the papers, Cowboy. You're even on TV, and you've still got no idea what's really going on."

"Okay, fine," he said. "Then tell me what's really going on."

She narrowed her eyes as she mulled it over and tried to settle down. "A fifteen-year-old girl was raped and murdered. Unfortunately, the detective assigned to her case is incompetent, might even be crazy, and has an ax to grind with the rich. Instead of pursuing the sex maniac, he's badgering legitimate businesspeople who are making a positive contribution to our city. Until he's fired and replaced, every family in the county—every one of us—is in danger."

The art of politics. The art of bullshit.

Sophia Ramirez hadn't been raped, but that didn't matter. Matt hadn't beaten up Lane Grubb tonight, but that didn't matter either.

Colon's eyes went dark. "There are three things that you can't beat, Cowboy. Me, the tax man, and your undertaker. The sooner you own that, the sooner you'll find true and lasting peace."

Matt kept his mouth shut. It looked like the driver had planned to circle Hollywood. He'd just made a left off the Strip and was heading for Santa Monica Boulevard. With any luck they were on their way back to the bistro and Matt's car.

Colon leaned closer. "You realize what's at stake, right, Detective?"

"You've already said it twice. You've got the chief's ear, and I'll lose my job."

"That's true," she said. "But I had something else in mind."

Matt shrugged. "Like what, councilwoman?"

A moment passed. From the smirk on her bodyguard's beat-up face, his English was just fine. And Colon's voice had changed, becoming quieter and, Matt thought, more suspicious. It suddenly occurred to him that Colon had been working from a script tonight. That the city councilwoman had been playing a card game with him and was about to throw her ace on the table.

"The Ramirez family," she said. "Losing your only child's gotta be tough, don't you think?"

Matt nodded, waiting for the card to drop. He hated the sordid woman.

"The toughest," he said finally.

"They're illegals, you know. They crossed the border a long time ago, but still, they've broken the law. Sonny Daniels knows they're illegals. Seems like everybody does except Immigration."

Matt turned to face her. "You're a piece of shit, Colon. A real piece of shit. They came here the same way you did."

She giggled. Somehow it seemed so vicious. "But I made something of myself, Cowboy, and they didn't. They're scum. They could be deported tomorrow."

Another long moment passed, the card on the table, Colon's dirty hand played.

Matt lowered his voice and gave her a look. "And if I back off Sonny Daniels and DMG?"

She shrugged. "Then we'll see."

Matt grimaced again as he chewed it over. "I don't work for you."

"Yes, you do," she said with another dark smile. "You just don't know it yet. You work for me, and you'll always work for me. I run this city."

"What about the mayor?" he said.

Colon glanced up front at her go-go boy, then turned back to Matt, winked, and lowered her voice.

"He watches me run it," she said.

THIRTY-FIVE

The limo stopped a block short of the bistro. Matt climbed out of the back seat without a word and slammed the door shut. Once the limo got lost in traffic, he checked his cell phone for text and voice messages and was surprised not to find any. He hoped that it meant his partner was home in bed and on his way to a decent night's sleep.

Matt walked down the sidewalk, passing the Yum Yum donut shop and entering the strip mall's parking lot. It seemed unusually dark tonight. Looking overhead, he noticed something was wrong with the lighting. He walked by an SUV and then a pizza delivery car. When his view cleared the pizza sign on the car's roof, he saw Robert Gambini leaning against his black Mercedes with his arms folded over his chest. Gambini's dark eyes were all over him. And there was no way out. The heroin dealer had backed his car in front of Matt's, blocking the street.

Gambini gave him a look up and down. "You got directions to Paradise, Detective? There's a club on Paradise. I've heard it's nice, you know. Pretty girls and pretty men. Supposed to be safe and real peaceful. You got directions to a place like that?"

Matt stopped ten feet out and met the man eye to eye.

"You'll never get to the club on Paradise, Gambini. You'll never make it. Not in a million years."

Gambini laughed. "Who says so, Detective? You?"

Matt remained motionless, still eyeballing the heroin dealer hard. He was dressed in the dark slacks and casual shirt he'd been wearing at Grubb's house. But now, standing this close, Matt could tell from the cut and quality of the fabric, everything was Armani. Everything except for the gold Rolex around his wrist.

"Why are you bothering me?" Gambini said. "Why aren't you chasing whoever murdered that little Mexican girl?"

"But I am chasing him. I'm looking at him right now."

Gambini shook his head in disappointment. "I don't mess with kids, Detective. No matter who they are or what they might have done. That's one of the rules."

"Rules?"

The heroin dealer nodded slowly in affirmation.

"What about Moe Rey?" Matt said. "Is there a rule for a guy like him?"

"Moe Rey's a schmuck who worked for my uncle. What about him?"

"He was murdered with the girl."

Gambini flashed a short smile. "I heard about that. You know what? Everybody's better off with a jackrabbit like Moe Rey gone. Less CO_2 in the air. Less dead weight to help the world spin around the sun."

"How's Lane Grubb spinning?"

Gambini gave him a long look. "You know as much about that as I do," he said finally. "You were there. You had a seat in the front row."

Matt paused a moment. He had followed both Grubb and Gambini into Hollywood Hills, but he'd given them more than enough distance. It seemed hard to believe that he'd been made.

"You knew I was watching?" he said.

"Sure," Gambini said. "I've had my eye on you all night. Me and Grubb. It was a command performance, don't you think?"

"You beat him up pretty good. You threatened his life. Seems like there might be rules for that, too."

Gambini didn't say anything. It looked like he was thinking something over. He glanced at the bistro, the windows dark and the CLOSED sign on the door, then turned to watch a police cruiser pass the lot heading south toward Melrose.

"No offense," he said after a while, "but guys like Lane Grubb and the two dimwits he's hanging with are stone-cold losers. If you want to break them, the only way to cut through all the noise is to scare the life out of them. It's all about their generation, Detective. They never grew up. You ever notice how they turn their women into mommies so they can suck their titties and go boo-hoo-hoo?"

Who's calling who crazy?

Matt let it go without saying anything. When Gambini's eyes dropped down to Matt's waste, he could tell that the drug dealer had spotted the .45 holstered to his belt.

"What do you want, Gambini? Why are you here?"

Gambini, with that MBA from Wharton, thought it over for a while.

"You're dirty, aren't you?" he said finally. "You're a dirty cop. You're in it with my uncle. You're in it with these three little fools at DMG. And I saw you tonight, Detective. I saw you with Dee Colon. You got in her limo. You took a ride up and down the Strip and had a real long talk. You've gotta be dirty."

Matt had lost his patience five minutes ago. And he felt no need to enlighten Gambini with the truth. The more he tossed it over, the more convinced he became that letting Gambini think he was dirty might even heat things up and prove to be useful.

"What do you want?" he repeated.

Gambini lowered his hands and took a step forward. Matt didn't move.

"I want you to give my uncle Joseph a message."

"What's the message?"

Gambini saw something and stopped. Matt turned and watched two cops walk into the donut shop, their cruiser parked on the street at the curb. When the door closed, Gambini leaned closer and lowered his voice.

"It's not gonna work, Detective. That's the message I want you to give my uncle. He can bankroll these three fools and try to muscle in on my business, but it'll never work. He never helped me, even when I needed it. He never helped me or my family. And now I'm bigger than him. I'm stronger than him, and I'm richer than him. So you tell your new best friend that if he wants to stick it to me, I'm gonna stick him back ten times harder. That's the message. That's how I do business. Ten times harder. Got it?"

Matt didn't say anything.

Gambini was seething, no doubt about it. Matt watched him get into the Mercedes and gun it through the lot. When he reached the street, he skidded to a stop and gazed through the window at the two cops in the donut shop ordering coffee. Matt couldn't really tell, but it sounded like Gambini was shouting at the cops through the glass. After a few minutes, the black coupe made a right onto Highland, its tires screeching as it vanished around the corner and headed north toward the Strip.

THIRTY-SIX

He tried not to think too much as he got the front door open and switched on the outdoor lights. He stepped into the dark house, found the lamp by the couch, and turned it on. As he entered the kitchen, it felt like he hadn't been home in a year.

He lowered his laptop case onto the chair by the table, then poured a drink over ice from the bottle of Tito's vodka he kept in the freezer. The first sip was strong and had a bite to it. He needed it to be strong. He needed it to taste like medicine tonight. But like most things in his life, change was built in, and the second sip tasted smooth as silk. He didn't mind that either.

He walked back into the living room, shaking his head. His mind was way too stoked to even think about going to sleep.

Something was wrong with this case. And he had a strange feeling about it. A feeling in his gut that when and if he ever figured it out, that new thing, that new piece to the puzzle, would be followed by doom.

It almost seemed like déjà vu. Almost the same feeling he'd had after talking to Val Burton, only worse.

Somewhere upstream was a storm. When he reached it, everything would seem tantalizingly familiar—and then everything would end.

He guessed as much the minute Robert Gambini showed up and started talking about that imaginary club on Paradise Road.

Matt had no doubt that Gambini was vicious. Just a few hours ago he'd witnessed the man's brutality firsthand. But after meeting Robert Gambini in the flesh, after talking to him, Matt knew something else about him that even his uncle Joseph didn't seem to get.

Robert Gambini wasn't crazy.

He was a serious man, albeit dangerous and angry, but he did things for a reason. His actions were planned, deliberate, and well thought out.

And that's when Matt began to sense the darkness that comes with an impending doom. It overwhelmed him in the car all the way home, and this time he couldn't shake it.

Robert Gambini had no interest in sending a message to his uncle tonight. Matt was certain of this. Gambini's message had been meant for him.

Matt switched off the lamp and sat down on the couch in the darkness. He could hear the coyotes stirring underneath his deck through the slider, the sound of the heater shutting down and the house becoming quiet and still except for the refrigerator humming in the background. Outside he could see the lights strewn across the charred basin leading east to the tall buildings downtown.

He took another sip of vodka, beginning to feel the glow.

He wondered if Gambini's message had been some kind of warning or threat. If, in the heroin dealer's mind, Matt was a dirty cop working with his uncle Joseph, a corrupt politician like Dee Colon, and the three partners at DMG, Gambini could have been saying that Matt's life was fair game, too.

It seemed to make sense. Still, there had to be more to it than that.

The missing piece. The missing thing. Something right in front of his eyes that he couldn't see yet.

Matt set his mind adrift.

A lot of people lease their cars these days. But Lane Grubb was renting his home as well. Why didn't he own anything?

There was something odd about that. Something wrong with it.

Matt wondered about the other two. Did Ryan Moore own his home, or was he renting? And what about Sonny Daniels? Did he own anything at all?

His cell phone started ringing. Matt dug it out of his pocket, read Mitch Burton's name on the face, and took the call.

"Channel four," Burton said. "Hurry."

Matt switched on a light, found the remote on the fireplace mantel, and powered up the TV mounted on the wall. Toggling up to channel four, he saw a video shot of Dee Colon sitting on the couch between Angel and Lucia Ramirez in their home. The camera and microphone were jammed into the Ramirez's faces. In this case, the shot was made from over a female reporter's shoulder. The graphic banner at the bottom of the screen was the same one every news station uses every day for every story, no matter how big or small.

BREAKING NEWS.

"I've got it," he said to Burton. "I'm there."

"Listen."

Colon had her arm around Lucia, who was wiping tears away from her eyes as she wept and tried to speak through her sadness. Matt couldn't help thinking that she looked frightened.

"We don't know what's going on," she said in a frail voice. "We miss our daughter very much."

The female reporter broke in. "What does it feel like to know that the detective in charge of your daughter's case may not be doing his job?"

Matt heard it. He couldn't believe that it had even been said, but he'd heard it and it had. He stepped closer to the TV.

Lucia nodded, still wiping the tears away, still looking frightened. "We don't know what's happening," she managed. "We don't know why the police aren't trying to catch the man who did this to our little girl."

Angel turned and looked directly at the camera. "We've got a sex maniac out there. He murdered my daughter. Why isn't anyone doing anything?"

For whatever reason, Angel looked frightened as well. Matt's eyes flicked back to Colon. The vile woman seemed pleased with herself as she milked the tragedy of a young girl's murder for her own financial benefit and whatever Sonny Daniels had cut her in for. Matt thought about Burton on the other end of the line and pressed the phone against his ear.

"That's it," he said. "We're dead."

"It looked forced to me," Burton said. "And both of them came off frightened. What Colon's implying with this spectacle isn't true. She's lying. The chief's a lot of things, Matt, but he's smart enough to see through this kind of crap."

"I'm not sure that's what matters this time around. What matters is that all of a sudden the chief's got a major PR problem. Colon went public with false information. She did it on purpose because she's being paid to do it. That doesn't change the fact that the chief's gonna have to deal with it now."

"We'll see," Burton said. "I'll give him a call tonight."

The production lights in the Ramirez's living room shut down, but the camera was still rolling. Angel Ramirez turned directly to the city councilwoman and started speaking off mike. He looked upset and appeared to be pleading his case.

"We did everything you said, right? We told them what you told us to say. Now we won't be deported, right? You promised that we—"

And then the camera shut down and the shot cut back to the studio.

Matt's body shuddered. "Did you catch that?"

"Now you know why they looked terrorized," Burton said. "Colon's blackmailing them. The whole thing was staged. We're not going anywhere, Matt. Not yet anyway. I'll let the chief know as soon as we hang up."

Matt spent the next ten minutes briefing the deputy DA on tonight's encounters with Lane Grubb, Colon and the threat she'd made, and then his face-to-face hookup with Robert Gambini. By the time he'd finished, his glass was empty, and he poured another.

He sat down at the kitchen table. "Gambini said he didn't kill the girl."

"They all say that, Matt. You know that."

Matt shook his head, then remembered that he was on the phone and Burton couldn't see him. "I'm not saying I believe him. I'm just thinking about things. I mean, what if we're seeing this wrong? What if Robert Gambini isn't the one?"

"We agree that the girl witnessed an execution, right?"

"We agree," Matt said. "That's why she's dead."

"Okay," Burton said. "Then it's all about Moe Rey. What motive would Sonny Daniels have for killing Moe Rey?"

Matt thought it over as he stepped back into the living room and started pacing between the slider and the fireplace.

"What if Sonny Daniels didn't want Joseph Gambini involved in their business?" he said finally. "What if Joseph Gambini was trying to muscle his way in without an invitation. What if Moe Rey had been working at DMG as Joseph Gambini's spy and Sonny caught him?"

"It's possible, I guess."

"But wouldn't that be enough reason for Sonny to want Rey dead?"

Burton didn't say anything for a while. Matt wondered if Burton was standing in front his window with that wide-screen view of the city as he thought things over. That big game-board view.

Burton cleared this throat. "Everything you just said is possible, Matt. More than possible. Except for one thing, and it's a big thing."

"What do you mean?"

"The crime itself."

"What about it?"

Burton lowered his voice. "The crime itself," he repeated. "The brutality of it. The way it happened. The things that were done. The condition the victims were in when they were pulled out of the ground. Think it over for a while. Sleep on it, Matt, and we'll talk in the morning."

Burton's phone clicked.

Matt pocketed his cell, then switched off the TV and the lamp. With the room lit by only what outdoor light passed through the windows, he sat down on the couch again and gazed at the city in the distance. He'd known what Burton was trying to say, just as he knew that he himself had made a mistake. The kind of mistake a detective makes when he's not basing his conclusions on hard evidence.

The execution of Moe Rey, followed by the murder of the girl who witnessed the killing, Sophia Ramirez, had been ferocious—the doer a savage. There weren't many people capable of committing a crime that harsh. Not many people who could reach the point of becoming merciless. While the idea that Sonny Daniels was involved in the murders might seem to fit logically, Matt began to see the possibility as flawed. At least for now, it had no basis in reality and deserved to be shelved somewhere in the back of a drawer.

The phone rang. Not Matt's cell this time but the house line. Matt grabbed the phone and switched it on, thinking Burton was calling back.

"How'd you get this number?" he said.

The caller didn't say anything. Matt sat down in his reading chair when it occurred to him that it might not be Burton on the other end of the line.

"Who is this?" he said, carefully.

Several seconds ticked off in a heavy silence. Then a male voice came on, sounding ultraweak and far away.

"Is this Detective Jones of the LAPD?"

The tone the caller had used to say "LAPD" appeared sarcastic, but Matt ignored it.

"This is Jones," he said.

"We need to meet, Jones."

"Who are you?"

The man didn't respond.

"Who are you?" Matt repeated.

The man let out a sigh. "Lane Grubb," he said.

Matt felt a sudden chill quake through his body. "What's going on, Grubb?"

"I'm done," he said. "I want out. I wanna come in."

"When? Where? Tell me how I can help you."

It hung there for a while. Matt guessed that Grubb had shot another load of smack and was in the twilight of his high.

"Let me help you, Grubb. Tell me what you wanna do."

"I want to meet in a place where I'll feel safe, Jones."

"I can think of a dozen places right now. How 'bout the station?"

"No way, man. No fucking way." He took a shallow breath and exhaled. "I'll find the place. I'll find it and call you in the morning. We'll meet in the afternoon."

"You sure you want to wait that long?"

"Tomorrow, Jones," he said. "You and me. Tomorrow afternoon."

The phone went dead. Matt checked the caller ID and read the words UNKNOWN CALLER.

He returned the phone to its charging base, took a long swig of vodka, and started pacing through the living room again.

His brain was all hopped up, his stomach on fire and churning. No way was he ready to fall asleep and take another meeting with the Grim Reaper.

THIRTY-SEVEN

Matt entered the station using the back door off the lot and headed straight for the conference room. It was early, 6:00 a.m., and he was loaded with goods from his favorite street vendor—a tall cup of piping-hot coffee and a poppy seed bagel toasted over charcoal with lox and cream cheese.

He set his laptop down on the table. While he waited for the machine to boot, he pulled a file from his laptop case and spread the papers out beside his pad and pen so that he could read them at a glance.

Matt had managed to get four hours of deep, dreamless sleep last night, which he was more than grateful for. But before all that, with a bit of luck and good timing, he'd also managed to get something done. He'd called back Burton with the news that Grubb wanted to come in, then spent another hour briefing Cabrera and Lieutenant McKensie on everything that had happened since he'd walked out of the station yesterday and decided to take the long way home. Everyone seemed to agree that even if the case wasn't breaking their way just yet, it had taken on direction.

But Matt had done something even more last night. Working with Jimmy Kim, their contact at the phone company, and Keith Upshaw, a friend of David Speeks in the Computer Crime Section, they had been able to trace Lane Grubb's call to Matt's house. When Matt entered the number associated with the unknown caller, the message service for Yellow Brick Leasing came online. The recording stated that the office was closed until tomorrow morning and directed the caller to the company's automated message system.

Yellow Brick.

Matt typed the words into a search engine on his laptop and hit "Enter." A long list of irrelevant entries appeared on the screen that included the song by Elton John, "Goodbye Yellow Brick Road," T-shirts on eBay from the farewell concert of the same name, images from the movie *The Wizard of Oz*, long lists of novels and self-help books that appeared contrived and were written by people Matt had never heard of, a gardening center in Atlanta that had painted its bricks yellow and held a sale two years ago, and finally, on page five at the very end of the compilation, Matt learned that a warehouse had been available for sale or lease six years ago in a town fifteen miles south of Birmingham, Alabama, on Yellow Brick Road.

Matt thought it over as he took a first bite out of the bagel and sipped his hot coffee.

He went back to the search window and revised his entry.

Yellow Brick Leasing.

When the new list rendered on the screen, Matt could tell at a glance that almost nothing had changed. The leasing company hadn't made the list this time either, even though the six-year-old entry for the warehouse in Alabama had. It seemed more than just strange.

He took another sip of coffee thinking about Geeks, then killed the thought as quickly as he could. Returning to the search window, he made a slight revision and hit "Enter."

Yellow Brick LLC.

A long moment passed as Matt eyeballed the first two entries on a completely new list. He rolled his chair closer to the table. It felt like maybe he'd just hit pay dirt.

Yellow Brick Leasing was here, but it appeared to be overseen by a parent company, the Yellow Brick Legacy Group LLC. And while it looked like they kept a small office on Wilshire Boulevard, they weren't really involved in leasing houses or luxury cars. Yellow Brick was a family of hedge funds, the corporation headquartered on Wall Street.

Pay dirt.

Cabrera walked in, carrying his briefcase and a bag from a fast-food restaurant.

"Did Grubb check in yet?" he asked.

Matt shook his head. "He sounded pretty high last night. I'm thinking lunchtime, if we hear from him at all." He watched Cabrera yawn and set his things down on the table. "When you ran Sonny Daniels's plate and got his license, did they email any images?"

Cabrera pulled a file out of his briefcase. "I've got all three," he said. "I made a hard copy. What do you need?"

"I just want to know when their licenses were issued."

Cabrera leafed through his file and pulled a sheet of paper out. Rolling a chair over, he sat down and compared the dates on all three driver's licenses.

"You might be on to something, Matt. These were issued three years ago. On the same day, three years ago."

"Then they really aren't from LA."

"But where are they from?"

Matt turned back to his laptop. "New York," he said. "Wall Street. Give me a minute."

"Wall Street?"

Matt clicked the link on the search engine's list and opened the Yellow Brick Legacy Group's home page. After locating the site map at the bottom of the screen, he found a link called "About Us" and clicked through a series of pages until he hit the list of corporate officers.

More pay dirt.

All three of them were there. Lane Grubb, Ryan Moore, and Sonny Daniels.

Wall Streeters. A hedge fund company.

Matt couldn't believe what he was reading in their biographies. When he hit a link to the *Wall Street Journal*, he clicked it and an article about the three partners appeared from the business section. Matt checked the date and found that the piece had been written last year to celebrate Yellow Brick's ten-year anniversary on Wall Street. According to the journalist, the three partners had known each other since meeting at a prep school in Greenwich, Connecticut, and had become known in the world of high finance as the Brothers Grimm. They began as corporate raiders, had a reputation for being ruthless, and had made their fortunes before they were thirty. Four years later they started their first hedge fund under the name Yellow Brick Legacy Group LLC and never looked back.

Matt turned to his partner and pointed at the screen. "Look," he said. "Look how complicated things just got."

Matt went back to the keyboard and typed Sonny Daniels's name in the search window. When the list assembled, he spotted an article from the *New York Daily News* and hoped that it would be even more telling.

The headline above photographs of all three partners read THE BROTHERS GRIMM, along with the subheading, THESE THREE IDIOTS DON'T PAY TAXES.

Matt moved over so that Cabrera could read the article as well. From the first sentence to the last, the biography of the Brothers Grimm was a detailed portrait about greed. All three were rich, private school, country club types with chips on their shoulders. All three were spoiled brats. None of them had ever served in the military. None of the three could ever remember voting, and their tax returns obtained by the newspaper's legal department revealed that none of them had ever given a dime to a charitable cause. According to the journalist who interviewed them, not one of the three felt any sense of responsibility to their country, their community, or anyone other than themselves. The world was their oyster, they kept telling the writer. It was all about how much money they were making and how much fun they were having as they grabbed more and more cash out of other people's hands.

Cabrera stopped reading. "They're shitheads," he said in a quiet voice. "All three of them are shitheads. They think it's a game."

Matt pushed his coffee aside and sat back in his chair. "To them it probably is. And that might explain why they seemed so naive when we met them. They had no immediate sense of danger, remember? No street smarts.

No wisdom because they've never had to fight for anything. It also explains why Dee Colon wants in. The Brothers Grimm. She knew who they were from the beginning."

"But what could they possibly be doing out here?"

Matt nodded. "You mean, what are they doing in that factory? And what is Grubb afraid of? Why doesn't he want to just meet here?"

"That's easy. You said it yourself. Robert Gambini beat him up last night."

"That may be part of it, but I think it's these guys. Sonny Daniels, Ryan Moore, and now, Dee Colon. No way they'd want Grubb to talk to us. Not if they've got something going."

Cabrera tossed it over. "Has it occurred to you that their interest in Robert Gambini might have nothing to do with the illegal side of his business?"

"I think we're on the same page but keep going."

Cabrera glanced at the *Daily News* article on the laptop, then turned back. "After reading this, I can't see why three rich assholes from Wall Street would have any interest in opening up shop here in LA just to wean users off oxycodone with high-grade smack. They're already rich. Why would they take a risk like that?"

"Because they think they're smarter than everybody else," Matt said. "Because like we said before, life's a game and they think they can win every time. They think they're invincible. Let's face it, even the rich want to get richer. If you've got two million in the bank, you're gonna want ten, right?"

"But I'm guessing they've got more than that," Cabrera said. "Probably too much to count. That's why it still doesn't make sense."

Matt thought about it as he got up and walked over to the window. He could see McKensie walking into his office with Mitch Burton. The group waiting for Grubb's call had begun to assemble. Matt turned back to his partner.

"I can think of one way that it might work," he said.

"How?"

"What if they were trying to steal away Robert Gambini's license to sell weed? If they were going after his pot shops, if that's what they really wanted, then it would make a lot of sense."

Cabrera gave him a long look. "He's got pot shops all over LA, Matt."

"And in San Diego, San Francisco, Portland, and Seattle. And don't forget about Vegas and Colorado. See what I mean? He's got an MBA in business. When the rest of the country goes legal, he's got the infrastructure to be the one on top. The next Marlboro Man. The next Reefer Man. Who wouldn't want to steal that?"

A moment passed as a new reality settled into the room. Cabrera tossed his pen on the table.

"I see it," he said finally. "Making money with no risks. So what if a couple of people get murdered along the way. That's the price of doing big business, right?"

THIRTY-EIGHT

They had spent most of the day in McKensie's office. Burton had brought his work with him and had set himself up at the table by the window. Matt and Cabrera used the time to update their reports and enter everything into the Chronological Record. It was almost three, and Grubb still hadn't called.

McKensie glanced at his watch, then turned to Matt. "What if the only number he's got is the landline to your house?"

"It's call-forwarded to my cell. So is the phone on my desk."

Matt turned back to his laptop as he chewed it over. The truth was that he'd become worried about Grubb. Worried that Sonny or even Colon had gotten to him.

He let the thought go. He could smell someone brewing a fresh pot of coffee on the bureau floor and left the room to fill his office mug. Everybody seemed to be on pins and needles, even the guys at the homicide table not working the case. There was an edge to the entire day. Something in the air that had spread through the station. He took a quick sip of the fresh brew and started to head back to McKensie's office. But before he reached the door, his cell started vibrating in his pocket.

Matt hurried into the room and pulled out the phone. The words UN-KNOWN CALLER were blinking on the face. Matt shot Burton a look, then

Cabrera and McKensie. As he took the call, he switched on the speaker so everyone could listen.

"This is Jones," he said.

The caller didn't reply, but judging from the din in the background, he hadn't ditched the call and was still there.

"This is Matt Jones," he repeated. "Is that you, Grubb?"

Matt could feel the others moving closer. The lack of a response was excruciating.

"If it is you, Grubb, if you still want out, I can help you. I can keep you safe."

"Safe?" Grubb said in a shrill voice. "They're following me."

"Who's following you?"

"All of them."

"Are you okay?"

Grubb didn't answer the question. Matt lowered his voice.

"Are you stoned?"

Grubb sighed. "Maybe a little."

"Did you find a place to meet? A safe place to meet?"

"I think so."

Cabrera pulled out a pad and pen, ready to write down the address.

"Tell me where you'd like to meet," Matt said.

"It's a new café. It used to be called Café Pinot."

Matt knew the place. "On the corner of Fifth Street and Flower."

"Yeah," Grubb said. "That's it. On the corner by the park."

"That's a great place, Grubb. You couldn't have picked a better place. It's an open space."

Grubb didn't say anything for a while, then—

"I thought so, too. I need to be safe."

"Do you have a piece of paper handy? Can you write something down for me?"

"I guess so."

"We need an alternate location," Matt said.

"Why?"

"Just in case you get to the café and change your mind. There are a hundred reasons why you might change your mind, Grubb. We need another place to go just in case you do. A place that's safe."

Another stretch of silence went by. "I guess that makes sense. Where's the second location?"

"Another restaurant not very far away. The Red Dragon. It's in Chinatown on Bamboo Lane."

"I know the place," Grubb said. "I like that place. It's quiet."

"If you walk into the café and change your mind, you'll head straight for the Red Dragon, right? There's a private dining room in the back. Everybody knows me there. Tell them you're waiting for me, and they'll take good care of you."

"It's just me and you, right, Jones? You're coming alone."

"It's just us, Grubb. It's just me and you. Now what time do you wanna meet?"

"In an hour and a half," Grubb said. "Four thirty. I'll be waiting outside."

The phone went dead. Everybody looked at each other. But it was McKensie who seemed the most concerned.

"The sun goes down at four thirty," he said. "It'll be dark. And the park's filled with homeless people. Any chance this is a trap?"

THIRTY-NINE

The café was nestled on the corner of Fifth Street and Flower in Maguire Gardens, an urban park surrounding the Central Library in the heart of downtown Los Angeles. The park featured numerous fountains, open lawns, and walkways lined with benches and low walls meant for additional seating. On the downside, McKensie had been right. In recent years the park had become a magnet for the homeless.

Matt let the thought go as he stepped off the sidewalk. Although he appeared to arrive alone and sat down on the wall in front of the café's entrance on Fifth Street, he was wired for sound and had an audience. Cabrera was watching with three members from the Special Investigation Section hidden in a converted taco truck parked across the street. Patrol units were out of sight and stationed around the corner on Flower. Both Fifth Street and Flower were one-way thoroughfares, four lanes wide. Lieutenant McKensie, along with a handful of detectives, were spread out on both streets in SUVs. In the park, ten more detectives dressed in plain clothes filled in the landscape. And in the café itself, Deputy DA Burton, along with two detectives borrowed from the Cold Case Unit, had a table by the windows and a front-row seat.

Matt adjusted the wire behind his shirt and checked the time. Even though he was ten minutes early, the sun had begun to set, and he could feel a chill in the air. He glanced at the taco truck, then at the heavy traffic on the streets. Grubb had picked an open place, but because of the time of day, because of the crowds of people exiting the buildings and filling the sidewalks, the setup seemed awkward and made Matt feel uneasy.

He took a deep breath and tried to focus, sifting through the sea of faces walking toward him and away. He glanced at the people in the park behind him, then at Burton with the two detectives inside the café. As his gaze moved down Fifth Street, he turned to his left and spotted Grubb walking south on Flower. He got to his feet and started down the steps to the sidewalk. Grubb looked up and nodded from a half block off as he reached the intersection and waited for the light to change.

And then Matt saw it.

The black Mercedes coupe, hidden in the gloom revving its engine on Flower another half block behind Grubb.

The light turned. When Grubb stepped off the sidewalk, the black coupe lurched forward and accelerated through the heavy traffic. Matt didn't need an interpreter to realize what was happening. He burst forward and ran toward the intersection, waving at Grubb and shouting at him to turn back. He could see the Mercedes bulldozing cars out of its way.

Horns started sounding, and then all the sirens—the loud, piercing noise echoing off the tall buildings and coming from everywhere at the same time.

Grubb seemed confused by the chaos and didn't appear to understand that he was in danger.

The black coupe barreled over the curb behind him and down the sidewalk, knocked over a mailbox, and bounced back onto the street, its tires screeching.

Matt kept shouting as he sprinted forward. But it looked like Grubb had become frightened now, and Matt watched the man freeze in the middle of the crosswalk.

The Mercedes rocketed toward its victim—the street clear ahead. Thirty yards away from the target soon became twenty, then only fifteen—and Grubb was just standing there.

Matt charged into the intersection and lowered his shoulder, trying to beat the car to its prey. He drove his upper body into Grubb's waist, thrusting him backward and tackling him onto the sidewalk. He could feel the hard rush of air as the Mercedes missed its mark by only inches and blew by them.

Grubb was down, but he looked okay.

Matt got to his knees and eyeballed the black coupe. It seemed like madness. The car was right in front of them, spinning in a controlled circle and sideswiping any other car that was in its way. When the front end swung around to Fifth Street, the engine seemed to light up and the Mercedes shot down the one-way street splitting oncoming traffic into two. Cars veered off the road. A city bus driver must have lost sight of the black coupe in the darkness, swerved at full speed, and plowed into the taco truck.

And then time stopped.

Matt could see it happening in slow motion—in utter disbelief. The bus rear-ending the taco truck and the gas tank bursting into flames.

He screamed at the top of his lungs.

He looked down at Grubb, still confused and panting on the sidewalk, then jumped to his feet and bolted over to the taco truck. The entire rear end was engulfed in flames. Ripping open the front door, he looked inside and saw all four people lying motionless on the floor under piles of shattered glass. The three SIS officers, two men and a woman, were facedown. Cabrera was on his back, his eyes open and pointed Matt's way but blank.

None of it good. None of it good.

Matt grabbed his partner's forearms and dragged him out the door, onto the sidewalk, and away from the burning truck. Police were beginning to arrive shouting that the gas tank was going to explode.

Matt pushed the cops out of his way, hard and fast, and in one case with a closed fist. Running back into the truck, he locked his hands around the woman's wrists, yanked her out of the shattered glass, and dragged her onto the sidewalk beside Cabrera.

The flames were getting bigger, the fire hotter, the truck ready to blow.

He dove back in, eyeballing both men as he rushed to turn them over. He knew from his time in Afghanistan that one of them was dead. The man's head was hanging off to the side, his eyes stuck to the roof of the taco truck. Matt wanted to scream again but didn't. Instead, he grabbed the dead man's wrist, and then the second man's arm, digging his heels into the floor and wrenching their heavy bodies out into the fresh air.

Seconds ticked by. Time jumbling down the drain. The taco truck had just started to make an odd whining sound. After a few moments, the strange noise stopped, the silence even more daunting.

And then night turned into day.

Matt heard the loud crack, saw the bright flash, and watched the taco truck lift off the street and explode before his eyes.

The concussion from the blast knocked people down. Matt could hear them screaming in terror on both sides of the street. Shattered glass and shards of metal began to fall out of the dark sky like frozen rain.

Matt wrapped his arms around Cabrera, shielding his partner from the storm. As the fireball rose over their heads, he saw his partner blink his eyes. He looked him over in the flickering light. He guessed that his right arm and leg were broken, and he spotted blood seeping through his shirt just below his rib cage.

He looked up at the cops staring at the fireball. "Hey, hey, hey," he shouted. "We need help over here. What are you guys doing? Where the hell are the EMTs?"

Matt ripped open Cabrera's shirt and examined the wound. Blood was oozing out of a slice that might have been caused by broken glass during the crash. The wound looked shallow and didn't appear to be life threatening.

"Can you talk?" he said.

Cabrera nodded.

"Say something."

He shook his head, writhing in agony. "I can't."

"You just did," Matt said. "I want you to move your left hand. Not your right. Just your left hand."

"You think my neck's broken?"

"Just try moving the fingers on your left hand."

"Oh my God, Jones. Oh my God."

Cabrera's eyes dropped to his left hand. A long moment passed as he appeared to struggle. But then his fingers moved.

The relief was overwhelming, and Matt saw a tear drip down his partner's cheek. Matt closed his eyes for a moment. He couldn't catch his breath and felt dizzy. He shook his head and looked away. He could still see the black coupe and the open path the car had cut all the way down Fifth Street. All the wrecked cars, some of them on fire, lining both sides of the street. When the Mercedes made a turn onto Grand Avenue and disappeared, Matt looked around for a cruiser and realized that no one was even in pursuit.

His skin flushed. His entire being lit up.

He tried to pull himself together and turned to check on Grubb but didn't see him on the sidewalk. He grabbed hold of a street sign and pulled himself to his feet. When he turned, he spotted Grubb racing across the intersection into the park. Burton and McKensie were on the corner but unable to stop him as he sprinted by and vanished into the night.

Matt glanced back at Cabrera, then gazed across the intersection until his eyes stopped on a limousine idling safely on Flower Street. The rear window was down, but it didn't need to be. Matt knew exactly who was riding in the back seat and who was sitting beside her.

He watched the limo pull into the open street, the traffic behind it at a standstill. As the car drove off, free as a bird, the flames from the burning taco truck filled the limo's interior with bright red light.

That's when he saw her eyes. Her brutal face.

The city councilwoman had been here tonight.

FORTY

Matt watched two EMTs lift the gurney and roll Cabrera into the ambulance. As they closed the doors, one of them gave Matt a hard look.

"You sure you don't want to come with us, Detective?"

"I can't," Matt said. "I don't have time."

"But you need medical attention."

"What are you talking about?"

The EMT shot him another look. "Have you seen your face?"

Matt wiped his cheek, felt his skin stinging, and saw the blood on his fingertips.

"I'll stop by later," he said. "I've gotta meet somebody first."

The EMT shrugged. "Suit yourself, pal."

Matt watched the man hop in behind the wheel. The engine was already idling, the LED light bars, flashing. When the ambulance drove off without a siren, Matt took it as a sign that his partner might be banged up and broken but would be okay in the end.

He turned and started walking down the sidewalk. Burton and McKensie were standing on the corner with a handful of plainclothes detectives. It sounded like they were planning their delayed pursuit of the Mercedes. McKensie had ordered the choppers in, along with providing a description of the banged-up car to everyone on the ground. Matt wished that he could have avoided them because he wasn't sure how much time he had, if he had any at all. Lane Grubb would be making that decision for him.

"I've gotta go," he said.

McKensie grabbed him by the shoulder and pulled him back, his voice tainted by sarcasm. "Where?"

"The Red Dragon."

"Do you really think Grubb's gonna show?"

Burton shook his head. "I saw him run away, Matt. He didn't look like he was gonna stop running anytime soon."

"That's why we picked a backup location, right? I'll see you guys later."

Matt didn't wait for a reply and started jogging down Flower Street. He'd parked in the garage halfway down the block and just this side of the California Club. Within five minutes he was barreling through the city headed for Chinatown. At one point when he'd reached a red light and was buried three cars back, he glanced in the rearview mirror. He didn't recognize himself at first and turned away. When he looked back, he eyeballed the specks of blood from small cuts peppering his cheeks and forehead. He thought about the shattered glass and shards of metal that rained out of the sky. When it occurred to him how lucky he'd been that his eyes were spared, he turned away and never looked back.

Bamboo Lane was a narrow one-way street between Hill and Broadway at the north end of Chinatown. Matt spotted the street and skidded into a parking spot on Broadway. Before getting out of the car, he checked his piece, then holstered the pistol and took a moment to look up and down the street. He eyed the traffic carefully, then got out of the car and gave the street another long look. If the Mercedes had been here, he felt confident he would have seen it.

He looked back at the two-way traffic, picked his spot, and made a harrowing run through the passing cars until he reached the other side of the street. It could have been his imagination, but Bamboo Lane seemed dark tonight. As he walked down the narrow road, he could feel his heart beating in his chest. The Red Dragon was on the left, almost at the end of the block.

Matt passed the restaurant, gazing at the red door and through the windows at the people seated at tables. He wanted to come in from the back. Picking up his step, he walked around the corner, then entered the alley behind the buildings.

The passageway was tight and gloomy. Avoiding a long series of the trash cans, discarded building materials, and lawn chairs set around charcoal grills, he kept his eyes on the buildings and started counting. When he thought he had the right place, he peered through the screen door into the kitchen and walked in.

An old man working an oversize wok whom he recognized said something to him in Mandarin and pointed at the door to the private dining room. Matt met the old man's eyes.

"Alone?"

The old man nodded. "We take care of him, like you say."

Matt bowed his head slightly in gratitude—or was it relief?—then exhaled as he stepped through the kitchen and pushed open the door.

His eyes swept through the dark room. He found Grubb seated at a table in the corner with a single place setting and a single candle illuminating the entire room. Lowering his gaze, he realized Grubb was pointing a Beretta 9mm pistol at him.

Matt grimaced. "Why the gun?" he said.

Grubb's eyes looked dead as he stared back at him. "I need to feel safe."

"Put it on the table, Grubb."

The man shook his head back and forth without saying anything.

Matt checked the room again, just to confirm that they were alone. His vision had adjusted to the darkness. When he turned back, he noticed the syringe and five bags of smack laid out on the wooden table beside a glass of water and the place setting. Looking Grubb over, he saw that he'd already rolled up his right sleeve and wrapped a rubber tourniquet above his elbow. Already emptied one of the five bags of white powder into a soupspoon.

"Are you gonna shoot up?" Matt said.

"Why the hell not?"

"Because you won't be safe."

Grubb laughed, exposing his rotten teeth. Then he laughed even more, like he'd just heard a good joke.

"Why are you doing this, Grubb? How could you let this happen to yourself? You already have all the money you could ever need. What are you doing in LA?"

Grubb's eyes rose from the table and burrowed in. "Is this the part they call the interrogation, Detective? If it is, you can stop with all the stupid questions. I'm not in the mood right now."

"Would you mind if I sat down?"

"Not at this table," he said, looking the place over. "That one."

Matt pulled a chair out and sat down at the table in front of Grubb's. "What about the piece?"

"What's a piece?"

"The gun."

"The gun stays here."

"What about pointing it at something other than me? You know, just in case it goes off."

Grubb nodded, panning the muzzle to the empty table beside Matt. "Good?" he said.

Matt shook his head. "No, Grubb. It's not good, but it's better."

Grubb picked up the glass of water and took a sip. After resting the glass on the table, his eyes seemed to dim, and he remained quiet.

Matt leaned forward in his chair. "I'm gonna need to know what's going on," he said. "I can't help you if I don't know what's happening."

The man looked at him, then looked away. He appeared to be thinking something over and having difficulty doing it. Matt guessed that it was the heroin already in his system—the back end of his afternoon high.

"I overheard you talking," Matt said. "You got into it with Sonny last night. You were saying something about the risks. There weren't supposed to be any."

"He promised. Sonny told us that it was gonna be easy. He said there was nothing to worry about."

"How's Dee Colon fit into your trouble-free life, Grubb?"

The man shrugged. "After you showed up with those pictures of Robert Gambini, we realized that we needed protection. It was supposed to be a single payment, but she could smell the money. You know, the way politicians do these days. She has the knack and wanted more. She wanted in."

"Is she in?"

Grubb shook his head. "Nobody gets in. That's the way it is. That's the way it has to be. Sonny's trying to stall, but she's not buying it."

"What about Robert Gambini? Are you in with him or not?"

"Not even close, Jones," he said. "And for the record, that's another stupid question."

Matt took the hit but ignored it. He'd figured out who Grubb was a long time ago.

"Gambini beat you up last night," he said. "What's he want out of this?"

Grubb's hollow eyes narrowed. "Everything."

"You mean a big piece. Fifty, maybe seventy-five percent."

"No," Grubb said. "I mean he wants everything."

Matt looked across the table, sizing Grubb up and still baffled by the idea that three Wall Street assholes, the Brothers Grimm, could be so naive. The idea that these idiots thought they could walk into LA and muscle in on the drug business without risk or worry seemed so ludicrous.

"What do you know about the murders of Moe Rey and Sophia Ramirez?"

"Are you talking about that stupid Mexican girl?"

Matt winced as he heard Grubb say the words. He noted the anger in the man's voice. The hate.

Matt steadied his gaze. "What do you know about their deaths?" he repeated.

"If that stupid kid hadn't gotten herself killed, none of this would be happening right now. That's what I know about it."

Now there was new anger settling into the room. Not just in Grubb's voice but the storm crashing through Matt's body. He wished Robert Gambini had hit him a couple more times in the face last night.

"What are you trying to say, Grubb?"

The man sat back and sighed. "Nothing, Jones. I can see you wouldn't get it, so why waste time. The only thing you need to know is that I want out. Are you gonna help me or not?"

Matt didn't answer the question. Instead, he'd reached the point of self-doubt and needed to think it over. Grubb wasn't worth helping. And it no longer seemed worth the bother of keeping him safe either. That was the bottom line. Unfortunately, these ideas went against everything Matt had always stood for, everything he had learned as a soldier and then again as a cop and a detective. He was there to serve all things living, even if he felt like killing them. Shooting them. Beating the crap out of them.

His mind surfaced, and he gazed across the two tables at Grubb. The man had given into his wants and needs and had placed the Beretta beside his napkin. Now he was holding the soupspoon filled with white powder over the candle.

"You sure you want to do this, Grubb? Why don't we just walk out now? We'll drive over to police headquarters. It's just a couple of blocks away."

"We'll do that later. Order something to eat. It's on me."

Grubb's hands were quivering as he began filling his syringe with the hot load. Matt thought about going for his .45, but Grubb's pistol was still too close.

"You know the smack they sell out here is stronger than the crap they sell you guys on Wall Street."

Grubb gave him a look with those dead eyes of his. "I can handle it, Jones. You think I'm a pussy?"

"I think you're a lot of things, Grubb. The problem with smack is you just never know."

Grubb tightened the rubber tourniquet and slapped his arm in search of a fresh vein.

"You're an asshole, Jones. Trying to scare me like that. Wow. Cops. I've read all about you. I guess that's what happens when your momma dies on you, and your rich daddy walks out on you. Shit, you grew up dirt poor like a stupid welfare brat."

Grubb found the vein, stabbed it with the needle, backed blood into the syringe, and gave the plunger a hard push. Matt watched the smack rush down the barrel and vanish into Grubb's arm. Grubb gave him a look and had a wiseass smirk on his face. He started to laugh, even giggle, but it was short-lived—maybe only a second or two. Then the stupid man fell back in his chair and collapsed onto the floor.

FORTY-ONE

It felt like someone was watching him from behind his back. Like he'd been transformed into a machine that had been programmed. He could see himself stuffing Grubb's pistol inside his belt, then moving over to the body on the floor.

It wasn't about Grubb anymore. It made no difference who he was or even how he got there. The number of zombies walking the streets these days had become quantifiable over the past four years at a steady 30 percent.

But everything had changed over the last ten seconds.

Matt knew that it was about him now—who he was as a person and his ability to rise above the fray.

He turned Grubb's body over, pulled the needle out of his arm, and slapped him across the face. When the man didn't open his eyes, he stripped off Grubb's shirt and rubbed his knuckles over his chest bone as hard as he could.

Grubb wasn't responding, and that feeling came back in waves. The idea that he was being tested for something he didn't understand.

He could see himself eyeballing the man's lips and fingertips and noting that they hadn't turned blue yet. He could see himself checking for a pulse, then lowering his head to Grubb's chest and listening to his breathing. Grubb's vital signs had slowed down significantly but were still functioning.

He pulled out his phone and punched in 911. Once he'd spoken with the dispatcher, he gave Grubb another hard look and thought it over. Response times in LA varied because of traffic congestion. Given the time of day—the height of rush hour—it was entirely possible that the EMTs wouldn't get there for more than ten minutes. As Matt weighed the odds, he thought about that Narcan kit he kept in the back of his car ever since he'd worked narcotics.

No doubt about it. Grubb didn't look like he had ten minutes.

Matt jumped to his feet, found the kitchen empty, and burst into the ally. Sprinting around the corner and down the narrow road, he reached Broadway and ran into the street. The car horns started, followed by a lot of angry, loud voices. But as Matt grabbed the Narcan kit, what concerned him most was the din of the city. He didn't hear a siren. Not even the faint hint of a siren somewhere in the distance.

He let the thought go, then raced back across the street, down the road, and up the ally. Rushing through the kitchen, he pushed the door open and hurried over to Grubb's body.

That sensation was back. That feeling that someone was standing over his shoulder watching him.

Matt ripped open the kit as if on autopilot. The plastic delivery device wasn't much more than a syringe without a needle. He pried the yellow caps off, then grabbed a cartridge filled with the antidote naloxone, removed the red cap, and screwed it into the barrel of the syringe. Tilting Grubb's head back, he sprayed half the drug into his left nostril, then hit the right nostril with the rest.

Seconds clicked off. After almost a minute nothing had happened, and Matt felt a chill rocketing up his spine.

He slapped Grubb across the face again. When he didn't get a response, he gave him another hard slap, but the man was just lying there like a rag doll. Matt took a deep breath and exhaled. Setting the timer on his watch for three minutes, he grabbed another cartridge of the antidote and prepped the syringe with a second dose.

The wait for his alarm to go off was hard to handle. He could see his fingers trembling as he held the syringe in his hand and wondered how three minutes could take so long to get here. As he wiped the sweat from his forehead, he became aware of a siren approaching. But the relief only lasted for a second or two. When the timer on his watch started vibrating, he knew that he couldn't wait.

And he knew what he had to do.

He tilted Grubb's head back and sprayed a half dose into his left nostril. The dining room doors burst open behind him, and the overhead lights switched on. Matt looked over his shoulder as a pair of EMTs began rushing toward him. He turned back to Grubb, inserted the syringe into his right nostril, and pushed the plunger all the way through the barrel.

"Heroin," Matt said in a loud voice. "He OD'd ten minutes ago."

A female EMT knelt down beside him. "How many doses have you given him?"

Matt turned to her and saw the concern showing on her face. "Two," he said. "Three minutes apart. No response. Nothing."

The EMT eyed Grubb for a moment, then gave her partner a long look. "We'll take over from here, Detective. Please step back."

Her partner rushed in with a canvas bag, showing the same concern on his face. Matt began to wonder if something was going on beyond Grubb's overdose. A stethoscope came out, and after a moment of probing the man's chest, the female EMT gave her partner another grave look. Matt watched them trying to revive him but could see it happening before his eyes.

Grubb was dying.

The dining room doors snapped open with a punch. Matt turned and saw two men in suits with hard faces storm in with their badges up and out like a pit bull's tail. They looked like seasoned detectives, both of them in their fifties—the kind of guys who've seen everything in the world two or three times over and have no time or interest in talking about it. Matt didn't have to read their IDs to know that everything in the case had changed, and these detectives were from the LAPD's elite Robbery-Homicide Division.

"Are you Jones?" the meaty one said in a gruff voice.

Matt nodded as they approached.

"I'm Jack Raines, and this is my partner, Billy Hudson. You're out. The case was bumped up to RHD."

"When?"

"About ten minutes ago. What's that behind your belt?"

"His gun," Matt said.

Raines reached for the gun and pulled it out. "Better leave this here with us, Jones. Your best bet is to get some medical attention. Once you're fixed up, we'll need to talk. As a matter of fact, I'll have an officer drive you to the hospital and bring you back."

Matt sized Raines up, noting his white hair and goatee, his steely blue eyes and tanned skin. He didn't like the man's tone or attitude.

"I can drive myself," he said.

Raines shook his head. "Not tonight, Jones. Tonight, we're doing it my way."

The female EMT seemed to know who had just taken charge of the case and turned to Raines.

"This guy's DOA, Detective. This guy's dead."

FORTY-TWO

The cop they'd picked to drive Matt to the hospital seemed young and nervous. As Matt opened the passenger door, the cop protested.

"I'm sorry, Detective. But you're gonna have to ride in back."

Matt didn't say anything. When the cop opened the back door of his black-and-white cruiser, Matt slid onto the seat thinking it felt a lot like he'd just been arrested. He turned away from the cop without asking his name or even reading the plate pinned to his shirt. He was too angry and had no intention of talking to the guy.

He turned to the window and gazed across the street. Cops had already shut down the block and stretched crime scene tape at both ends of Bamboo Lane. An evidence collection truck from the Forensic Science Division had arrived about five minutes ago, along with a handful of crime scene techs. But even more strange, two additional teams of detectives from RHD were on site. Matt had seen them enter the restaurant as he and the young cop crossed Broadway.

It didn't feel like a test anymore. Grubb was dead, and Matt had lost control of the case.

After what happened tonight, he understood that the situation had become radioactive. But why would it take six detectives from RHD to investigate a heroin overdose? Why had Raines insisted that Matt be escorted to the hospital and driven back? Why didn't Raines and his partner, Billy Hudson, trust him enough to get his face cleaned up and return to the crime scene on his own? And why was he sitting in the back seat of this cruiser instead of the front?

Matthew Trevor Jones.

He took a deep breath and exhaled. As the car pulled away from the curb heading south for USC Medical Center, he watched the city go by in a jumbled blur.

He'd lost the case. His case. And he'd let Sophia Ramirez down—a fifteen-year-old girl—he'd let her down.

Matt tried to shake it off but couldn't. After ten minutes he saw the sign for the emergency room and watched the cop pull in front of the entrance. When Matt tried to open the back door, he realized that he'd been locked in. He gave the young cop a heavy look, trying to maintain his cool even though he was still enraged.

"Open the door," he said in a quiet voice.

"I'm supposed to keep an eye on you."

Matt grimaced. "Let me tell you how this is gonna work tonight, Officer. I'm going in that door to see a doctor. You're gonna go to the hospital's front desk over there to find out how my partner's doing. Then we'll meet back here. Got it?"

"They told me that I have to stay with you at all times."

Matt shook his head. "Open the goddamn door, kid, or I'm gonna mess with you. Open it and do it in a hurry."

The cop looked frightened again, but the door clicked, and Matt climbed out of the back seat.

"Now go find out how my partner's doing. Denny Cabrera. And don't come back until you do."

Matt walked away from the cruiser, the cop staring at him from behind the wheel. When the door to the emergency room slid open and he saw

McKensie waiting for him in the lobby, he knew that the night still had legs and wouldn't end soon.

"They took our case," Matt said. "RHD stole our case."

"I'm afraid it's worse than that, Jones. Follow me. You're already checked in. They're waiting for you, so let's go."

Matt followed McKensie past the front desk and down the hall into a large room. The lights had been dimmed here, and doctors and nurses were sitting behind a counter in the center of the room monitoring about twenty patients in beds separated by thin walls. A young nurse greeted them as they entered, pulled the curtain open in the third bay on the left, and pointed to the bed. As Matt sat down, she stepped closer and examined his face.

"It's not that bad," she said. "This is from shattered glass, right?"

He nodded.

"It looks like most of it grazed your skin and kept going. But I don't want to stain your shirt. Let me get you a smock, and I'll be right back."

The nurse crossed the room and vanished down a second hallway. Matt noticed his supervisor staring at the TV mounted on the wall.

"Your partner's in surgery," McKensie said.

"How is he?"

McKensie turned, his face showing concern and worry. "You're not gonna see him tonight."

"Is he okay?"

"His arm's broken, but they seem to think that's an easy fix."

"Then what's the problem?"

McKensie gave him a look with those emerald-green eyes of his. "His leg, Jones. It's broken in two places. They said that it'll be a long time before he can walk again."

A moment passed as Cabrera's fate settled into the small room. Matt turned to his supervisor and tried to get a read. The concern and worry showing on McKensie's face seemed worse than before. Something was wrong. Something more than the weight of Cabrera's injuries.

"What is it?" Matt said. "Why are there six detectives from RHD investigating a heroin overdose?"

McKensie lowered his eyes like he couldn't hold the gaze. "Cause of death won't be determined until his autopsy tomorrow morning."

"But I was there. I saw it. Grubb overdosed."

McKensie didn't say anything for a while. When he spoke, his voice seemed unusually quiet. "It might be more complicated than that, Jones. You could be in trouble. They're gonna debrief you at headquarters. I've asked Burton to be there."

"But what happened? What's going on?"

Matt looked up. When he followed McKensie's eyes to the television, he began to feel more than uneasy. It was city councilwoman Dee Colon, holding a press conference outside police headquarters. Enlarged photographs of Lane Grubb and Matt had been set on a pair of easels to the left and right of a portable lectern.

"Turn up the sound," Matt said.

"You sure?"

Matt nodded. "Turn it up."

McKensie grabbed the remote attached to the bed and raised the volume. Matt forced himself to listen.

Colon was just stepping up to the microphone with a crowd of people behind her. Like most power mongers, she stood before her audience and looked them over for a while. When she finally began speaking, she came off smug and self-righteous—a real woman of the people whose tone of voice was cut with plenty of sarcasm.

"In all my years in public service," she was saying, "in all my years of fighting for the people of this great city, I have never seen such a miscarriage of justice in my life. Here we stand tonight, just two weeks into the new year, and this good man, Lane Grubb, is dead because a member of the LAPD fell asleep at the wheel. That's right, Lane Grubb, a taxpayer, a respected member of the business community here and in New York, a childhood success story by anybody's count, is dead tonight because LAPD detective Matt Jones didn't do his job. And that's not an exaggeration. *He didn't do his job.* Let me put this in perspective for you fine people, the people I work so hard for every single day. A teenage girl is brutally murdered. There's a maniac out there. A sex killer. And what's Detective Jones up to? To tell you the truth, nobody's really sure. We know he's bothering some of the best and brightest people in business right now. We know he's running around the city telling everybody that he's a big shot and he's in charge. So where do we stand? I say this to you. If Detective Jones had listened to his superior officers and focused the investigation on hunting down the sex maniac who killed this teenage girl, Lane Grubb would be alive tonight. You heard it from me, and you know I always say it the way it really is. I speak the truth, and nothing but the truth. Lane Grubb would be alive today, but he isn't because Matt Jones killed him."

McKensie hit the "Mute" button. "I can't listen to this crap," he said. "She knows damn well that the girl wasn't raped. Her office requested a copy of the autopsy report from the chief two days ago."

Matt shrugged but didn't say anything. Instead, he concentrated on controlling the rage burning through his body. The adrenaline rushing through his veins. He'd always taken pride in his ability to read people. He'd always trusted that feeling in his gut, and tonight was no different. As he had watched Colon speak, he could tell that the entire press conference had been scripted. She'd looked into each camera on cue. She'd changed her tone of voice on cue. And she'd stared at the photo of Grubb and even wiped a fake tear away on cue.

He chewed it over. He tried to understand what could possibly motivate someone like Colon to be what she had become. He knew money and power played a big role, a defining role, but guessed that something had been added to the mix. Something more twisted. More perverted. After a while, he surfaced and found McKensie still watching the press conference even though the sound had been muted.

"How could she possibly know that Grubb's dead?" Matt said.

"What are you talking about, Jones?"

"Grubb died, what, an hour ago? His body is still laid out on the floor at the crime scene."

"So what?"

"So how did she know he's dead?"

"News travels fast, I guess."

Matt shook his head. "Somebody's talking to somebody," he said. "I'll bet she's got somebody on the inside. A lot of somebodies. And I'd bet she's got something on everybody."

"If she didn't, she would have been indicted a long time ago."

Matt glanced at Colon on the TV monitor, then turned back to his supervisor. "So what do you think she's got on the chief?"

McKensie turned and gave Matt a long look but didn't say anything.

FORTY-THREE

Matt walked into **Interrogation Room 3B** at the police headquarters building in downtown LA. Raines and Billy Hudson had told Burton he could watch through the one-way glass but couldn't enter the room. This seemed odd because Burton worked as a prosecutor, not a defense attorney, and had become an integral part of the case.

Raines tossed a legal pad on the table by the pitcher of water and paper cups, then pulled out a chair. "If you want anything, Jones, now's the time to speak up."

Matt stared at the detective as he sat down. He didn't like the guy, but now he realized that he didn't trust him either.

"No thanks, Raines. I'm good."

He took a deep breath and exhaled as Hudson closed the door, pulled a seat away from the table, and sat down behind his back. Matt may have been a rookie, but he knew exactly what Hudson was trying to pull. He knew that the detective would never say anything. Hudson would just sit back there like a thorn in Matt's side, trying to play with his nerves and hoping that he'd make a mistake. The idea that this was going to be a friendly conversation now seemed ludicrous.

Matt turned back and gazed across the table at Raines. "So why does it take six of you guys to investigate a drug overdose?"

Raines laughed. "We'll get to that, Jones. Make sure you're ready when we do. I just need to know a couple of things first."

"What things?"

"You were the last one to see Grubb alive, right?"

Matt had considered some of the pitfalls he might face as McKensie drove him from the hospital and they left that young cop behind. If Raines was trying to trap him, his first question seemed to be the most likely way in.

"Do I need to speak up, Jones? You were the last one to see Grubb alive, right?"

"Maybe," he said.

The answer seemed to bother Raines. "What are you talking about, Jones? What maybe? You were the last one to see him alive. Yes or no?"

Matt shrugged. "Maybe," he repeated.

Raines was upset now. He shouldn't have been showing it, but he was.

"Is this how it's gonna be all night, Jones. You're gonna pull stuff like this out of your rookie ass? You're not gonna have the professional courtesy to help us figure out what happened?"

Professional courtesy. Matt grimaced and stood his ground.

"That depends, Raines. That depends on a lot of things, like the reason you won't tell me why it takes six detectives from RHD to investigate a heroin overdose. I was there. I saw it."

"If you were there, Jones. If you saw Grubb stick the needle in his arm, then why didn't you try to stop him?"

"You saw the gun he was carrying. Why would you ask a question like that? It's stupid, Raines. What's wrong with you?"

"Okay, Jones, okay. He had the gun. I'll give you that."

"Have you picked up Robert Gambini yet?"

Raines narrowed his eyes. "Why would we?"

Matt wondered if they were messing with him in some way. There's no question that both Raines and Billy Hudson would have been briefed on the players when the case was pulled out of Hollywood and bumped up here.

"Have you been watching TV?" Matt said. "Do you have any idea what happened downtown?"

Raines met his gaze. "So what?"

"So Gambini tried to run down Lane Grubb tonight."

Raines traded looks with his partner, then glanced at his legal pad for a moment.

"Let's get back to Grubb's death, Jones."

"His overdose," Matt said.

Raines laughed again. "Okay, you win. The rich guy's overdose."

Matt noted the sarcasm in Raines's voice—the way he'd called Grubb's death "the rich guy's overdose." He gazed at the one-way glass, wishing he could speak with Burton. Before they entered, Burton had suggested that he refuse to say anything at all without representation. Matt thought it would be okay to cooperate, that he'd know the right time to pull out if he needed to. The fact that no one read him his rights had seemed encouraging at first. Now he wasn't so sure.

Raines filled a paper cup with water and took a sip. "Why do you think a member of the city council has gone public saying you're responsible for killing Grubb?"

Matt sat back in his chair and looked the detective over. "I've got no idea, Raines."

"The EMTs seem to think Grubb had been dead for at least five minutes before they got there. They told us you were spraying shit into the dead guy's nose. Why would you spray shit into a dead guy's nose unless you were worried about the way things looked?"

Matt leaned against the table. "The shit you're talking about was the antidote, Raines. I didn't know Grubb was dead. I had a Narcan kit. I was trying to help him."

Raines gave him a look like he didn't get it. "Help him?" he said. "Why would you want to do that? From what we heard you beat the crap out of him last night?"

Matt slapped the table with an open hand and stood up. They'd spoken to Colon. Or worse, she'd spoken to them. Matt tried to reel it all in before speaking in a horrifically quiet voice.

"If that's what you heard," he said, "it could only have come from one place, Raines. A very dark place. It would mean that Colon bought you off.

It would mean that you guys are on the take. That you're dirty cops. You got the tape rolling? We're almost done here."

"What are you talking about, Detective? And sit down."

"The idea that I beat up Grubb could only come from Colon because it's a lie and because it's wrong and because it's stupid. Robert Gambini roughed him up, just like he tried to run him down tonight. I saw him do it."

"You mean you were at Grubb's house, Jones? You were watching? And you didn't try to stop that either?"

"You'd have done the same thing. Two people of interest in a double homicide. You would've let them go at it for hours taking in everything they said to each other."

"Really?"

"Well, maybe not you, Raines. Not if you've got your hand up Colon's—whatever—take your pick."

"Sit down, Jones, and chill."

Matt finally took a seat. Raines dropped his pen on the table and stared back at him. Matt tried to get a read on the guy, but his rough face remained completely blank. It seemed strange. Matt had tossed one insult after the next his way, yet there wasn't even a hint of anger in his demeanor. After a minute or two, Raines finally spoke.

"Where did the Narcan kit come from, Jones?"

Matt met Raines's eyes. "My car," he said.

"So you left Grubb alone in the restaurant and ran out to your car?"

Matt nodded but kept his mouth shut.

"Where were you parked?"

"A block away on the other side of Broadway."

"How long were you gone?"

"Five or six minutes," he said. "Maybe a couple more."

"Did you see anyone around?"

"No."

Raines took another sip of water. "Do you see where you made your mistake, Detective?"

"What are you talking about?"

"You left the restaurant. That's the first thing you should have told me. I asked you a question. I asked it twice. Were you the last person to see Lane Grubb alive or not? Yes, or no?"

"I didn't make a mistake, Raines. The answer is maybe, and it's still maybe."

"Because you left him alone in the restaurant."

"Yes."

It hung there for a moment. As Matt replayed the last few minutes in his head, he thought Raines might be about to confirm what he'd been thinking all along—why did it take six detectives to investigate a heroin overdose? He glanced over his shoulder at Billy Hudson, then turned back at Raines.

"What are you guys up to?"

"We're just trying to take your statement and sort things out, Jones."

"Grubb didn't die of an overdose, did he. That's why you needed the extra help."

Hudson got up from his chair and took a seat at the table beside his partner. Raines was shaking his head. That blank expression the detective had been wearing for the past half hour was gone now but was still something worth admiring. It came from years of experience, Matt realized, and a great deal of talent.

"We believe it's a homicide, Jones. And we expect the coroner will back us up after the autopsy tomorrow morning."

"Why a homicide? I saw him shoot up. He collapsed before he could even get the needle out of his arm."

Hudson cleared his throat. "Before you ran out for the Narcan kit, did you check his vitals?"

Matt nodded. "Everything had slowed down, but when I left him, he was alive. His heart was beating. His breathing seemed shallow but steady."

Raines turned his legal pad over. "We found an empty bag of smack on the table."

"There should have been four more," Matt said. "Not empties, but four more loads."

Raines nodded. "They're empties now, Jones. We pulled them out of a trash can in the kitchen, along with a pair of nitrile gloves. The investigator from the coroner's office examined Grubb's arm before they bagged him up and found five fresh tracks. The one he made while you were watching him get loaded, and the four the doer added when you left the room."

Matt sat back in the chair and thought it over. Like a shadow, Gambini had been there the whole time. He'd found an opening—a five-minute window—and finished Grubb off. Now there was only Ryan Moore and Sonny Daniels to deal with. The Brothers Grimm had been reduced to two.

Raines's cell phone started vibrating on the table. He glanced at the face, took the call, said the word "right" two times, and switched off his phone. As he set it back down on the table, he glanced over at Matt and reached out to shake his hand.

"The chief wants to see you and Burton, Jones. Good meeting you."

FORTY-FOUR

Matt followed Burton into the elevator. After the doors closed, he turned to the prosecutor with concern.

"What do you think that was really about?"

Burton met his gaze. "Grubb was murdered. You didn't know it at the time but somehow sensed it when you asked why they needed six detectives to investigate an OD."

"They were playing me. I knew something was wrong when Hudson decided to sit behind my back."

Burton smiled. "Raines had the gloves and the empty bags and knew that the last one to see Grubb alive killed him."

"But I answered 'maybe.'"

"Yes, you did. And you just beat two of the best detectives in the division. That's why I think you ought to be an attorney, Matt. You belong in a courtroom."

The doors opened onto the top floor. As they started down the hall, Matt shook off the idea and glanced at the photographs neatly framed and hanging on the walls—a display that depicted the entire history of the LAPD from 1869 to the end of last year. Matt couldn't help feeling a sense of pride as they reached the chief's suite of offices at the end of the hall and stepped inside.

They were greeted by the deputy chief, who ushered them through the lobby and into the chief's corner office. Chief Logan was standing by a bookcase looking through the window at the city glowing in the night.

Behind him Matt could see three TV monitors mounted to the wall. One was switched to CNN. The second, to Channel Four, an NBC affiliate broadcasting the late-night news. But it was the third monitor that caught Matt's attention. The third screen was switched to Interrogation Room 3B. Matt could see and hear Raines collecting his pad and pen and walking out. The chief had watched the entire interview from his desk chair.

Matt turned and saw the deputy chief close the door on his way out.

"Have a seat," the chief said in an even voice.

There were two chairs placed before the chief's desk. As he and Burton sat down, the chief began pacing. He seemed extremely irritated and high strung. After several moments he turned and stared at Matt with those dark eyes of his.

"We met when, Detective? Was it yesterday afternoon?"

"Yes, sir."

"And what did I ask you to do? I want Burton here as a witness. What were your orders, Detective?"

Matt understood that there was nothing to be gained by glossing over what had happened. "You told me to leave the three partners at DMG alone."

"I believe there was more to it than that."

"Yes, sir," Matt said. "You ordered us to pull back the surveillance unit and no longer consider any one of the three men as persons of interest."

"And, of course, you followed that order because you know that's how things work in this police department or any other police department anywhere in the world. When a superior officer gives you an order, you follow the order. The reason it makes so much sense is that following orders is logical, wouldn't you agree?"

Matt hesitated. "Yes, sir. Following orders is logical."

The chief nodded and flashed a strained smile that hurt to look at.

"I'm not sure if you've noticed, Detective, but the city's burning right now. You see the flashes of light behind those two buildings? Those are car fires still being cleaned up after what happened on Fifth Street tonight. We have two deaths, including one of our own, and thirty-three people injured, including your partner, Detective Cabrera. On top of all that, now we've got another murder."

The chief glanced up at the TV monitor set to Channel Four. Councilwoman Colon was being interviewed by a reporter in studio. After a moment, he turned back to Matt.

"What was a relatively small homicide investigation with a few loose ends—a teenage girl found in a shallow grave—has become a high-profile case that's infecting the city. Right now, Councilwoman Colon is blaming you for the murder of her dear friend, Lane Grubb, and, because you've proven yourself to be incompetent, she's taking credit for getting you kicked off the case. According to Colon, you're the Lone Ranger and a disgrace to the entire department. I'm sure you don't want me to turn up the sound. I know I have no interest at all in what she's saying or hearing her say it. What you need to keep in mind is that everything Colon touches turns into something ugly, Detective. And because she's got a dirty mouth, because she's a serial liar, she owns nothing. No matter what the reality, it will always be your fault, not hers. What I'm saying is that we need to find a way to shut her down and do it as soon as we can. Before we go on, I've gotta ask. Did you do something to her? Is there a reason why she's going after you so hard?"

Burton cleared his throat. "I asked him the same thing, Chief. It seems so visceral."

Matt shook his head. "I'd never even met her before the other night."

"You're sure?" the chief said.

"Yes, sir. I've been thinking about it, though. Now I'm wondering if it's something else."

"Like what?"

"The amount of money that's at stake. I overheard Gambini talking to Grubb. He thinks the three partners at DMG are trying to muscle in on his business."

The chief nodded like he understood. "And Colon being a parasite wants in."

"That's what Grubb told me before he died. They've already made one payment to her, but she wants more."

"Of course, she does."

Burton turned to the chief. "The way she's been acting, it would have to be a lot more."

The chief nodded again and, for whatever reason, had the hint of a wicked smile working across his face.

"Sir?" Matt said.

"What is it?"

"I don't understand why we're hands off on Gambini."

The chief glanced at his computer as a text message popped up. "We're not hands off, Detective. We just can't locate him. The lab's working on the pair of nitrile gloves they found at the restaurant. They're hoping to lift the killer's prints off the inside of the gloves but said it'll take time."

The chief read his text message and looked up.

"So here's where we stand," he said. "Colon takes credit for your fall, Detective. The case goes to Jack Raines and Billy Hudson in RHD. Mitch, anything they need, you'll help them with, right?"

Burton nodded. "Of course, Chief. Anything they need."

"Good," he said. "That's the way the story will appear in the *Times* tomorrow. That's the official story."

Burton raised a brow. "Official?"

The chief turned to Matt and sat down on the end of his desk. "Jones, you're off the case because everything went to shit tonight. Like I said before, it's become a high-profile investigation. But if Colon's on the take, I trust her even less tonight than I ever did. So officially, you're off, Detective—you're back on medical leave. Okay? But unofficially, you passed the test with Raines tonight. Unofficially, I want you and Burton to keep at it. And I mean do whatever it takes to close this case out and get it off the table. Everyone involved is now a person of interest. But no rough stuff—keep your footprints small. I don't want to know what you're doing or how you're doing it. If Colon wants the Lone Ranger, we'll give her one. But if it blows back in your face, you're on your own, Detective. Do you understand what I'm saying?"

Matt glanced at Burton, then met the chief's eyes and nodded.

The reins were off. Proceed with caution.

FORTY-FIVE

It was the only next step that made sense. Despite the risk, it seemed like the only way forward.

Matt was standing behind a row of bushes pressed against the wall outside Robert Gambini's home off Bundy Drive in Brentwood. It was a dark, moonless night, around 12:30 a.m. He had parked a few blocks away and spotted the two SIS teams watching the house on his way in. The first had been easy to pick out—a dark van that looked empty parked at the curb two doors down. But the second team had been harder to make. The house next door was under construction from the ground up. Matt had noticed that the windows and walls had been framed out, but the structure itself provided no cover. As he moved through the gloom, he noticed the dim light from a cell phone switch on and off in the contractor's trailer. Peering through the rear window, he saw two members of the surveillance team they'd used outside the DMG facility staring across the side yard at Robert Gambini's house.

Matt had backed away, keeping to the shadows and now finding himself hidden on the street before a five-foot-high wall. He peered across the lawn, surprised by the size of Gambini's home. It was a big modern job that stretched across a wide lot and included a terrace with a pool and hot tub. But what really mattered right now were the large oak trees and the darkness. Although the outdoor lights were switched on, Matt thought he had enough lanes of shadow to make it across the front yard unseen.

He looked back at the house. A single lamp was on, lighting up the two windows by the front door. The driveway was empty, the garage doors closed. Although Matt couldn't be certain, the place had the look and feel houses get when the owners are away on vacation. It was almost as if the building itself had gone to sleep.

He heard a car approaching in the night. As the headlights swept through the tree branches above, Matt rolled over the wall onto Gambini's front lawn. Picking out a lane of darkness, he cantered through the gloom and around to the back of the house. The two surveillance units were stationed out front and off to the side. Matt knew that they were either waiting for Gambini to show up or looking for some sign that he was already here hiding out. It seemed odd that they weren't covering the back of the house. But after several minutes of searching, Matt became satisfied that the backyard was clear. Stepping out of the darkness, he walked over to the garage and gazed through the window.

A white Ford Mustang was parked in the first bay. The black Mercedes coupe, nowhere to be found.

He took a deep breath and turned back to the house, eyeballing the second-floor windows as he considered a new and unwelcome set of possibilities. Someone could be in a bedroom sleeping. Someone he didn't expect.

Proceed with caution.

He crossed the driveway and stepped up to the kitchen door. Through the window above the dead-bolt lock Matt could see a keypad mounted on the wall inside the house. The green lights on the interior panel were blinking in succession, indicating that the security system was armed.

Matt dug his cell phone out of his pocket, opened his speed dial list, and called Keith Upshaw, Speeks's friend and the former hacker who now worked in the Computer Crime Section. Upshaw picked up on the first ring.

"You're there?" Upshaw said.

"I'm here, with two SIS teams out front."

"You knew they'd be watching. Is the security system armed?"

Matt told Upshaw that it was and gave him the name of the manufacturer.

"That's an easy one," he said. "The technology's five years old. Give me a minute to dig out the password."

Matt could hear Upshaw's fingers working a keyboard. As he waited, he took cover in the gloom across the drive and kept his eyes glued to the second-floor windows.

"Do you know how to pick a dead-bolt lock?" Upshaw said.

Matt felt the set of picks in his jacket pocket. "If I have to."

"Well, you can forget about it."

"Why?"

"We're in luck. Robert Gambini owns a smart house."

"What do you mean?"

"It means that the locks, the doors, the TV, even the lights and phone can be controlled by his cell phone. It means he can let the UPS guy open the door, leave a package inside, and rearm the system from anywhere in the world. I just found his password. I can do everything we need to do from here. Which door would you like me to open?"

Matt thought about the Mustang in the garage. "I'm standing outside the kitchen, but don't do it, Upshaw. Someone could be upstairs sleeping. Ring the phone and let's see if anyone answers."

"You got it."

Matt heard Upshaw enter Gambini's phone number, then listened as the phones inside began to ring through the house. After six rings the house went silent.

"The call bumped over to his service," Upshaw said. "By the way, his outgoing message doesn't mention anyone but himself."

"Let's make sure. Do it again."

Matt heard Upshaw reenter the number, then listened to the phones ringing in the house. After another six rings they stopped.

"If someone's inside, Jones, they're either drunk or they're dead."

Matt took a last look at the second-floor windows and stepped out of the darkness.

"Open the kitchen door," he said.

"Here we go."

Matt looked through the window at the keypad mounted to the wall in the kitchen. As he watched Upshaw disarm the system, as he watched the green lights shutting down one after the next, he couldn't help but feel amazed. Once the system switched off, the dead bolt clicked, the door opened, and Matt stepped inside.

"I'm in."

"Good," Upshaw said. "Call me back when you're out and you want to rearm the system. No one will ever know you were there."

"Thanks."

"It was easy, Jones. Too easy. What kind of world do we live in?"

Matt switched off his phone and slipped it into his pocket. Except for the light by the front door, the house was cast in dark shadows and lit by only the outdoor lights feeding in through the windows. Still, as he moved out of the kitchen and into a dining room, he tried to keep in mind which windows could be seen by the surveillance units outside. Breaking into Gambini's house wasn't anything he wanted to get caught doing. Tonight was purely a fishing expedition. He needed to know more about who Robert Gambini was. More about the man's intent and purpose, and where he might be hiding. They already had the used bags of smack, the hypodermic needle, and the gloves used to murder Grubb, so he wasn't focused on finding anything specific.

First things first, he had to be certain that he was alone.

Matt pulled his cell phone out, switched on the flashlight, and made a quick but thorough sweep through the first floor. The rooms were big and included a living room and a library with a fireplace, a comfortable pair of reading chairs, and built-in shelves overflowing with books. He found Gambini's office attached to the library, then passed through a den and TV room, a large pantry, and back around to the kitchen. As he took in the furnishings and eyed the art on the walls, he realized that Robert Gambini had taste and style. The art was an eclectic mix of impressionistic watercolors cut against a modern realism depicted in oils with bold, vibrant colors. Matt couldn't explain why the intelligence he saw behind the things Gambini owned wasn't a surprise. For whatever reason, after meeting the man he'd expected it.

He stepped out of the kitchen.

He'd covered every inch, and the first floor was clear. Before heading back to Gambini's office for a more careful look around, he climbed the stairs and started down the hallway. The door to each room was open. Moving quickly, he counted three bedroom suites and then, at the end of the hall, the master suite. In each case the beds were made and, as he swept his hand over the pillows, cool to the touch.

Matt entered Gambini's master suite, stepped around a stack of books on the floor by the bed, and peeked out the window. He could see the terrace and pool, the trees surrounding the backyard so thick and lush that they blocked out the homes on the other side of the wall. Wrestling with his curiosity, he turned back to the books on the floor and glanced at the titles. There was a biography about Willie Mays here, and another about Abraham Lincoln. A book of poems by Rainer Maria Rilke came next, along with three Lena Gamble thrillers and a copy of Ken Follett's *A Dangerous Fortune*. Robert Gambini's taste in reading matched his eclectic taste in art, only this time Matt couldn't help being surprised. He shook it off and straightened the stack of books, then backed out of the room. Moving down the hallway quickly, he turned and noticed a door he'd missed along the way.

Even worse, unlike every other door on the second floor, this one was closed. He gave it a good look. Judging from the width of the opening, it wasn't a closet.

Matt pressed his ear to the wood and listened. After several moments, he turned the handle and cracked open the door. Then he sighed with relief.

It was a laundry room. Like the first floor, the second floor was clear. He was alone. He was safe.

He took the stairs two at a time and made his way back to Robert Gambini's home office. At a glance he could tell that Gambini was well organized. The entire room was laid out in a smart but simple way and devoid of clutter. Although there were several files stacked on the desk beside a laptop computer, most were neatly set in a tray on the credenza.

Matt sat down in the desk chair and skimmed through the tabs. Passing over anything that looked personal, his heart started pounding when he found a file labeled "DMG." He pushed the others aside and laid out the DMG file in a patch of light feeding in from the windows.

They were photographs. Surveillance photographs.

Many of them probably taken the day Sophia Ramirez and Trey Washington shot that video of Robert Gambini laid out on the grassy bank overlooking DMG's facility down the hill.

Matt leaned over the desk for a better look.

They were close-up images taken with a long lens of the workers loading those mysterious fifty-five-gallon drums onto small unmarked trucks. Other images included close-ups of each of the partners, Lane Grubb, Ryan Moore, and Sonny Daniels, with Daniels issuing orders to the drivers as the trucks pulled out.

But Robert Gambini had taken a lot of photographs from a lot of different places on a lot of other days.

Matt separated them from the rest and laid them across the top of the desk. Then he pulled his phone out again and switched on the flashlight. The pictures told a story as Gambini followed the trucks out of the city into the desert. It looked like Gambini had found the underground mine the Brothers Grimm had mentioned a few days ago. The gold mine outside Palmdale that had been modernized to accommodate the size of their small trucks. Towering chain-link fences topped with rings of barbed wire surrounded the place. A sign by the front gate warned anyone passing by that this was a hazardous-waste site. Trespassing was forbidden and dangerous to your health. Gambini had covered the entire trek from Elysian Park into the desert—the trucks passing through the gate in the fence, then entering the facility through a pair of heavy steel bay doors before they vanished underground.

Matt found the images fascinating but didn't know what to make of them. After digging through the papers to the bottom of the file, he reached a number of photocopies taken from newspapers.

Robert Gambini had figured out who they really were. He'd read the same articles Matt had pulled up on his computer. Gambini knew that

Grubb, Moore, and Sonny Daniels owned Yellow Brick Legacy Group LLC, a hedge fund on Wall Street. He'd found the Brothers Grimm.

"Would you like some more light, Detective?"

Matt nearly jumped out of his skin and looked up. It was Robert Gambini. He was standing in the shadows by the doorway holding a Glock .45 in his right hand.

FORTY-SIX

"How long have you been standing there?" Matt said.

Gambini smiled. "About five minutes," he said. "By the way, you broke into my home."

Matt stared back at him. "I just stopped by for a visit."

"I saw the surveillance teams on my way in. I'm guessing that after what happened tonight, you're not with them. You got the boot, friend. You're off the case. What may or may not have happened is none of your business anymore."

Matt didn't say anything.

"Well, which is it, Detective? Should I turn on the lights and let the LAPD know we're here? Or should I just call nine-one-one?"

"You don't want them here anymore than I do, Gambini."

"You're probably right about that."

"Why don't you put the gun down?"

Robert Gambini shook his head. "No," he said. "And while we're at it, slide yours across the floor."

Matt gave him long look. After several moments, he pulled his .45 out and slid it across the floor.

Gambini picked up the pistol and gave it a look. Then he ejected the mag and dumped the bullets onto the floor.

"You can have it back when I leave, Detective. I have no reason to keep your gun and embarrass you."

Matt watched Gambini slip the .45 into his pocket.

"What's going on with these pictures you took, Gambini?"

"Which do you mean?"

"The trucks. The fifty-five-gallon drums. The mine in the desert."

"Hazardous waste would be my guess. They're burying it underground so that we'll all be safe."

"I don't think so."

Gambini laughed. "I don't either."

Matt watched Gambini cross the room and open a closet door to reveal a freestanding safe bolted to the floor. Using his cell phone for light, Gambini dialed in the combination and swung the heavy door open. Even from a distance, Matt could see that the safe was filled with cash. As Gambini began loading a black Halliburton case with the money, Matt noticed the mustard-colored cash straps and realized that they were packets of hundred-dollar bills worth ten K each.

"You're gonna hide out?" Matt said.

"Until this blows over? Sure. Why not?"

"Blows over? You murdered Grubb tonight."

"Why would I do that?"

"You said it yourself last night. Grubb and his partners are trying to muscle in on your business."

Gambini laughed, still loading packets of cash into the Halliburton case. "I had Grubb exactly where I wanted him, Detective. I scared him off. He called you for help, right? He was ready to leave on his own. Why bother killing the fool?"

A moment passed as Gambini's way through the motive settled into the room.

Matt shook his head. "Let's get back to those fifty-five-gallon drums, Gambini. What's in them?"

Gambini turned and gave him a look. "What do you think is in them?"

"You don't know?"

"I saw you in the plant the same day they had an accident. One of the drums fell over. You were there. What spilled out?"

"That had to be staged. I didn't know it then, but I do now."

"Staged?"

Matt nodded.

"Do you know how much oxycodone is worth these days, Detective?"

Matt sat back in the chair. Although he was well aware of the answer, he wanted to hear Gambini's take on it.

"Oxycodone hit the market more than ten years ago and made forty-five million dollars for the pharmaceutical company that manufactured it. Four years later, sales reached one-point-one billion. Six years after that we're talking about three-point-one billion. You see where I'm going, Detective?"

Matt nodded. "You think those drums are filled with oxycodone."

"I haven't opened one up to see. Not yet anyway. But given the fact that these three losers—what do they call themselves, the Brothers Grimm? Given the fact that all three are preppy shitheads from Wall Street and don't want to get their hands dirty, oxycodone seems more likely than heroin. Do the math. A single eighty milligram tab is worth over fifty bucks, Detective. What's the price of a single bag of smack? Almost nothing compared to that."

Matt remembered the words Grubb had used when he overheard him arguing with Sonny Daniels. Grubb had said the same thing to him at the Red Dragon. Sonny had promised both Grubb and Ryan Moore that there wouldn't be any risks to what they were doing. No doubt about it, dealing heroin came with an automatic set of risks.

Matt looked up and watched Gambini snap the Halliburton case shut and then the safe. After locking the closet door, he stepped before Matt still seated at his desk. Matt glanced at the gun he was holding, then looked back up at Gambini's face.

"You want their product," Matt said. "That's what this is all about? You told Grubb you wanted all of it."

"I want everything, Detective. Every single drum. Every single pill. This is my market. There's no room for anybody else."

"Sonny told me they were keeping it in Palmdale."

"In a place so remote you'll never find it. Not even after looking at the photographs I took."

"What about the guys driving the trucks?"

Gambini flashed a knowing smile. "There are only two, and I know where both of them live. Besides, they're not in on it. They think they've been hauling hazardous waste."

Gambini crossed the room, then turned back from the door. "I'll leave your gun in the bushes beside the garage. If you're smart, you'll give me five minutes to get out of here. It's your call. I don't care one way or the other. I'll win, you'll lose—no matter what goes down."

Matt didn't say anything. Once Gambini disappeared down the hall, Matt gathered the photographs and returned them to the file. Then he walked over to the doorway and listened. He could hear the kitchen door open and close, the house going silent again. After a beat or two, he stepped into the kitchen and watched Gambini drop his piece into the garden, then vanish into the night.

He gave Gambini two minutes. Then he walked out of the house, retrieved his .45, and slipped into the darkness. It took almost ten minutes to work his way past the surveillance teams and back to the car. Tossing Gambini's file on the passenger seat, he cruised through the neighborhood until he reached Sunset, heading west, heading home.

He switched off the radio and listened to a hard wind breaking against the car. He thought about his partner, laid up in the hospital and probably worried that he'd never walk again. He thought about the way Lane Grubb had died.

He felt numb inside, and it worried him.

FORTY-SEVEN

Matt unlocked the front door and walked inside without switching on the lights. Dropping Gambini's photographs on the kitchen table, he snapped open the freezer, grabbed the bottle of Tito's vodka, and poured a glass over ice.

After a first sip, he felt his stomach begin to glow and stepped into the living room. Out the window he could see that the marine layer had swept by and filled in the entire basin from rim to rim. The night was pitch-black, the sky filled with stars. But his eyes were locked on a handful of buildings at the other end of the city that were tall enough to poke through the heavy blanket of fog.

On any other occasion he would have called the sight remarkable, even surreal and inspiring. But right now, it just seemed spooky.

He took another sip of vodka, thinking about what had happened tonight. All those separate horrible things. Worst of all, he'd let Gambini walk away. While it may have been true that he'd searched the house and found it empty, how could he have ever taken his mind off where he was? How could he have ever let himself become so absorbed in the photographs Gambini had taken that he didn't hear the man enter the house? Despite the darkness, how could he have not known somewhere deep inside himself that Gambini was standing in the doorway watching him?

Gun drawn, ten feet away—for five minutes.

How could he call himself a detective?

And if the truth be known, if he hadn't left Lane Grubb alone at the Red Dragon, the man probably would have still died from an overdose. But at least it would have been by his own hand and not Gambini shoving four more hot loads up his arm in a hideous act of murder.

If the truth be known . . .

He turned away from the window. Bypassing his reading chair and even the couch, he headed for the bedroom. And that's when he began to sense that someone else was in the house. It hit him before he even started down the hall.

He stopped and listened.

He could smell her.

The scent of her skin and hair wafting through the air.

He stepped over to the doorway and gazed into the dark room. He could see her lying on his bed. He looked at her back and hips. Her long legs spread across his comforter.

Val Burton was laid out on his bed wearing a white blouse and tight jeans. And she was turning over, leaning on her elbow and measuring him from head to toe with an amused smile on her face.

"It's actually not the way it looks, Matthew."

He nodded. "Okay," he said. "How's it look?"

"Like I came over to seduce you. Like I want to have sex with you behind my husband's back."

She seemed so straightforward about it. Matt tried to shut down his senses. Crossing the room, he sat on the arm of the chair by the window.

"Is that what you want?" he said. "Is that why you're here?"

She laughed. "Good heavens, no. You're working with my husband, and I'm a happily married woman. I love Mitch, and I always will."

"How did you get in?"

She laughed again. "I found a spare key in the old shoe by your front door. Where did you think that one up?"

He smiled at her. He couldn't help it.

"What are you drinking?" she asked.

"Vodka."

"May I have a sip?"

Matt passed over the glass. As she took a sip, her wide-open eyes never left his face. After a second sip she passed the glass back. He glanced at her body wrapped in those tight jeans. She seemed so overwhelmingly beautiful in the dim light.

"You like looking at me, don't you," she whispered.

A moment passed, and then another.

"Why are you really here?" he said finally.

She appeared to need time to think it over. But after a short while, she sat up and moved to the end of the bed, her eyes dancing all over his face.

"On the news tonight, they said you were kicked off the case."

Matt shrugged. "That's just the party line."

"I know," she said. "Mitch told me what happened."

"Then what made you come over?"

"He couldn't reach you on the phone. He got worried. He's got an early meeting with the DA tomorrow and got tied up. I told him I'd drive over."

"So he knows you're here?"

She met his eyes and nodded. "Of course," she said. "But I've been here for quite a while. I thought you'd come straight home after you and Mitch left the chief's office. I started to get tired and needed to lie down for a few minutes. I'm sorry for the way it looked when you walked in."

He could see the concern on her face. It seemed genuine.

"What is it?" he said. "What's wrong, Val?"

Her blue-gray eyes glistened in the darkness, and she lowered her voice. "Mitch thinks you're in danger."

He gave her a long look without saying anything. Then he set down the glass, got off the chair, and sat beside her on the end of the bed.

"Did he say anything else?"

She reached for the glass and took another sip. "He thinks you're being set up."

"For what?"

"He's not sure. He just said that cops don't work alone. They always have somebody backing them up. He said that what they're doing isn't right.

Mitch thinks that the chief might be in on it. That tonight the chief made you think he was giving you a break. But that's not what it is at all. Tonight, he threw you into the wind."

Matt shook his head as he chewed it over. "Why didn't Mitch say something to me when we left?"

"He didn't say anything to me either. He knew how much it would upset me. He just told me that you weren't really thrown off the case."

"Then where is all this other stuff coming from?"

"He called a defense attorney on your behalf. He wanted his advice."

"Who?"

"Buddy Paladino. Have you ever heard of him?"

Matt nodded but didn't respond. He'd heard plenty of things about Buddy Paladino. Paladino was the best defense attorney in Los Angeles. He was the attorney you called when you were hurdling through the air toward the proverbial wall. The attorney you called when it looked like you might run out of tomorrows.

Matt's mind surfaced as he felt Val's arms wrapping around his shoulders and pulling him closer in the darkness. When he turned, he found her staring out the window at those eerie tall buildings poking out of the fog at the other end of the city. Her voice was still low, still not much more than a whisper.

"Before tonight I would have said you needed a woman, Matthew. Someone to be with. Someone to share your life with. But now, after all this, Mitch is probably right. You need an attorney."

FORTY-EIGHT

Matt walked past the front desk, down the hall, and around the corner into Burton's office. It was 7:25 a.m.—early morning after a hideous day and a brutal night's sleep. As Matt entered, Burton looked up from his desk and appeared relieved to see him.

"I've got a meeting with the DA in five minutes that I can't get out of," Burton said. "Walk with me."

Matt nodded, relieved himself that Val Burton's warning had been at the direction of her husband. That beyond the playful banter and whatever troublesome thoughts he may have entertained, Val's intentions last night had been genuine and righteous. He watched the prosecutor collect his files and grab a coffee cup and then followed him out the door. When they reached the hallway, Burton checked his back before speaking in a voice that wouldn't carry.

"Where were you last night? I called and you never picked up. When Val got there, she said she had to wait a couple of hours."

Matt met Burton's gaze. "Gambini's," he said. "We spoke. I was in his house and had my phone turned off."

"And?"

"He had a gun. He came back for the cash he keeps in a safe."

They stepped around the corner and passed two prosecutors who didn't even seem to notice them. Still, Matt waited until they were out of earshot before leaning closer to Burton and lowering his voice.

"The Brothers Grimm are storing oxycodone in a facility somewhere outside of Palmdale. Gambini wants it. He wants all of it. The hazardous waste business in Elysian Park is just a front for what's in those fifty-five-gallon drums. Grubb's dead. That leaves Ryan Moore and Sonny Daniels."

They reached the DA's office. Burton stopped and gave Matt a worried look.

"That's good work, but it's not my concern right now. You've got a problem, Matt. Something's going on that shouldn't be going on."

Matt didn't say anything. He watched Burton check the hallway again and turn back, his voice sounding anxious.

"Paladino agrees with me. Something's going on that's not natural. Colon's personal attacks toward you are too high pitched to be directed at someone she never had contact with. Your interview in the interrogation room last night was laughable, if not illegal. They never read you your rights. And who knows how the chief really fits into all this? You're off the case, but then you're back on—only it's our little secret. You see what I mean? Things don't work that way when it's clean."

Matt could feel his heart pounding in his chest. "How do you want to handle this?" he said. "What's your best advice?"

Burton pulled a business card out of his pocket and passed it over. Matt glanced at the name printed on the face. It was Buddy Paladino's law firm, along with contact information that included Paladino's cell number written in ink.

"This is who you call if you're in trouble," Burton said. "And don't wait on it. If something happens, call Paladino right away. You'll be in good hands. He's the best defense attorney in the business."

"And until something happens?"

"That's been the problem with this case from the beginning, hasn't it? Everyone on the list seems to be bought and paid for. Everybody wants something. As far as I can tell, they're all suspects at one level or another." Burton checked his watch. "I'm late. I've gotta go. We'll talk later."

"Any other advice?"

Burton turned back, thinking it through as he spoke. "Pick your moments, Matt. Don't let them pick you."

Matt watched Burton walk into the DA's office and disappear through the waiting room. As he stood there, his new reality weighing down his back, the self-doubt that he'd been wrestling with last night began to prey on him again. People were walking up and down the hall, glancing at him in a way that he wasn't used to. Like just maybe they'd been watching the news last night or even early this morning. Like just maybe they knew what Colon had accused him of. Like just maybe they bought into the vile woman's bogus trip.

LAPD detective Matt Jones fell asleep at the wheel, and now an innocent man was dead.

The anger percolating through his body felt particularly raw. He grimaced and tried to shake off the bad vibes. All the lies. Hustling over to the elevator, he got out of the building as quickly as he could and made it to his car in the lot on First Street. The coffee he'd filled his mug with at home still felt warm, and he took a sip. Pulling his cell phone out of his pocket, he found David Speeks's number over at the crime lab and hit "Enter." Speeks picked up after two rings.

"If you're calling about lifting prints from inside the nitrile gloves, we're still working on it, Jones."

Matt set the mug down in the cup holder. "How long do you think it's gonna take?"

"No predictions."

"Anything else going on?"

"Now that you mention it, something curious came up this morning."

"Like what, Speeks?"

"It's the cash we found at Moe Rey's house."

"The hundred-dollar bills."

"That's right," Speeks said. "I don't know if it means anything, but every one of them came from the same bank."

"Where?"

"That's what got me going. The cash came from offshore. It came from a bank in Bermuda."

It meant something—and Matt let the news settle in as he sat back in his seat. Bermuda was a tax haven for Big Pharma. Many of the most well-known drug companies—the same companies advertising on American television everyday—were headquartered there to avoid paying taxes in the States. But what mattered most was that one of those companies had made their mark in the production of a single drug.

Oxycodone.

Moe Rey's brutal execution now seemed to be tied directly to the Brothers Grimm and their turf war with Robert Gambini.

"Are you still there, Jones?"

Matt heard Speeks's voice and snapped out of it.

"I'm here, Speeks, thanks. Have you heard anything about Grubb's autopsy?"

"If it's an overdose, you know better than me how long it takes to get the results back. Two weeks, if we're lucky."

"Right," Matt said. "But they would've checked out the tracks on his arm and been able to make a good guess. Is the autopsy over?"

"They're releasing the body in an hour or two."

Matt started the car. "Grubb lost his wife, Speeks. I don't think he has any family. Who's picking up the body?"

"You got me. Besides, you're off the case, Jones. I shouldn't even be talking to you."

"Maybe not, but you owe me. You left Moe Rey's body in the ground."

"I know I owe you."

Matt pulled out of the lot and into the street. "When you lift those fingerprints off the gloves, I'm your first call, right?"

Speeks paused to think it over. "Maybe," he said finally.

"No maybes, Speeks. I'm your first call."

FORTY-NINE

Matt worked his way through downtown traffic, heading east for the county coroner's office. He wanted to know who was going to take charge of Lane Grubb's corpse. And he wanted to see them do it.

He crossed a narrow stream of water, what remained of the Los Angeles River, and made a left on North Mission Road. The land was desolate and burned out here—a real long way from all the money that was being poured into downtown or even the Valley. Out the windows on either side, he could see empty lots of sand, trash, and piles of contaminated soil. As he began passing one auto wrecking company after the next, he realized that there wasn't a single object, a single sign or surface, that hadn't been tagged with spray paint. If Los Angeles had an anus, this section of the city had to be it. Everything about the place reeked of being at the end of the line.

He spotted the gas station ahead on the left and then the Jack in the Box fast-food restaurant. The coroner's office was directly across the street surrounded by a white wall and fencing.

Matt pulled before the security gate, showed the guard his badge, and cruised to the far end of the lot. There was an open parking space here with a bird's-eye view of the facility. From here he could see a black hearse backed up to the loading dock. A handful of emergency vehicles were parked along the curb. But it was in the lot by the building's entrance that he found what he had been hoping for.

Ryan Moore's BMW i8 and Sonny Daniels's Aston Martin DB11. They were parked in two spots reserved for the handicapped by the front door. Daniels and Moore were here in all their rudeness.

Matt lowered his seat, checked his watch, and settled in. He spent the first twenty minutes trying not to think about the jeopardy he might be in and the downward slide his career seemed to have taken. But even more, he tried to forget the looks he'd seen on people's faces as they passed him in the hallway outside the DA's office. The power Colon seemed to have to bury, if not ruin, anyone who didn't sign on and become a willing partner to her corruption. Her brand of lies, ignorance, and evil.

His efforts to shed these thoughts only seemed to bring them into sharper focus. It occurred to him that he might run across the street to the Jack in the Box for a fresh cup of coffee and maybe even an early burger. But after checking the time on the dash, he saw the rear doors on the loading dock open and bolted up in his seat.

A temporary casket, the aluminum battered by time and heavy use, was being wheeled outside on a dolly by two men in scrubs. Daniels and Moore followed them out, watching the driver from the funeral home fumble with his keys before raising the hearse's rear gate. As Matt measured the two remaining Brothers Grimm from a distance, he wouldn't have called either one of them grieving. Instead, they appeared uncomfortable, even nervous. And they kept fidgeting and looking over their shoulders.

Matt wondered if they were keeping an eye out for Robert Gambini. Maybe it was the sight of the battered casket that spooked them. Maybe they thought that with Gambini still out there, they might be next.

What were the promises Sonny Daniels had made to his two partners less than a week ago? How did he put it? There were no risks to what they were doing. The whole thing was a game. They were all supposed to make money and have a good time.

Easy Street.

Matt watched the two men in scrubs roll the casket off the dock and into the hearse. When the driver lowered the gate, Daniels and Moore led the way back into the building and the doors closed.

Matt turned to the front entrance. After about five minutes the doors opened, and Daniels and Moore stepped out. Then, remarkably, he spotted Councilwoman Colon walking toward them with a group of supporters and three or four TV news cameras. Colon reached out to shake Sonny Daniels's hand.

And that's when it happened. Daniels looked across the lot and straight through Matt's windshield.

A nervous moment passed.

Matt watched Colon follow Sonny's gaze, the sympathetic look on her face morphing into a twisted mire of hate as her eyes drove through the glass and locked onto his face.

"What are you doing here?"

Matt could hear her voice even with the windows closed and the engine running. Colon wasn't shouting. It was more of a screech or scream as she played to the cameras and feigned outrage.

"What is this man doing here?" she repeated. "Why are you here? Are you planning to attend the funeral, Detective? A funeral for the man you killed?"

Matt watched Sonny Daniels step in beside Colon. The crowd was moving toward him quickly. Backing out of the parking space, he tried to reach the exit but ran out of time. Fifteen, maybe twenty of Colon's supporters were pounding their fists against the windows and the hood of his car.

"You're out of control," Colon was saying. "You're a disgrace. I got you kicked off the case, and now I'm gonna get you booted off the force. Do you understand me, Detective? I cannot tolerate you. I will not tolerate you."

Matt grit his teeth, idling through the crowd. When a man with a video camera stepped in front of the car, Matt didn't go for the brakes but continued forward. He heard the man let out a scream, then watched him leap to safety with the camera flying off his shoulder and hitting the asphalt.

Colon pounded her fist against the driver's side window again. Matt turned and looked at her shrieking at him. Their eyes met, and he held the glance because he wanted to remember the moment. He'd seen it before, but never so clearly. He could see what hate does to the human face. He could see the transformation.

The deformity.

"I'm gonna destroy you because I can," she was saying. "Take that to the bank, Detective. The people's bank. This is my town and my city. You better believe it, honey. Don't mess with me or my business."

Matt remained calm, reaching the gate finally and pulling onto North Mission Road. He never checked the rearview mirror. Instead, he let the sound of the rabble fade out as the din from the street took over and reset the tone. On the other side of the wrecked landscape, just a few miles beyond the desolation, he could see the tall buildings downtown rising into the clear blue sky and glistening in the bright sunlight.

He knew there would be trouble. He knew Colon could make something out of nothing and wondered if he should turn off his phone.

FIFTY

Colon didn't eat as much as she fed.

Matt had followed her limo to the Sunset Cantina, a cafeteria-style restaurant south of Hollywood on Western Avenue. The city councilwoman was with a small group whom Matt guessed were local business owners from her district. As Matt watched her from his car, he noted that she liked to eat, talk while she chewed, and point. But what struck him most were the faces of the people she was seated with. They were listening and nodding the way troops listen and nod when receiving orders from their commanding officer. By all appearances, when it came to Colon, she didn't work for them as their representative. They worked for her and did as they were told.

Matt was just grateful he was watching all of this on an empty stomach.

His cell phone pulsed and then stopped. He pulled it out of the cup holder and checked the face. He had forty-three unread text messages and nineteen voice messages that he hadn't listened to. Returning the phone to the cup holder, he turned up the heat and tried to settle down.

His plan for the night was vague. He wanted to spend the early hours keeping an eye on Colon. Later, when things quieted down, he wanted to drive back to the medical center and see how Cabrera was doing.

He glanced at the clock on his dash—10:03 p.m.—then back across the street. Colon had just exited the restaurant and was marching down the steps to her limousine. Apparently, her bodyguard was the designated driver tonight, and her go-go boy, the mayor of Los Angeles, had decided to stay home.

Matt watched the limo drive off, heading for Sunset. He waited for a car to pass, then pulled away from the curb. After a few minutes, he realized that the limo was heading for the Hollywood Freeway. Following them down the ramp, he didn't become concerned until they exited onto the 110 Freeway, and then again onto Solano Avenue. It seemed obvious that Colon was planning to visit Sophia Ramirez's family. And at this late hour, the reason for her visit couldn't be good.

He watched the limo circle the block from a distance. When it turned up Casanova Street, he spotted the news van parked outside the Ramirez's home, switched off his headlights, and pulled to the curb.

He waited a few minutes until Colon and her bodyguard were ushered into the house. His stomach was going, the feeling of impending doom back again at full strength. Slipping out of the car, he crossed the street and hurried through the gate into the park. Bushes five feet high bordered a low chain-link fence, and he moved quickly up the lawn. When he reached Sophia's house, he knelt down and parted the branches.

His view was up close and personal. He could see the camera operator and sound technician preparing to shoot a scene in the Ramirez's living room. Colon was seated on the couch between Sophia's mother and father. A producer was talking to them with a female reporter standing beside him reading her notes.

Matt checked his watch. At 11:00 p.m., the camera lights went hot, the producer stepped aside, and the reporter took her seat in front of the couch. They were up, and it didn't take much for Matt to realize that the broadcast was live.

He sat down on the grass—his eyes wide open. Although he couldn't hear what they were saying, he had a good idea of the gist. Just as she had controlled the conversation at the Sunset Cantina, Colon was doing all the talking while pointing her finger at just about everybody in the room.

Sophia's mother, Lucia Ramirez, had begun weeping the minute the lights went hot and the reporter held out her mike. Sophia's father, Angel, listened to Colon with his eyes narrowed and kept nodding in agreement.

No doubt about it. Colon was taking Matt down just as she promised.

Matt hustled down the row of bushes, through the gate, and climbed back into his car. He could see the bright camera lights casting shadows onto the Ramirez's front lawn and across the street. He waited in the darkness, his stomach churning. After a few minutes, the camera lights shut down. Five minutes after that, Colon was marching across the lawn to her limo with her bodyguard-turned-driver in tow.

Matt lowered his head until the limo passed, then turned his car around and began to follow a safe distance behind. He guessed that Colon's bodyguard wasn't paying much attention, but he let another car fall in between them just in case. Matt's first thought was that they were making a return trip to Hollywood, but they passed the entrance to the freeway and continued south until they reached the Santa Monica Freeway.

Maybe Colon had done enough damage and was on her way home for the night.

The limo exited onto Western Avenue, then snaked its way through the neighborhoods on surface streets. When they reached South Gramercy Place, the limo turned up the drive before a Spanish-style house in the middle of the block. Matt shut down his headlights and pulled over. He could see an electronic gate opening. Once the limo vanished behind the wall, the gate closed, and the houselights came on.

Matt looked up and down the street. It was a quiet neighborhood of large homes—some, he guessed, might even be called grand. Each home was different than the next, and all were set six to ten feet above street level, with steps leading up from the sidewalks. Palm trees towered above, lining both sides of the street. Even at a glance, Matt could tell that a city councilwoman who had crossed the border as a child with nothing more than what she was wearing couldn't afford to live in a neighborhood like this one. The price of Colon's house couldn't be bought and paid for on her salary.

Matt glanced at the clock on the dash and decided to hang out until the bodyguard left. As he waited, memories of what had happened over the past few days began to surface. Looking back at the house, the city councilwoman's corruption seemed so over the top and so out in the open—he had to admit that in a certain way he was fascinated by her. He settled back in the seat. He wasn't sure if it was a fascination with evil or just the shock that people like Colon exist in the world and that so many of them seem to get away with it. As he thought it through, the idea that somehow their past would catch up with them almost seemed too naive to say aloud.

Of course, Matt realized that this was exactly the same dilemma his uncle, Dr. Baylor, had wrestled with before he went insane and became a serial killer. The former plastic surgeon had obviously concluded that if he couldn't rely on karma to rid the world of this blight—if he lived in a place where someone's past atrocities were never going to come to light—then it was his duty to weed the garden on his own.

Matt started to count the number of murders his uncle had committed in order to, as the doctor put it, make the world a better place, but stopped himself. The idea that he had covered the same ground and arrived at the same place as his uncle sent a chill up his spine.

He tried to let the thought go. He didn't want to kill Colon. It hadn't even entered his mind.

He glanced out the window, wishing he had a cigarette. He could hear police sirens in the distance, along with the sirens from an emergency vehicle and a fire truck.

He turned back to Colon's house and noticed a set of headlights switch on near the garage on the other side of the wall. The electronic gate opened, and a Honda Accord started to amble down the drive. Matt watched the car pull into the street and head off in the opposite direction. The bodyguard-turned-designated-driver didn't seem like he was in too much of a hurry tonight.

Matt kept his eyes on the taillights. Once they vanished around the corner, he turned back to the house and started the car. He was about to pull away from the curb when the sound of the sirens and a sea of flashing lights engulfed the entire neighborhood. Matt sat back in the seat and saw first responders running toward Colon's house. Someone slammed their fist into the driver's side window and shouted at him. He turned, startled, and found Jack Raines glaring at him through the glass.

"What are you doing here, Jones?"

Matt jumped out of the car. "What is it? What's wrong?"

Raines started running toward Colon's house with his partner, Billy Hudson. Matt chased after them, watching a crew of cops pounding on the front door. When no one answered, one of the heavier men kicked the door down.

And then they were in. Running through the house, shouting, and clearing rooms until they'd worked their way to the family room off the kitchen.

That's when everyone stopped. That's when Matt felt the Grim Reaper touch him between his shoulder blades.

They were dead. Murdered and left in a way that seemed particularly gruesome.

The bodyguard was lying on the floor with his eyes open and his tongue hanging out of his mouth. Blood was draining from the hole in his forehead and pooling on the tiled floor. The city councilwoman had been laid out on her back. Her eyes were jutting out of their sockets, her neck heavily bruised and obviously broken. When Matt took a step closer and knelt down, he could see that the back of her head had been crushed in and that she had died the same hideous death as Sophia Ramirez.

"What are you doing here, Jones?"

Matt looked up and saw Raines still glaring at him.

FIFTY-ONE

They wouldn't let him leave. His keys had been taken away from him, along with his badge and gun. For the second time in as many nights, Matt was sitting in the backseat of a patrol unit with its LED light bar flashing.

Only this time he could feel the dread.

A crew from the Forensic Science Division had been there for two hours. The investigator from the coroner's office had arrived an hour and a half ago with two assistants and the meat wagon. A handful of cops in uniforms had canvassed the street, talking to neighbors and rushing back to Colon's house to turn in their field interview cards.

He could feel the dread all right.

Despite the late hour, most of Colon's neighbors were standing outside watching the investigation and flashing hard and guilty looks at Matt sitting in the cruiser. Although the street had been sealed off, news that a member of the city council had just been murdered tended to attract media attention quickly. And now, every TV station in the city, every newspaper and blog, was camped out on the corner. The glare from their camera lights was impossible to escape—the neighborhood so bright that it could have been high noon.

Matt tried to keep his head turned away but wasn't sure that it would help. Even from this distance, every camera on every tripod could reach out with their long lenses and get their close-up.

Matt couldn't seem to settle down—his heart was pounding in his chest, his mind sprinting ahead of itself.

He kept thinking about what Val had told him. The warning both she and Burton had delivered.

You're being set up. Something's going on that shouldn't be going on. It's not natural. Everybody on the list is bought and paid for. When Raines and Hudson interviewed you in the interrogation room it was laughable, if not illegal. And what's with the chief? You're off the case, but then you're back on—only it's our little secret. Things don't work that way, Matt.

Not unless you're being set up.

The car doors snapped open, and Matt flinched. He watched Raines take the seat beside him, then Billy Hudson climbed in behind the wheel. Raines tossed a large manila envelope on the floor and started leafing through the pages on his clipboard.

"Doesn't look good," Raines said in a big voice. "Doesn't look good, Detective."

He turned and gazed at Matt for a long time. "There's a brand-new Escalade parked beside Colon's limo. It still has that 'new car' smell. The vehicle's registered to the bodyguard. You see the size of that guy, Jones? The man didn't drive a Honda."

Matt looked away. "I just told you what I saw, Raines."

Raines poked him in the chest with a finger. "The trouble is, Jones, no one in the neighborhood saw a Honda. They saw you. They saw your car but no Honda. This is a murder case. If you're gonna make things up, you gotta do better than that."

Matt shook his head. "I'm not making anything up."

Hudson laughed from the front seat. "Come on, Jones. You had every reason in the world to kill that stupid bitch."

Matt glanced at Hudson, then back at Raines. "From what I could tell, you could fill the Rose Bowl with the number of people who wanted Colon dead."

"Yeah," Raines said. "But none of them were following her around tonight, and you were. We've got witnesses who saw you in your car outside the Sunset Cantina. Two neighbors say you ran into Elysian Park outside the Ramirez's house. They said you were hiding in the bushes, Jones."

"And what if I was?"

"Why didn't you answer your phone all night? Why didn't you reply to a single text message?"

Matt turned and met Raines's gaze. "Maybe I didn't feel like it."

Raines laughed. "Didn't feel like it, Jones? I think you killed the bitch. I think you'd had enough of her bullshit. After what she did to you today, anybody would've had enough of her bullshit. I think you were trying to make it look exactly the way that girl died. The bodyguard gets a bullet to the head just like Moe Rey did. Colon gets strangled and beaten to death just like Sophia Ramirez. Too bad you didn't have time to throw them in a hole somewhere and let the neighborhood dog sniff them out."

Hudson leaned closer and whispered. "Sort of your warped signature kind of thing, right, Jones? Detective School 101? Connect the two double murders and we're so stupid, we draw a line from dot to dot and you're free and clear."

Raines shook his head. "It'd be easier if you just said you did it, Jones. The coroner's investigator examined Colon's body. She's got a broken neck, a broken face, and half her skull fell out of her head. He called the murder personal. He called the killer angry. You hear that—just like you."

"I'm not angry, Raines. I was just sitting out here enjoying the fresh air and waiting for the moon to rise."

"Yeah, sure, Jones. Sitting here playing with yourself. Let's face it—with your uncle and all—it's in your blood, man. You killed the bitch. It doesn't matter that she deserved it or even that the world's a better place now. Sooner or later you're going down for it."

Matt's mind cleared suddenly. "What do you mean, sooner or later?"

Raines looked back at him and shrugged.

Matt grimaced. "You don't have enough to hold me, do you?"

Raines lowered his head and appeared to be chewing it over. "Not yet," he said in a quieter voice.

"I want my things back. I want everything back."

Raines looked like he was in pain as he passed over the large manila envelope. Matt ripped it open and dug out his badge, his keys, and gun.

"You know what, Raines?"

"What, Detective?"

"There's no physical evidence in that house because I never went inside until you guys got here."

"That's your side of the story, Jones."

Matt opened the door, got out of the cruiser, then turned back and looked inside.

"Did it ever occur to either one of you guys that Gambini wanted me out of the way just as much as he wanted Colon dead? Tonight, he got both."

Raines shook his head but didn't say anything.

"By the way, Raines, I carry a forty-five. The hole in the bodyguard's head was made by a twenty-two."

Raines nodded. "The same caliber as the gun the bodyguard was licensed to carry. And it was fired tonight. Nice touch, Jones, killing a guy with his own goddamn gun."

Matt turned away and walked off. Glancing at the media people on the corner, he got into his car and lit up the engine. The other end of the street looked clean—just a handful of cruisers and a couple of barricades. Matt decided that he'd take the clean way out and drove to the other end of the block. When he made the turn at the corner, he noticed that his fingers were trembling. He could barely hold on to the steering wheel.

FIFTY-TWO

Visiting Cabrera at the hospital would have to wait for another day—if there was another day. Matt headed home, well aware that he was being followed. When he looked at the rearview mirror, he could see three patrol units right behind him.

He tried to ignore them but had to admit that with Gambini missing, he wasn't really sure what to do. The feeling that there was something wrong with the case seemed so overwhelmingly out in the open now. With every curve in the road, with every turn, he checked the rearview mirror and the patrol units were still there. Again and again—all the way home.

Chasing the wrong man. Everything upside down.

Matt looked ahead to his house and saw two black-and-white cruisers parked in front of his lawn. As he pulled into the carport, the cops were staring at him from inside their cars. He could see them talking on their cell phones. The expressions on their faces were blank, mean—no need for a trial to decide who's guilty this time around.

We just know it's him.

Matt unlocked the front door and stepped into the living room without turning on the lights. Lowering the venetian blinds, he peered through the slats and watched the three patrol units that had been following him park in the shadows underneath the oak trees on the other side of the street. Even more disconcerting, two cops got out of their cars and started walking around the side of the house.

Matt stepped into the kitchen, carefully avoiding the LED lights from the clock on the stove. Through the window he could see the two cops moving to the base of the deck and examining the steps and sliding door. One of them was whispering into his cell phone.

His home had become a prison, and he needed to break out.

He stepped into the hallway, closing the kitchen and bedroom doors to mask the light from his cell phone. Thumbing through his speed dial list, he found Burton's number, and hit "Enter." After two rings, the prosecutor picked up and, despite the late hour, didn't sound tired.

"Are you okay, Matt?"

"I need to get out of here."

"I'll open the gate."

"I'm being followed."

"I expect you are," Burton said. "But unless they've got paperwork, they'll have to wait outside."

Matt slipped the phone into his pocket, opened the kitchen door, and fished through his laptop case for his meds. Popping three pills into his mouth, he downed them with bottled water and glanced out the window. The two cops who had walked around to the back of the house had multiplied by three. Now there were six of them out there keeping watch in the darkness.

It was an eerie feeling. Matt being a cop, a homicide detective—and here he was watching himself check the mag on his .45 and slip three more into his pocket like a lowlife readying for a shoot-out.

He took another deep breath and exhaled. If he was doing what he had to do, why was he sweating?

He holstered his pistol, walked through the living room, and switched on the outdoor lights. Then, fighting off the shakes, he walked outside to his car and backed out of the carport. As he started up the block, he could see the six cops sprinting around the house to their patrol units. After a few minutes, he checked the rearview mirror and saw that all five cars were in line and openly following him.

It took half an hour to reach Burton's place on Mulholland Drive. Matt pulled through the gate, ignoring his entourage and arming his car alarm. Then he climbed the steps two at a time and found Burton waiting for him by the open front door. They nodded at each other while Burton locked the door behind them. When they entered his study, Val was already here, sitting in a chair by the desk. Matt noted the TV mounted on the wall as he crossed the room—the picture was on with the sound off. It looked as if the news had been reduced to a single story tonight. City councilwoman Dee Colon had managed to get Detective Matt Jones thrown off a homicide case and ended up savagely murdered.

Like Hudson said, connect the dots. One plus one equals twenty to life, or better yet, the needle.

Burton pointed to the chair beside Val, and Matt sat down.

"Don't say anything to me, Matt. Not one word, okay? I'm a prosecutor. An officer of the court. Anything you say to me could be used against you, and you know it. They'd force me to testify, and I'd have to do it."

Matt wiped the beads of sweat off his forehead as he glanced at Val, then back at Burton. He was trapped, and he knew it. He was nervous.

Burton leaned against the window. "Your arrest is imminent. It's one thirty. I expect they'll be ready by seven. It's time to call an attorney. It's time to call Paladino."

Matt shook his head back and forth, deep inside himself. "It's no good," he said. "Not now. Not yet."

Burton sat down on the corner of his desk and appeared more than concerned. "Listen to me, Matt. Listen to me. It's time to make arrangements with the police for your surrender."

"Not yet," Matt said. "Not tonight. Not until I can explain all this."

Burton glanced at his wife—worried—then turned back. "Do you want me to turn up the sound on the TV? Do you want to hear what they're saying about you? Dee Colon was on the city council, Matt. They're not calling it a murder. They're calling it an assassination. Do you understand the danger you're in? Any cop on the street could shoot you."

Matt didn't say anything. He just wanted to get out of there and bolt. He could remember being ambushed and shot at in Afghanistan—

completely outnumbered by the Taliban. He could remember his unit running away from the firefight and not knowing what was safe and what wasn't until they got there.

Where was the *there*? Where was it tonight?

Burton leaned closer. "I can call Paladino myself. He'll make the calls on your behalf. He'll make sure that your surrender is done safely and bring you in himself."

Matt stood up. "I've gotta go."

Val shook her head. "Please, Matthew. Don't do this."

"I've gotta go," he repeated.

His body had gone numb. He'd lost his focus. His ability to think. He needed to get out of here and run until he was there. Until he was safe.

FIFTY-THREE

The entourage was back in place as Matt left Burton's house, leading the way east on Mulholland Drive. As they ambled up the street through the twists and turns in the hills high above the city, Matt had a chance to settle down.

He knew that he was missing something. That the key was right in front of him, but he couldn't see it.

It occurred to him that in a murder case, the way things look are often more important than the way they really are. Most people, including cops, don't pay attention and become victimized by their first impressions. If they start believing something, and they're given enough time to believe it, what was real and true can slip away with the chance of never being recovered.

And that was the problem. Like so many innocent people who were found guilty and sent to prison, it could take ten years or even a lifetime before anyone decided there was a problem and sorted this case out.

Matt let the idea fade. The nightmare.

What mattered was that Colon and her bodyguard were dead and done and now irrevocably linked to the murders of Moe Rey and Sophia Ramirez. Raines and Hudson had said it themselves. The two double murders were identical. The problem was that neither detective saw or understood the significance of their own words. Instead, they assumed Matt had a reason for killing Colon and was using the first double murder to cover the second.

Why were they forgetting about Robert Gambini? Why couldn't they see that he was reducing the number of players and killing off the field in order to take everything for himself? And if Gambini really wanted it all, why did he take off? Where was he hiding out?

Matt wanted a look at the oxycodone Sonny Daniels and his remaining partner were moving in those fifty-five-gallon drums. He wanted to open one up and see for himself.

He checked his rearview mirror and stared at the cops following him in the night. He needed to lose these guys but thought his best chance would be on the other side of the Hollywood Reservoir. The roads were narrow there, with sharp bends that snaked through the entire canyon on both sides of the mountain. The cops would probably assume that Matt was looking for a way out of the hills. Beachwood Drive would make the most sense to them because of its proximity to three freeway entrances. But what if he lost them just long enough to cut back and head for the Valley? What if he could get them to chase his ghost into Hollywood while he slipped through Burbank and headed back to the DMG facility in Elysian Park?

He tossed it over. At least on the surface, it seemed doable.

The downside, of course, was that Matt knew he wouldn't just *look* guilty anymore. He'd be making a run for it. He'd be underlining their belief that he really was guilty.

He passed over the Hollywood Freeway and started up the hill toward the reservoir, still mulling it over.

It was doable, he told himself. It might be grim, but it was doable.

We watched the road straighten out before him. Passing a string of homes, he glided around the bend and down a short incline to the reservoir. As he followed the road around the water and then up another ridge, he increased his speed slightly and started looking for the right moment, the right place. Another string of homes whizzed by. Then the bends sharpened as he entered Hollywood Hills and began his steep descent into Beachwood Canyon.

Matt gave the rearview mirror another look as he pushed air in and out of his lungs and wiped the sweat off his hands. The patrol units weren't close enough to keep him in view as the road began to zigzag. For ten, maybe twenty seconds, he was in the clear. Invisible.

He saw the next bend, hit the gas, and then he hit it harder.

When he spotted Ledgewood Drive, he made a hard right, pulled into the first driveway, and killed the headlights.

He turned, eyeballing the street and waiting with his teeth clenched. After several seconds, the five patrol units sped by with their lights flashing. Matt knew that he only had a short time before they realized what he had done and doubled back. Jamming the car into reverse, he pulled onto the road and gunned the engine until he was back on top of the ridge.

There was another road there. A smaller road that looked like it led up the mountain and toward the Valley. Matt made a hard right, his tires screeching, and barreled forward. The road curved to the left and then to the right. Gazing into the sky, he didn't see a chopper but guessed they would have been called in by now and were probably less than fifteen minutes away. It seemed like he might have a chance if he didn't run out of time. But then he hit a straight patch in the road, looked over his shoulder, and saw the flashing lights. Two of the five cruisers were behind him, closing fast.

Matt floored it around another bend and realized that he'd reached Mount Lee Drive. The road ran all the way up the mountain to the Hollywood Sign but was a dead end. Out of options, he accelerated up the mountain until he heard a loud bang and felt the car lurch forward. Checking his mirrors, he realized that the first patrol unit had slammed into his bumper, the cop signaling him to pull over.

Matt grit his teeth, the fear washed away by rage. Rocketing forward, he saw the Hollywood Sign getting bigger, and still bigger.

And then he caught a glimpse of it. A possible exit. A possible way out.

With his headlights switched off, he couldn't tell if it was a hiking trail or a fire road carved out of the dirt. In the end, he decided that it didn't really matter. He spun the car to the right and gunned the engine. The way was narrow, the edge horrifically steep. He could hear the tires digging up sand

and stones—the debris beating against the underside of the car and leaving a thick cloud of dust in his wake.

He felt another hard hit and swerved to stay on the dirt path. Looking over his shoulder, the first patrol unit had smashed into his car again. He couldn't believe that the cop—the stupid goddamn cop—was intentionally trying to bulldoze him off the cliff.

Matt screamed out loud and hit the gas, still eyeballing the patrol unit. The cop had just slammed into the side of the mountain, skidded forward, and bounced onto the dirt path behind him.

Matt turned back and spotted a fork on the trail, the lights from the Griffith Observatory at the bottom on the mountain. While he couldn't be certain, it looked like bearing right might lead down to the parking lot.

A moment passed as the grade steepened and the earth seemed to tilt downward. Giving the rearview mirror a nervous check, he noticed that both patrol units had pulled to a stop and were backing up. It didn't make sense until he felt the car pitch forward. He looked ahead and saw that he was on a dirt fire road that had been heavily eroded by the last rainstorm. The surface was deeply cratered with long crevices running along the edge.

He tightened his grip on the wheel and tried to slow down. The car was hurdling forward, the steering column vibrating between his knees. He could feel the tires skipping up and off the ground. There was a loud banging sound, and then he crashed through the branches of a fallen tree.

For several seconds he thought he might be airborne. Everything went black, and his stomach vaulted into his throat. When the windshield cleared, he watched the car hop the curb and slammed his foot on the brake pedal.

The car skidded fifty feet across the observatory's empty parking lot. Matt lowered his head and closed his eyes. He was hyperventilating, and the world seemed to be spinning round and round. When everything finally began to slow down, he climbed out of the car on shaky legs and gazed up into the hills. He could see the flashing lights just to the right of the Hollywood Sign at the very top of the mountain. All five patrol units were up there.

His body shivered in the cold night air, and he turned away.

Somehow, he'd made it.

He walked around the car, quickly checking the tires and eyeballing the scratches and dents and the thick layer of dust coating the roof and fenders. His cell phone let out a pulse, but he never bothered to dig it out of his pocket. Instead, he climbed back into the car, switched on the headlights, and sped out of the parking lot. It took twenty minutes to reach Elysian Park using surface streets—a ride that included passing Dodger Stadium and, ironically, the Police Academy. All the same, he made it to the picnic area at the top of the hill and was still breathing. Still in one piece.

He got out of the car, glancing at Sophia's grave site under the pine trees as he crossed the lawn and checked his watch. It was 2:33 a.m. He couldn't help noticing how quiet it was up there. How peaceful it could be at this time of night.

He climbed the grassy bank and gazed down the hill at the factory. He gave the place a long look.

The bay doors were open, and all the lights were on. Sonny Daniels and his partner, Ryan Moore, had shown up for work early. They had their sleeves rolled up and were loading a pallet's worth of fifty-five-gallon drums onto a truck with the help of the three goons they'd hired. It seemed like they were in a hurry. But what struck Matt most was what he didn't see.

No one handling the drums was wearing a hazmat suit.

Matt winced as he pulled out his .45 and rocked back the slide. Cantering through the woods, he hit the road and started down the hill. He didn't much care if Sonny Daniels was in a hurry. He wanted a good look at that oxycodone, and it didn't matter if it took all night.

FIFTY-FOUR

Matt raised his .45, then stepped through the open bay door and moved down an aisle of wooden pallets stacked ten feet high. When he reached the main floor, all five men turned. Matt's eyes flicked to the three rough-looking thugs with pistols strapped to their shoulders and stayed there.

"I know what you're thinking," Matt said as he approached them. "There's three of us and only one of him. The trouble with that idea is timing. This is a forty-five, and it's already out. By the time you reach yours, all three of you guys are gonna be dead. That's why it's a bad idea, especially on a night like this one when I'm so pissed off. The truth is, killing something would make me feel better right now. Killing anything would set me free and make my night."

Their faces changed, and the three guards raised their hands. The older one in the middle, a man whom Matt guessed was in his early forties, took a step forward with great care. When he spoke, his voice was surprisingly low key.

"We don't want any trouble, mister. This is just a job for all three of us. A temp job that goes away at the end of the week. It's not worth dying over. It's not worth making trouble for you or us."

Sonny Daniels slammed his fist down on top of a drum in protest. "What do you idiots think I'm paying you for?"

The man turned. "You're paying us to keep an eye on whatever rotten slop is in these barrels. And I know who this guy is. He's a cop."

Sonny Daniels mouthed the word *loser*, flashed a wicked sneer, and took two steps toward the guard as if reaching for the man's gun. Matt gave the trigger on his .45 three quick pulls, blowing out the entire glass wall in the office above their heads. The sound of the gunshots echoing off the high walls and ceiling was deafening. Daniels stopped dead in his tracks, watching the glass rain down onto the floor, then stepped away from the guard.

Matt pointed the gun directly at his head. "The next one's all yours, Sonny."

No one said anything. Matt took a quick look around, spotting a box of heavy-duty cable ties on the supply shelf beside bins of disposable gloves and rags.

"Here's what we're gonna do right now. Sonny, you and your little friend are gonna sit down on the floor and lean back on your hands. You three guys are moving over to these drums. I'm sure you know the drill. Hands on the top, then step back until you're at a forty-five-degree angle."

Everyone, including Sonny Daniels, did as they were told without a word. Once the three guards were leaning forward, Matt stepped behind each one, removed their pistols from their holsters, and patted them down. Dumping the cable ties on the floor, Matt tossed all three pistols into the empty box and gave it a kick.

Everyone seemed to have their eyes on that box as it slid across the broken glass. When it finally came to a stop on the other side of the floor, Matt turned to the oldest of the three guards.

"Grab a couple of cable ties," he said. "I want you to cuff your friends' wrists, then both of them can sit down."

The guard followed Matt's instructions, threading the tie through the head and pulling it tight. When the two men sat down on the floor, Matt turned to Ryan Moore.

"Get over here, Moore."

Moore gave him a look and shook his head. It was the sullen look of a spoiled fifteen-year-old man-boy with no manners and no respect. Matt walked over and slammed the barrel of the gun over his head. Moore cringed in pain and let out a yelp. Blood splashed onto his shirt from the gash in his scalp.

"This isn't a game, Moore. Get over here and tie off the third guard or you're gonna meet your maker."

"What kind of cop are you?"

"The kind you see in your nightmares, Moore. Now do it."

Matt prodded him with his piece. After a brief stare down, Moore got to his feet and cuffed the guard's wrists. Once the man sat down, Moore returned to Sonny Daniels's side, the gash in his head still bleeding.

Matt walked over to the first fifty-five-gallon drum beside the forklift and turned to Daniels.

"Okay," he said. "Okay, Sonny. Now you and Moore are gonna open this up."

Sonny's eyes got big. "Are you out of your mind? That stuff's lethal. Can't you smell it?"

Matt noted the concern growing on the three guards' faces.

"Open it, Sonny."

"But I can't," he said. "It's too dangerous. You were here that day. You saw what happened. We could all get sick."

Matt acknowledged the three guards as he stepped over to Daniels and knelt down. Pointing the .45 at his head, he leaned closer and whispered in Daniels's ear.

"I'll bet that's what you tell everybody who works here, Sonny. It's hazardous waste. It's poison. A possible death sentence ten years down the line. I'll bet you and your buddy here spray that stench on the drums after everyone goes home at night. When they come back in the morning, they don't know the difference. It keeps them on their toes. It keeps them from looking inside. I've gotta admit, the hazmat suits were a nice touch. Now cut the bullshit and open the drum, or I'll blow your head off."

Sonny Daniels grit his teeth, shaking in anger.

Matt took a step back and glanced at the guards, who now looked terrified.

"Relax, fellas. Believe me. The sky's not falling in tonight."

Sonny Daniels stood up with Moore. "They should be scared. Especially if any of this crap splashes out onto the floor."

Matt nodded. "Keep your mouth shut, Sonny. Just open the drum."

Ryan Moore grabbed a screwdriver off a nearby workbench and began prying open the clips holding the top in place. After several minutes, the rim popped free. Matt could see how uneasy both Daniels and Moore had become, their eyes big and wild and more than anxious.

"Lift off the lid, Sonny. Then you and Moore can step back over to the truck. And Moore, don't be a loser. Toss the screwdriver onto the workbench."

The air in the factory seemed to double in weight, the tension electric. Sonny lifted the lid off the drum and rested it on the pallet. Once he and Moore stepped away, Matt moved in for a closer look.

The contents were sealed in what appeared to be an industrial-strength black plastic bag. Matt ripped the tape away, opened the flaps, and gazed inside.

For a moment it almost seemed like the world had stopped turning. He could feel the rush of adrenaline flooding his body—the shock and awe he experienced when standing on a precipice and watching the air force drop a 21,000-pound bomb on the Taliban in Afghanistan. But even more, there was that moment, that split second in time, when he first set eyes on the contents and everything finally became clear. After all that had happened this week, after counting the number of people who had been murdered and were laid out in the morgue, after remembering Sophia Ramirez's face as she was pulled out of the ground—it came down to this.

The fifty-five-gallon drum didn't contain hazardous waste. And it didn't appear as if the Brothers Grimm had any interest in engaging Robert Gambini in a turf war over drugs. Matt didn't see anything at all like that in the drum. No oxycodone—no bags of white powder—not even a single pill.

He pushed the plastic away to widen his view, then leaned closer.

All he could see was cash.

Crisp, new bundles of $100 bills, sealed in Cryovac bags and identical in every way to the two bags found in Moe Rey's house. When they had counted the money in Rey's kitchen, each bag contained one hundred thousand dollars. Matt remembered that Moe Rey had worked here for a few weeks before getting the boot. That the floor manager had said that Rey was never where he was supposed to be. Somehow, Rey had stumbled onto the money and got himself murdered for it.

It finally made sense, but as Matt chewed it over, there was still gray to it, too. Moe Rey was a small-time punk. It seemed clear that Rey would never have been smart enough to have found this place on his own.

Matt filed the idea away for later. As he dug through the bags of cash and saw that they went all the way to the bottom of the drum, he heard Sonny Daniels stirring by the truck.

"Are you trying to count it, Jones?"

Matt looked his way but didn't say anything.

"It's two million dollars," Daniels said. "Two million in each drum. And you can have that one as my gift, if you'll just walk away and leave us alone."

Matt remained quiet, eyeballing the drums and appraising their inventory. He could remember the night Ryan Moore told Cabrera that each one of the downsized trucks had a thirty-drum capacity and made fifteen trips to the mine in the desert outside Palmdale. He looked over at the cargo container against the rear wall, his mind burning through the numbers in disbelief. Each trip into the desert added up to sixty million dollars. In the end, the Brothers Grimm were moving a total of $900 million in cash.

A moment passed as Matt glanced back at Daniels and once again thought about the lives that had been lost.

"You did all this for the money?" he said in a voice that cracked and burned. "Money that you already own?"

Daniels seemed to be thrown off by Matt's response and didn't say anything.

Matt picked up a bag of cash, measuring its weight his hands. "You guys run a hedge fund. If these bills match what we found in Moe Rey's house, then this cash came from Bermuda. That's the whole point, right? That's what this was always about. You're moving money into the States tax-free."

Sonny Daniels lowered his voice. "Over the past ten years we've saved six-point-eight billion dollars, Jones. We own a small insurance company in Bermuda. Money moves from the hedge fund to the insurance company, then gets reinvested in our hedge fund. The profits we earn are tax-free. There's nothing wrong with that."

"There's a lot wrong with it, Sonny. A fifteen-year-old girl is dead because of this money. An innocent kid."

"I sure hope you're not talking about that Mexican girl, Jones."

"What?"

"You know what I'm saying."

Matt gave him a long look, repeating to himself that he had a gun in his hand, took an oath as a police officer, and needed to remain cool.

"You're gonna go to prison, Sonny. You and your freak pal over here. Your lawyers might get you guys out on bail before the trial, but both of you are gonna be locked up for a long time. You know better than anyone here that the minute you brought this cash back into the country, you committed multiple financial crimes that led to one murder after another. The question is, why? Why, when you already have so much? What's it worth to you? I'm guessing that you moved nine hundred million in that container over there. How much is it worth tax-free?"

"An additional twenty percent, more or less."

"So that's what? Another hundred and eighty million?"

Sonny nodded like he was proud. "Give or take," he said. "By the way, you're not as dumb as Colon said you were."

"Colon's dead. She was murdered tonight."

"So I heard. My offer's still on the table, Jones. Take everything in that drum as a personal gift from me and my partner. All you have to do is—"

Matt felt the muzzle of a gun touch the back of his neck and froze. He didn't need to turn around to know who was holding the pistol. He could see the man's reflection in the shattered glass on the concrete floor.

Robert Gambini had come in from the cold.

FIFTY-FIVE

As Matt watched Gambini take his pistol away from him and jam it behind his belt, a memory surfaced.

It was something Burton had told him when they were standing in the hallway outside the district attorney's office.

Pick your moments, Matt. Don't let them pick you.

At first glance, the timing of the memory seemed odd. But as he thought it over, as he kept his eyes on Gambini, he understood why Burton's words had resurfaced.

Robert Gambini couldn't stop looking at the money.

No doubt about it, he'd come here hoping to steal a truck filled with opiated meds, and now, to his great surprise, it was pure, unadulterated cash. He seemed mesmerized by it. His eyes were glazed over like he'd taken something. But Matt knew that the wild glint had nothing to do with drugs. It was all about the cash. The number of $100 bills, and the number of fifty-five-gallon drums—what appeared to be the last load of thirty—awaiting their trip to that reconverted gold mine in the desert.

$60 million—before his eyes.

$60 million—free and clear.

$60 million—*and it's only the beginning.*

Gambini smashed Ryan Moore in the face, knocking him onto the concrete floor. As Moore started cowering, Gambini dragged him over to the passenger-side door of the truck.

"Do you know how to be a hostage?"

Moore couldn't look him in the eye and was shaking in terror—the blood from his head wound still oozing through his hair and dripping down his face.

"What are you talking about?" he murmured.

Gambini smashed him in the face again. "Shut up and sit still, you prick."

Matt watched Gambini swagger across the floor, waving his pistol at the three guards, then pointing the muzzle at Sonny and finally back at him. It looked like a Glock 22, a .40-caliber semiautomatic that carried fifteen rounds in the mag. The pistol was lighter than a .45 but still packed a punch. From where Matt stood, no one on the floor had any doubt who was in charge right now.

Still, Gambini was distracted.

He'd just given the money another look as if he couldn't believe his good fortune—like just maybe he'd been crowned the King of LA tonight. He stopped and turned and appeared to be thinking about his options the way kings do. Twenty-four drums had already been loaded onto the truck. The remaining six were set on a pallet close by. Matt followed his eyes up the steps of the loading dock to the work shed directly behind them.

A moment passed with Gambini's wheels still turning. Then he walked back over to Sonny and gave him a hard push into Matt.

"Cuff his wrists, Jones. Then do yours. And hurry up about it."

Matt slipped a tie around Sonny's wrists and gave it a yank. Then he wrapped another tie around his own wrists, pulling it tight with his teeth.

Gambini returned to the open drum. After another quick peek at the cash, he began herding everyone up the steps into the shed. Matt could see Moore collapsed on the floor by the truck watching them with his glassy eyes. From the pathetic expression on his face, it seemed as though he had some idea of his fate and had given into the inevitable.

Matt felt himself being pushed through the shed door with the others and turned to catch a glimpse of the lock. It was a simple gate latch, and once Gambini slammed the door shut behind them, he heard the latch arm swing down and click. The shed was nearly dark, the only light coming from the loose-fitting door and a keypad. He took a quick look through the gloom, thinking about that day he and Cabrera toured the building and recalling that this was a temporary structure made of plywood to house the digital X-ray machine.

Matt gave his wrists a futile tug and noticed that the three guards were whispering among themselves and seemed nervous. Sonny had moved to the far corner, brooding in silence. Matt stepped back to the door and peered through the gap in the doorjamb.

He could see Gambini berating Moore as he dragged him over to the forklift. After a hard slap across the face for motivation, Moore finally climbed onto the seat and seemed to know enough about operating the machine to raise the pallet in the air and guide it into place. The drums looked heavy. As the two men began rolling them onto the truck, Matt noticed that Moore couldn't stop sniveling. When they got to the last drum, his hands were shaking so violently that he lost his grip and just stood there as the barrel dropped off the truck. Gambini eyed the bags of cash strewn across the floor, became enraged, and bashed Moore in the face again. But then the drug kingpin did something Matt found even more disturbing.

After ordering Moore to get down on his hands and knees and pick up the cash, Gambini walked out. He strode past the restrooms and the dumpster, pushed the double doors open, and vanished into the office area.

Why? Why did he leave the floor?

Matt remembered the day he and Burton spent with Robert's uncle Joseph in the visiting room at Terminal Island. He remembered the crime boss talking about the "mean Gambini" gene. He called his nephew vicious and cruel and said that the gene had been passed down from his father. He went on to say that it was a family trait with a long history. That Robert had been raised in near poverty and, like his father, always hated anyone he thought he couldn't beat. That he took real pleasure in stabbing them in the back because that's where the feeling of power came from.

Why did Robert Gambini leave the floor? Even worse, how could he let himself take his eyes off the money? His money?

Something was in the air. Matt could sense it.

"You know there's a way to get out of these, don't you?"

Matt turned. The older of the three guards was standing beside him with a band of light from the crack in the door cutting down his right eye and cheek.

"How?" Matt said.

"Well, you've gotta be strong. Young and strong. I bet you could do it."

Matt nodded as he took another quick look through the gap in the door. Robert Gambini was just entering the floor. As the double doors swung shut, he saw clouds of smoke following him in from the office area. Gambini was going to torch the place. Matt could see him opening a can of something and pouring the liquid all over a stack of pallets, then lighting a rag and tossing it on the wood.

Matt turned back to the guard, holding his bound wrists up. "Show me."

The guard spun the cable tie around until the head was centered between Matt's arms.

"The head of the tie is the weak spot," he said. "It has to be on top and right between your wrists. And the cable tie's gotta be pulled tight."

Matt gave the door a hurried check. The factory was burning. And though the bags of cash had been picked up, the last drum hadn't been loaded yet and was still set on the floor.

Matt turned back to the guard and watched the man pull his cable tie tighter.

"Now what?" he said.

"You're gonna raise your hands into the air—high as you can get them."

Matt raised his hands over his head, the plastic band cutting into his skin like a carving knife.

"That's it," the guard said. "Now you're gonna drop your hands down as hard and fast as you can. The idea is to drive your forearms into your hips and, on impact, snap your wrists apart. You need to make it hurt, Jones."

Matt took a couple of deep breaths, his eyes still locked on the guard. And then he did it—but nothing happened.

A daunting moment passed. He could smell smoke in the air. He could see it funneling into the shed through the gap in the door.

"You need to do it again," the guard said.

"He's burning the place down."

"You need to do it again. Harder. Faster."

Matt noticed that everyone in the shed was watching and looked frightened. The smoke had become thick enough that one of the younger guards had started coughing. Matt grit his teeth as he raised his hands in the air, then groaned as he thrust his arms down and slammed them against his hips. For a split second, all he noticed was the pain. But then he saw the broken cable tie on the floor. When he glanced at his wrists, he gave them a turn and realized that he was free.

He rushed to the door and peeked through the gap. Moore was on the forklift, inching toward the last drum with the factory engulfed in flames. Matt turned back to Sonny and the three guards.

"We can deal with the cable ties later," he said quickly. "We need to get out of here first. All of us."

Matt took three steps back, then drove his shoulder into the door. The lock was a cheap gate latch, but it didn't give.

"I'm gonna need help," he said.

The oldest of the guards stepped forward again. Matt looked him over. He might have been in his forties, but he had some weight to him.

"What's your name?" Matt said.

"Gene," he said. "Gene Harvey."

"We're gonna go on three, Gene. You ready?"

"I'm ready."

Matt counted from one to three and both men charged forward, driving their shoulders into the plywood door. The gate latch snapped, and the door blew open.

Gambini looked up, pulled out his gun, and fired two quick shots into the work shed. When everyone retreated, Moore raised the last drum in the air and scurried off the forklift. Once the drum was loaded onto the truck, Gambini slammed the rear doors shut.

Matt looked at the four men crouching behind the plywood wall. "I'll keep him distracted," he said. "You guys need to make a run for it."

He crept to the door, peering through the heavy smoke. Gambini was shouting at Moore over the sound of the fire, telling the man to get into the passenger seat of the truck. When Gambini finally turned away and headed for the driver's side door, Matt sprinted forward and jumped off the loading dock. He reached the back of the truck and then around the side. Gambini was just about to open the door. Matt rushed toward him, grabbing his shoulders and yanking him down to the ground. He could see Gambini's knees buckle and twist, and heard him groan. As the man rolled over, Matt reached for the gun Gambini had stuffed behind his belt—his own .45—but watched it being batted away. The pistol skidded across the floor.

And that's when the world started spinning again. Gambini must have been waiting for him with his fist closed around his own pistol. When Matt turned toward the truck, Gambini hammered him in the face with the handle.

It was a knockout punch. A hard, vicious blow, and everything went black. Matt could feel panic quaking through his body. Through the smoke he could see Gambini opening the door and climbing in behind the wheel. Behind the truck, Sonny Daniels and the three guards were running through the blaze toward the open bay doors. He looked up and saw the entire ceiling burning overhead.

He rolled over onto his belly, still dazed. He started coughing but somehow managed to get to his feet. Searching for his gun, he spotted it through the haze and snatched it off the floor. Then he heard the truck's parking brake release and turned just in time to see Gambini wave goodbye with a wicked smirk on his face.

Matt raised the .45 and pulled the trigger, but the truck started moving. He didn't know what to do. He could feel the panic still washing through him in waves. Gambini was going to get away.

He fired another round into the front cab, but the truck kept rolling through the blaze and across the warehouse floor.

Matt grit his teeth and rushed forward, diving onto the front fender and grabbing the upper lip of the hood. His stomach was in his throat, his feet dangling in the smoky air. The floor moving beneath his legs suddenly turned into gravel and then asphalt as they reached the narrow road. The outdoor air was cold, the wind hardening as the truck began to pick up speed. Matt swung his legs around until he could feel the front bumper underneath his feet. And then he looked up and gazed through the windshield into the cab.

His eyes moved from Moore in the passenger seat to Gambini behind the wheel. They seemed so close. He could see Gambini's sneer becoming deeper and better defined. When Matt looked down, he saw the man lifting his gun off the seat and raising it in the air.

FIFTY-SIX

Gambini pulled the trigger.
The gunshot sounded more like a pop as it blasted through the safety glass and turned the entire windshield into a solid web of shattered glass. The truck pitched to the right, then swerved back and slowed down.

Matt ducked behind the hood and watched Gambini punch his pistol through the glass, trying to clear it away so that he could see the road again. Because the truck was moving, the sheets of shattered glass were flying back into the cab. Matt could hear Moore screaming in panic while Gambini ordered him to get off his seat and help. When the two men became quiet, Matt looked up and caught Gambini peering at him eerily through an open patch in the glass. The man's dark eyes twitched, and he flashed a cruel smile. Then the truck began swerving to the left and right, hard zigzags with Gambini trying to shake Matt loose.

The truck picked up more speed. The road appeared to be littered with potholes, the truck vibrating and bouncing up and down. Everything was shaking and jittering.

Matt drew his pistol out from his belt holster, approximated Gambini's position behind the wheel, and pulled the trigger three times. Both Moore and Gambini screamed, the truck veering left and almost crashing off the narrow road. But after hitting a pothole the size of a shallow grave, the front wheels rolled back onto the asphalt again. When Matt leaned forward to check the cab, his eyes widened, and his nerves spiked. He could see Gambini's pistol poking through the shattered glass in the darkness. The Glock .40 fired two times, then two times more—all four shots at point-blank range. Matt dropped below the hood, trying to twist his body out of the way. But the real tell was the stinging sensation in his upper right arm. The streak of blood staining his shirt.

He'd been hit.

He took a moment to collect himself, heaving air in and out of his lungs. He watched the muzzle retreating through the hole in the glass. As he tried to examine the gunshot wound in his arm, the truck made a sudden loud noise and began shaking violently. Matt checked the road ahead. The asphalt appeared to be heavily cratered, the stretch of potholes as endless as a walk on the moon. Jamming the pistol in his holster, he tightened his grip on the hood and tried to hold on. He could see the factory burning at the bottom of the hill now. But even more, as the road curved, he could see that three black Lincoln Continentals had fallen in behind them. Despite the sounds of distant sirens approaching and what looked like an LAPD chopper a mile or so off with its searchlight already fired up and beating against the ground, nothing about the three Lincolns or the hard-looking men driving them felt like law enforcement.

Everything about everything had turned harsh and grim.

He heard glass shatter and peered back over the hood. Gambini had cleared the rest of the windshield away and was aiming his pistol ready to fire. Even worse, the LAPD chopper had found them, the searchlight as bright as the sun. Matt realized that he no longer had any place to hide. He could feel his heart beating in his chest. The monsters waking up in his head.

He needed to do something. And he needed to do it in a hurry.

He lunged through the open windshield, grabbing Gambini's right hand and trying to pry his fingers away from the gun. He could hear Gambini grunting and groaning as they wrestled for control of the pistol. After a moment, Moore jumped in, wrapping his arms around Matt's back and trying to yank him out of the cab onto the hood.

The .40-caliber pistol fired three times, punching holes into the roof and flooding the interior of the cab with the chopper's white light. The truck began veering out of control.

Then two more shots exploded through the cab and Moore screamed. As Matt glanced his way, he found the man glaring at his thigh and what looked like a gunshot that had grazed his leg. Moore seemed to go crazy after that and started hurling punches.

Matt tried to fend them off, thrusting his knees against the dash and piling onto Gambini—the truck swerving wildly back and forth. He slammed Gambini's head into the seat, seized the hand gripping the gun, and began smashing it against the dashboard.

Another loud gunshot rang out, ripping a fourth hole through the ceiling.

Matt bashed Gambini's hand down again, breaking off the knobs on the radio. Then again and again and again until Gambini finally lost his grip, flinging the pistol through the air and out the windshield. Matt punched him in the face, but the heroin-dealer-turned-King-of-LA only smiled. When Gambini grabbed him by the neck, Moore started shouting something about how Matt was going to get them all killed and started using his legs to help Gambini push him back onto the hood.

Gambini tightened his grip on Matt's throat and dug his nails in. Matt tried to pull his fingers away but started choking. When he finally broke the hold, he was out the windshield clinging to the lip in the hood with his legs dangling in the air again.

He found the front bumper with his feet, began to hear the sirens getting closer, and turned. Three fire engines were barreling toward them down the narrow road with their lights flashing.

Gambini laughed like a madman and punched down the accelerator, the truck moving faster and faster over the rough road. Once he upped the speed, he began wrenching the steering wheel back and forth—violent shifts to the left and right all over again.

The fire engines were racing toward them and obviously not going to stop. Judging by the insane glint in Gambini's eyes, the "mean Gambini gene" had been cut loose for the night, and Matt knew that the maniac had no plans to stop either.

He turned and started looking for a place to jump or, even more important, a place to land. To the right a solid wall of rocks and stone followed the road as far as Matt could see. If he hit the wall, he'd die on impact. When he checked the railroad tracks beginning to cut in on the left, he noticed piles of fresh sand and mulch.

He turned and gave Gambini another hard look, then Moore as the spoiled man-boy mouthed the words *fuck you* at him. Ignoring the taunt, he glanced up at the chopper, then down at the fire engines. They were closing fast and now riding those deafening horns.

Time was slipping away quickly and chewing up the distance. One hundred yards became fifty yards, and in an instant, there were only twenty-five left.

Matt turned and gazed at the piles of sand and mulch around the railroad tracks. He shivered in the cold air, the monsters awake and alive in his head. He needed them to be with him now. He needed them to—

Matt let out a death scream. Leaping into the black, he thrashed his arms in the wind trying to keep his balance. Trying to spread his wings and fly.

FIFTY-SEVEN

It was a hard landing—the flight fast and filled with terror—the shock of the fall quaking through his body from head to toe. He'd hit the ground and bounced forward onto a pile of mulch. For several moments, he just lay there on his back, watching and trying to focus on what seemed more like a hallucination than anything real.

He could see Gambini picking a lane on the right side of the road, sparks flying as the truck careened off the wall of rocks and stone. But when the fire engines passed, the truck never stopped moving and never lost speed. Then the three Lincoln Continentals took their turns working the narrow gap and following Gambini into the night one by one.

Several moments passed with Matt thinking that he might actually be dead and basking in a light so bright it had to be heaven. Once he noticed that he was in pain, he looked up into the sky and realized that the light was coming from the LAPD's chopper.

He couldn't understand why they had ended their pursuit and come to a standstill hovering above him like a mother ship. He squinted and raised his left hand over his face to shield his eyes. He could feel the rush of air from the rotors, hear the grating sound of the engines, and smell the chopper's foul exhaust. But even more, as the seconds ticked by, as the taillights from Gambini's truck and the three Lincolns began to fade into the night and then vanish entirely—he could feel the anger in his bones.

The outrage.

He sat up, bending his arms and knees and making sure he hadn't broken any bones. Holding his right arm into the light, he examined the gunshot wound and felt a small degree of relief that the bullet had only shaved off a layer of skin.

He gazed back up at the chopper, wondering if the pilot and crew were idiots. Whether they might be dimwits or blithering fools, masquerading as police officers.

They were letting Gambini get away.

They were aiding and abetting a man who had murdered five people outright, injuring and killing even more with his Mercedes the other night.

Matt heard the sirens and saw the patrol units approaching at high speed, their tires kicking up walls of dust behind them. Then the loudspeaker on the chopper sounded off.

"Stay where you are, or you will be shot."

Matt shook his head and stood up. They really were brain dead.

"Do not move, or you will be shot. Raise your hands in the air."

Matt took a deep breath and exhaled, waiting for the patrol units to arrive. There were five of them, and it suddenly occurred to him that they might be the same units who had chased him through the hills above Hollywood. If that was the case, there was a better than even chance that they could be amped up and dangerous. He watched them skid to a stop, noticing the dents in the side of the lead car. The doors burst open and ten cops with their guns raised started racing toward him.

They were all young. All jacked up and crazy.

It had to be them.

Matt looked at the cop who had been behind the wheel in the lead car, the man who had tried to bulldoze him over the edge of the mountain. He was charging forward with more verve than the others. He had ultrapale skin, a shaved head, and blue eyes that were set a half inch too far apart to be normal.

He looked stupid and seemed way too angry. They all did.

They were shouting at him, ordering him to get down on the ground, screaming like they were deranged. When the cop with the shaved head spotted the .45 in Matt's belt holster, it felt like the man's engine blew and those eyes of his got big and scary.

"He's gotta gun!" the cop shouted. "Gun, gun, gun!"

Matt raised his hands in the air and knelt down on his knees. He could see his fingers shaking. He looked at the ten cops with their pistols out and ready. He looked at their faces, hoping he would remember them when this was over.

"I'm a police officer," he said in a loud voice. "And I'm wounded. I need medical—"

The cop with the shaved head kicked Matt in the head with his boot and knocked him down to the ground. When he spoke, he was shouting at the top of his lungs.

"Shut up and keep still, or I swear I'll shoot you!"

"I'm a police officer," Matt said, trying to catch his breath. "And I'm wounded."

"I told you to keep your mouth shut. You're charged with the murder of a city councilwoman and her bodyguard, you sick piece of scum. You ran out on us. You tried to get away from me. Nobody gets away from me. Do you understand that, you dirty piece of crap? Nobody!"

The cop grit his teeth and gave him another hard kick, this time in the ribs. And then another. Matt let out a groan and covered his head and face with his arms, but there were ten of them. And they were working like a gang—kicking and squealing and swinging their batons at his head. The blows were relentless, the beating out of some nightmare. He could feel the cop with the shaved head taking his pistol away from him. For reasons impossible to guess, the act of confiscating Matt's gun appeared to make the cop even more angry. The kicks and punches carried extra weight now. Killer weight. One of them, the skinniest of the ten, seemed to be taking great pleasure in stomping on Matt's gunshot wound with the heel of his boot. He was laughing and whining and squealing the way animals do.

At a certain point, the world began to darken and turn black. Matt could still hear them kicking him. He could hear their clubs whooshing through the night and landing on his body. He could hear them laughing like they were giddy and so revved up they just couldn't make themselves stop. He could hear them—but as he began to fade into the gloom, he couldn't feel them anymore.

And then something odd happened.

He heard a loud noise, followed by a definite thud. The kicking stopped after that, along with the pounding from their batons. He tried to open his eyes, but it felt like his lids had been glued shut. After fighting it some, he managed to part his eyelashes slightly and see a faint, narrow image through the slits.

The cop with the shaved head had collapsed onto the ground. Matt could see a bullet hole in his forehead right between those vicious blue eyes of his. The cop had that thousand-yard stare going now, and his teeth were jutting out.

Someone rolled Matt over onto his back.

He wasn't sure if he screamed or not. He knew that he was afraid because he couldn't move or fight back. But even worse, his body had gone numb for a while, and that was beginning to slip away now. He could feel a river of pain rushing in to fill the void.

He looked up through the slits in his eyelids.

The nine cops who were still alive had formed a line and were trying to catch their breaths and calm down. They were facing the road with their hands in the air. Matt could hear someone shouting at them. He tried to see who it was but couldn't turn his head. After several moments, a barrel-chested man wearing a police uniform stepped into view holding a Beretta .45 in his right hand. He had three other cops with him, and all three wore leather jackets to go with their grim faces and hard eyes. All three were carrying shotguns.

Matt looked back at the cop with the .45, noting the shock of white hair and his emerald-green eyes. Despite the man's age, he looked like a street fighter, and right now, he looked invincible. He looked fierce and tough—a real meat eater ready to gnaw on a fresh kill.

The man knelt down. Matt could feel him looking at him.

"Are you okay?" the man said finally.

Matt tried to speak but couldn't make his mouth work. As he struggled to say something, he gazed at the cop's face. After a while, it dawned on him that he knew him. The man with the shock of white hair was his supervisor, Lt. Howard McKensie.

McKensie shook his head. "I'm sorry, Jones," he said. "I'm sorry that they did this to you. They'll never do it to anybody again. You have my word on that. They'll never get the chance."

Matt nodded at him, even though he didn't believe it and knew that at some point, when these nine freaks thought all was forgiven, he'd have to deal with them himself. He pushed the nightmare aside—his thirst for revenge. Somehow, he managed to whisper without moving his jaw.

"Robert Gambini."

McKensie leaned closer. "What about him?"

Matt shut his eyes and opened them again, the pain evolving into agony. When he spoke, his voice was barely audible.

"I almost had him," he said. "He's getting away."

FIFTY-EIGHT

Matt saw the batons swinging through the air and tried to cradle his head in his arms to protect his already banged-up face. But tonight, his arms wouldn't work or even move, and so he took the beating straight up. The blows kept coming. The laughter from the cops brutalizing him sounded giddy again and more demented than he remembered. Their faces clown-like and deformed.

He could almost see it. Almost feel it.

And then his body quaked and shuddered.

He rolled over in bed and tried to shake off what had become yet another nightmare. Another lost night in a long line of lost nights.

Flashbacks. Night sweats. Ghouls and ghosts visiting his bed. The Grim Reaper checking on him every hour to see if he was *ready*, or was the word *done*. Even last night in the hospital after he found out that Sonny Daniels had lawyered up and was already out on bail, after the doctors had given him enough morphine to knock a horse down—the demonic haunting lingered in the darkness and carried on.

He gazed up at the ceiling, reliving key moments and remembering the unforgettable. He looked at the shadows cast above his head from a tree outside his window dancing in the wind. The different shapes and—

Someone started pounding on the front door.

Matt's eyes rocked across the bed to his cell phone set on the charging base of his clock radio. It was 4:33 a.m., and sunrise was still a long way off. Reaching for the holster slung over the bedpost, he drew his .45.

After the beating he'd taken yesterday, he'd arrived at a new motto. He wasn't sure if it was temporary or had the legs to last a lifetime.

Shoot first and keep on shooting. Deal with what comes next when the bullets run out.

The heavy pounding on the front door started again, and then Matt's cell phone lit up. After two rings, he saw McKensie's name begin blinking on the face and grabbed it.

"It's four thirty in the morning, Jones. You're not gonna make me wait out here in the cold, are you? Now get out of bed and open the goddamn door."

"Right."

Matt switched off the phone, slid his pistol back into the holster, and grabbed a T-shirt off the chair. As he stepped down the hall and through the kitchen, he began to notice the flashing lights bouncing off the walls. Out the living room window, he could see McKensie waiting by the front door. But parked at the curb were two patrol units with the same three cops McKensie had brought with him last night. They were standing by their cruisers, wearing leather jackets and carrying those shotguns again.

Matt's mind started going. Trouble ahead.

Feeling his body tighten up, he threw the locks and swung the door open. McKensie brushed past him and walked into the living room like he owned the place.

"Turn on the lights, Jones. It's dark in here."

Matt switched on a table lamp and found McKensie sizing him up with those sharp green eyes of his. His supervisor was standing by the slider, the deck behind him still lit up because Matt kept the outdoor lights on all night.

"You've come to arrest me for killing Colon," he said.

McKensie thought it over as he appraised him. When he spoke, his voice was scary quiet and overloaded with suspicion.

"But you couldn't have killed her, Jones. The results are in from her autopsy. She died exactly the same way the girl died. Art Madina performed the autopsy himself. He said everything about the two murders was identical. They died hard. They died like twins."

"But that's my genius," Matt said. "My alibi and my way out. I made the murders look the same because I was at the girl's autopsy and knew exactly what to do."

McKensie's eyes narrowed. "The way you're selling it, Jones, if it ever went to trial, I bet it would play really well with twelve of our finest."

"I had a reason to want her dead."

"A good reason, Jones. Colon was a piece of shit."

Matt gave McKensie a measured look. "So you're arresting me."

McKensie took a moment to think it over, then shook his head.

"Not tonight," he said.

"Why not tonight?"

"Because of Colon's bodyguard."

Matt leaned against the fireplace mantel. It occurred to him that something had happened, and McKensie was getting off on watching him twist in the wind.

"What about the bodyguard?" he said.

McKensie crossed the room and switched on the lamp beside the couch. "The bodyguard was licensed to carry a twenty-two-caliber pistol. According to Madina and then ballistics, the slob was killed by a twenty-two-caliber pistol—same make and model. It sure looks good on paper, doesn't it? The trouble is the slugs don't match, and they never will."

"Raines told me that it had been fired that night. He accused me of shooting him with his own gun like I'm some kind of deadbeat."

"Raines gets off on drama because he thought he could get you to fold. But Speeks found the slug from the bodyguard's piece when he went back on his own the next day. It passed through the wall and ended up in a can of Goya refried pinto beans."

Matt felt the hairs on the back of his neck begin to stand on end.

"What about the slug found in the bodyguard's head?"

McKensie flashed a short, dry smile. "That's why I know you're not good for Colon's murder, Jones. By the way, your sales job was bullshit."

Matt shrugged. "Tell me what's going on."

"You ready for this, Jones? I mean, you look like you got decked in a prizefight and no one blew the whistle. Your eyes are still swollen shut."

"I can see just fine," he said. "Tell me what's going on."

"Okay, so here it is in black and white. You were right about some things. Turns out, a lot of things. The slug they pulled out of the bodyguard's head matches the slug they pulled out of Moe Rey's head. Ballistics called in the match. Same bullets shot from the same gun. One hundred percent certainty, perfect as the day is long."

Matt sat down in a chair and took a moment to let it settle in. He noticed that his fingers had begun trembling slightly. His heart felt like it was racing in his chest. When he spoke, his voice sounded rough, but he couldn't have cared less.

"What do you mean, same gun? Did you find Robert Gambini?"

McKensie shook his head. "Not yet, but we've got the gun. We searched his house. One of the guys found it in a drawer by Gambini's bed."

The revelation hung there for a long time. Finally. They'd put it together and Gambini was locked in. Matt needed it so much, he almost couldn't believe it. He turned and caught a reflection of his face in the mirror by the front door. No doubt about it, the ordeal he'd been through had cost him this time around.

"What about the gloves found at the Red Dragon?" he said. "What about Lane Grubb's murder?"

"Speeks is still working on it, but the DA says he doesn't need it right now. The slugs and pistol are enough to get Gambini convicted. Besides, they'd try the cases separately, just in case they screwed one of them up or got a dog judge. Two murder cases means two chances to put the piece of shit away. You used to work narcotics—you already know all that."

Matt thought it over. What he knew was that Gambini had expected to find opiated meds, not cash, when he showed up to steal the truck. But that hardly mattered now. Gambini's knowledge of what was being dealt and traded—the Grimm Brothers' sick scheme to feed their greed and squeeze even more cash out of a fortune they already owned—had become irrelevant for good reason: at the time of each murder, Gambini had a righteous motive for wanting all four people dead. Whether they were somehow tied to what he assumed was a turf war over his drug business, or a witness to an execution that he had committed, or the bodyguard to someone like Dee Colon who was sticking her dirty nose into everybody's business and demanding a slice of the pie—Robert Gambini had a reason to kill each one.

Matt got up from the chair and looked out the window at the three cops standing before their patrol units with those shotguns.

"If this is just a briefing," he said, "and you have no plans or reason to arrest me, then why make the drive way out here? Why do it at four thirty in the morning? And why did you bring company? Why the heavy artillery? Why the shotguns?"

McKensie gave him another long look with those green eyes of his.

"Because Gambini's still out there," he said. "And this is one of those cases, isn't it? When are you seeing your shrink?"

"Why are you here?"

McKensie walked back over to the slider. Matt followed his gaze through the glass to the tall buildings all lit up at the other end of the basin.

"You're still not ready for prime time, Jones. I can see it. You've still got those monsters swimming in your head. You need time to heal, time to forget—but I need a favor."

"What kind of favor?"

McKensie turned back and looked at him with a spark in his eyes. "Once you finish your paperwork, you're on leave again, you know."

"You told me that at the hospital," he said. "What's the favor?"

"I was hoping you might drive out to Gambini's house in the morning and take a look around. It was the chief's idea, too. It's bad PR for the department that we let Gambini get away, especially after what happened to you. There's a chance there's something at the house, something he left behind that points to where he was going. Something the guys searching the place are missing."

Matt didn't need to think it over. Robert Gambini might be brutal, but Matt felt certain that the heroin-dealer-turned-King-of-LA didn't do anything without a plan. Worse still, time was rolling, and Gambini knew where the Brothers Grimm were keeping their money in the desert. Sonny Daniels, whom Matt guessed was unaware of Gambini's knowledge, was trying to avoid prison time and had refused to talk.

"I want something in return," Matt said.

McKensie shrugged as he opened the front door to leave. "Like what?"

"I want to notify the Ramirezes that Gambini killed their daughter. I want them to hear it from me before it leaks out and ends up on the news."

"I've got no problem with that. But go over to Gambini's first. The house is wide open. Speeks and his crew will probably be working the place all week."

McKensie acknowledged the three cops standing by their patrol units carrying those shotguns and turned back.

"You want these guys out here to hang around?"

Matt shook his head. "No, thanks. I'm good."

"Yeah, you sure look good, Jones. I'll talk to you later."

McKensie walked out and closed the door behind him. Matt watched them drive off with their lights flashing in the night. When they vanished around the corner, he checked the time. It was almost five, but he wasn't tired anymore and didn't want to take the chance that he might slip down the rabbit hole again, launching another series of nightmares. Instead, he stepped into the kitchen, turned the light on over the stove, and brewed a fresh pot of hot coffee. Then he sat down at the table and opened the file he'd taken from Gambini's house with all those photographs of the refurbished gold mine somewhere in the vicinity of Palmdale. After an hour of close examination, Matt realized that Gambini had been right. He couldn't find a single landmark in any of the images. Sonny Daniels's underground storage site could have been anywhere in the desert. Only Daniels and his remaining partner, Robert Gambini, and a couple of drivers whom Matt guessed were already dead knew where it was, so finding all that cash seemed like a shot in the dark.

FIFTY-NINE

There was something odd about Gambini's house.

Matt couldn't pin it down as he walked up the driveway. All he knew was that he'd sensed something peculiar the moment he got out of his car and set eyes on the place.

He didn't think that it had anything to do with the lab's evidence collection truck parked in front of the garage. Nor did he think the feeling was coming from the crime scene tape wrapped from tree to tree around the yard.

It must have been the house itself that spooked him.

It occurred to him that he'd experienced something similar the last time he'd been here—the night he broke in and found the house empty before Gambini showed up and surprised him. The place had the look and feel houses get when no one's home. It was almost as if the building itself had checked out and fallen into a deep sleep.

But the more he chewed it over, that really wasn't it either.

Matt shook it off and continued up the driveway.

He knew with certainty that today Robert Gambini wouldn't be showing up to surprise him. But even more, he doubted that the drug baron had left any trail at all. Everything about McKensie's "favor," as his supervisor had put it, seemed fabricated when weighed against the events of the past few days.

The chopper pilot and the cops who disgraced themselves hadn't just stopped Matt and let Gambini get away. They'd turned their heads while a person of interest in more than a handful of murders drove off carrying $60,000,000 in stolen cash with another $840,000,000 waiting for him in the desert.

The words *fuck up* didn't begin to describe the debacle. Matt guessed that it was a PR disaster that would live on the front page of the *Los Angeles Times* for a long time. And what about McKensie shooting a bad cop? That would play itself out on the front page, too.

Matt walked around to the back of the house and held the kitchen door open for a crime scene tech who was pushing a handcart outside loaded with three evidence cartons.

"Where's Speeks?" Matt said.

"In the next room."

Matt entered the house, stepped through the library, and spotted Speeks in Gambini's home office rummaging through a chest of drawers.

"You find anything?"

Speeks turned and gave his battered face a long look. "Jesus Christ, Jones. What did they do to you? Are you okay?"

Matt nodded. "Sure, Speeks. Never better. What's the holdup on the gloves you guys found at the Red Dragon?"

Speeks closed a drawer he'd been searching through and opened the next one down. When he spoke, he sounded disappointed.

"We had to send them out," he said. "They went to the crime lab at Quantico."

"I guessed that, but why is it taking so long?"

"We're not at the top of the list. Especially now since ballistics came through."

Matt sat down at Gambini's desk, more irritated than angry. "I'm glad everybody in ballistics did their job, Speeks. You know what I'm saying?"

"Actually, I'm not sure, Jones."

"I want the results from the gloves used to kill Lane Grubb."

"But even the DA doesn't think we need to put a rush on it. Ballistics gave them everything they need."

"We don't want anything to get lost, Speeks. Not in a case with a body count this big. Not with one of our own dead, and another, my partner, Speeks, with a broken leg. I want you to call the crime lab and tell them to push it through. If they give you a hard time, let me know and I'll call them myself."

Speeks shook his head. "Okay, okay," he said. "I'll give them a call right now."

Matt slid open the top desk drawer, found Gambini's weekly planner, and opened it. "Before you go, Speeks, how about answering my question."

The criminalist turned and gave him an odd look. "What question?"

"How are you guys making out?"

Speeks's face changed. "You know what it's like?" he said. "It's like we got called to the table on Thanksgiving after everybody else had eaten."

Matt kept his thoughts to himself. Speeks was saying exactly what Matt had been thinking ten minutes ago.

"He's not coming back, Jones. And he knew he wasn't coming back. It's pretty obvious that he went through everything and cleaned house."

"In his business, he may have just lived that way, Speeks. A lot of them do. Besides, he didn't know he had a truckload of cash until he got there. If it had been drugs it would have been business as usual with no reason to run."

"Maybe," he said. "I forgot you used to work narcotics. But what a lousy way to live."

Matt nodded, looking back down at Gambini's weekly planner and leafing through the pages. "Go call the lab, Speeks. Tell them the clock hit midnight, and we're out of time."

As the criminalist left the room, Matt noticed that Gambini kept an orderly planner, which seemed to underscore his idea that the heroin dealer had every intention of returning home until he realized it was about truckloads of money. Names may have been reduced to initials or, in some cases, converted to numbers, but times and dates for meetings, dinners out, doctor's appointments, and even errands like trips to the market or the dry cleaner were all neatly listed. Paging through the weeks and months, Matt had to keep reminding himself that this was still only January. Gambini's entire year seemed to be sketched in.

He tossed the planner back in the drawer and got out of the chair. On top of the chest of drawers he noticed a handful of family photographs set in silver frames. It occurred to him that Gambini probably lived a lot like his own uncle, Dr. Baylor. One was a drug dealer turned murderer, the other a serial killer, but both lifestyles would have required living in two separate worlds with two unique identities. Both lifestyles required a place to escape that was worry-free when trouble knocked on the door.

Matt stepped into the hallway, found the staircase, and walked through the entire house, examining each room in the light of day. Early in the process, after only a bedroom or two, he began to sense something.

That peculiar feeling was back. Stronger now. Fuller. Almost otherworldly. The impression seemed so palpable, and he couldn't shake it. It wouldn't fade or go away.

Even so, by 3:00 p.m. he thought he'd seen enough to know that Gambini's trail was ice cold. Nothing had been left behind that pointed to that second world where the drug baron might have fled. Matt imagined that with the cash Gambini had stolen, the man could get lost for a long time—maybe even find that place in paradise he'd mentioned—and never look back or be found.

He walked through the kitchen, passing several crime scene techs who were removing the drawers beside the dishwasher and sink. Once outside, he crossed the drive for a look through the window at Gambini's Mustang in the garage. The sun was kicking off the glass, and he had to move closer and cup his hands. For several moments he peered into the darkness, not sure about what he was actually seeing.

The white Mustang was gone. But that's not what made the view through the window so confusing.

It was the car parked on the other side of the garage. The car that shouldn't have been there. The car that should have been lost or stolen or driven off the Santa Monica Pier after midnight.

Matt realized that he was staring at Gambini's black Mercedes coupe.

He heard someone and turned away from the window. It was a crime scene tech placing another evidence carton on the truck. Matt pointed at the door on the side of the garage.

"You guy's got a key?"

The man nodded. "It should already be open."

Matt tried the handle. When it turned, he gave the door a push and stepped inside. Still eyeballing the Mercedes, still incredulous, he switched on the overhead lights.

Gambini's car was not damaged, and Matt didn't know what to make of it.

He opened the bay door for even more light, stepped closer, and examined every inch of the hood and fenders. The black Mercedes coupe that had tried to run down Lane Grubb had been bashed in and wrecked as it bulldozed every other car on the street out of its way.

Gambini's car remained untouched. And after close inspection, he saw that the hood and fenders were not new, nor were they the result of a recent repair. The wear and tear on the car's body appeared normal in every way. A small dent here, a light scratch there—normal, in every way.

SIXTY

The sun had set an hour ago, the air an unusual thirty-five degrees—way too cold for a January night in Los Angeles. Matt turned up the heat as he exited the freeway.

He had been trying not to let his mind skip ahead, struggling to keep his imagination in check for the entire drive across town. It wasn't until he reached Elysian Park and made the turn onto Casanova Street that he managed to pull himself together and calm down.

He could see the Ramirez's home halfway up the block and thought about the first time he'd met Sophia's parents, Angel and Lucia. They had already known that their young daughter was murdered and had spent the day watching the news on TV and waiting for someone to knock on their door.

Yet tonight wouldn't play like a next-of-kin notification. Matt expected it to be far more difficult.

The pain and emotion—the weight of a mother and father's love for their child and their loss—would always be something the Ramirezes would have to live with. But tonight, they would be hearing for the first time who murdered their daughter and why. Tonight, they would realize what a horrific twist of fate their daughter's death turned out to be. That her murder wasn't the result of anything she had done. That she was a complete innocent who, on the night of her fifteenth birthday, showed up at the wrong place at the wrong time and was murdered for something she saw.

Matt pulled in front of the house, wondering why all the lights were on and the front door was standing open. When he got out of the car, he heard Lucia screaming.

He ran into the living room and saw a man roughing her up on the couch. Without a single wasted motion, he horse-collared the intruder and yanked him down to the floor. Flipping him onto his back, he saw Sonny Daniels screaming at him and hurling his fists into the air.

"What the hell are you doing, Sonny?"

Sonny spoke through clenched teeth. "Getting these animals out of here."

The words settled into the room like poison gas. Matt met Sonny's eyes and realized that they'd gone dead. But even more, he could feel something exploding inside his body. Something fierce and uncontrollable. And then he snapped.

He kicked Sonny in the face, and then kicked him again even harder. As the man tried to block the blows with his arm, Matt struck him again and again until his nose burst open and the blood started to flow. It dawned on him that he was hurting Sonny exactly the way he'd been hurt—outmatched and unable to defend himself—giving into his anger and rage. He needed to get a grip on himself. He needed to end this quickly. Grabbing Sonny by the collar, he jacked him up to his feet and began running him through the living room. When they reached the front door, Matt drove him across the porch and tossed him into the street. Then he bent over and pointed his finger in the man's face, his voice low and dangerous.

"Get the fuck out of here, Sonny. Get up and go home. Go home, or you'll spend the night handcuffed to a tree in a place where no one, not even your dumb-ass lawyer, will ever find you."

Sonny didn't say anything. He just lay there, staring at Matt with those frenzied eyes and trying to catch his breath.

Matt walked back inside and closed the door. Lucia was still screaming, still hysterical, still unable to control herself in a way Matt had only seen on the street with drug overdoses. It almost seemed as if Sonny was still in the room, still shouting at her and slapping her around. He took a quick look about the room. And then his eyes stopped on the wall over the fireplace mantel.

Angel's shotgun was missing. The Remington 870 Wingmaster.

Something catastrophic was happening.

Matt raced over to the couch. "Where's Angel, Lucia? Where's your husband?"

It was almost like she couldn't hear him. She sat there trembling and repeating Sophia's name. She kept calling out to her little girl. Tears were streaming down her face, and she appeared to be in a state of deep psychosis.

Matt sat down beside her, pressing his hands against her cheeks and trying to get her to focus. "You have to tell me what's happening, Lucia. Quickly. Where's Angel? Where's your husband?"

She couldn't make it. She couldn't concentrate. She pointed in the direction of her daughter's bedroom and called out Sophia's name again.

Matt got up and raced through the kitchen into the bedroom. The computer was playing a video loop that had been uploaded onto a social media website. Matt could feel his soul collapsing as he rushed toward the desk.

It was a video of Sophia's murder.

A video shot from the camera on the helmet she used to record her skateboarding runs. The helmet they had been looking for but could never find.

Matt sat down on the bed, watching his world crumble. Sophia had witnessed everything. He could see Moe Rey underneath the tree branches being forced to dig his own grave at gunpoint. The man was on all fours, pushing the dirt to one side in a huge pile. When it looked like he'd finished, he clasped his hands behind his back and bowed, his body convulsing in fear. Matt could hear Rey begging for his life and weeping, but it didn't matter. The killer was standing behind him with the pistol aimed at the back of his head. The muzzle flash came first, followed by the sharp sound of the gun blasting in the night. All it took was a single shot to finish Moe Rey off, his dead body flopping onto the ground.

But even more harrowing, Matt could see the moment Sophia tried to back off and run away. The moment the killer heard her from underneath the trees and knew that she was out there. He could see the killer begin to race after her, the camera on her helmet turning away and bouncing up and down. He could hear Sophia shrieking in terror and crying out for help—the killer grunting and groaning and chasing her through the woods.

And then he finally reached Sophia and tackled her down to the ground.

The killer must have ripped her helmet off to get to her throat. The image rolled over and over again until the helmet seemed to hit something and came to a sudden stop. And that's when the killer wrapped his hands around Sophia's neck and started banging her head into the ground.

What the image hadn't stolen from Matt's soul, the reality of the murder did. He could see the killer's face now—the man gritting his teeth and straining under the pressure—his body shaking in a mad animal-like fury as he squeezed the life out of a fifteen-year-old girl on her birthday.

Everything about the moment cut to the bone. Especially when it was all over—when Sophia's body became still and lifeless and the killer turned to the helmet and noticed the camera. For more than a minute, he just sat on the ground staring at the lens and trying to compose himself.

Deputy District Attorney Mitch Burton.

It took Matt's breath away.

SIXTY-ONE

It almost seemed as if fate had reset the clock to half past midnight. Like reality was rippling through a distorted lens. Everything straight in the world was now bent. Everything bent had somehow become straight. Matt turned away from the computer and saw Sonny Daniels standing in the doorway.

"I thought I told you to go home."

Sonny just stood there, his dead eyes pulling away from the computer, landing on Matt's face, and burrowing in.

Matt shook his head. "I don't have time for this."

He grabbed Sonny by the arm and pulled him through the living room, then out the front door onto the porch.

"Be smart, Sonny. Let it go, and just get out of here."

Matt knew that as much as he would have liked to, he couldn't stay there for Lucia. Jumping into his car, he lit the engine up and floored it down the street. As he sped by, he caught a glimpse of Sonny stumbling down the sidewalk and felt a certain degree of relief that at least Lucia was safe for now.

The drive to Burton's house was a scrambled blur of grim memories and even darker thoughts. He couldn't believe what he'd just witnessed. He couldn't believe that anything like this could be happening.

He had been chasing Robert Gambini, but it was Mitch Burton all along. The same Mitch Burton who worked in the district attorney's office and helmed the Organized Crime Unit. The man who had been standing right beside him.

Matt's body shivered in the face of this new horrific reality.

As he climbed the hill and rolled around the corner, Burton's house seemed normal enough. But then he lowered his gaze to the driveway and saw that Angel Ramirez had crashed his pickup truck through the gate.

As he skidded to a stop, he heard the cannon-like blast of a shotgun followed by two quick bursts from what sounded like a large-caliber pistol. Burton and Ramirez were shouting at each other. Drawing his .45, Matt leapt up the steps and ripped open the front door. The moment he stepped inside, Val called out his name and rushed toward him. Her face and eyes were bruised and swollen—she'd obviously taken a hard beating.

"Who did this to you?" Matt said. "Mitch or Ramirez?"

She seemed confused. Panic stricken. Trembling in his arms.

"Mitch," she whispered. "I found the helmet in the back of his car. I saw the video, Matthew. I saw it. I put it on the web so everyone could see it, too. How could he do this? Why is this happening?"

The shotgun pounded again, followed by two more pistol shots. Burton shouted something at Angel, and Angel shouted back.

"He's in the study," Val said. "He's only got one gun, but I saw a lot of bullets. They looked big to me."

Matt gazed into her eyes and pulled her closer. "I want you to call nine-one-one," he said. "Then I want you to get out of here, okay? Over to a neighbor's, Val. Anywhere that's not here, right?"

She nodded and fled into the kitchen wiping the tears off her cheeks. Matt turned and started down the hallway with his .45 up and ready. He noticed that his hands were sweating and realized that he'd never been in a situation like this before. He didn't want to shoot Angel, and he didn't want to become Burton's judge and jury and gun the man down. Not in a case like this one. He filled his lungs with air and exhaled. When he spoke, his voice had hardened and become loud.

"Angel Ramirez, this is LAPD detective Matt Jones. I want you to back out of there before you do anything you'll regret."

Ramirez shrieked at the outrage and sounded all jacked up. "But he killed Sophia! He murdered my little girl!"

"If you don't back out, Angel, I'm coming in. And don't fool yourself into thinking that what Burton did will make a difference. It won't. If you've got that shotgun in your hands, I'm gonna shoot you and keep on shooting you until you're dead. Do you understand?"

Two gunshots rang out. Burton.

Matt started around the corner. The lights were dimmer there. Everything hard to see.

"But he killed her," Angel said, his voice distraught. "He took my little girl's life away. My Sophia. She's all we had."

"Are you listening to me, Angel? Your wife has already lost a daughter. Do you really want her to lose you, too? How do think she's gonna handle that?"

Two more gunshots rang out from the pistol, and Matt grimaced in anger when he thought he heard someone groan.

He stopped and gazed into the darkness. "Knock it off, Mitch! Goddamn it! Stop shooting! Angel? Are you coming out or not?"

A moment passed, the silence heavy and corrosive. But then Matt saw a figure passing through the darkness into the dim light. It was Angel, staggering toward him with the shotgun pointed at the floor. He was pressing his right hand against his left shoulder. Blood was dripping down his shirt.

Matt pulled him over to the window and turned him into the light. "Let me see it," he said.

Angel looked terrorized, lifting his hand to expose the gunshot wound. As Matt examined it quickly, it was a through-and-through a half inch below the skin. And Val had been right about the size of the bullets. Still, when Matt glanced back at Angel's face and noticed that he was weeping, he guessed that it had nothing to do with being shot or the size of the wound.

"I want you to go into the kitchen," Matt said. "I want you to sit down and press a towel against your shoulder until help gets here. They're on their way."

"But he did it. He killed Sophia. My little girl. I saw her body stop moving. I saw my girl die."

Matt tried to keep it together, tried to stay cool in the face of an emotional overload. He took charge of the shotgun and stepped into the man's face.

"I know what you saw," he said. "I know what you saw, Angel. And by now, trust me, everybody knows what he did. Now I want you to go into the kitchen. I want you to hold on until the EMTs get here."

The man was a wreck, trembling from head to toe. Matt watched him stumble around the corner. After inspecting the shotgun, he gave it a pump, checked the magazine, and realized that all four shells had been fired. Leaning the unloaded weapon against the wall, he stepped into the darkness with his .45 and worked his way to the door to Burton's study.

Burton fired his pistol, the bullets exploding into the wall a foot beside Matt's head. Matt fired three shots into the office and leapt to the other side of the door.

"You just shot at a police officer, Mitch. Are you out of your fucking mind?"

"What difference does it make now?"

"You're right about that. You'll get the needle for what you've done. I just want to know why. What made you do it?"

"I'm taking it with me to the grave. I've got no plans to walk out of here alive. And there's no way I'm sitting through the humiliation of a goddamn trial. I'm gonna make you kill me, Matt."

Matt was peering through the doorway. He could see Burton in the dim light jamming a fresh mag into a pistol and firing three more quick shots into the hall. Matt lost his balance and fell against the doorjamb. When he recovered, he'd lost sight of where Burton was in the room.

"What made you do it, Mitch? Why did you kill Moe Rey? That's where this starts, right?"

Burton didn't say anything. Matt couldn't tell what he was doing, but it sounded like he might be moving furniture around. As he thought it over, he wondered if Burton was trying to barricade himself in the room. Val had said that he had a lot of ammunition. Maybe he was preparing for a shoot-out when backup arrived. Maybe he really did want to be killed.

But then Matt heard a table fall over and saw Burton's shadow begin swaying across the wall. He took a jittery peek around the corner and flinched, then raced into the room.

Burton had tied a noose around his neck and was hanging from one of the ceiling beams, his feet dangling six feet overhead. Matt couldn't believe what he was seeing as he watched Burton point his gun in the air, scream like a madman, and blast off ten maybe twelve rounds into the ceiling. The sound was horrendous. When Burton ran out of bullets, he tossed the pistol onto the floor and began twitching.

SIXTY-TWO

A moment passed as the cloud of spent gunpowder floated through the room. Matt glanced at the pistol on the floor, then turned back to Burton, hanging from a rope lashed to the wooden beam high in the air.

"So what are you doing, Mitch? Taking the hero's way out?"

Burton looked down at him, his eyes big and glassy. The jump from the table he'd placed on his desk hadn't broken his neck. But judging from the color of his cheeks, Matt guessed that the noose was beginning to cut off his blood supply.

"Screw you. Sometimes a guy's gotta do what a guy's gotta do."

"Sounds like a TV commercial for a really bad beer, Mitch."

Matt stepped closer, watching Burton's body sweep through the gloom. The view of the city out the wall of glass was remarkable tonight. It seemed like Burton had positioned himself so that he could gaze out the window as he died.

But Matt couldn't help thinking about the photograph on the wall in Burton's office. "You and Joseph Gambini go way back, don't you, Mitch? You guys were in it together from the beginning."

"What are you talking about?"

"You and the old crime boss. How did it start?"

Burton didn't say anything, but Matt could tell he was thinking about it.

"He was your snitch, wasn't he, Mitch? He helped you win convictions. You helped him consolidate his power."

Burton gave him a wild look. "Yeah, maybe."

"I'm guessing he came up with the idea. He did the research and knew what Sonny Daniels was up to all along. But then the feds stepped in. What's his name? That freak prosecutor who thinks screwing people is his ticket into politics. He took everything Joe had and put him away for two more years. Joe needed help from the outside and was willing to cut you in."

Burton grabbed the rope above the noose, straining to pull himself up and loosen the grip on his neck. "He needs money. Cash. A way to live when he gets out."

"But that doesn't explain why you did this, Mitch. Joe's in a prison cell at Club Fed, and you're out here doing all the dirty work."

Burton almost seemed outraged. "I need the money, too! I'm tired. I've been doing this nonsense for thirty years and wanna retire. How are me and Val gonna make it? Sell this place and move into a one-bedroom piece of crap in West Hollywood?"

"You didn't save enough to get by?"

Burton looked down at him with those big eyes. "Sooner or later, Matt, I think you'll find that people, no matter how smart or stupid, no matter how good or bad, will do just about anything for money. And I mean anything. Everybody who's breathing, anyone who's walking around on two legs, wants money. And when they get it, they want more of it. They like the feel of it. The smell of it. They can't get enough of it. They'll steal for it. They'll screw for it. They'll sell their souls for it—and yes, if that's what it takes, they'll kill for it, too. Because money's the only real way to happiness we've got left. Money's better than God. Money's bigger than God. Money actually answers your prayers and makes everything good again. Clean again. Money's what makes the world go round."

Matt didn't say anything. After a while, he leaned against the back of the couch and looked up. Burton had let go of the rope and was kicking his legs, his body swaying through the shadows like a swing.

"So I was right. You guys knew what the Brothers Grimm were up to all along. You knew that it was never about a turf war over drugs. It was about the cash."

"Not at first," he said, pulling at the rope above the noose again. "We sent Moe Rey in to check things out."

"Ah, I got it now. You sent Moe Rey in, but he did more than figure it out. He stole two bags of cash—two hundred grand—and made the mistake of telling you about it."

"He was a stooge. The crumbs at the bottom of a bag of chips. I couldn't take the chance that he might tell someone else. I never said anything to Joe about it. I just knew that Moe Rey needed to be eliminated."

Matt laughed in irony. "Is that the way you mobbed-up guys say it these days? Moe Rey needed to be eliminated?"

"Whatever," Burton said. "And stop laughing at me. You know I might have made a mistake doing this. I'm having trouble breathing. Maybe you should cut me down."

"I'll think about it."

"No, I mean it. I'm starting to feel dizzy."

"That's because the rope's cutting off the blood supply to your head."

"Well, Jesus Christ, I don't wanna turn into a goddamn vegetable, Matt. Cut me down."

"Maybe later. I wanna know what happened first. You made Moe Rey dig his grave and shot him in the back of the head. You heard Sophia Ramirez running away. You knew she'd witnessed the murder."

"She screamed, but I don't want to talk about her."

"Why not? You killed her. You squeezed the life out of her with your bare hands."

Burton closed his eyes as if replaying the murder in his head. "I don't want to talk about the girl."

"But you strangled her to death."

"I couldn't help it. She saw everything, and I panicked. I couldn't let her get away."

Burton shook his head back and forth like he was trying to free himself of the demons in his head. When he opened his eyes, his voice wasn't much more than a whisper.

"I killed her," he said. "Let's leave it at that. You need to cut me down, Matt. I don't want to die like this. I don't want Val to see me like this."

Matt picked up the table that had fallen over and placed it back on the desk beneath Burton's feet. While it may have taken the weight off the prosecutor's neck, the rope remained taught and Burton was trapped with no way down.

"If you don't talk to me, Mitch, I'm taking the table away, and you can die the death you deserve. Now what about the city councilwoman? What about Dee Colon and her bodyguard?"

"What about them?"

Matt shrugged. "Why did you murder them?"

"Who said I did?"

"Nice try, but I mean it. I'll take the table away and walk out of the room. Now why did you kill Colon?"

He seemed to need to think about it and didn't say anything.

Matt shook his head in disgust. "The gun that greased Moe Rey is the same gun that greased the bodyguard. You probably haven't heard, but ballistics matched the slugs. You let me take the heat for the murders, then planted the gun in Robert Gambini's house. That's the only way all this could have happened. I heard that they found the gun in a drawer by his bed."

Burton remained silent, but it looked like his wheels were turning. A guilty man chewing over his options with a rope around his neck.

"I thought it was a nice touch," he said finally.

"Which part?"

Burton tried to loosen the noose, but it was still too tight and wouldn't give.

"All of it," he said in a scratchy voice. "Dee Colon was a psychotic bitch addicted to herself and other people's money. One of those 'mirror-mirror on the wall' types, right? She knew that something had to be going on with Sonny Daniels. It was only a matter of time before she figured things out. Her big mistake was that she went after you and did it publicly. I'll never know why she seemed to hate you so much."

"I think she felt the same way about a lot of people. Users and takers and backstabbers usually do."

"True enough, but her hate for you was different. It seemed like she was jealous of you. Like she was competing with you in a race only she could see. And by that time, you were becoming a problem, too. When they let you walk after Lane Grubb was murdered, when we sat in the chief's office and he told us that you were off the case, but you were really still on—something had to give."

"And so you set me up."

Burton laughed and gave him a quick look. "It was easier than I thought it would be. But please don't hold it against me, Matt. I really do need to be cut down now."

Matt pulled the table away. Burton's eyes got big as his body began to swing through the dim light again.

"Tell me how easy it was to set me up, Mitch. I wanna hear it in your own words."

"It seems like you're taking it personally. I asked you not to do that."

"You know the more you kick your legs, the more strain you're putting on your neck. If you're not careful, it could snap."

"Please, Matt. Put the table back on the desk or cut me down."

"Tell me how easy it was to set me up for a double murder."

Sweat was percolating all over Burton's face. From the glint in his eyes, terror had set in like an infection.

"Well just think about it," he said. "You were fascinated by Colon. You were following her. You were trying to figure out why she was putting so much effort into destroying your career—it was just perfect. After I did her, after I killed them, I drove down the driveway and saw you parked at the curb. I could hear the sirens in the distance. It was just so perfect. By the way, she died like a bitch, whining and begging for her life. My only regret is that I didn't drive a stake through her heart."

A moment passed, Burton's body still drifting through the shadows. Matt took a step closer and looked up.

"It's time to talk about Lane Grubb," he said.

"He OD'd on heroin."

"He was murdered."

Burton shook his head. "I didn't say that he wasn't. I just meant that I don't know anything about it."

"You didn't shoot him up?"

"I wouldn't have known how to shoot him up. I thought Robert Gambini got rid of Grubb. He tried to run him down in the street earlier that night. I was sitting at a table by the window in the café with those detectives. You were on the sidewalk. We saw the whole thing. Everybody did."

An image surfaced. Gambini's Mercedes parked in the garage the way it shouldn't have been. Matt kept his thoughts to himself.

"Yeah, I guess we did," he said. "We saw Robert Gambini drive off. And now, after everything you've done, after all this, he got away with all the money. You and his uncle Joe ended up with squat. How's that feel?"

Matt's eyes were pinned to Burton's as he asked the question. When Burton's face remained blank, waves of doubt began to surface on their own.

Who were the three men driving the Lincoln Continentals?

Where was Robert Gambini?

Where was all that cash?

But even more, why, when Matt had walked up Gambini's driveway earlier in the day, why did he get that odd feeling that the house had gone into a deep sleep? Was it a premonition? A sign?

SIXTY-THREE

Two shots from a pistol rang out. Matt could hear Angel Ramirez shouting at someone. Then two more shots pinged off the walls in the hallway. Matt heard the sound of people running and turned to the door with his gun up and ready. Angel burst into the room first, then tripped and fell onto the floor. Behind him, a man holding a pistol in his right hand was breaking through the darkness.

Matt pointed his .45 at the man's chest. "Drop the gun, Sonny."

Sonny Daniels couldn't keep his mad dog eyes off Angel. "It's his fault," he said in a loud voice. "Everything that's happened is his goddamn fault. He doesn't belong here."

Matt grimaced, trying to hold back his anger. "He's a material witness in a double homicide, Sonny. He's not going anywhere. I told you to go home. Now I'm telling you to drop the gun."

"But I've lost my money."

Matt could hear the sirens approaching and guessed that they were still a mile off.

"What about the mine in the desert?"

"It's his fault. I've lost everything."

Matt tried not to show anything on his face, but it was difficult. The Brothers Grimm had been cleaned out.

"Shut your mouth and drop the gun, Sonny."

The pistol was shaking in Sonny's hand. As Matt measured the man, a grim thought flashed through his head, rekindling all the rage and darkness within him—the idea that all the violence and all the deaths, including Sophia's murder, could be reduced to Sonny's sick attempt to milk more money out of a personal fortune he already owned. He looked at the greedy man who had just lost an estimated $900 million, then looked at him some more. He seemed so petty. So rotten, cheap, and small.

Matt's cell phone started vibrating in his pocket. The rhythm to the pulse indicated that the call was urgent. Matt kept his .45 pointed at Sonny and, with great care, fished the phone out of his pocket. When he saw David Speeks's name blinking on the face, to everyone's amazement, he took the call.

"I'm busy, Speeks. I'm in a situation right now."

"I just thought that you needed to know something."

"What do I need to know?"

"The FBI came through, Jones. The crime lab. The report on the gloves is in, and you won't believe the results."

"Try me."

"They lifted the fingerprints of the man who shot Lane Grubb up with all those bags of smack, and they don't belong to Robert Gambini."

Matt could feel it in his soul now. Like a mind reader or a fortune-teller or a blackbird riding the upper winds in the light of the moon, he could have switched off the phone because he already knew.

"Who do the prints belong to, Speeks?" he said quietly.

A moment passed with guns drawn. Everyone in the room was staring at him incredulously. Everyone was listening to his side of the conversation. Angel, Burton, and Sonny. All in shock that he took the call.

"Who do the prints belong to?" he repeated.

Speeks cleared this throat. "Sonny Daniels, Jones. He killed his own partner. He murdered Lane Grubb."

"Are you sure?"

"One hundred percent. Sonny was arrested in college for sexually assaulting a woman. His prints are in the system."

"Thanks."

Matt slipped his phone into his pocket. He'd known the answer the minute he set eyes on Gambini's Mercedes in the garage. Lane Grubb wanted out of the Brothers Grimm. He wanted out of the scheme, and he'd been afraid of his partners. Despite his addiction to drugs, he'd known that he wasn't safe. He had called Matt and wanted to come in. He'd said that he was ready to talk—ready to tell Matt everything.

And Sonny ran things. Sonny couldn't let that happen. Somewhere in this world, Sonny Daniels kept a black Mercedes that needed body work.

Matt looked up at Burton, still wrestling with the noose around his neck. Glancing down at Angel on the floor, he saw him staring up at Sonny with his hands raised in the air. It was almost as if Angel thought he could block the bullets if the gun fired. But then Matt's eyes worked their way back to Sonny and stayed there. Except for the sound of the rope rubbing against the wooden beam above their heads, the room had gone completely silent. Time seemed to have stopped, everything white hot and radioactive now. When Matt spoke finally, his voice was low and slow and burning like a grass fire.

"Give me the gun, Sonny. Do the smart thing. Hand it over so we can call it a night."

It happened slowly—so very slowly—Sonny turning away from Angel and pointing his pistol at Matt, then giving him a look and shaking his head.

"Because of his daughter, Jones, because of him, I lost my money. A lot of money. I'm not going anywhere."

Matt grimaced again, his .45 hot and ready. "I've asked you three times, Sonny. Maybe it's four times or even five—I really don't remember. Lower the gun to the floor and step away."

Sonny gazed back at him with those eyes of his and shook his head again. When the corner of his lips turned, he looked just like Satan.

"Wrong answer," Matt said.

He pulled the trigger three times, the heavy .45-caliber rounds exploding into Sonny's chest as the sound of thunder cracked and roared through the room. Then he pulled the trigger four more times just to make sure. Matt saw the muzzle flashing and could smell the cloud of gunpowder rising in the air. Sonny was out of luck and didn't have time to respond. His body snapped back on its heels and dropped onto the floor like a bag of dirt.

There was no real need to check. Sonny's face had "forever dead" stamped all over it. But Matt checked anyway, then looked up at Burton still hanging from the noose.

"You ready to come down, Mitch?"

Burton didn't say anything. He just stared back at him with those big glassy eyes of his and then nodded. Matt raised the .45, aimed at the rope lashed to the beam, and fired a single shot. As Burton plunged to the floor and rolled onto his side, Matt could hear the cars and trucks pulling to a stop on the street out front. He slipped the .45 into its holster and helped Angel get to his feet. Then he cuffed Burton and switched on the lights. He didn't want the first responders to enter a dark house. He was hoping that there wouldn't be any more shooting tonight.

SIXTY-FOUR

It was 6:17 a.m., still more than a half hour before sunrise, and Matt had gone another night without sleep. Knowing that he would be back on medical leave after he finished his report and updated the Chronological Record in the murder book, he had left the crime scene at Burton's house and driven directly to the station in Hollywood. He took a sip of coffee as he sat before his laptop and tried to put what had happened over the past two days into words. There were moments he knew that he would carry with him until the end of time. There were memories he knew that as long as he lived, he could never—

"We need to take a drive, Jones."

Matt looked up and saw McKensie staring back at him.

"What is it?" Matt said.

McKensie flashed an ironic smile. "Hollywood Reservoir. Some Wall Street guy who works East Coast time went jogging about an hour ago. He says he saw two bodies floating in the water. Two dead guys. I thought you might want to be there when we fish them out."

Matt shut down his laptop and grabbed his coffee. The drive to the reservoir on top of the mountain should have taken fifteen minutes, but McKensie was jacked up and made it in ten. Two open workboats with outboard motors were lashed to the dock, the first skiff being used by Ed Gainer and two assistants from the coroner's office, along with a pair of LAPD divers ready to go in their wetsuits, masks, and scuba gear.

They began their search for the two bodies at the spot where the jogger claimed to have seen them. Matt wasn't surprised when they struck out. The reservoir had the look and feel of a large lake. He imagined that the corpses were on the move, drifting with the currents. After exploring the reservoir from one end to the other, they followed a bend into a small cove.

And that's when Matt saw them.

They were hovering about three feet below the water's surface facedown. Still, Matt had a pretty good idea who they were going to turn out to be. When he glanced over at McKensie, he could tell that they were on the same page.

The sky had become lighter, the sun rising on the other side of the mountain.

Matt gazed into the water from his seat on the second workboat. The corpses were fully clothed. Despite the cold water, decomposition had begun to set in and the bodies were beginning to bloat some.

He turned and watched the divers slip into the water from the first skiff. Using boat hooks, they rolled the corpses over and began guiding them back to the surface.

Matt gave McKensie a nudge and pointed. "It's them," he said. "That's Robert Gambini, and that's Ryan Moore."

"Looks like they've seen better times, Jones. Every dog has his day, I guess."

The divers gathered the corpses into fishnets, keeping everything in place. Once the victims were wrapped, Gainer's assistants hoisted them onto the skiff.

"Let's get them back to shore," Gainer said. "By now Speeks should have the tent set up, and we'll take a quick look."

The water's surface was as smooth as glass, the low hum from the small outboard motors filling the canyon. With the mist rising into the cooler air—the sky clear and a deep blue—the morning seemed peaceful enough. But as Matt looked up and saw the hills littered with patrol units and their flashing lights, as he lowered his gaze and eyed Gambini and Moore through the fishnets—dead as dead gets—the feeling was two or three times past eerie.

No one said anything the entire way in. Just the hum of those outboard motors and the sound of the wake they were leaving behind in the calm waters.

Matt could see the lab's evidence collection truck parked beside the coroner's van. Under the trees a large tent had been pitched that included lights mounted on stands and a long worktable.

The two boats came into their slips side by side. Matt followed McKensie onto the dock, standing back as the bodies were lifted onto gurneys and rolled up the ramp. Once the work lights were fired up, everyone entered the tent and the flap was lowered for privacy.

It took five minutes to extract the corpses from the fishnets and another five minutes to empty their pockets and check their IDs. Because everything was wet, evidence bags were set aside until later. As Gainer began his preliminary examination of the bodies, Matt didn't see any evidence of foul play and stepped closer.

"Why don't you save us some time, Ed."

Gainer turned to him. "What are you asking me to do?"

"Roll them over and let's get a look at the back of their heads."

"You mean you want to cut to the chase, Jones?"

Matt caught the wry smile, the glint in his eyes, and nodded. "I think everyone here's got a good idea of what happened to these guys."

Gainer's smile broadened, and he rolled the bodies over with the help of his two assistants. As Speeks broke out a handful of UV flashlights and eye protection, the tent went dark.

Matt switched on his UV flashlight and stepped closer. But the truth was he could see what happened to both Gambini and Moore from two feet away in the dark. Blood was still oozing out of the small holes in the back of their heads. The double murder was exactly what it appeared to be at first glance.

McKensie stepped in beside Matt, eyeballing the victims. "They were executed," he said.

Gainer nodded. "With a low-caliber pistol. Most likely a twenty-two. A bullet small enough to go in, bounce around, and not bother the shooter or anybody else by coming back out."

"But now the money is really lost," McKensie said. "The only one who could possibly know where it's stashed will never talk."

Matt slipped on a pair of vinyl gloves. Then he spread Gambini's wet hair away from the entrance wound and leaned in. "You mean Joseph Gambini?"

McKensie nodded. "He'll never talk."

Matt shrugged as he chewed it over. He was thinking about the three rough-looking guys driving the Lincoln Continentals and guessing that they were in the wind never to be found as well. But he was also thinking about the "mean Gambini gene"—who had it, and who didn't. He could imagine the look on Joseph Gambini's face when he was tried for the four murders Mitch Burton committed on his behalf, plus the executions of his nephew and Ryan Moore, which Matt bet he'd ordered on his own. While it was true that Joseph Gambini would be leaving Terminal Island soon, he probably didn't understand that he would be moving into a maximum-security penitentiary until the trial was over and the state decided when to end his miserable life. Matt wondered if it was worth a drive down to Terminal Island to let him know that they knew he had the money, and that in the end, it didn't matter anymore. All Matt really wanted was to see the wicked glint in Gambini's eyes when he realized that his life as a man of great wealth would be short and sweet, and that in all his days he would never see a single dollar.

Chump change. That's all he'd be left with. All he'd ever have.

Matt pulled the flap away and stepped out of the tent into the sunlight. He was spent. Weary. Tired of all the blood and all the dead bodies. Tired of all the questions that kept surfacing in his head.

SIXTY-FIVE

Matt pulled into the carport, killed the engine, and strained to lift himself out of the front seat. It was just past noon. Before heading home, he'd driven down to the USC Medical Center to see his partner. Once he arrived, the front desk had told him that Cabrera was in surgery and wouldn't be out of recovery until early evening. Disappointed that it didn't work out, Matt had stopped by Burton's house to check on Val. He'd seen the evidence collection truck parked in the drive, the guys from the lab still processing the crime scene. When he looked in the garage, Val's car was gone.

And so he ended up here. Home in the middle of the day.

He unlocked the front door and stepped inside. He was having balance issues and feeling dizzy. Chills were running up and down his back and working their way through his spine. When he caught a glimpse of his banged-up face in the mirror, he turned away quickly because he didn't want to remember it.

He walked into the kitchen, opened the freezer, and poured a glass of chilled Tito's vodka over ice. Setting the bottle on the counter, he took a first sip and felt his stomach begin to glow. Then he topped off the glass, walked through the living room, and went out the slider onto the deck. It was chilly, but the sun was out and the breeze off the ocean had pushed the foul odor from the wildfire deeper into the basin. The cool salty air actually smelled clean today.

He sat down on the chaise longue, put his feet up, and rested his head against the cushion. After a few moments, he could feel his body beginning to let go. He wasn't sure how much time had gone by. But when he opened his eyes, his glass was empty, and he saw a man standing at the other end of the deck with a drink of his own. The man was leaning on the rail and seemed to be taking in the view of the charred canyon and all the burned-up homes.

Matt blinked his eyes, wondering who the man was and thinking that he might not even be there because this whole thing could be a dream. But then the man turned, and Matt's eyes hit his face and stopped.

It was his uncle. It was Dr. Baylor. A serial killer who had murdered two more people in a cheap motel outside of Pittsburgh on the same night Sophia Ramirez had been killed.

"What are you doing here?" Matt said.

"Taking you away."

"Where?"

"To a place I know not far from here."

"You came to kill me?"

The doctor laughed. "Why would I want to do that, Matthew?"

Matt shook his head. "I don't know," he said. "I'm not well."

Baylor smoothed his hand over Matt's hair, the way an uncle might do to his beloved nephew. Matt looked up at him and wasn't afraid.

"Why are you here?"

Baylor's eyes sparkled in the sunlight. "You need a plastic surgeon, Matthew. And I'm still the best there is."

ALSO BY
ROBERT ELLIS

City of Stones

The Love Killings

City of Echoes

Murder Season

The Lost Witness

City of Fire

The Dead Room

Access to Power

ABOUT THE AUTHOR

Robert Ellis is the international bestselling author of *Access to Power* and *The Dead Room*, as well as two critically acclaimed series—the Lena Gamble novels *City of Fire*, *The Lost Witness*, and *Murder Season*, and the Detective Matt Jones Thriller Series, which includes *City of Echoes*, *The Love Killings*, *The Girl Buried in the Woods*, and *City of Stones*. His books have been translated into more than ten languages and selected as top reads by *Booklist*, *Kirkus Reviews*, *Library Journal*, *Publishers Weekly*, National Public Radio, the *Baltimore Sun*, the *Chicago Tribune*, the *Toronto Sun* (CA), *The Guardian* (UK), *People* magazine, *USA Today*, and *The New York Times*. Born in Philadelphia, Robert moved to Los Angeles to work as a writer, producer, and director in film, television, and advertising. He studied screenwriting with Walter Tevis, author of *The Hustler*, *The Man Who Fell to Earth*, *The Color of Money*, and *The Queen's Gambit*, and with John Truby, author of *The Anatomy of Story*. After ghostwriting the final draft of *Nightmare on Elm Street 4: The Dream Master*, Robert turned to writing novels and debuted with *Access to Power*, a national bestseller. His books have won praise from authors as diverse as Janet Evanovich and Michael Connelly.

For more information about Robert Ellis, visit him online at: https://www.robertellis.net

AUTHOR'S NOTE

The Girl Buried in the Woods was inspired by a true story—the murder of Connie Evans on her fifteenth birthday in the suburbs outside Philadelphia. Her body was found in a shallow grave beneath a grove of pine trees on a country road about a mile from my home. At the time Berkley Road was a desolate street between empty fields of grass that I used to ride my bicycle on every day. I was only a boy at the time of the murder, only ten years old. It took me a year to find the courage to get off my bike and step underneath those pine trees for a look at her grave. In my mind, my imagination, I can still see her hair strewn through the soil, just as it was described by the man who discovered her body with his dog. This is an image that I have carried with me ever since. While this novel isn't the story of Connie Evans's life and death, her murder shook me to the bone and changed my life forever.

ACKNOWLEDGMENTS

Many thanks go to John Truby, author of *The Anatomy of Story* and my good friend, for his in-depth take on the first draft of this work. *The Girl Buried in the Woods* is a better story and a better novel because of him. I'd also like to thank Michael Conway, whose notes were more than helpful from page one to the end. This novel wouldn't feel authentic without the help from many professionals working in forensic labs and law enforcement agencies across the country. I'd been holding back on some of the most fascinating forensic details and waiting for the right moment to bring them out and let them shine. *The Girl Buried in the Woods* seemed to be that time. But even so, readers should keep in mind that this is a work of fiction. Any technical deviation from facts or procedures is my responsibility alone, and almost always, a matter of choice for the sake of story.

Printed in Great Britain
by Amazon